THE HOUSE WITH A CLOCK IN ITS WALLS

"Newly orphaned, Lewis is a plump ten-year-old who has come to live with his Uncle Jonathan; he finds himself very much at home in the old, odd mansion and he quickly becomes fond of both Uncle Jonathan and his next-door neighbor . . . Mrs. Zimmermann. But there's something odd going on: the ticking noise in the walls of the house, the strange things Uncle Jonathan does; Lewis discovers that his uncle has magic powers, that he himself has acquired some occult ability, and that there is a major power struggle between their well-meant white magic and the dire plans of an extinct (but haunting) former owner. Black magic against white, good against evil, the mood and suspense are artfully created and the illustrations exactly right for the eerie tale."
— *Bulletin of the Center for Children's Books*

"What the author has done that's so special is to touch both the intellect and the feelings. He has dusted off the paraphernalia of ancient magic and made us newly aware of the differences between good and evil. His dialogue goes snap, crackle, and pop. He sets chilling scenes with suspense that tightens like a screw. . . . *The House With a Clock in Its Walls* will cast its spell for a long time."
— *The New York Times Book Review*

THE HOUSE
WITH A CLOCK
IN ITS WALLS

JOHN BELLAIRS
pictures by Edward Gorey

Puffin Books

PUFFIN BOOKS
Published by the Penguin Group
Penguin Books USA Inc., 375 Hudson Street, New York, New York 10014, U.S.A.
Penguin Books Ltd, 27 Wrights Lane, London W8 5TZ, England
Penguin Books Australia Ltd, Ringwood, Victoria, Australia
Penguin Books Canada Ltd, 10 Alcorn Avenue, Toronto, Ontario, Canada M4V 3B2
Penguin Books (N.Z.) Ltd, 182–190 Wairau Road, Auckland 10, New Zealand

Penguin Books Ltd, Registered Offices: Harmondsworth, Middlesex, England

First published in the United States of America by The Dial Press, 1973
Published in Puffin Books, 1993

7   9   10   8   6

LIBRARY OF CONGRESS CATALOGING-IN-PUBLICATION DATA
Bellairs, John.
The house with a clock in its walls / by John Bellairs;
illustrated by Edward Gorey.   p.   cm.
Sequel: The figure in the shadows.
Summary: A boy goes to live with his magician uncle in a mansion
that has a clock hidden in the walls which is ticking off the
minutes until doomsday.
ISBN 0-14-036336-X
[1. Magic — Fiction.]   I. Gorey, Edward, 1925–   ill.   II. Title.
[PZ7.B413Ho   1993]   [Fic] — dc20   92-26794

Printed in the United States of America
Set in Janson Text No. 55

For Priscilla, who lets me be myself

*The House
with a Clock in Its Walls*

CHAPTER ONE

Lewis Barnavelt fidgeted and wiped his sweaty palms on the seat of the bus that was roaring toward New Zebedee. The year was 1948, and it was a warm, windy summer evening. Outside, that is. Lewis could see the moonlit trees tossing gently beyond his window, which was sealed shut like all the windows on the bus.

He looked down at his purple corduroy trousers, the kind that go *whip-whip* when you walk. He put his hand up and rubbed it across his hair, which was parted in the middle and slicked down with Wildroot Cream Oil. His hand was greasy now, so he wiped it on the seat again. His lips were moving, and he was saying a prayer. It was one of his altar-boy prayers:

Quia tu es Deus fortitudo mea; quare me repulisti,
et quare tristis incedo, dum affligit me inimicus?

For Thou O God art my strength; why have you
cast me off, and why do I go sorrowful, while the
enemy afflicts me?

He tried to remember more prayers, but the only one
he could come up with was another question:

Quare tristis es anima mea, et quare conturbas me?

Why art thou sorrowful O my soul, and why do you
trouble me?

It seemed to Lewis that all he could think of these
days were questions: Where am I going? Who will I
meet? Will I like them? What will happen to me?

Lewis Barnavelt was ten years old. Until recently he
had lived with his parents in a small town near Mil-
waukee. But his father and mother had been killed suddenly one night in an auto accident, and now Lewis was
on his way to New Zebedee, the county seat of Capharnaum County in the state of Michigan. He was going
to live with his Uncle Jonathan, whom he had never
met in his life. Of course, Lewis had heard a few things
about Uncle Jonathan, like that he smoked and drank
and played poker. These were not such bad things in a
Catholic family, but Lewis had two maiden aunts who
were Baptists, and they had warned him about Jonathan.
He hoped that the warnings would turn out to be unnecessary.

/ 4 /

As the bus rounded a curve, Lewis looked at his reflection in the window next to his seat. He saw a moony fat face with shiny cheeks. The lips on the face were moving. Lewis was saying the altar-boy prayers again, this time with the wish that they might make Uncle Jonathan like him. *Judica me Deus* . . . Judge me O God . . . no, don't judge me, help me to live a happy life.

It was five minutes to nine when the bus pulled up in front of Heemsoth's Rexall Drug Store in the town of New Zebedee. Lewis got up, wiped his hands on his trousers, and tugged at the enormous cardboard suitcase that hung out over the edge of the metal rack. Lewis's father had bought the suitcase in London at the end of World War II. It was covered with ripped and faded Cunard Line stickers. Lewis pulled hard, and the suitcase lurched down onto his head. He staggered back across the aisle with the suitcase held perilously in the air; then he sat down suddenly, and the suitcase landed in his lap with a *whump*.

"Oh, come on! Don't kill yourself before I have a chance to meet you!"

There in the aisle stood a man with a bushy red beard that was streaked in several places with white. His Big Mac khaki trousers were bulged out in front by his pot belly, and he was wearing a gold-buttoned red vest over a blue work shirt. Lewis noticed that the vest had four pockets; there were pipe cleaners sticking out of the top two, and a chain of paper clips was strung between the lower pair. One end of the chain was hooked to the winding knob of a gold watch.

Jonathan van Olden Barnavelt took his steaming pipe out of his mouth and held out his hand.

"Hi, Lewis. I'm your Uncle Jonathan. I recognized you from a picture your father once sent me. Welcome to New Zebedee."

Lewis shook hands, and noticed that the back of Jonathan's hand was covered with a springy mat of red hair. The coat of hair ran right up his sleeve and disappeared. Lewis wondered if he had red hair all over his body.

Jonathan hefted the suitcase and started down the steps of the bus.

"Good Lord, what a monster! It ought to have wheels on the bottom. Unh! Did you pack some of the bricks from your house?"

Lewis looked so sad at the mention of his house that Jonathan decided to change the subject. He cleared his throat and said, "Well, now! As I was saying, welcome to Capharnaum County and beautiful, historic New Zebedee. Population six thousand, not counting . . ."

A bell overhead began to strike the hour.

Jonathan stopped talking. He froze on the spot. He dropped the suitcase, and his arms hung limp at his sides. Lewis, frightened, looked up at him. Jonathan's eyes were glazed.

The bell continued to toll. Lewis looked up. The sound was coming from a tall brick steeple across the street. The arches of the belfry made a howling mouth and two gaping eyes; below the mouth was a large, glowing clock face with iron numerals.

Clang. Another stroke. It was a deep-throated iron bell, and its sound made Lewis feel hopeless and helpless. Bells like that always did. But what was wrong with Uncle Jonathan?

The tolling stopped. Jonathan broke out of his trance. He shook his head convulsively, and with a jerky motion raised his hand to his face. He was sweating profusely now. He mopped his forehead and his streaming cheeks.

"Hmh . . . hah! Hrumph! Ooh! Sorry, Lewis, I . . . I just remembered that I had . . . that I had left a kettle boiling on the stove. I always phase out like that when I remember something I've forgotten, or vicy versy. Bottom of the pot's probably ruined by now. C'mon. Let's get moving."

Lewis looked hard at his uncle, but he said nothing. Together, the two of them started to walk.

They left the brightly lit Main Street, and before long they were trotting briskly down a long, tree-lined avenue called Mansion Street. The overhanging boughs made Mansion Street into a long rustling tunnel. Pools of lamplight stretched off into the distance. As they walked, Jonathan asked Lewis how his schoolwork was coming, and whether he knew what George Kell's batting average was this year. He told him that he would have to become a Tiger fan now that he lived in Michigan. Jonathan did not complain any more about the suitcase, but he did stop frequently to set it down and flex his reddened hand.

It seemed to Lewis that Jonathan talked more loudly in the darkness between the streetlights, though why he did this Lewis couldn't say. Grownups were not supposed to be afraid of the dark, and anyway this was not a dark, lonely street. There were lights on in most of the houses, and Lewis could hear people laughing and talking and slamming doors. His uncle was certainly a strange person, but he was strange in a likable way.

At the corner of Mansion and High, Jonathan stopped. He set down the suitcase in front of a mailbox that said: FOR DEPOSIT OF MAIL ONLY.

"I live at the top of the hill," said Jonathan, pointing up.

High Street was well named. Up they went, leaning forward and plodding slowly. Lewis asked Jonathan several times if he could carry the suitcase, but each time Jonathan said, no, thanks, he could manage it. Lewis began to be sorry that he had packed all those books and lead soldiers.

When they got to the top of the hill, Jonathan set down the suitcase. He took out a red bandanna handkerchief and mopped his face with it.

"Well, there it is, Lewis. Barnavelt's Folly. What do you think of it?"

Lewis looked.

He saw a three-story stone mansion with a tall turret on the front. The whole house was lit up, downstairs, upstairs, and upper upstairs. There was even a light in the little oval window that was set, like an eye, in the bank of shingles at the top of the turret. In the front yard grew a large chestnut tree. Its leaves rustled in the warm summer breeze.

Jonathan was standing at parade rest, his hands behind him, his legs wide apart. Again he said, "What do you think of it, Lewis? Eh?"

"I love it, Uncle Jonathan! I've always wanted to live in a mansion, and this is sure some mansion!"

Lewis walked up to the frilly fence and touched one of the iron pompons that ran in a row along the top. He stared at the sign that spelled out "100" in red glass reflectors.

"Is it real, Uncle Jonathan? The house, I mean."

Jonathan glanced at him strangely. "Yes . . . yes . . . yes, of course it is. It's real. Let's go inside."

Jonathan lifted the loop of shoestring that held the gate shut. The gate squeaked open, and Lewis started up the walk. Jonathan followed close behind, lugging the suitcase. Up the front steps they went. The front hall was dark but there was a light at the far end of it. Jonathan set down the suitcase and put his arm around Lewis.

"Come on. Let's go in. Don't be bashful. It's your house now."

Lewis walked down the long hall. It seemed to take forever. At the other end he emerged into a room full of yellow light. There were pictures in heavy gilt frames on the walls; there was a mantelpiece covered with a wild assortment of junk; there was a big round table in the middle of the room, and over in the corner was a gray-haired woman in a baggy purple dress. She was standing with her ear to the wall, listening.

Lewis stopped and stared. He felt embarrassed. It was as if he had walked in on someone who was doing something he shouldn't be doing. He thought that he and Jonathan had made a good deal of noise coming in, but it was very apparent that the lady, whoever she was, had been surprised when he entered the room. Surprised and embarrassed, like himself.

Now she straightened up, smoothed her dress, and said cheerfully, "Hi there. I'm Mrs. Zimmermann. I live next door."

Lewis found himself staring into one of the wrinkliest faces he had ever seen. But the eyes were friendly, and all the wrinkles were drawn up into smile lines. He shook hands.

"This is Lewis, Florence," said Jonathan. "You remember Charlie writing about him. The bus was on time for a change. They must have gotten the driver drunk. Hey! Have you been stealing any of my coins?"

Jonathan walked over to the table. Now Lewis noticed that the red checkered tablecloth was covered with heaps and stacks of coins. All kinds of coins, most of them foreign. Doughnut-shaped Arabian coins with Boy Scout knots all over them; a heap of dark-brown copper coins, all of which were stamped with the picture of a bald man who wore a handlebar moustache. There were big heavy English pennies that showed Queen Victoria in various states of chinniness, and there were tiny silver coins no thicker than your fingernail. There was an egg-shaped Mexican silver dollar and a genuine Roman coin, covered with green rust. But most of all, in shiny golden stacks, were brass coins with *Bon Pour Un Franc* printed on them. Lewis liked the phrase, and since he didn't know any French, it got twisted around in his mind till it came out *Bon Sour One Frank*.

"No, I have not been stealing any of your precious Brasher doubloons," said Mrs. Zimmermann in an irritated voice. "I was just straightening up the stacks. Okay, Brush Mush?"

"Straightening up the stacks. I've heard *that* one before, Hag Face. But it doesn't matter, because we're going to have to divvy up the coins three ways. You play poker, don't you, Lewis?"

"Yes, but my dad won't . . ." He stopped. Jonathan saw tears in his eyes. Lewis choked down a sob and went on, "My . . . my dad wouldn't have let me play for money."

"Oh, we don't play for money," said Mrs. Zimmermann, laughing. "If we did, this house and everything in it would belong to me."

"Poop, it would," said Jonathan, shuffling the cards and puffing clouds of smoke from his pipe. "Poop, it would. Get 'em all divided up, Frumpy? No? Well, when you're ready it's going to be dealer's choice, and I'm the first dealer. No ladies' games, like Spit-out-the-Window or Johnny's Nightshirt. Straight five-card draw. Nothing wild." He puffed some more and was about to deal the first hand when he stopped and looked at Mrs. Zimmermann with a mischievous smile.

"Oh, by the way," he said, "you might bring Lewis a glass of iced tea, and get me a refill. No sugar. And bring out another plate of chocolate-chip cookies."

Mrs. Zimmermann stood up and clasped her hands subserviently in front of her. "How would you like your cookies, sir? Stuffed down your throat one by one, or crumbled up and sifted into your shirt collar?"

Jonathan stuck out his tongue at her. "Ignore her, Lewis. She thinks she's smart because she's got more college degrees than I have."

"I would be smarter than you in any case, Weird Beard. Excuse me, folks. I'll be back in a minute." She turned and walked to the kitchen.

Jonathan dealt a practice hand while she was gone. When Lewis picked his cards up, he noticed that they were old and worn. Most of the corners were missing.

But on each faded blue back was a round golden seal with an Aladdin's lamp in the middle. Above and below the seal were the words:

CAPHARNAUM COUNTY

MAGICIANS SOCIETY

Mrs. Zimmermann returned with the cookies and iced tea, and the game began in earnest. Jonathan gathered up the cards and cut them together with a very professional *zzzzzit!* He shuffled and started to deal. Lewis sipped his iced tea and felt very comfortable, very at home.

They played until midnight, by which time Lewis had red and black spots in front of his eyes. Pipe smoke hung in layers over the table and rose in a column from the shade of the floor lamp. It made the lamp seem magic, like the one on the playing cards. And there was something else magic about the game. Lewis won. He won a lot. Usually he had rotten luck, but in this game he got straight flushes, royal flushes, four of a kind. Not all of the time, but enough to keep winning steadily.

Maybe it was because Jonathan was such a lousy poker player. What Mrs. Zimmermann had said was certainly true. Whenever Jonathan had a good hand, he snortled and chortled and blew smoke out of both corners of his mouth. When he had a bad hand, he sulked and chewed his pipestem impatiently. Mrs. Zimmermann was a crafty player who could bluff you under the table with a pair of deuces, but that night she just wasn't getting the cards. Maybe that's why Lewis was winning. Maybe. But he had his doubts.

For one thing, he could have sworn that once or twice when he was reaching out to turn over a card that had been dealt to him, the card had changed. It had changed —just like that—while he was picking it up. This never happened when Lewis was dealing, but it did happen when Jonathan or Mrs. Zimmermann was dealing. And more than once he had been about to throw in a hand when, after a second look, he discovered that the hand was a good one. It was odd.

The mantel clock cleared its throat with a *whirr* and started to chime midnight.

Lewis shot a quick glance at Uncle Jonathan, who was sitting there perfectly composed, puffing his pipe. Or was he composed? He seemed to be listening for something.

The other clocks all over the house joined in. Lewis sat entranced, listening to high-pitched dings, tinny whangs, melodious electric doorbell sounds, cuckoos from cuckoo clocks, and deep sinister Chinese gongs roaring *bwaoww! bwaoww!* These and many other clock sounds echoed through the house. Now and then during this concert Lewis looked at Jonathan. Jonathan did not look back. He was staring at the wall, and his eyes had that glazed look again. Mrs. Zimmermann sat through the whole thing with her eyes fixed on the tablecloth.

The last clock to strike was the grandfather clock in the study. It made a noise like a steamer trunk full of tin plates falling slowly and solemnly down a flight of stairs. When it stopped striking, Jonathan looked up.

"Hm. Yes. Where were we? Well, Lewis, it's midnight, isn't it? Game's over. Time for bed."

Jonathan cleared the table briskly. He gathered up the playing cards, stacked them, and put a rubber band around them. Snap! Then he reached under the table and came up with a red tin candy box with a picture of the New Zebedee County Courthouse on the lid. He scraped the clattering coins into the box, snapped the lid shut, pushed back his chair, rapped out his pipe into a saucer, and folded his hands in his lap.

"Well! And what do you think of 100 High Street, Lewis?"

"I think it's wonderful, Uncle Jonathan. I like the house, and I like the town, and I like you two an awful lot."

Lewis wasn't lying. In spite of Jonathan's strange behavior and the eavesdropping habits of Mrs. Zimmermann, he had had a very good time during his first evening in New Zebedee. In fact, for most of the evening, he had had a great deal of trouble keeping himself from jumping up and down in his seat. He had been told that it was a bad thing to do in company.

Jonathan took Lewis's suitcase upstairs, and Lewis got his first look at his new room. There was a tall black bed with battlements at the top of the headboard and foot-board. In the corner was a black mirror that matched the bed, and near it was a black marble fireplace with a coffin-like black clock on its mantelpiece. Up against one wall was a tall glazed bookcase full of old books, and on top of the bookcase was a vase with cattails in it. In the mid-dle of the floor was a large hooked rug. The pattern re-minded Lewis of a map of the United States—a map of the U.S. done by a crazy person. Many children might have been put off by the dark woodwork of the old room, but Lewis loved it. He imagined that this was the sort of room Sherlock Holmes would have slept in.

Lewis got into his pajamas, put on his bathrobe and slippers, and shuffled down the hall to the bathroom. When he got back, he found that Jonathan had just finished building a fire in his fireplace.

Jonathan got up and brushed twigs off his vest. "Well, Lewis, there you are! Need anything else?"

"Gee, no, I guess not, Uncle Jonathan. This is a great room. I've always wanted a room with a fireplace in it."

Jonathan smiled. He went over to the bedside table and turned on the reading lamp. "Read as long as you like tonight, Lewis. Remember, school doesn't start for another three weeks."

"I don't know if I'll read much after all the poker playing," said Lewis, yawning. "But thanks anyway. Good night, Uncle Jonathan."

"Good night, Lewis."

Jonathan started to close the door, but he stopped. "Oh, by the way, Lewis. I hope all these clocks don't keep you awake. They're kind of noisy, but . . . well, I like them. Good night." He closed the door.

Lewis stood there with a puzzled frown on his face. There was something going on in this house that he couldn't quite get hold of. He thought of Jonathan standing paralyzed while the clock in the church steeple tolled; he thought of Mrs. Zimmermann listening at the wall. It was strange.

Oh, well, he thought, shrugging his shoulders, people are funny sometimes. Lewis climbed into bed and turned off the light. A few minutes later he turned it back on. He realized that he was still tense, excited, and wide awake.

He climbed out of bed and walked over to the shaky-looking bamboo bookcase that stood by the closet door. What a lot of old dusty books! He pulled one out and wiped the dust off with his sleeve. The faded gilt letters on the black buckram spine said:

John L.
Stoddard's
Lectures

VOL. IX
Scotland
England
London

Lewis opened the book and flipped through the slick glossy pages. He held the book up to his nose. It smelled like Old Spice talcum powder. Books that smelled that way were usually fun to read. He threw the book onto his bed and went to his suitcase. After rummaging about for a while, he came up with a long, narrow box of chocolate-covered mints. He loved to eat candy while he read, and lots of his favorite books at home had brown smudges on the corners of the pages.

A few minutes later Lewis was sitting up in bed with his pillows propped behind him. He was reading about how the Scotch nobles had murdered poor Rizzio right in front of Mary, Queen of Scots. Stoddard compared Rizzio to a purple-velvet plum spurting plum juice in all directions. The nobles dragged the poor man, kicking and screaming, into the hallway, where they stabbed him some more. Fifty-six times, said Stoddard, though he didn't say who counted the stabs. Lewis flipped the page and bit into a peppermint patty. Now Stoddard was talking about the permanence of bloodstains and wondering whether or not the stain on the hall floor in Holyrood really was Rizzio's blood or not. Lewis began to yawn. He turned off the light and went to sleep.

But he was awakened—quite suddenly—a little while later. He had been dreaming that he was being chased by the Queen of Spades. Now he sat up, wide awake. He was scared, and he didn't know why.

Creak, creak. Someone was tiptoeing down the hall.

Lewis sat still and listened. Now the sound was outside his door. Now it was going away down the hall. *Creak, creak, creak.*

Lewis slid out of bed. As slowly and carefully as he could, he tiptoed to the door. He opened it, just as slowly and carefully. He didn't open it far. Just a crack. He looked out.

The hall was dark, except for a glimmering gray window down at the far end. But Lewis could hear someone moving. And now he saw the faint, pale circle of a flashlight beam moving over the wallpaper. Frightened, Lewis pulled the door shut and then opened it just a crack. The flashlight beam had stopped. Now the figure with the flashlight brought his fist down on the wall—hard. Lewis heard little clots of plaster falling down into the space between the walls. The figure pounded again, and again. Lewis stared and opened the door wider.

Now the shadowy intruder stepped back, and Lewis saw a bulky shadow against the hall window. A bulky, bearded shadow with a pipe in its mouth. Jonathan!

Lewis closed the door as softly as he could and leaned against it, shaking. He hoped Jonathan hadn't seen him. A horrible thought came into his mind. Was Jonathan crazy?

Lewis went to the wing chair by the fire and sat down. He watched the black honeycombs as they crumbled into deep red wells. *What if Jonathan were crazy?* His parents had always warned him against crazy people, the type that lured you into their cars and offered you candy with glue in it. Or was it glue? He couldn't remember. But Jonathan didn't really seem like *that* kind of person. Or the kind that sneaked into your room at night and stabbed you to death. Lewis sighed. He would just have to wait and see what happened.

He went back to bed and had a dream in which he and Jonathan were running round and round the block that had the church on it: the church with the monster-faced steeple. All the houses on the block were lit up, but they couldn't go into any of them to hide. Something tall and dark and shapeless was following them. Finally they stopped in front of the church, and the tower began to sway as if it were made of rubber. The howling face got closer and closer . . . and then the dream changed. Lewis was sitting in a room full of glittering coins. He let them run clinking through his fingers until morning came.

CHAPTER TWO

Lewis woke up the next day with confused memories of the previous night running around in his head. In general, his impression was a happy one, despite the dark things that lurked in the corners of the picture.

He got dressed, went downstairs, and found Jonathan and Mrs. Zimmermann at breakfast. It seemed that Mrs. Zimmermann always came over to cook Jonathan's breakfast because Jonathan was such a terrible cook. Well, that was fine with Lewis. He sat down to pancakes and sausages, and before long he was figuring out how best to use the three weeks of freedom that were left before school began.

Lewis soon found out that three weeks was not nearly

enough time for exploring the town of New Zebedee and the house at 100 High Street. In three weeks he barely got started.

To begin with, the town was marvelous. It was the sort of place he had always wanted to live in. Lewis's old hometown in Wisconsin looked as if it had been built yesterday; all the houses were the same size, and the main street was just a row of bars and gas stations. New Zebedee was different. It was full of tall, elaborately decorated old houses. Even the ordinary white-frame houses had things that made them seem different—a stained-glass window or a bouquet of iron flowers on top of a cupola. And so many of the houses seemed to be hiding secrets.

Jonathan took Lewis for some walks around the town, but more often he just let Lewis find out things for himself. Sometimes Lewis just walked up and down Main Street and stared at the high, elaborate, false fronts of the stores. One of the stores had an abandoned opera house in its upper stories. Jonathan said that the old scenery was still up there, leaning against cases of Mounds bars and five-cent writing tablets. At one end of Main Street was the Civil War Monument, a fantastic stone object shaped like an artist's easel. Each of the joints and corners of the easel had a soldier or sailor standing on it, threatening the rebel army with a musket or a sword or a cannon swabber or a harpoon. The flat part of the easel was covered with the names of Capharnaum County residents who had died in the Civil War. There was a small stone arch near the monument, and it was called the Civil War Monument Annex, because it contained the names that the carvers hadn't been able to get on the big monument. Jonathan's grandfather had fought in the war with the Fifth Michigan Fire Zouave Lancers, and Jonathan was full of stories about the old man's exploits.

As for the house at 100 High Street, it was every bit as wonderful as the town, besides being strange and more than a little bit scary. There were lots of rooms to explore: third-best upstairs front parlors and second-best back bedrooms; linen closets and playrooms and just plain rooms. Some of these were empty and full of dust, but there were others that were crammed with antique furniture. There were marble-topped tables galore, and upholstered chairs on squeaky casters, and doilies pinned to the backs of the chairs, and stuffed partridges under glass bell jars. Each room had its own fireplace made of marble that looked—depending on the room—like blue cheese or fudge-ripple ice cream or green hand soap or milk chocolate.

One afternoon Lewis was walking down the back staircase in the south wing of the mansion, when he came to a stained-glass window on a landing. There were quite a few stained-glass windows in the house. Lewis found them on back staircases like this one, or in unused bathrooms or at the ends of hallways. Sometimes he even found them set in the ceiling. He had seen this one before, or rather, he had seen another window where this one was now. That was why he stopped and stared.

He remembered the other window very well. It had been a big oval window that showed a red tomato sun setting into a blue sea the color of old medicine bottles. The oval frame was still there, but in it Lewis found a window that showed a man fleeing from a forest. The forest was plum colored, and the grass under the man's feet was bright green. The sky in the picture was a squirming, oily, brownish-red. It reminded Lewis of furniture polish.

What had happened to the other window? Did Jonathan go around changing them during the night? It was pretty strange.

Another thing that was strange was the coat rack in the front hall. At first Lewis had thought that it was just an ordinary coat rack. It stood about six feet high, and it had a little round mirror on the front. There were pegs for coats and hats, and there was a little wooden compartment in the front for rubbers. It looked very ordinary. But one day when Lewis was hanging up his raincoat, he looked at the mirror and saw a Mayan step pyramid in a steaming green jungle. He knew that the pyramid was Mayan because he had a picture of it among his Viewmaster slides. Only this scene was not fake three dimensional, the way the slides were. It looked as if you could reach through the mirror and touch the vines. As

Lewis watched, a brilliant red bird with a long tail flew from one tree to another. Waves of heat made the pyramid ripple. Lewis blinked and stared again. He was looking at the reflection of the rainy gray window behind him.

Lewis thought a lot about the stained-glass windows and the coat rack. Were they magic? He believed in magic, even though he had been taught not to. His father had spent one whole afternoon explaining to Lewis that ghosts were caused by X rays bouncing off distant planets. But Lewis was a stubborn boy, and besides, hadn't he seen the Aladdin's lamp on the back of Jonathan's playing cards, and the words *Capharnaum County Magicians Society?* He was convinced that magic was at the bottom of this mystery.

Lewis was also convinced that he would have to solve another mystery before he could tackle the problem of the coat rack and the stained-glass windows. He would have to find out why Jonathan prowled the house every night with a flashlight in his hand.

Lewis had discovered that the strange incident on his first night in New Zebedee was part of a regular pattern. Every night after twelve, Jonathan was out there searching. What he was searching for, Lewis couldn't say.

Again and again, as on that first night, he had heard the floor boards creak outside his door. Again and again he had heard Jonathan tiptoeing stealthily down the hall, entering rooms, closing doors. He heard him overhead on the third floor, where Jonathan hardly ever went during the day. Then he would be back downstairs, poking around, stumbling into furniture. Maybe he was scared of burglars. Maybe so, but then why did he pound on the wall? Burglars seldom got into walls.

Lewis had to find out what was going on. And so, one night a little after twelve, Lewis lowered himself silently from his bed to the cold floor boards. As stealthily as he could, he tiptoed across the room, but the warped boards complained under his feet. By the time he got to the door, he was thoroughly shaken. He wiped his hands on his robe several times and turned the knob. He took a deep breath, let it out, and stepped out into the dark hallway.

Lewis clamped his hand over his mouth. He had stepped on the protruding head of a nail. It didn't really hurt much, but Lewis was scared of tetanus. When his panic had died down, he took another step. He began to edge his way down the hall.

But Lewis was no better at stealthy creeping than you might think and, by the time he had bumped his head against a heavy, gilt picture frame for about the third time, Jonathan called to him from one of the distant rooms.

"Oh, for heaven's sake, Lewis! Stop playing Sherlock Holmes! You make a better Dr. Watson. Come on and join me. I'm in the bedroom with the green fireplace."

Lewis was glad that his red face didn't shine in the dark. Well, at least Jonathan wasn't mad.

Lewis picked his way down the hall until he found an open door. There was Jonathan, standing in the dark with a flashlight in his hand. He was playing the light over the mantel clock, a boxy black affair with gold handles on the sides, like a coffin.

"Evening, Lewis. Or morning, as the case may be. Would you care to join me on my rounds?"

Jonathan's voice sounded tight and nervous. Lewis hesitated a moment and then he plunged in. "Uncle Jonathan, what are you doing?"

"Stopping the clocks. During the day it's nice to have clocks ticking all over the house, but at night it keeps me awake. You know how it is, Lewis, with faucets and . . . and the like."

Still chattering nervously, Jonathan turned the clock around, reached into the back of it, and halted the stubby pendulum. Then he motioned for Lewis to follow him and, waving the flashlight a little too cheerfully, walked on to the next room. Lewis followed, but he was puzzled. "Uncle Jonathan, why don't you turn the room lights on?"

His uncle was silent for a minute. Then he said, in that same nervous voice, "Oh, well, you know how it is, Lewis. If I were to go from one room to another snapping lights on and off, what would the neighbors think? And what about the electric bill? Do you know that you get billed for an hour's worth of electricity every time you snap the lights on and off?"

This explanation did not sound convincing to Lewis. In the first place, Uncle Jonathan had never before given any sign that he cared what the neighbors thought about anything he did. If he wanted to sit in the glider under the chestnut tree and play a saxophone at 3 A.M. he was likely to do just that. In the second place, Jonathan had more than once left the floor lamp in his study burning all night. He was a careless man, and not the sort who worried about big electric bills. It was true that Lewis had only known his uncle for three weeks, but he felt that he already had a pretty good idea of what Jonathan was like.

On the other hand, he couldn't very well say, "Uncle Jonathan, you're lying through your teeth!" so he silently followed his uncle to the next room, the second-best upstairs bathroom. It had a fireplace too—a white tile one—and there was a small, white plastic clock buzzing on the mantel. Jonathan unplugged it without saying anything and went on to the next room, where he stopped a cherrywood clock with a pendulum that used three columns of mercury as a weight. And then on to the next room.

The last clock to be silenced was the grandfather clock in the study. Jonathan's study had a very high ceiling, and all the walls were lined with books. There was a fat, slouchy, brown-leather easy chair that hissed when you sat down in it and, of course, there was a fireplace, and there was still a fire burning in it. Over in a corner by the sliding doors that opened into the dining room stood the tall gloomy clock. The brass disk on the pendulum flashed dimly in the light of the dying fire. Jonathan reached inside and grabbed the long black rod. The clock stopped.

Now that their strange tour was over, Jonathan lapsed into silence. He seemed to be thinking. He walked over to the fireplace, stirred up the fire, and put on another log. He threw himself down into the leather chair and waved his arm at the green easy chair on the other side of the fireplace.

"Have a seat, Lewis. I'd like to have a talk with you."

Lewis wondered if he was going to get bawled out for sneaking up on his uncle. It didn't seem likely. Jonathan looked and sounded friendly, though his voice was still a little edgy. Lewis sat down and watched as Jonathan lit up his hookah. Lewis always liked to watch him do this. The hookah was shaped like a Spanish galleon, and the crow's nest on the mainmast was the bowl. The body of the ship was full of water for cooling the smoke, and up on the bow stood the tiny ceramic figure of a boatswain with his pipe to his lips. A long hose was plugged into the ship's stern, and there was a black rubber mouthpiece on the end. When you blew into the hose, the burning tobacco in the crow's nest sent up a long column of smoke, and the boatswain went *fweee!* on his little pipe. Sometimes, when Jonathan made a mistake and filled the boat too full of water, the boatswain went *blp!* and blew bubbles.

When Jonathan had the pipe going good, he drew in a big mouthful of smoke, let it out slowly, and said, "Lewis, I think it would be better for you to be scared than it would be for you to think of your uncle as a crabby old lunatic."

"I don't think you're crabby," said Lewis.

Jonathan laughed. "But you *do* think I'm off my rocker. Well, after tonight I wouldn't blame you."

Lewis blushed. "No, Uncle Jonathan! I never meant that! You know I don't think . . ."

Jonathan smiled. "Yes, of course, I know. But all the same, I think it would be better if you knew something about this clock business. I can't tell you all about it because I don't know all about it. In fact, there are times when I think I don't know much about it at all. But I'll tell you what I know."

He crossed his legs, sat back, and puffed some more at his pipe. Lewis sat forward in the big green chair. He kept clasping and unclasping his hands and he stared hard at Jonathan. After a brief dramatic pause and a particularly long drag at the galleon-hookah, Jonathan began.

"I haven't lived in this house always, Lewis. In fact, I only moved here five years ago. I used to live down on Spruce Street, near the waterworks. But when the old owner died, and the place was put up for sale cheap, and it meant a chance to live next door to my best friend, Mrs. Zimmermann—"

"Who was the old owner?" asked Lewis, interrupting.

"I was going to get around to that. His name was Isaac Izard. Initials I.I., like a Roman numeral II. You'll find his double *I* carved or painted or stamped on all sorts of things all over this house: the wainscoting, the floorboards, the insides of cupboards, the fuse box, the mantelpieces—everywhere. You'll even find a Roman numeral II worked into the tracery on the wallpaper in the upstairs front hallway." Jonathan paused for a second and looked thoughtful. "Have to get that paper replaced some day . . . oh, well, back to what I was saying. Old Isaac Izard—his name is odd, isn't it? Mrs. Zimmermann thinks that it comes from *izzard*, which in some parts of England is the word for *zed*, which is the word the English use to identify the letter Z. I go along with Mrs. Zimmermann's theory because I can't think of a better one. And besides, she is a Z-lady, so she should know. But, as I was saying, and I will get around to saying something *sometime*, Lewis . . ." He puffed on his pipe some more and wriggled around in the chair to get comfortable. "As I was saying, old Isaac was a warlock."

"What's that?"

Uncle Jonathan looked very serious. "It's the word for a male witch."

Lewis shuddered. Then, out of nowhere, a strange

thought came to him. "Are you one too?" he asked in a tiny, frightened voice.

Jonathan looked at him with a strange smile. "Would it scare you if I said I was?"

"No. I like you an awful lot and you can be a warlock if you want to be one, I guess. You wouldn't be a bad one, I know."

"That depends on how you mean 'bad,' " said Jonathan, chuckling. "If you mean that I wouldn't be an evil one, you're right. If you mean that I wouldn't be too bad at wizarding . . . well, I don't know. I'm pretty much of a parlor magician, though I have a few tricks that go beyond rabbits and playing cards."

"Like stained-glass windows and coat racks?" said Lewis, grinning.

"Yes. Exactly like those. And just to make you *perfectly* secure, let me inform you that Mrs. Zimmermann is also a wizard, though in her case the term should be witch."

"Couldn't you find a better name?" asked Lewis timidly.

"Well, she prefers 'maga' or 'enchantrix,' but I can't use such words without breaking up, so she's old witch Florence to me. She's really a much more serious wizard than I am. Got her D.Mag.A.—that's *Doctor Magicorum Artium*—from the University of Göttingen in Germany in 1922. I just have an A.B. from Michigan Agricultural College."

"What in?" asked Lewis, as if he were interviewing Jonathan for a job. Actually he was interested in Jonathan's college work. Both of Lewis's parents had gone to college, and they always talked a lot about their college work.

"What in?" said Jonathan, blushing. "What in? Why, Agricultural Science. Animal Husbandry and all that. I was going to be a farmer till my grandpa died and left me a pile of money. But back to Isaac Izard. You're still interested, aren't you?"

"Oh, yes! Of course! Please tell me. I want to know."

"Isaac, as I say, was a wizard. He fooled around with black magic, the worst kind of thing a wizard can do. I can't tell you about anything bad that I absolutely know he did—for sure—but if one wizard can judge another, I'd say he was an evil one. A very evil one. Mrs. Zimmermann thinks so too. She lived next door to him for years, remember. You'll have to ask her about him yourself, of course, but there were many evenings when she and I would stand in her back yard and look up and see old Isaac's evil face in the window of the cupola on top of the house. He'd be holding an oil lamp and just staring out at the night. Mrs. Zimmermann claims that he would sit for hours in the cupola during the day. He seemed to be taking notes."

"Gee, that *is* weird. What was he taking notes for?"

"Lord only knows, Lewis. But I'm sure it wasn't anything good. At any rate, to get on with my story. . . . It must be getting pretty late by now, but without the clocks I have no idea what time it is. Where was I? Oh, yes. Old Isaac died during a wild thunderstorm, one of the worst in the history of Capharnaum County. You can look it up in the New Zebedee *Chronicle* if you want to: roofs blown off barns, trees uprooted, and a bolt of lightning melted the iron doors on the tomb Isaac is buried in now. I'll have to show you that tomb some day. Ugly old dump—one of those little stone houses for the respectable dead. There are several of them up in our cemetery, some of them really fancy. This one was built by Isaac's family in the 1850's, but it was never used till they put his wife in there. She died before he did."

"What was she like?"

"Pretty strange, as you'd have to be to choose Isaac Izard for a husband. I don't remember anything about her but her eyeglasses."

Lewis stared. "Her eyeglasses?"

"Yes. I passed her once on the street and she turned and looked at me. It might have been the way the sun caught her spectacles, but I remember two freezing circles of gray light burning into me. I turned away and closed my eyes, but those two cold spots stayed there. I had nightmares for a week after that."

"How did she die?" Lewis imagined Mrs. Izard falling from a cliff during a hurricane, or flinging herself from the cupola of the house.

"How? Quietly and mysteriously. No funeral. Some

strange-looking people from out of town came and helped Isaac bury her. After that, he went into seclusion. Further seclusion, that is. He and she had always been hermits, but after her death he really shut himself up. Built a big high board fence between this house and Mrs. Zimmermann's. I had it torn down as soon as I moved in." He smiled contentedly. Lewis felt that his Uncle Jonathan was happy living at 100 High Street, despite the fact that old Isaac Izard had made the place his castle.

"Is that all there is to the story?" asked Lewis cautiously.

"Oh, my, no. We're just getting to the good part. Look, here I am selfishly puffing away at this boat, and you have nothing. Let's go out to the kitchen and get a couple of glasses of milk and some chocolate-chip cookies. Okay?"

"Sure!" said Lewis, who liked chocolate-chip cookies even more than he liked Welch's Fudge Bars.

In a few minutes they were back in the study, sitting by the quietly crackling fire and munching cookies. Suddenly a book fell out of the bookcase. *Flop*. Two more fell out. *Flop. Flop*. Lewis stared at the black gap in the row of books. A long, withered, bony hand appeared. It seemed to be groping for something.

Lewis sat rigid with terror, but Jonathan merely smiled. "A little to your left, my dear. That's it. Now you've got it."

A latch clicked and a large section of the built-in book-case swung outwards. More books fell to the floor. And there stood Mrs. Zimmermann, with a strand of cobweb hanging from her left eyeglass. Her sleeve was covered with whitish dust.

"Fine way to build a secret panel," she grumbled. "With the latch on the room side instead of on the passage side."

"It adds to the mystery, Doll Face. As you might have guessed, Lewis, this house has a secret passageway. You enter it through the china cupboard in the kitchen. Come on in, Florence. I was just going to tell Lewis about the clock in the walls."

Mrs. Zimmermann gave him a look as if to say, "Do you think that's a wise thing to do?" But she shrugged and helped herself to the cookies and milk.

"Good cookies," she said, munching. "Very good."

"She always says that because she makes them," explained Jonathan, helping himself to two more. "And now that everyone's mouth is stuffed, including mine, I guess I'll go on. Where were we? Oh, yes. Well, I had no sooner moved in here than I felt that something was wrong. The house had a kind of listening stillness. And then I heard it."

"Heard what?" This was Lewis, who had worked himself to the edge of his chair. He had even stopped eating his cookie.

"The clock. You know how you can be in a room with

a clock ticking, and you won't notice it for a long time. Then, when things are very, very quiet and you aren't thinking about anything in particular—there it is!"

Lewis jumped up and looked around wildly. "Where?"

Jonathan laughed. "No, no, no. I didn't mean to frighten you like that. I mean I heard it for the first time in this room. It was ticking away in the walls. You can go over to that wall and listen for it, if you like."

Lewis got up and walked over to the book-lined wall. He put his ear to a row of black leather volumes and listened. His eyes opened wide.

"It *is* there, Uncle Jonathan! It is!" He was excited by the discovery, but then his face changed. He looked afraid. "What is it for, Uncle Jonathan? What does it do?"

"I haven't the faintest idea," said Jonathan, "though I know that I want to blot it out. That's why I have all these stupid clocks. I didn't used to be so fond of incessant ticking and sudden, loud, hell raising every hour on the hour. But I prefer my clocks to his."

Jonathan's face had turned grim. He shook his head, smiled a little half-hearted smile, and went on. "You may be wondering why I don't just tear down the wall and rip out the clock. Well, it wouldn't do any good. It sounds like it's behind every wall: up in the attic, down in the cellar, in the closets and storerooms and parlors. And sometimes it seems to be slowing down. I keep hoping it will stop. But then it picks up and keeps going.

I don't know what to do." There was a note of real despair in his voice. For a minute Lewis thought his uncle would cry. Then Mrs. Zimmermann broke in.

"I'll tell you one thing you ought *not* to do, Jonathan Barnavelt. You oughtn't to frighten Lewis with something you don't know anything about. After all, the ticking may be some leftover magic from the old coot's experiments. Or death-watch beetles. Or an illusion of some kind, like in houses that have whispering galleries. I get a funny kind of hum in my head now and then. It goes *dooooo* for a while and then it goes away."

Jonathan looked irritated. "Oh, Florence, there's no need to kid around. You don't think it's something harmless and neither do I. I wouldn't have told Lewis just to frighten him. But I thought it would be better for him to know about the clock than to think that his uncle was getting ready for the loony bin. You see, he caught me making my nightly rounds."

"Well," said Mrs. Zimmermann, "I don't know about the loony bin, but Uncle Jonathan had better be getting ready for beddy-by if he's going to take us on a picnic tomorrow." She reached into the folds of her dress and pulled out a silver watch on a long chain. She popped the lid open and announced that it was three A.M.

Jonathan looked up with surprise. "It is? Good grief, I had no idea——"

"Please, Uncle Jonathan," said Lewis, interrupting. "Can you tell me one thing more?"

"Sure, Lewis. What is it?"

Lewis looked fidgety and embarrassed. "Well . . . if the clocks are supposed to drown out the noise of the clock in the walls, why do you stop them at night?"

Jonathan sighed. "I don't stop them every night. Some nights I just walk around checking all the rooms. It makes me feel secure, somehow. I can't explain it. But some nights, like this one, I get the urge to stop all the blasted everlasting ticking. I get the feeling that if I were to make the house quiet—perfectly quiet—then maybe I could hear the real clock, the magic one, ticking behind one particular wall, or in some cubbyhole. But it never works, and I always feel half crazy for trying."

Lewis still looked puzzled. "If it's a magic clock," he said slowly, "then wouldn't it be invisible? I mean, wouldn't it be something you couldn't actually put your hands on?"

Jonathan shook his head. "Not really, Lewis. Most magic is accomplished with solid everyday objects. Objects that have had spells said over them. One witch I knew tried to obliterate her enemy by leaving a photo of him under the running water of her gutterspout. Her reasoning was that he would die when the face on the picture was wiped out. It's a common method. No, Lewis. This is a clock as real as grandpa over there. Only it's enchanted. But what it is enchanted to do I don't for the life of me know."

"Well, *I* know something, Weird Beard," said Mrs.

Zimmermann, dangling her watch like a pendulum before Jonathan's eyes, "I know that if we don't catch just a little, teeny bit of shut-eye, we're all going to be wearing our crabby caps in the morning. Lewis, off to bed. Jonathan, same with you. I'll rinse the cookie plates and put away the milk."

Later, up in his room, Lewis stood in the middle of the floor staring at a patch of flowered wallpaper near the fireplace. He walked quickly over to the wall and put his ear to it. Yes, the ticking was here too. He walked across the room and listened to another wall. More of the same.

Lewis walked back to the center of the room and then, abruptly, he began to pace. He paced in quick strides with his hands behind his back, the way he had seen his father do when he was upset. He paced and tried to think logically. But logic wasn't much help where the clock in the walls was concerned, so at last Lewis gave it up. He jumped into bed and went to sleep.

CHAPTER THREE

On the first Monday after Labor Day, Lewis started going to school in New Zebedee and, before long, he had forgotten all about the mysterious clock in the walls. He had troubles enough of his own.

They weren't new troubles. They were the troubles that a fat boy who can't play baseball carries around with him from place to place. Lewis had always been overweight. He couldn't remember a time when he hadn't been. All his life—all ten years of it—he had been listening to children who chanted:

> Fatty, fatty, two by four
> Can't get through the kitchen door.

Sometimes he wanted to beat up the kids who made fun of him, but he couldn't box and he wasn't very strong. That was another problem. But the worst problem of all was the baseball problem. Lewis still spun all the way around when he swung at a ball, and he threw his bat. At first he tried to excuse himself by saying, "Watch out, I'm gonna throw the bat!" But the other kids said, "Look, you throw the bat and we're gonna beat you up. You hang onto it when you swing or you can't play."

That is what they said when they let him play, which was not very often. Most of the time when he lined up to be chosen he was the last one left, and the captain of the side that was supposed to take him usually said, "Why do we hafta take *him?* He can't field, he can't hit, he can't pitch. He can't even run. Come on, we'll play one man short."

What they said about Lewis was true. Sometimes a new boy or a kind boy would get to be captain, and he would choose Lewis for his team. But when Lewis came to bat, he usually struck out. If he hit the ball, it popped up and the pitcher caught it. Or he might ground out to first base. When his team was out in the field, the boys made Lewis play right field, because not many balls got hit out that way. But when one did, Lewis always dropped it, unless it hit him on the head. He would stagger back and forth as he tried to keep track of the ball that hung there, high over his head, but he always got dizzy and covered his face with his glove and screamed "No! No!" as the ball came down. After a while even the kind boys turned him down.

One afternoon, when the usual routine had been gone through, and Lewis had run off the field sobbing because they would not let him play, he found himself standing at home plate on a baseball diamond that wasn't being used that day. At his feet was a bat, a thick old club with a split handle that had been wrapped up with black friction tape. There was a softball nearby, or what was left of one: a black, sticky, egg-shaped lump covered with string. Lewis picked up the ball and bat. He threw the ball into the air and swung at it. He missed. He picked the ball up and tried again. Again he missed. He was about to try for the third time when someone said, "You're doin' it all wrong."

Lewis turned and saw a skinny boy about his own age squatting next to the bicycle rack. There was a big fluff of brick-red hair on top of the boy's head, and his right arm was in a sling. The boy was Tarby.

Everybody in the school knew who Tarby was. Even Lewis knew, and he had only been in New Zebedee for a couple of months. Probably everyone in New Zebedee and most of the people in Capharnaum County knew who Tarby was. At least, that was the impression that Lewis got. Tarby was the most popular boy in the school. He was a daredevil, the kind of boy who rode his bicycle through bonfires and hung by his knees from the limbs of trees. All the girls liked him, and he was the big home-run hitter in the softball games. He got chosen first so often that most of the time the boys made him a captain, just to avoid all the fighting over who got to have Tarby on their team. But here he was with his arm in a sling, watching Lewis as he tried to hit the ball.

"I said, you're doing it all wrong. You're supposed to keep your feet planted flat. Then you swing from the hips. Here. Let me show you."

Tarby scrambled to his feet and walked over to where Lewis was standing. He grabbed the bat and hefted it in one hand, choking up on it a bit.

"Okay," he said, "get out there and pitch. Just lob it up here."

Lewis had never seen anyone trying to hit a ball with the bat held in only one hand. He was afraid that Tarby would miss and get mad and go home. With a nervous grin on his face, Lewis lobbed the ball toward the plate. Tarby swung and the bat connected. *Clack!* It struck the ball with that rickety hollow sound that split bats have. The ball shot on a line toward center field. It would have been a clean single.

"See? And that's just with one arm. You ought to be able to do that well with two. C'mon. I'll pitch."

Lewis walked in from the pitcher's mound and took the bat from Tarby's hand.

"I didn't know your arm was broken," said Lewis shyly. "How'd you do it?"

"Fell out of a tree. I was hanging by my knees. Upside down, like in the monkey house. It's okay. It'll heal up."

Tarby walked out to the mound. Lewis pounded his bat on the plate and waved it the way he had seen George Kell do in Briggs Stadium in Detroit. But when Tarby threw the ball, Lewis missed as usual.

Every day for the next two weeks Tarby met Lewis after school, and they practiced batting. Slowly, gradually, Lewis's swing got better. He even managed to hit a few line drives. But something even more important was happening. Lewis and Tarby were getting to be friends. Tarby liked Lewis's jokes, and Lewis found out that Tarby hated some of the kids that he hated. Lewis liked Tarby's imitation of Mrs. Fondrighter, a mean teacher at school. Mrs. Fondrighter always called her husband "Jerrold," which was a funny thing to do. Tarby made a loop in the end of a green twig and pretended it was an eyeglass on a stick. Then he would stare through the loop at Lewis and say, in a high voice, "How *deah* you say such things to me, Jer-*rold!*"

Then Lewis and Tarby would sit around planning how they were going to take care of Carol Kay Laberdeen, a snotty girl in the sixth grade who got away with murder because her father was on the school board. It was usually dark by the time Lewis and Tarby said goodby to each other by the mailbox at the bottom of High Street.

One afternoon early in October, Lewis and Tarby

were out at the athletic field playing flies and grounders. Lewis had gotten good enough so that he could hit Tarby some pretty long fly balls. Tarby's arm was still in a cast, but he picked off the line drives and caught the pop flies as easily as if he had had two hands.

Lewis was out in the field. It was getting dark, and he was having trouble seeing the ball, and besides he was a little bored. He stood there thinking, or "doping off" as Tarby called it.

He wanted to do something nice for Tarby. Something nice that would really impress him and make him a stronger friend than ever. Maybe he could get Uncle Jonathan to do a magic trick for Tarby. Sure, that would do it. Lewis hesitated a minute, remembering Jonathan saying that he was only a "parlor magician." The kind that pulled rabbits out of hats and told you what card you were holding in your hand. But then he *had* said that he knew a few tricks that went beyond that. . . .

Lewis thought some more. Oh, well, Jonathan could probably do it. Anyone who could make windows change their pictures could do what Lewis had in mind. And anyway, Lewis thought that he remembered hearing Jonathan say that he had done such a thing once.

"Hey, Lewis! I hit the ball out to you about six hours ago. Did you go to sleep?"

Lewis looked up. "Huh? Oh, gee, I'm sorry, Tarby. Say, how would you like to see my uncle eclipse the moon?"

Tarby stared at him. "What did you say?"

"I said . . . oh, c'mon, Tarby, let's go home. It's too dark to see the ball. C'mon and I'll tell you all about my Uncle Jonathan. He's a real wizard."

The two boys walked back under the streetlights, playing catch as they went. Lewis tried to explain about Uncle Jonathan's magic powers, but he could see that Tarby was not convinced.

"Boy, I'll *bet* your uncle can eclipse the moon. I'll just *bet* he can. He prob'ly sits up in his room drinking beer, and then he goes out in back and stares up at the moon, and boy does it go rround . . . and . . . rraounnd." Tarby staggered out into the street and rolled his eyes.

Lewis felt like hitting him, but he knew that Tarby could beat him up, so he just said, "You wanta see him do it?"

"Yeah," said Tarby in a sneery voice. "I wanta see him do it."

"Okay," said Lewis. "I'll ask him tonight. When he's ready to do it, I'll let you know."

"Gee, I hope I won't have to wait too long," said Tarby sarcastically. "I really do want to see Old Lard Guts eclipse the moo-hoo-hoo, moo-hoo-ha . . . ."

"Stop it. Stop making fun of my uncle." Lewis's face was red, and he was almost crying.

"Make me," said Tarby.

"I can't, and you know it," said Lewis.

Tarby went on moo-hooing until they reached the

khaki-colored mailbox at the foot of High Street. This time when they split up to go home, Lewis didn't say goodby to Tarby. He didn't even wave. But by the time he was inside the gate at 100 High Street, Lewis had gotten over his mad—more or less—and so he went straight inside to see his uncle. He found Jonathan laying out a game of solitaire on the dining-room table. It was a complicated game called "Napoleon at St. Helena," and the layout covered most of the ivory-colored oilcloth pad. Jonathan looked up and smiled as Lewis walked into the room.

"Hi, Lewis! How's baseball these days?"

"Getting better, I guess. Tarby helps me a lot. Say, Uncle Jonathan, do you suppose we could do something nice for Tarby? He really is a good friend of mine."

"Sure, Lewis. We'll invite him to dinner. Is that what you mean?"

Lewis blushed and fidgeted. "Uh . . . well, yeah . . . kind of. Do you think that maybe after dinner we could . . . uh, that is, *you* could . . . eclipse the moon for him?"

Jonathan stared at him. "Did I tell you I could do *that?*"

"Yes. Remember, one night when you were bragging . . . er, talking to Mrs. Zimmermann about whether earth magic was stronger than moon magic? You said that a moon wizard could eclipse the moon any time he felt like it, and that you were a moon wizard."

Jonathan smiled and shook his head. "Did I say that? My, my, how I do run on. Let me see, I do seem to recall eclipsing the moon one night in 1932. That was during a picnic out at Wilder Creek Park. I remember the date, April 30, which is Walpurgis Night. That's the night when witches and warlocks all over the world get together for whoop-te-doos. Ours was just a convention of the Capharnaum County Magicians Society, but some of them are real wizards. At any rate, to get back to what I was saying . . ."

"Never mind," said Lewis, turning away with a pouty look on his face. "I'll tell Tarby that you can't do it."

"Oh, Lewis!" cried Jonathan, throwing the pack of cards down on the table. "You are the most easily discouraged boy I ever met. If I did it once, I can do it again. It's just that it's not a normal occurrence. And everything has to be just right. In the heavens, that is."

"Oh."

"Yes, oh. Now, as soon as I have won this silly game from myself, you and I will go to the library and consult the almanac. So be quiet for a minute."

Lewis fidgeted and clasped and unclasped his hands and stared at the light fixture until Jonathan finished his game. Then the two of them went to the library, slid back the panelled doors, and entered the marvelous room that smelled of damp paper, wood smoke, and Turkoman's Terror, Jonathan's personal tobacco blend. Jonathan moved the stepladder to the part of the wall that contained his magic books, climbed up, and pulled down a thick dusty volume labelled:

HARDESTY'S

Universal Omnium Gatherum

Perpetual Calendar, Date Book,
Almanac, and Book of Days

He flipped to the section on eclipses, did some rapid mental calculations, and said, "You're in luck, Lewis. 1948 is a good year for lunar eclipses. The planets will be favorable next Friday. Invite Tarby to dinner for that night. I'll be ready."

Friday night came around, and Lewis brought Tarby home for dinner. There was nothing especially magic about the meal, except that the cider jug on the table burped a lot, and that might have been because the cider was getting hard. After the dishes were cleared away, Jonathan asked Lewis and Tarby to help Mrs. Zimmermann carry some kitchen chairs out into the back yard. Then he walked out into the front hall and consulted his cane rack, a blue Willoware vase full of walking sticks of all sizes and shapes. Some had ivory or bone handles, some were tough, crooked old pieces of hickory or maplewood, and some had thin springy swords concealed inside. But only one cane was magic.

It was a long black rod of some very hard wood. At one end was a ferrule of polished brass, and at the other was a glass globe the size of a baseball. It seemed to be snowing inside the globe. Through the swirling little flakes you could see, now and then, an odd little miniature castle. The globe burned with an icy gray light. Jonathan picked up the cane, hefted it, and walked back toward the kitchen with it tucked under his arm.

Out in the back yard, the audience was ready. Mrs. Zimmermann, Lewis, and Tarby sat in straight chairs facing the birdbath. It was a chilly, clear October night. All the stars were out, and a large full moon was rising over the four elm trees at the far end of Jonathan's yard. The screen door slammed, and everyone looked up. The magician had arrived.

Without saying a word, Jonathan went around to the north side of the house. An old mossy rain barrel stood there against the sandstone wall. Jonathan looked into the barrel, breathed three times on the dark water, and with his left forefinger cut the faintly shimmering surface into four quarters. Then he leaned low over the mouth of the barrel and began whispering in a strange language. The three spectators had not left their chairs—Jonathan had told them to stay where they were—but they craned their necks around a good deal trying to figure out what the wizard was doing.

The whispering, weirdly magnified by the mouth of

the barrel, went on for some time. Lewis twisted way around in his chair, but all he could see was the dark shape of Uncle Jonathan and the faintly glowing gray globe of the magic cane. Finally Jonathan returned. In one hand he held the cane, and in the other he had a saucepan full of rain water.

"Is your uncle going to wash his hair?" whispered Tarby.

"Oh, be quiet!" hissed Lewis. "He knows what he's doing. Just you watch."

Tarby, Lewis, and Mrs. Zimmermann watched anxiously as Jonathan poured the saucepan into the birdbath. Then he went back to the rain barrel for more. *Dip. Splash*. He came back with another panful. He emptied it. And he went back for a third.

The third panful seemed to be enough. Jonathan set down the empty pan and picked up his cane, which had been leaning against the birdbath. The glass ball glowed and sent out a ray of dusty gray light. The ray rested on the surface of the water in the birdbath. Jonathan made signs over the water with the cane and started muttering again.

"Come on and look," he said, motioning to the three spectators. They got up and walked over to the birdbath. The water in the flat, shallow concrete pan had started to heave and pitch, like ocean water in a storm. Lewis was surprised to see tiny whitecaps forming. Then long rollers began to crash silently into the rim, sending pin-point flecks of foam out onto the grass. Jonathan watched for a while along with the rest. Then, suddenly, he raised the cane and cried, "Peace! Peace to the waters of the earth! Show unto us the round disk of the moon, even as she now appeareth in the heavens above!"

The water calmed down. Soon it was a flat pool again, and floating on the still black surface was the cold reflection of the full moon. Now Jonathan did something very unlikely. As the others watched, he bent over and pulled a small boulder out of the pile of rocks at the base of the birdbath. Then, lifting it high in the air, he shouted, "Stand back!" and dropped the rock. *Splash!* Water slopped everywhere, and Lewis did not get out of the way soon enough to keep from getting some on his shoes.

When the water had calmed down again, Jonathan picked up the rock and looked into the pool. There, wobbly and creased with ripples, was the moon's reflection.

"Still there?" said Jonathan, grinning. "Well, we'll just see about that!"

He reached down into the water and picked up the reflection. It might have been a trick, but the cold, icy-gray disk he held up looked like the reflection that had floated in the pool a moment before. And sure enough, when Lewis looked into the water, all he saw now was a shiny blackness.

Jonathan held up the reflection and turned it back and forth as if it were a dinner plate. The disk burned cold and bitter, and sparkled like freshly fallen snow. It hurt Lewis's eyes to stare at it for very long. Now Jonathan snapped his wrist and sent the disk flying across the yard. It sailed clear across to the dark thicket in front of the four elm trees. Then Jonathan, cane in hand, ran off after the disk. It was a long yard and, even in the moon-light, the boys and Mrs. Zimmermann could not see what he was doing down there.

Suddenly the air was filled with the inane glockling and blockling of bamboo wind chimes. There was a set of them hanging from one of the elm trees, and Jonathan had given it a good hard yank. Now he came dancing back up the yard, dueling with shadows and saying things like, "Ha! Have at you in your bladder for a blaggardly slacker! Hoo! Hunh! And the third in his bosom!"

He stopped in front of the birdbath and held the ball of the cane up under his chin so that his face looked like an actor's face when it is lit from below by footlights. Slowly he raised his right hand and pointed at the sky. "Look!" he cried.

All three of the spectators looked up. At first they saw nothing strange. Then, slowly, a black, tarry, drippy shadow oozed down over the face of the surprised moon. In no time at all the moon was dark, completely dark, blacked out, without even the faint brownish umbra that marks its place during an ordinary eclipse.

And now Uncle Jonathan's back yard came to life. It was full of strange sights and sounds. The grass glowed a phosphorescent green, and red worms wriggled through the tall blades with a hushing sound. Strange insects dropped down out of the overhanging boughs of the willow tree and started to dance on the picnic table. They waltzed and wiggled in a shaking blue light, and the music they danced to, faint though it was, sounded to Lewis like "Rugbug," the famous fox trot composed by Maxine Hollister. This was one of the tunes that Jonathan's parlor organ played.

Uncle Jonathan walked over to the tulip bed, put his ear to the ground, and listened. He motioned for the others to join him. Lewis put his ear to the damp earth, and he heard strange things. He heard the noise that earthworms make as they slowly inch along, breaking hard black clods with their blunt heads. He heard the secret inwound conversations of bulbs and roots, and the breathing of flowers. And Lewis knew strange things, without knowing how he came to know them. He knew that there was a cat named Texaco buried in the patch of ground he knelt on. Its delicate ivory skeleton was falling slowly to pieces down there, and its dank fur was shrivelled and matted and rotten. The boy who had buried the cat had buried a sand pail full of shells near it. Lewis did not know the name of the boy, or how long ago he had buried the cat and the pail, but he could see the red and blue pail clearly. Blotches of brown rust were eating up the bright designs, and the shells were covered with green mold.

After a long while, Lewis sat up and looked around. Tarby was kneeling near him, his ear to the ground and his eyes wide with wonder. But where was Uncle Jonathan? Where, for that matter, was Mrs. Zimmermann? At the far end of the yard, in the shadow of the four elm trees, Lewis thought he saw them moving around. He tapped Tarby on the shoulder, pointed, and the two boys silently got up and went to join the magicians.

When they found them, Jonathan was arguing with Mrs. Zimmermann, who argued right back, though her ear was pressed flat to the ground.

"I say it's the old storm sewer system," she muttered. "It was lost track of in 1868 because the charts got thrown out with the wastepaper."

"Well, you can think what you like, Frizzy Wig," said Jonathan as he knelt down for another listen. "*I* say it's an underground stream. Capharnaum County is full of them, and it would account for the fact that Sin-and-Flesh Creek is much bigger when it leaves New Zebedee than it is when it enters it."

"You're full of beans, Fatso," said Mrs. Zimmermann, whose ear was still pressed to the ground. "I think I know the sound of water rushing through a brick tunnel. It's all vaulty and hollow."

"Like your head?"

Lewis and Tarby pressed their ears to the ground, but

all they could hear was a sound like the one you hear when you press your ear against an inner tube that you are floating on in a lake. Lewis felt very excited. He wanted to be all over the garden at once, touching things and smelling them and listening. The magic in the back yard lasted for over an hour. Then the phosphorescence changed to plain old ordinary moonlight, and the moon floated high overhead, free from enchantments.

As they walked back into the house, Lewis asked his uncle if the police department didn't get mad when he eclipsed the moon. Jonathan chuckled and put his arm around Lewis.

"No," he said, "strangely enough they don't. I've never been quite sure why, but maybe it's because the eclipse is only visible in this yard."

"You mean it's not real?"

"Of course, it's real. You saw it, didn't you? But one of the troubles with human beings is that they can only see out of their own eyes. If I could be two people, I'd station the other me across town to see if the eclipse was operating over there."

"Why don't you ask Mrs. Zimmermann to go watch?"

"Because she'd be crabby. She always wants to be in on things. Don't you, Pruny?"

"Yes, I do. And right now I'd like to be in on some chocolate-chip cookies. Why don't you all come over to my place?"

And that is what they did. Lewis was happy to have a chance to show off Mrs. Zimmermann's house to Tarby. It was not a mansion, by any means. Just a little two-story bungalow with a screened-in front porch. But it was full of strange things, most of them purple. Mrs. Zimmermann had a thing about the color purple. Her rugs, her wallpaper, her staircase runner, her toilet paper, and her bath soap were all purple. So was the large surrealistic painting of a dragon that hung in her living room. It had been done for her specially by the French painter Odilon Redon.

As they munched their cookies and drank their milk and walked around looking at the purple things in Mrs. Zimmermann's house, Lewis noticed that Tarby wasn't saying much. When it came time for him to go, Tarby shook Jonathan's hand while staring at the carpet, and he mumbled, "Thanks for the cookies" to Mrs. Zimmermann in such a low voice that he couldn't be understood. Lewis saw Tarby to the front gate. He knew this was odd behavior for Tarby, who was usually loud and sassy-acting, even in front of grownups.

"Thanks for the magic show," said Tarby, shaking Lewis's hand and looking very serious. "It was kind of scary, but it was fun. I take back all the things I said about your uncle, I guess. Well, see you around." And with that, Tarby went trudging down the hill.

Lewis stared after him with a worried frown on his

face. He hoped that Tarby had had a good time. Most people do not like to be proven wrong, even when they enjoy themselves in the process. Tarby was a popular boy, and he was used to being right about everything. He had turned out to be wrong about Jonathan's magic powers. Now what would he do? Lewis didn't want to lose his only friend.

CHAPTER FOUR

It was the last week of October, and Tarby's arm had almost healed. Lewis saw less and less of him now. He still waited for him on the baseball diamond out behind the school, and sometimes Tarby showed up, and sometimes he didn't.

Of course, Tarby couldn't be expected to be very interested in flies and grounders at this time of year. The football season was getting underway. Lewis had seen Tarby playing football with the other boys after school. Needless to say, Tarby was always the quarterback. He threw long passes and made end runs and pulled off tricky plays, like the "Statue of Liberty."

Lewis had thought of trying to join the football game,

but he remembered what had happened back in Wisconsin. Whenever anyone charged over the line at him, he fell to the ground and covered his head with his hands. He couldn't catch passes and, if he tried to kick the ball, he usually wound up bunting it with his knee. Maybe if he got really good at baseball, he could get Tarby to teach him football next year.

But he wasn't going to learn much about baseball without Tarby. Of course, these days he wasn't learning much even with Tarby's help. On those rare occasions when Tarby showed up to play ball with Lewis, he seemed to want to get the game over with in a hurry. Lewis knew that he was losing Tarby, but so far he hadn't figured out how in the world he was going to hang on to him.

One Saturday afternoon when the two of them were poking around in the cemetery, Lewis had an idea. New Zebedee's beautiful old cemetery was on a high hill just outside of town. It was full of elaborate gravestones that showed weeping women leaning on urns and cupids extinguishing torches. There were pillars made to look as if they had been broken, and there were pillars with hands on top, pointing up. There were little tombstones made in the shape of lambs, and these were over the graves of children. Some of the lambs had been there so long that they were worn into grimy white blobs that reminded Lewis of soap.

On this particular day, Lewis and Tarby had been

inspecting a lot where all the gravestones were carved to look like wood. Each grave was marked by a little granite log, complete with bark and rings and knotholes. The curb around the lot matched the tombstones, and in the center of everything rose a broken tree of stone. The top was jagged, as if lightning had struck it, and a stone woodpecker was whetting his beak on the realistically carved bark. Lewis and Tarby had been playing in this petrified forest for a while, but now they were getting tired. The sun, red as the tomato sun in Jonathan's stained-glass window, was setting between two crooked pine trees. Lewis shivered and zipped up his jacket.

"Let's go back to my house," he said. "Mrs. Zimmermann can make us some cocoa, and I'll show you some *real* petrified wood. My uncle got it in a forest out west that was actually turned to stone."

Tarby looked bored, and he also looked mean. "Who wants to go back to your old uncle's house? It's a pretty crazy place, if you ask me. And how come old Mrs. Zimmermann is over there all the time? Is she in *luuvv* with him?" Tarby threw his arms around the stone tree and started kissing it with loud smacks. Lewis felt like crying, but somehow he managed to keep down the tears.

"I . . . I bet you think all my uncle can do is eclipse the moon," said Lewis. It sounded silly, but he couldn't think of anything else to say.

Tarby looked interested, in a bored sort of way. "Well," he said, "what else can he do?"

Lewis did not know why he said what he said next. It just came to him.

"My uncle can raise the dead."

Tarby did a somersault over one of the log-shaped markers. "Oh, sure he can," he snorted. "Look, your uncle is a fake. That night when he made it look like the moon had gone out and all that other stuff was happening, he just had us *hypnotized*. My dad told me that was prob'ly what happened."

Lewis stared at him. "You said you'd never tell anyone about what we did that night. Remember? I made you promise."

Tarby looked away. "Oh, yeah, I guess I did promise. Sorry."

Both of them sat quietly for a long while. There was nothing left of the sun but a faint red afterglow. A night wind had sprung up, and it stirred the long grass on the graves. Finally Lewis got up and spoke. His voice came from way down in his throat.

"What if I were to raise a dead person by myself?"

Tarby looked at him. He giggled. "Boy, that would be some fun. I can see you runnin' down Main Street in the middle of the night with a ghost after you." Tarby got up and waved his arms. "*Woo-oooo!*" he wailed. "I am the ghost of miss-terr-reee! *Woo-oooo!*"

Lewis's face was getting red. "Wanta see me do it?"

"Yeah," said Tarby. "I do. When are you gonna do it?"

"I'll let you know," said Lewis, although he didn't have the faintest idea of what he was going to do, or when he was going to do it, or how he was going to do it. All he knew was that he had to try, if he was going to hang on to his only friend in New Zebedee.

During that week before Halloween, Lewis spent a lot of time in his uncle's study. Normally it was okay for Lewis to browse in the library, but if Jonathan had known what books Lewis was looking at now, he would have stopped him. Lewis knew this, so he always waited till Jonathan was out visiting, or raking leaves, or tying up corn shocks in the garden. When he was sure he would not be disturbed, Lewis would slide back the paneled walnut doors, tiptoe into the study, and roll the step-ladder down to the section of the library wall that contained Jonathan's magic books. Jonathan had forbidden Lewis to look through these books without his permission, so Lewis felt very bad about what he was doing. He felt bad about the whole business. But he went ahead anyway.

He looked through all the strange old volumes, with their pentacles and pentagrams, their anagrams and talismans and abracadabras and long incantations printed in Old English lettering. But he spent most of his time with a big black leather volume entitled *Necromancy*. Necromancy is the branch of magic that deals with the raising of the dead. The frontispiece of the book was an engraving that showed Dr. John Dee, personal astrologer to Queen Elizabeth I of England, as he and his assistant,

Michael Kelly, raised the spirit of a dead woman in an English churchyard at midnight. The two men were standing inside a chalk circle drawn on the ground. The border of the circle was covered with strange symbols and words. Just outside the charmed circle hovered a figure in a long nightgown. On her head she wore an odd ruffly bonnet, the kind they once buried women in. Lewis kept turning back to the illustration because it frightened him. But he read the rest of the book. He read it all, and he memorized some of the charms. He even copied one of the pentagrams and the spell that went with it onto a piece of notepaper and put it in his pocket.

Halloween was a windy dark day. Lewis sat in the window of his bedroom and watched the wind strip the trees of the few ragged brown leaves that remained. He felt sad and scared. He was sad because he had disobeyed his uncle, who was always kind to him. And he felt scared because he had promised Tarby that he would meet him in the graveyard at twelve o'clock on Halloween night, so that the two of them could raise up the spirit of a dead person. Or try to. Lewis didn't think it would work, and he was kind of hoping that it wouldn't.

They had the grave all picked out. It was a mausoleum stuck into the side of the hill the graveyard was built on. Lewis didn't know anything about who was buried in the tomb. Neither did Tarby. There wasn't even a name on the door. But whatever the name was, it probably started with O, because there was an O in the triangle over the heavy old stone arch. It was a funny kind of O, and it looked like this:

At dinner that night, Lewis did not say much. This was odd because he usually talked his head off about everything under the sun, especially those things he didn't know anything about. Jonathan asked him if he was all right, and Lewis said that of course he was all right, anybody could see that. Jonathan and Mrs. Zimmermann exchanged worried glances and stared at him again, but Lewis went on eating with his head down. At the end of the meal, he pushed his chair back and announced that he was not going trick-or-treating, because he was too old for it.

"Does that mean that you're not coming over to my place for cider and doughnuts?" asked Mrs. Zimmermann. "Because if it does, I'll show up at midnight at the foot of your bed in my role of Grinning Griselda, the resuscitated cadaver. It's a horrible thing to see."

Lewis looked up. There was a wild look on his face, but he managed to force his mouth into a smile.

"No, Mrs. Zimmermann," he said. "I wouldn't miss one of your cider-and-doughnut parties. Not for the world.

But right now I've got to go up to my room and finish one of John L. Stoddard's books. I've gotten to the exciting part." Whereupon he jumped up, excused himself, and ran upstairs.

Jonathan looked at Mrs. Zimmermann. "I have a feeling," he said, "that something is up."

"Hooray for your lightning-quick mind," said Mrs. Zimmermann. "Yes, something is up, and *I* have a feeling that we won't know what it is till it's over with."

"Maybe not," said Jonathan as he lit his pipe. "But I can't believe that Lewis is mixed up in anything bad. And I'm certainly not going to grill him like a mean stepfather. Still, I'd like to know what he's up to."

"So would I," said Mrs. Zimmermann thoughtfully. "Do you suppose it has anything to do with Tarby? The boy's arm is healing, and he'll probably be going back to play with the other boys soon. That leaves Lewis out."

Jonathan scratched his chin. "Yes, maybe that's it," he said. "I'll have to have a talk with him. Oh, by the way, have you noticed that the clock is louder now?" He was trying to sound nonchalant, but Mrs. Zimmermann could read the look in his eyes.

"Yes," she said, trying hard to smile. "I've heard it too. And maybe if we ignore it, it'll just die down. It has before, you know. One thing for sure: you're not going to do any good by barging around the house with a crowbar, prying open the wainscot and peering between floorboards."

"I suppose not," said Jonathan, sighing. "Though I might come across the blasted thing by sheer persistence. On the other hand, that would mean wrecking the house, and I'm not quite ready to do that. Not until I have some clearer idea that the clock is something that can do us harm. And so far, I'm just guessing. I'm even guessing when I say it's a real, physical clock, and not just some illusion left here by old Isaac Izard to drive people mad."

"It's best not to think about the thing," said Mrs. Zimmermann. "Not until you have to, at any rate. You can't prepare for all the disasters that might occur in this frightening world of ours. If the devil appears or if we find that the End of the World is at hand, we'll do something."

"Mm-hmmm. We'll hide in the cellar. Come on. Let's wash the dishes."

Lewis came down from his room at ten o'clock and went next door to have cider and doughnuts. He found Jonathan and Mrs. Zimmermann waiting for him in the dining room. There was a big round oak table at one end of the long room, and it was covered with a clean checkered tablecloth. On the table stood a gallon jug of cider and a plate of powdered doughnuts, or "fried cakes," as Mrs. Zimmermann called them. At the other end of the room, a violet fire crackled in the fireplace. Purple shadows rushed back and forth over the hearthrug and, over the mantelpiece, the purple dragon in the painting seemed to writhe and squirm. He looked very fierce indeed.

"Evening, Lewis," said Jonathan. "Pull up a chair and dig in."

After Lewis had eaten two or three doughnuts and downed four big glasses of cider, Jonathan announced that tonight's entertainment would be Historical Illusions, or Famous Scenes From the Past. He asked Lewis what past scene he would most like to see.

Lewis answered immediately. "I want to see the defeat of the Spanish Armada. Not the battle scenes, because I've read all about them in John L. Stoddard. But he doesn't tell what happened when they had to sail all the way around England and Scotland to get home. I want to see that part."

"Very well," said Jonathan. "Let's go over and sit by the fire."

They got up and walked over to the fireplace, where three big comfortable chairs waited for them. When they were all settled, Jonathan pointed his pipe at the two electric candles over the mantelpiece. Slowly the power began to drain from them. They flickered and went out. Then the bulbs in the chandelier over the table began to do the same thing. It was like watching the house lights dim in a theater. Lewis felt something tickling his nostrils and his tongue. It was the smell and taste of salt. Grainy blowing mists filled the room, and Lewis found himself standing on a grassy headland. Jonathan was on his left, and Mrs. Zimmermann was on his right. Before them a cold gray sea tumbled and tossed.

"Where are we?" asked Lewis.

"We are standing on John O'Groats," said Jonathan. "It is the northernmost point in Scotland. The year is 1588, and out there is the Armada, or what is left of it. You'll need the telescope to see them."

"Telescope?" said Lewis, and then he realized that they were standing on a little stone platform behind a curving waist-high wall. It was the kind of wall you find on scenic lookout points in state parks. And mounted on the wall was a small pay telescope with a set of instructions under glass. Lewis bent over and peered at the little card, which said:

SEE THE ARMADA
Last chance this year
Deposit five shillings, if you please.

Jonathan fumbled in his vest and dug out two large silver coins. He handed them to Lewis. They were half crowns, and each one was worth two and a half shillings in old-fashioned British money. Lewis slid the coins into the slot. There was a whirring sound. He put his eye to the telescope and looked.

At first all he saw was a milky blur but, after he had fiddled with the adjusting wheel a bit, Lewis could see several big galleons ploughing sluggishly through the waves. Their sails were ripped and torn, and their tattered rigging flew about crazily in the wind. The long rows of gunports were closed tight against the battering sea, and

Lewis could see patches on the sides of three or four ships. One lumbering hulk had a cable passed around its middle, presumably to hold it together.

As Lewis watched, the ships wallowed on. Now he could see their tall ornamented sterns. Saints and bishops and dragons supported gilded window frames or clung to scrolled corners. Lewis noticed that several statues had arms or hands or heads missing. One scowling bishop was wearing his miter at a rakish tilt.

Lewis turned the telescope. Now he was looking at a strange little man. The man was pacing the quarterdeck of the biggest, richest-looking, but most badly damaged ship of all. He wore a black cape that barely reached to his knees, and he was shivering. His whiskers were long and weepy, and he looked very worried.

"Who is the man on the biggest ship?" asked Lewis.

"That," said Jonathan, "is the Duke of Medina-Sidonia. He is the Captain General of the 'Ocean Sea,' which means that he is the commander of the Armada. The whole, shot-riddled, sinking mess. I'll bet he wishes he were at home right now."

Lewis felt sorry for the poor Duke. When he was reading John L. Stoddard in bed the night before, he had wished that he could be there in the Narrow Seas, commanding a stout English galleon. He would have emptied broadside after broadside into the Duke's flagship, until she sank. But now he wanted to help the man, if he could.

While Lewis stood thinking, Jonathan tapped him on the shoulder and pointed to something Lewis had not seen before. There, mounted on the wall, stood a cannon. A brass twenty-four pounder with a wooden, step-sided carriage and ropes running from rings in the base of the carriage to rings in the wall. The ropes were to keep the gun from rolling down the hill after it fired.

"Come on, Lewis," said Jonathan, smiling. "Let's have a shot at the Armada. Isn't this what you've always wanted to do? It's all loaded and ready to fire. Come on!"

Lewis looked as if he were going to be sick. Tears came to his eyes. "Oh, no, Uncle Jonathan! I couldn't! The poor Duke and his men. Can't we do something for them?"

Jonathan stared at Lewis and rubbed his chin. "You know," he said slowly, "for a boy who loves to play at sieges and war, you are remarkably peaceable. When confronted with the real thing, that is. Fortunately for you, however, this isn't the real thing. It's an illusion, as I may have said before. We're really still in Mrs. Zimmermann's dining room with the table at one end and the purple fire at the other. If you go feel that rock there, it will feel remarkably like an armchair. The Duke and his ships out there are less real than smoke and mist, and so is that cannon. Go on. Have a shot."

Lewis brightened up now. This would be fun. A soldier appeared out of nowhere, dressed in the red costume of an English Beefeater. He handed Lewis a smoldering wick on a long rod. Lewis applied it to the touchhole of the cannon. *Boom!* The cannon jerked back against its ropes. Bitter smoke drifted past. Jonathan, who was fighting with Mrs. Zimmermann for the use of the pay telescope, said, "I think that—oh, g'wan, Florence, find your own peephole—I think . . . yes, you have brought down his fore-topgallant spritsail."

Lewis felt pleased, though he didn't know what a fore-topgallant spritsail was. The soldier reloaded, and Lewis fired again. This time he knocked a wooden bishop off the heavily ornamented poop deck. He fired several more times, and then Jonathan gestured, and another Beefeater came running up the hill carrying a wooden bucket full of sizzling, red-hot cannon balls, or "hot potatoes," as the Elizabethan sailors used to call them.

The two soldiers loaded the cannon. First they poured in a kegful of powder. Then they stuffed in wet wadding to keep the cannon ball from setting off the powder. Then came the cannon ball itself. It hissed and steamed when it touched the wadding. Lewis applied the linstock again, and the gun leaped backwards. He watched the cannon ball as it whizzed toward the Duke's galleon. It looked to him like a tiny insane harvest moon. When the ball hit, the ship burst into flames. The weepy-bearded Duke sailed up toward heaven, playing a harp and sitting on a powdered doughnut. And now Lewis, Jonathan, and Mrs. Zimmermann were back in the dining room by the fire.

"Well!" said Jonathan, rubbing his hands. "And what would you like to see next?"

Lewis thought a bit. He was so excited and happy that he had almost forgotten about what he had to do later that night. "I'd like to see the Battle of Waterloo," he said.

Jonathan waved his pipe and the lights went out again. Now they were standing on a muddy hillside in Belgium. The year was 1815. It was raining, a steady smoking drizzle that half hid the high hill opposite the one they were standing on. In the valley below were little red squares. As they watched, blue arrows crashed into these squares, dented them, turned them into parallelograms, trapezoids, and rhombuses, but did not break them. Little puffs of smoke sprang out on the opposite hillside. They reminded Lewis of mushrooms. Behind him he saw geysers of dirt and chipped rock fly up.

"Napoleon's artillery," said Jonathan calmly. More mushrooms sprang up on their hillside as Wellington answered with his own cannons. Rockets exploded overhead, green and blue and sizzling white, and, of course, lovely purple. Flags rose in the valley, dipped, rose, and fell again. Lewis, Jonathan, and Mrs. Zimmermann watched the whole thing from behind a low wall that looked a great deal like the wall on John O'Groats.

After what seemed like a long time, Lewis became aware of a figure standing off to their right. A tall skinny man in a cocked hat and a black cutaway coat.

Lewis recognized him immediately. It was Wellington. He looked exactly the way he did in John Clark Ridpath's *History of the World*.

Wellington scanned the horizon with his telescope. Then he sadly clicked the telescope shut and took out his watch. The watch, which resembled the one Mrs. Zimmermann wore on a chain, dinged eight times. Wellington rolled his eyes toward the sky, put his hand on his heart, and said gravely, "Oh, that Blücher or night would come!"

"Why did he say that, Uncle Jonathan?" asked Lewis. He had looked at all the illustrations in Ridpath's book, but he had never read the account of the battle.

"Blücher is a Prussian general who is coming to aid Wellington," said Jonathan. "Napoleon has sent Grouchy off to keep Blücher busy."

Lewis giggled. "Why is he called Grouchy?"

"Because that's his name," said Mrs. Zimmermann. "Only it's pronounced Groo-*shee* because it's a French name. Fat Ears here knows that, but he's trying to be funny. Well, Jonathan, do you think Wellington will win this time?"

"Dunno, Florence. Wait and see."

Since it was Jonathan's illusion and not the real battle, and since he was feeling silly that evening, he decided to let Napoleon win for a change. Night fell with a clunk like a book falling out of a bookcase, but Blücher did not come. The blue arrows sliced into the red squares, split them up, tore them to pieces. Now the blue arrows turned into an army marching up the hill, an army of tall men wearing bearskin hats that made them even taller. They had long black moustaches and carried muskets with bayonets on the end. They were coming for Wellington, who now looked very red-faced and crabby. He tore off his hat and stomped on it. He threw his watch on the ground and stomped on it too.

"Ooh-*waah!*" he screamed. "Greenwich Mean Time! Very mean time! I want to go home *now!*"

Whereupon the scene changed, and Lewis and Uncle Jonathan and Mrs. Zimmermann were back in the dark shadowy dining room by the warm fire. The purple china clock on the mantel whanged tinnily eleven times. The whole show had taken only an hour.

Jonathan got up, stretched, yawned, and suggested that they all go to bed. Lewis thanked Mrs. Zimmermann for the wonderful party and went home with Jonathan. He went upstairs to bed, but he did not sleep.

CHAPTER FIVE

As the luminous hands of his new Westclox bedside clock
crept around toward midnight, Lewis lay, fully dressed,
under his covers. The room was dark. His heart was
pounding, and he kept saying over and over to himself,
"I wish I didn't have to do it. I wish I didn't have to
do it."

He felt in his pants' pocket for the piece of paper with
the magic circle copied on it. There was a fat piece of
yellow chalk in his other pocket. What if Uncle Jonathan
came to his room to see if he were all right? He'd just
have to pull the covers up to his chin and pretend that he
was asleep. *Tick-tick-tick-tick.* Lewis wished that it was
next week, and that he had never made his stupid promise

to Tarby. He closed his eyes and stared at the patterns that formed on the insides of his eyelids.

Minutes passed. Suddenly Lewis sat up. He threw back the covers and stared at the clock. It was five minutes after twelve! He had promised to meet Tarby in the cemetery at midnight, and now he was going to be late! What could he do? Tarby wouldn't wait for him. He would go home, and tomorrow he would tell all his friends how Lewis had chickened out.

Lewis rubbed his face and tried to think. The cemetery stood atop a long ridge that rose just on the other side of Wilder Creek Park. You had to walk half a mile beyond the city limits to get to the road that ran up the ridge. There was a short cut, of course, but Lewis hadn't intended to take it. Now he had no choice.

Slowly, carefully, Lewis eased himself down onto the floor. He knelt down and groped under the bed for his flashlight. It was a long, old-fashioned flashlight with a fluted handle and a big round lamp on the end. The metal felt cold and slimy in his hand. He went to the closet and put on his heavy jacket. It would be cold up on Cemetery Hill.

Lewis opened the bedroom door. The hall was dark, as usual, and from the next room he could hear Uncle Jonathan snoring. Lewis felt awful. It was like being sick to your stomach. He wished with all his heart that he could run into Jonathan's room, wake him up, and tell him all about the adventure he was going on, and why he had to go through with it. But he didn't do any of these things. Instead, he tiptoed across the hall and opened the door that led to the back stairs.

It didn't take long for Lewis to get to the other side of town. When he had reached the CITY LIMITS sign, he poked around by the side of the road until he found a little wooden staircase that ran down the gravel bank to Wilder Creek Park. The creek was fairly shallow at this point, so Lewis waded across. The water was freezing on his ankles. When he got to the other side he looked up. His hands felt sweaty, and he almost turned around and went home.

He was looking at Cemetery Hill. It was a high, flat-topped ridge cut across in two places by a narrow dirt road. It wasn't a hard hill to climb: New Zebedee children went up and down it every day during the summer. But to Lewis, who was scared of heights, it might as well have been Mount Everest.

Lewis looked up at the dark hill, and he swallowed a couple of times. Maybe if he took the long way around . . . no, he was already late, and Tarby might get bored and go home. The last thing Lewis wanted was to be in the cemetery alone at this time of night. He got a tight grip on his flashlight and started to climb.

At the first landing, Lewis stopped. He was breathing hard, and the front of his jacket was soaked through.

There were black smudges on the knees of his trousers, and there was a twig in his shoe. Two more stages. Lewis gritted his teeth and went on.

At the top of the hill, he dropped to his knees and crossed himself several times. The sweat was running down his face, and he could feel his heart thumping. Well, he had done it. It was no great triumph because Tarby had probably scaled the ridge in a tenth of the time it had taken him. But at least he had done it.

Lewis looked around. He was standing at the edge of a long avenue lined with willow trees. The bare strings of the willows swayed in the wind, and Lewis shivered. He felt very cold and very alone. At the far end of the avenue, the gray gate of the cemetery glimmered. Lewis started to walk toward it.

The cemetery gate was a heavy arch of stone covered with elaborate carving. On the lintel were inscribed these words:

THE TRUMPET SHALL SOUND

AND

THE DEAD SHALL BE RAISED

Lewis pushed open the squeaky iron gate and walked quickly past the rows of white headstones. The mausoleum was on the other side of Cemetery Hill, the side that looked out across the deep valley beyond the town. A little narrow path led down to the stone platform in front of the tomb door. Where was Tarby?

As Lewis looked around, someone said, "Boo!" Lewis almost fainted. It was Tarby, of course, hiding in the shadow of the stone arch on the front of the mausoleum.

"Hi! You sure took long enough," said Tarby. "Where were you?"

"It was hard work climbing," said Lewis, staring sadly down at his wet and dirty trousers.

"It's always hard climbing for fatsoes," said Tarby. "Whyncha lose some weight?"

"Come on, let's do what we're supposed to be doing," said Lewis. He felt depressed.

The cracked and mossy stone slab that lay at the doorstep of the tomb was in the shadow of the hillside now. Everything around it lay in bright moonlight. Lewis turned on the flashlight and played the pale beam over the ugly iron doors. A heavy chain held the doors together, and it was fastened by a large, heart-shaped padlock. Lewis flashed the beam up. There was the strange-looking *O* on the cornice. The wind had died down. Everything was quiet. Lewis handed the flashlight to Tarby and knelt down. Out came the scrap of paper and the chalk. He drew a big circle and then a smaller one within it, like this:

As Tarby held the flashlight steady, Lewis filled in the border of the magic circle with symbols from the piece of paper. When he had chalked in the last strange sign, there was still a blank space in the border. Lewis had read in Jonathan's book that you were supposed to fill in the space with the name of the dead person. But he didn't know the name.

"Well," said Tarby, "I don't see any dead people."

"It's not finished," said Lewis. "We've got to put in the name."

Tarby looked disgusted. "You mean you don't know it?"

"No, I don't," sighed Lewis. "Maybe if we sit here for a minute or two it will come to us."

They knelt silently at the door of the tomb. A sudden gust of wind rattled the dead leaves on an oak tree that grew nearby. Minutes passed. Lewis's mind was completely blank. Then, for some reason, he picked up the chalk.

"Hold the flashlight down here," he said.

Slowly, carefully, he spelled out a name. The funny thing was that he was not thinking of a name at all. It was as if someone else was guiding his hand. With one last down-stroke of the chalk he completed the word: *Selenna.* It was a strange name. Lewis had never known anyone called Selenna. He didn't even know how to pronounce the name. But there it was.

He stood up with the creased paper in his hand. Now

he started to chant in a high-pitched nervous voice: *Aba bēbē bachabē* . . .

He stopped. Tarby, who was crouched beside him, grabbed his arm and squeezed it hard. From deep within the tomb came a sound. *Boom!* A deep hollow sound. The iron doors jolted, as if they had been struck a blow from inside. The chain rattled, and there was a *clunk* on the pavement. The padlock had fallen off. And now, as the boys knelt, terrified, two small spots of freezing gray light appeared. They hovered and danced before the doors of the tomb, which now stood ajar. And something black—blacker than the night, blacker than ink spilled into water—was oozing from the space between the doors.

Tarby shook Lewis and squeezed his arm harder. "Run!" he shouted.

They tumbled over the bank and started to scramble down the hillside. Part of the way Lewis slid on his belly, with roots scratching at his face. He clawed at the wet slippery grass, but he could not get a handhold. Then he was tumbling over and over, and then he was sliding on his back. Rocks scraped his shoulder blades and bumped the back of his head. And then he was sitting on the dirt road, thoroughly shaken and sick and scared.

The moon drifted out from behind a thin veil of clouds and stared down at Lewis as if it were scared too. Tarby was sprawled near him in a weedy ditch. He got up quickly and stared back up the hillside. Now he was tugging at Lewis's arm. "Come on! We've got to get out

of here! It might come after us! Oh, come on! Please come on!"

Lewis was dazed and shaken, but he got up and followed Tarby over the next stage of the hillside, and the next one. They waded across the stream and were soon on the gravel road that led back to New Zebedee.

As they walked along, Lewis kept stopping and shuddering. Tarby told him to quit it.

"I can't help it," said Lewis in a sick voice. "Did you see it? It was awful!"

"I don't know what I saw," said Tarby sullenly. "Maybe it was the moonlight or something."

Lewis stared at him. Was Tarby kidding, or was he trying to deny to himself that he had seen what he really had seen? Lewis didn't know, and he didn't care. All he knew was that he was terribly frightened.

Lewis sneaked back into the house a little before three A.M. He tiptoed up the back stairs, checked to make sure that his uncle was asleep—he was—and quietly opened the door of his own room. Just as quietly, he shut it behind him. Then he slowly began to strip off his wet and dirty clothes, which he wadded up and threw into a dark corner of his closet. Where was his flashlight? Tarby must have taken it. He would get it back from him later. As for the clothes, he could get them cleaned without Jonathan knowing about it.

Lewis went to bed. He tried to sleep, but all he could see when he closed his eyes were those two burning circles of light. Finally he did drift off, but he had a strange dream. Clock hands and skeleton bones were chasing him around and around a high stone tomb. Lewis awoke with a start and, for a moment, it seemed that his room, and the whole house, was filled with a loud ticking noise.

CHAPTER SIX

The next morning, when Lewis came down to breakfast, Uncle Jonathan was reading an article on the front
page of the New Zebedee *Chronicle.* Curious, Lewis
leaned over his shoulder and this is what he read:

TOMB DESECRATED BY VANDALS

Answers Sought to Senseless Act

Last night vandals broke into the Old Izard
mausoleum in Oakridge Cemetery. The doors
of the tomb were found standing ajar, with
the padlock lying shattered on the pavement.
This incident has sadly marred what was

> otherwise a Halloween remarkably free from
> incidents of vandalism and wanton destruc-
> tiveness. What these human ghouls hoped to
> attain lies mercifully beyond conjecture, but
> it may be hoped . . . .

"Morning, Lewis," said Jonathan, without looking up. "Did you sleep well?"

Lewis turned pale. Did Jonathan know?

Mrs. Zimmermann was sitting across the table, munching her Cheerios. "Does it say whether they disturbed the coffins?" she asked.

"No, it doesn't," said Jonathan. "The caretaker probably just shoved the doors shut and fastened them with a new padlock. I don't blame him. I wouldn't want to look inside old Isaac Izard's tomb."

Lewis sat down. There were too many things whirling around in his head, and he was trying to get them straightened out.

"I . . . I was up in the cemetery with Tarby a couple of times, Uncle Jonathan," he said cautiously, "but I didn't see any tomb with 'Izard' on it."

"Oh, well, he didn't want his name on the tomb. When he had it fixed up for his wife's body, he brought in a stonecutter who chiseled off the family name and carved an omega."

"An omega?" said Lewis. "What's that?"

"It's the last letter of the Greek alphabet, and it's used a lot by wizards. It looks like an O, except that it's open at the bottom. It is the sign of the Last Judgment—the End of the World."

Lewis sat there staring at the little *O*'s floating in his bowl. He forced himself to eat a few of them.

"How come he wanted something like that on his tomb?" asked Lewis. He was trying to conceal the tremble in his voice.

"Lord knows, Lewis," said Jonathan. "Say, you're not scared about this tomb-breaking business, are you? Old Isaac Izard's dead and gone. He's not going to bother us."

Lewis looked at Jonathan. Then he looked at Mrs. Zimmermann. He knew, as well as he knew anything, that they couldn't wait for him to go off to school so they could discuss the matter alone. So he finished his breakfast, mumbled goodby to them both, grabbed up his books, and left.

Jonathan and Mrs. Zimmermann did indeed want to discuss the break-in alone. Any tampering with the tomb of two powerful wizards like Isaac and Selenna Izard was a matter for serious discussion, and they didn't want to frighten Lewis with their talk. But they had no idea of what Lewis had done. Jonathan was not in the habit of peering in at the sleeping form of his nephew during the night, so he had no idea that Lewis had been out of the house. Of course, he and Mrs. Zimmermann had been concerned for some time about Lewis's strange behavior. But they did not connect it with what had happened on Halloween night.

After their discussion—which came to no conclusions at all, except that there was dirty work afoot—Jonathan and Mrs. Zimmermann decided that it would be nice to take Lewis on an evening ride around Capharnaum County. They knew he loved to ride, and since they hadn't taken him out in some time, they thought that maybe an excursion would shake some of the gloom out of his system.

But when Lewis came home from school that day, he was depressed and worried. He had been thinking about the tomb business all day long. So, when Jonathan pushed back his chair after dinner and asked Lewis if he'd like to go for a nice long ride, Lewis merely shrugged his shoulders and said, "Yeah, I guess I'd like to go" in a dying-cat sort of voice.

Jonathan stared at Lewis for a minute, but he said nothing. He merely got up and went to get his car keys. Soon all three of them—Jonathan, Mrs. Zimmermann, and Lewis—were crammed into the front seat of Jonathan's 1935 Muggins Simoon, a big black car with running boards and a windshield that could be cranked open. The car, spewing clouds of bluish smoke, backed down the rutted driveway and into the street.

They drove for hours, as the afterglow of sunset stayed and stayed, and the hollows filled with purple mist. They drove past barns with big blue signs on their sides that said: CHEW MAIL POUCH. They drove past green John Deere tractors parked in deep muddy ruts. Up hill and down hill they drove, over bumpy railroad crossings with X-shaped signs that said: RAIL-SING CROS-ROAD if you read them the wrong way, through little towns that were no more than a church, a food store with a gas pump outside, and a flagpole on a triangle of green grass where the roads met. By the time it got dark, they were miles from New Zebedee.

They were on their way home when—for no reason that Lewis could see—Jonathan stopped the car. He turned off the motor and sat there staring at the row of green dashboard lights.

"What's wrong, Uncle Jonathan?" asked Lewis.

"I keep imagining that I hear a car somewhere," said Jonathan. "Do you hear it, Florence?"

"Yes, I do," said Mrs. Zimmermann, giving him a puzzled look. "But what's so odd about that? They do let people drive these roads at night, you know."

"Do they?" said Jonathan in a strange voice. He opened the car door and stepped out onto the gravel. "Stay here," he said to them. He walked up the road a little ways and stood there, listening. Even with the car door open, Lewis could hear nothing but the wind in the roadside trees and the clattering of a tin sign on a barbed-wire fence. The car was parked near the top of a high hill, and now Lewis could see headlights rising out of a gully and then dipping into the next one.

Jonathan came running back to the car. He slammed the door and started the motor. With a squealing of tires, he turned the car around and headed back the way they had come.

Lewis was frightened. "What's wrong, Uncle Jonathan?" he asked.

"Ask me later, Lewis. Florence, what's the best way—other way—back to New Zebedee?"

"Take the next side road to your right. That's Twelve Mile Road, and it runs into the Wilder Creek Road. And step on it. They're gaining."

Many times, when he had been out riding with his father and mother, Lewis had pretended that they were being followed by some car or other. It was a good game to pass the time on long dull evening rides, and he remembered how he had always felt disappointed when the mystery car turned away into a side street or a driveway. But tonight the game was for real.

Around sharp curves they went, lurching dangerously far over and squealing the tires. Up hills, down hills, then seventy or eighty miles an hour on the straightaway, which was never straight for long on these winding country roads. Lewis had never seen Jonathan drive so fast, or so recklessly. But no matter how fast he drove, the two cold circles of light still burned in his rear-view mirror.

Both Mrs. Zimmermann and Uncle Jonathan seemed to know who or what was in the car behind them—or at least they seemed to know that it was someone that had the power to do them harm. But they said as little as possible, except to confer now and then about directions. So Lewis just sat there, trying to feel comforted by the green dashboard lights and the warm breath of the heater on his knees. Of course, he also felt comforted by the two wizards, whose warm friendly bodies pressed against his in the furry darkness. But he knew that they were scared, and this made him twice as scared.

What was after them? Why didn't Uncle Jonathan or Mrs. Zimmermann just wave an arm and turn the evil car into a wad of smoldering tinfoil? Lewis stared up at the reflected headlights, and he thought of what he had seen in the cemetery, and of what Uncle Jonathan had told him about Mrs. Izard's eyeglasses. He was beginning to have a theory about how all these things fitted together.

The car raced on, spitting stones from under its tires. Down into hollows bordered by dark skeletal trees, up over high hills, on and on while the setting moon seemed to race to keep up with them. They covered a large part of Capharnaum County that night, because the way around was a long way. After what seemed like hours of driving, they came to a place where three roads met. As the car screeched around the turn, Lewis saw—for a few seconds—a Civil War cannon white with frost, a wooden church with smeary stained-glass windows, and a general store with a dark glimmering window that said: SALADA.

"We're on the Wilder Creek Road now, Lewis," said

Mrs. Zimmermann as she put her arm around him. "It won't be long now. Don't be afraid."

The car raced on. Dead roadside stalks bent in its hot wind, and overhanging branches whipped along the metal roof. The burning white holes danced in the mirror as before, and it looked like they were getting closer. They had never, since the start of the chase, been more than two or three car lengths away.

Jonathan shoved the accelerator to the floor. The needle moved up to eighty, which was dangerous, to say the least, on these roads. But the greater danger was behind, so Jonathan took the big roundhouse curves as well as he could, and the tires screeched, and the fenders almost touched the crumbling asphalt at the side of the road. This was blacktop, and you could go faster on it than you could on loose gravel.

At last they came to the top of a high hill and, there below them, glimmering peacefully in the starlight—the moon had gone down some time ago—was Wilder Creek. There was the bridge, a maze of crisscrossing black girders. Down the hill they barrelled, faster and faster. The car behind followed, just as fast. They were almost to the bridge when the lights in the rear-view mirror did something headlights had never done before. They grew and brightened till the reflection was a blinding bar of white light. Lewis clapped his hands to his eyes. Had he been struck blind? Had Jonathan been blinded too? Would the car crash, or . . .

Suddenly Lewis heard the rolling clatter of the bridge boards under the car. He took his hands away from his face. He could see. Jonathan was smiling and putting on the brakes. Mrs. Zimmermann heaved a deep sigh of relief. They were across the bridge.

As Jonathan opened the door to get out, Lewis twisted around in his seat and saw that the other car had stopped just before it got to the bridge. Its headlights were dark now, except for two smoldering yellow pinpoints. Lewis could not tell if there was anyone in the car, because the windshield was covered by a blank silvery sheen.

Jonathan stood there, his hands on his hips, watching. He did not seem to be afraid of the other car now. Slowly the mysterious car turned around and drove away. When Jonathan got back to the Muggins Simoon he was chuckling.

"It's all over, Lewis. Relax. Witches and other evil things can't cross running water. It's an old rule, but it still applies."

"You might throw in the fact," said Mrs. Zimmermann in her most pedantic tone, "that Elihu Clabbernong built that iron bridge in 1892. He was supposed to be doing it for the county, but he was really trying to make sure that the ghost of his dead uncle, Jedediah, didn't cross the stream to get him. Now Elihu was a part-time warlock, and what he put into the iron of the bridge . . ."

"Oh, good heavens!" cried Jonathan, covering his ears.

"Are you going to go through the whole history of Capharnaum County at four A.M.?"

"Is it *that* late?" asked Lewis.

"That late or later," said Jonathan wearily. "It's been quite a ride."

They drove on toward New Zebedee. On the way they stopped at an all-night diner and had a large breakfast of waffles, eggs, American fries, sausage, coffee, and milk. Then they sat around for a long time talking about the narrow escape they had just had. Lewis asked a lot of questions, but he didn't get many answers.

When they got back to New Zebedee, it was dawn. Dawn of an overcast November day. The town and its hills appeared to be swimming in a gray grainy murk. When Jonathan pulled up in front of his house he said, "There's something wrong, Florence. Stay in the car with Lewis."

"Oh, dear!" she cried, wrinkling up her mouth. "What more can happen?"

Jonathan swung back the iron gate and marched up the walk. From where he was sitting, Lewis could see that the front door was open. This could easily be explained, since people in New Zebedee never locked their doors, and sometimes the latches didn't hold when they closed them. Jonathan disappeared into the house, and he didn't come back for ten full minutes. When he did reappear, he looked worried.

"Come on, Florence," he said, opening the door on her side. "It's safe to go in, I think. But the house has been broken into."

Lewis burst into tears. "They didn't steal your water-pipe, did they? Or the Bon-Sour coins?"

Jonathan smiled weakly. "No, Lewis, I'm afraid it's not as simple as all that. Someone was looking for something, and I think they found it. Come on in."

Lewis expected to find the house in wild disorder, with chairs and lamps smashed and things all scattered around. But when he got to the front hall, he found everything in order. At least, that's the way it looked. Jonathan tapped him on the shoulder and pointed toward the ceiling. "Look up there," he said.

Lewis gasped. The brass cup that covered the place where the ceiling fixture met the ceiling had been pried loose. It dangled halfway down the chain.

"It's like that all over the house," said Jonathan. "Every wall sconce and ceiling light has had its cup jimmied loose. A few chairs were overturned and a couple of vases were broken, just to make it look like this was an ordinary break-in. But we ought not to be fooled. Whoever it was had a general idea of where to look. Come here."

Jonathan led Lewis and Mrs. Zimmermann into the front parlor, a more or less unused room full of fussy little red-velvet chairs and settees. On the wall over the parlor organ was a brass light fixture like all the others in the house: a tarnished cup-shaped thing fitted to the wall, and a crooked little brass tube sticking out of it. On the end of the tube was a socket and a bulb with a frilly pink shade.

"I thought you said the cup was loose," said Lewis.

"It was. It is," said Jonathan. "In this case Whosis tried to fit it back just the way it was, which was kind of stupid, seeing as how all the other cups in the house are at half mast. Some of them are slid all the way down to the socket. But I think Whosis was trying, in a clumsy way, to keep me from looking too closely at this one."

Jonathan pulled over a chair and stood up on it. He slid the cup out and peered inside. Then he got down and went to the cellarway for a flashlight. When he got back, Mrs. Zimmermann and Lewis had taken turns looking into the cup. They both were puzzled. What they saw inside the dusty bowl was a greenish rust blot. It reminded Lewis of the stuff in the cracks and crevices of the copper Roman coins they played poker with. It was the mark of something that had lain concealed inside the old brass cup for a long, long time. The mark looked like this:

"It looks like a clock key," said Lewis in a weak, throaty voice.

"Yes, it does," said Jonathan. He played the light around inside the cup and squinted hard.

"Uncle Jonathan, what does all this mean?" Lewis sounded as if he were about to burst into tears.

"I wish I knew," said Jonathan. "I really wish I knew."

CHAPTER SEVEN

It rained a lot in New Zebedee that November. Cold rain fell steadily through each night and left the sidewalk a glaze of ice in the morning. Lewis sat in his window seat and watched the rain peck at the chipped slates of the front porch roof. He felt sick inside. It was an empty, black feeling in the pit of his stomach. He was eaten up with guilt and remorse because he knew what he had done—or thought he knew, at any rate. He had let Mrs. Izard out of her tomb, and now she had stolen the key. The key that wound up the magic clock ticking in the walls of Jonathan's house, ticking away morning, noon, and night; sometimes loud, sometimes soft, but always there.

What was going to happen? How could anyone stop her? Had she used the key? What would happen if she did? Lewis had no answers for any of these questions.

It might have helped if he had been able to talk the whole matter over with Jonathan, but then he would have had to admit what he had done. And Lewis was afraid to do that. It was not that Uncle Jonathan was such a hard man to talk to. He was easier to talk to than most people Lewis knew, easier by far than Lewis's own father had ever been. Then, why was Lewis afraid?

Well, he was afraid because he was afraid. Maybe it was because his mother had once threatened to send him to the Detention Home when he was bad. The Detention Home was a big white house on the outskirts of the town that Lewis and his parents had lived in. It stood on a high hill and had bars and chicken wire over the windows. Bad boys and girls were sent there—at least, that's what everyone said. Lewis had never known anyone who had actually gotten sent there. Of course, Lewis's mother would never have sent him there for being bad. Not really. But Lewis didn't know that, and now when Lewis thought of telling his uncle about Halloween night, he thought of the Detention Home, and he was afraid. It wasn't a reasonable fear, considering the kind of man Jonathan was. But Lewis had not known him for very long, and anyway, people are not always so reasonable.

And there was another thing that added to Lewis's despair. He had lost Tarby. He had lost him in spite of all his sneaking and planning—or maybe he had lost him because of it. It was one thing to say that you could raise the dead, but when you did it—well, ordinary people have never cared much for the company of wizards. Tarby was afraid of Lewis now, or else he was enjoying himself with the other boys, the boys who could hit home runs and catch fly balls. Whichever way it was, Lewis had not seen Tarby since Halloween night.

The month wore on, the rain kept falling, and nothing mysterious or evil happened. Until one day—the third of December it was—when the Hanchetts moved out.

The Hanchetts lived across the street from Uncle Jonathan in a boxy, dark-brown house with tiny windows, the kind of windows that have little diamond-shaped panes and swing out instead of sliding up and down. The Hanchetts were a friendly, middle-aged couple, and they liked Jonathan and Mrs. Zimmermann a lot, but one morning they were gone. A couple of days after their disappearance a truck came and a couple of movers in gray uniforms packed all the Hanchetts' furniture into it, and drove off. A real-estate man came around and hung a big red and white sign on their front door. The sign said:

HI THERE!

I'M FOR SALE

Call Bishop Barlow Realtors

Phone: 865

Bishop Barlow was not a real bishop. Bishop was just his first name. Lewis knew the man: he was a fat loud-mouth who wore sunglasses all the time, even on rainy days. He smoked cheap smelly cigars and wore sports coats that looked like awnings.

Jonathan seemed really upset at the departure of the Hanchetts. He phoned their son, who was a lawyer in Osee Five Hills, and he found out that the Hanchetts were living with him. The frightened couple would not talk to Jonathan over the phone, and they seemed to blame him for whatever had made them leave. The son did not seem to know much about the matter. He muttered something about ghosts and "messing around with magic" and hung up.

One day Lewis was walking home from school when he saw a small moving van pull up in front of the empty Hanchett house. The big black letters on the side of the van said: TERMINUS MOVERS INC. Lewis was about to cross the street to watch the men unload the truck when he realized, with a shock, that he knew the driver. It was Hammerhandle.

All the children in New Zebedee knew Hammerhandle and, if they were smart, they were afraid of him. He was a mean old hobo who lived in a tar-paper shack down by the railroad tracks, and he had a reputation for being able to foretell the future. Lewis had stood once on the outskirts of a crowd of kids gathered about the door of Hammerhandle's shack on a hot summer day. He remembered seeing Hammerhandle seated in the doorway on a broken kitchen chair. He was telling stories about the World's Last Night, which, if you believed him, was not far off. Behind Hammerhandle, in the disorder and darkness of the old shack, stood ranks of smooth yellow poles: ax handles, hoe handles, hammer handles. He made them and sold them. That was how he got his name.

Lewis stood there wondering what he was doing driving a moving van. Hammerhandle slammed the door on the driver's side and walked across the street. He looked around him quickly and then grabbed Lewis by the collar. His bristly face was close to Lewis's now, and his breath smelled of whiskey and tobacco.

"What the hell you starin' at, kid?"

"N-nothing. I-I just like to watch people moving in." It was getting dark, and Lewis wondered if anyone could see him. If he yelled, would Jonathan or Mrs. Zimmermann come?

Hammerhandle let go of Lewis's collar. "Look, kid," he said in his harsh scraping voice, "you just keep yer nose on your side of the fence, okay? An' that goes f'ya fat uncle too. Just don't bother me, okay?" He glared at Lewis, turned, and went back to the truck.

Lewis stood there trembling for a few moments. He was sweating all over. Then he turned and ran in through the open gate, up the walk, and into the house.

"Uncle Jonathan! Uncle Jonathan!" he shouted. He

yanked open the doors of the study and looked. No Jonathan. He shouted into the front parlor and into the kitchen and up the stairwell. At last Uncle Jonathan appeared at the top of the stairs. He was wearing his bathrobe, which was made in the shape of the robes professors wear at graduation ceremonies, black with red stripes on the sleeves. In one hand he held a dripping, long-handled scrub brush. In the other, he held the book he had been reading in the tub.

"Yes, Lewis? What is it?" He sounded cross at first, but when he saw the state that Lewis was in, he dropped the book and the brush and clumped down the stairs to throw his arms around the boy. It was a damp embrace, but it felt good to Lewis.

"Lewis, my boy!" said Jonathan, kneeling in front of him. "What in the name of heaven is wrong? You look awful!"

Lewis, stuttering and breaking down several times, told Jonathan what had happened. When he was through, he watched Jonathan's expression change. There was a hard, angry look on his face now, but his anger was not directed at Lewis. He stood up, knotted his bathrobe tighter about him, and stalked to the front door. For a minute Lewis thought that Jonathan was going out to challenge Hammerhandle right then and there. But he merely opened the front door and stared across at the Hanchett house. The workmen were just hitching up the tail gate and getting ready to drive off. Apparently there hadn't been much to unload.

With folded arms Jonathan watched the truck drive away. "I might have known he'd be in on it," he said bitterly. Lewis stared up at his uncle. He didn't have the faintest idea of what was going on, and for some reason he was afraid to ask what Jonathan meant.

That evening at supper, Lewis asked Jonathan why Hammerhandle had acted so mean. Jonathan threw down his fork and said angrily, "Because he's mean, that's why! Do you have to have explanations? Just stay away from him and you'll be all right. And stay away . . . stay away . . . . oh, I don't know what I mean!" He got up and stomped out of the room. Lewis heard the study doors slam.

Mrs. Zimmermann reached across the table and laid her hand gently on Lewis's. "Don't worry, Lewis," she said. "He's not angry at you. But he does have a lot on his mind these days, and he hasn't been getting much sleep. Come on over to my house and we'll have a game of chess."

"Okay." Lewis was grateful for the suggestion.

They played chess till ten o'clock at night and, since Lewis won most of the games, he was in a happy mood when he went home. Upstairs he saw a line of light under the door of Jonathan's bedroom. He decided not to disturb him. When he had gotten ready for bed, Lewis

went to his window seat, sat down, and pulled back the heavy curtain.

It was a bright, cold, starry night. The water tower at the top of the hill glimmered in the moonlight, and the roofs of the houses were dark pointed shadows. There were lights on in the houses that stood on either side of the Hanchett house and, in one window, Lewis saw the gray aquarium-glow of one of those new television sets. Jonathan hadn't gotten one yet. The Hanchett house seemed to lie in deep shadow, except for faint patches of moonlight on the roof. By the light of a street lamp, Lewis could see that there was a car parked in the driveway.

He was about to close the curtain and go to bed when the porch light of the Hanchett house came on. The two frosted panes of the front door glowed yellow. Then one of the panels of the door moved inward. Someone stepped out onto the front stoop. Lewis watched as whoever-it-was stood there, just stood there, taking in the frosty air of the December night. He thought he caught the faint glitter of spectacles, but he couldn't be sure at this distance.

After a little while, the dark figure went inside and pushed the door shut. The hall light went out. Lewis sat there for a while thinking, then he lowered the curtain and went to bed.

CHAPTER EIGHT

The next day Jonathan was helping Lewis rummage in the front hall closet for his ice skates. Lewis had weak ankles, and he was terrified of falling down on the ice, but he had decided to try to learn to skate. If he got good enough he might be able to worm his way back into Tarby's favor. He had never seen Tarby ice skate, but he was sure that the team's greatest home-run hitter was also the champion ice skater of New Zebedee. He probably could sign his name across the ice of Durgy's Pond.

So Lewis and Jonathan threw warped badminton rackets, raccoon coats, galoshes, and picnic baskets into the hall. Finally Jonathan came up with what looked like a short aluminum ski for a midget. It was a beginner's skate, with two little ridges for runners.

"This it?"

"That's one of them. Thanks a lot, Uncle Jonathan. Now all we need is the other."

As they went on searching Lewis said, in what he thought was a casual way, "Who's living in the old Hanchett house?"

Jonathan stood up suddenly in the closet and banged his head on a shelf. When he had stopped rubbing his head and wincing, he looked down at Lewis and said, rather sharply, "Why do you want to know?"

"I just wanted to know," said Lewis shyly. Once again, he wondered what his uncle was angry about.

Jonathan stepped out of the closet with the other skate. He dropped it into a pile of clothes.

"So you just wanted to know, eh? Well, Lewis, there are some things it would be better for you *not* to know. So if you'll take my advice, you'll just stop poking around where you're not wanted. There's your other skate and . . . and good day. I have work to do in the study, and I've already wasted enough time answering your foolish questions."

Jonathan got up abruptly and stalked off to the study. He had slid back the doors with a loud clatter when he paused and went back to the closet, where Lewis was still kneeling with tears in his eyes.

"Please forgive me, Lewis," said Jonathan in a tired

voice. "I've been feeling really rotten lately. Too many cigars, I guess. As for the house across the street, I hear that it's been rented to an old lady named Mrs. O'Meagher. She acts kind of crabby—or so I'm told. I really haven't met her, and . . . and I just didn't want anything bad to happen to you." Jonathan smiled nervously and patted Lewis on the shoulder. Then he got up and walked to the door of the study. Again he stopped.

"Don't go over there," he said quickly, and then he stepped inside and slammed the double doors, hard.

Lewis felt crisscrossing lines of mystery and fear and tension hemming him in on all sides. He had never seen his uncle acting like this. And he wondered, more than ever, about the new neighbor across the street.

One night during the week before Christmas, after a heavy snow had fallen, Lewis was awakened by the sound of the doorbell ringing. *Brr-rr-rring! Brr-rr-rring!* It was not an electric bell, but an old, tired mechanical bell set in the middle of the front door. Someone was turning the flat metal key, grinding the stiff old chimes around. *Brr-rr-rring!*

Lewis sat up and looked at his bedside clock. The two luminous hands were straight up. Midnight! Who could it be at this hour? Maybe Uncle Jonathan would go down and answer it. Lewis felt cold just thinking of the drafty front hall. He bundled his quilt about him and shivered.

The bell rang again. It sounded like a whiny person

insisting on some stupid point in an argument. No sound from Jonathan's room. No waking-up sounds, that is. Lewis could hear his uncle's loud, steady snoring even though there was a thick wall between their rooms. Jonathan could sleep through an artillery bombardment.

Lewis got up. He threw back the covers, slipped on his bathrobe, and found his slippers. Quietly, he padded down the hall and then down the dark staircase. At the entrance to the front hall he stopped. There was a street-light burning just outside the front gate, and it threw a bent black shadow against the pleated curtain on the front door. Lewis stood still and watched the shadow. It didn't move. Slowly he began to walk forward. When he reached the door, he closed his fingers around the cold knob and turned it. The door rattled open, and a freezing wind blew in over his bare ankles. There stood his Aunt Mattie, who was dead.

Lewis stepped back as the old woman, her head cocked to one side as it always had been, tottered across the floor toward him. A shaking blue light filled the air around her, and Lewis, his eyes wide open in this nightmare, saw Aunt Mattie as she had been the last time he had seen her alive. Her dress was black and wrinkled, she wore heavy shoes with thick heels, and she tapped her bunchy, black umbrella as she went. Lewis even thought he smelled kerosene—her house, her furniture, and her cloth-ing had always reeked of it. The white fungus blotch that was her face shook and glowed as she said, in a horribly familiar voice, "Well, Lewis? Aren't you glad to see me?"

Lewis fainted. When he awoke, he was lying on his back in the cold hallway. The shaking blue light was gone. So was Aunt Mattie, though the front door was open. Skitters of snow blew in over the worn threshold, and the street lamp burned quiet and cold across the street. Had it all been a sleepwalker's dream?

Lewis didn't think so. He had never been a sleepwalker before. He stood there thinking for a minute, and then, for some reason, he shuffled out onto the front porch and started to pick his way down the snow-covered steps. His feet were so cold that they stung, but he kept going until he was halfway down the walk. Then he turned and looked at the house. He gasped. There were strange lights playing over the blank windows and the rough sandstone walls. They wouldn't have been strange lights at midday in the summer, but on a December night they were eerie. For they were leaf-lights, the shifting circles and crescents cast by sunlight falling through leaves.

Lewis stood and stared for several minutes. Then the lights faded, and he was alone in the dark, snow-covered yard. The chestnut tree dropped a light dusting of snow on his head, shaking him out of his trance. His feet were numb and tingling, and he felt, for the first time, the cold wind whipping through his thin pajamas and his half-open cotton bathrobe. Shuddering, Lewis stumbled back up the walk.

When he got to his room, he sat down on the edge of his bed. He knew he wasn't going back to sleep. There were the makings of a fire in his fireplace, and he knew where the cocoa was kept. A few minutes later Lewis was sitting by a warm, cheerful fire that cast cozy shadows over the black marble of his own personal fireplace. He sipped steaming cocoa from a heavy earthenware mug and tried to think pleasant thoughts. None came to him. After an hour of sitting and sipping and brooding, he plugged in the floor lamp, got John L. Stoddard's second lecture on China out of the bookcase, and sat reading by the fire until dawn.

The next morning at breakfast, Lewis saw that Jonathan was red-eyed and nervous acting. Had his sleep been disturbed too? Jonathan had not discussed the break-in or the car chase or the Izard tomb with Lewis, and Lewis was not about to bring up any of these subjects. But he knew that something was bothering Jonathan, and he also knew that, ever since the night of the break-in, Jonathan and Mrs. Zimmermann had been holding midnight conferences. He had heard their voices coming up through the hot-air register, although he had never been able to make out what was being said. He had thought a couple of times of hiding in the secret passageway, but he was afraid of getting caught. A passage that is entered through a china cupboard full of rattling dishes is not as secret as one might wish. And if some secret spring lock snapped shut on him, he would need to scream his way out, and then there would have to be explanations.

Lewis almost wished that something like that would happen, because he was sick of his secret. He was sick of it because it kept him away from Jonathan and Mrs. Zimmermann. He always felt that they were watching him, waiting for him to break down and tell them everything. How much did they know?

Christmas at 100 High Street was both good and bad that year. There was a big tree in the study and the glass balls on it were magic. Sometimes they reflected the room, and sometimes they showed you ancient ruins on unknown planets. Jonathan gave Lewis several magic toys, including a large pink Easter egg—or Christmas egg, if you wish—that was covered with sparkly stuff and what looked like icing, although it couldn't be eaten. When Lewis looked into the egg, he could see any battle in history. Not the battle as it really was, but as he wanted it to be. Though he didn't know it, the egg, like the balls on the tree, was capable of showing him scenes on other planets. But it was not until he was a grown-up man, working as an astronomer at Mount Palomar, that he was able to discover that property of the magic egg.

Jonathan did a lot of other things that Christmas. He put candles in all the windows of the house—electric candles, not real ones, since he liked the electric kind better—and he put strong lamps behind the stained-glass windows, so that they threw marvelous patterns of red and blue and gold and purple on the dark, sparkling snow outside. He invented the Fuse Box Dwarf, a little man who popped out at you from behind the paint cans in the cellarway and screamed, "Dreeb! Dreeb! I am the Fuse Box Dwarf!" Lewis was not scared by the little man, and he felt that those who scream, "Dreeb!" are more to be pitied than censured.

Needless to say, Jonathan put on a very good show with the coat rack mirror, though it had the habit of showing the ruins at Chichen-Itza over and over again. Somehow the mirror managed to pick up radio station WGN on its bevelled edges, so that when Lewis went out the door in the morning, he heard the Dow-Jones averages and livestock reports.

Lewis tried to enjoy himself that Christmas, but it was hard. He kept thinking that Jonathan's magic show was meant to cover up what was happening to the house. What was happening was hard to figure out, but it was strange and terrifying. After the night when Lewis saw— or dreamt he saw—Aunt Mattie, the house seemed stranger than it ever had. Sometimes the air in certain rooms seemed to shimmer as if the house was going to disappear in the next second. Sometimes the stained-glass windows showed dark and terrifying scenes, and sometimes Lewis saw in the corners of rooms those awful sights that nervous people always imagine are lurking just outside the borders of their eyesight. Walking from room to room, even in broad daylight, Lewis forgot what day it was, what he was after, and at times almost forgot who he was. At night he had dreams of wandering through the house back in the 1890's, when everything was varnished and new. Once or twice Lewis woke from such dreams to see lights flickering on his bedroom wall. They were not leaf-lights this time, but rags and patches of orange light, the kind that you see in the corners of an old house at sunset.

These strange things didn't go on all the time, of course; just now and then over the long cold winter of '48–'49. When spring came, Lewis was surprised to see that the hedge in front of the Hanchett house was wildly overgrown. It was a spiraea hedge, and had always had bristly little pink-and-white blossoms. This spring there were no blossoms on the hedge; it had turned into a dark, thorny thicket that completely hid the first floor windows and sent long waving tendrils up to scrape at the zinc gutter troughs. Burdocks and ailanthus trees had grown up overnight near the house; their branches screened the second-story windows.

Lewis still had not seen much of the new neighbor. Once, from a distance, he had caught a glimpse of a dark, huddled figure rattling a key in the front door. And from his window seat, he had seen her passing to and fro on the second floor. But, aside from that, the old woman had kept out of sight. Lewis had figured it would be like that.

She did have visitors though: one visitor. That was

Hammerhandle. Lewis had seen him coming away from Mrs. O'Meagher's back door late one night. And twice, on his way to the movies in the evening, Lewis had literally bumped into Hammerhandle, who was huddling along High Street toward the Hanchett house, his shabby overcoat buttoned up to the neck. Both times Hammerhandle had been carrying packages, odd little bundles wrapped in brown paper and twine. And both times they had collided because Hammerhandle kept looking behind him.

The second time they met this way, Hammerhandle grabbed Lewis by the collar, the way he had before. He pressed his unshaven muzzle to Lewis's ear and growled, "You little snip! You're lookin' to have your throat cut, aren't you?"

Lewis pulled away from him, but he didn't run. He faced Hammerhandle down.

"Get out of here, you rotten old bum. If you ever try to do anything to me, my uncle will fix you."

Hammerhandle laughed, though it sounded more like he was having a choking fit. "Your uncle!" he said, sneering. "Your uncle will get his sooner than he thinks! The End of the World is at hand. Don't you read your Bible like a good boy? There have been signs, and there will be more. Prepare!" And with that, he stumbled on up the hill, clutching his parcel tightly.

The day after this strange meeting was cold and rainy, and Lewis stayed indoors. Jonathan was over at Mrs.

Zimmermann's helping her bottle some prune brandy, so Lewis was alone. He decided to go poke around in the back rooms up on the third floor. The third-floor rooms were generally unused, and Jonathan had shut the heat off in them to save money. But Lewis had found interesting things up there, like boxes full of chessmen and china doorknobs and wall cupboards that you could actually climb up inside of.

Lewis wandered down the drafty hall, opening and closing doors. None of the rooms seemed worth exploring today. But wait. Sure! The room with the parlor organ. He could go play it; that would be fun.

One of the disused parlors on the third floor had a dusty old parlor organ in it. It was one of the few pieces of furniture that was left from the time Isaac Izard had lived in the house. Of course, there was the parlor organ downstairs—the good one—but it was a player organ, and often refused to let Lewis play what he wanted to play. This one up here was wheezy, and in the winter its voice was only a whisper. But you could sometimes get good tunes out of it if you pumped hard.

Lewis opened the door.

The parlor organ was a bulky shadow against one wall. Lewis found the light switch, and the light came on. He wiped some dust off the seat and sat down. What would he play? "Chopsticks," probably, or "From a Wigwam." His repertoire wasn't very large. Lewis pumped the worn treadles, and he heard a hissing and puffing that came from deep inside the machine. He touched the keys, but all he got was a gaspy tubercular sound. Darn.

He sat back and thought. Over the keys was a row of black organ stops with labels that said things like *Vox Humana, Salicet,* and *Flute.* Lewis knew that these stops were supposed to change the sound of the organ in various ways, but he had never pulled any of them out. Well, now was the time. He grabbed one of the black tubes and tugged gently. It wouldn't budge. He wiggled the stop and pulled harder. The whole thing came out in his hand.

Lewis sat there staring stupidly at the piece of wood. At first he felt bad about breaking the organ, but then he looked more closely at the stop. The end that had been in the organ was blunt, smooth, and painted black. There was no sign that it had ever been hooked up to anything.

What a cheesy outfit, Lewis thought. I wonder if they're all like that. Let's see. He pulled at another. *Pop!* He pulled them all out. *Pop! Pop! Pop! Pop! Pop! Pop!*

Lewis laughed. He rolled the black tubes back and forth over the keyboard. But then he stopped and thought. He had read a story once where a car had had a dummy dashboard that came out so you could hide things behind it. What if this organ . . . ?

He got up and went downstairs. He went all the way down to the cellarway, where Jonathan kept his tools. He opened the toolbox and took out a screwdriver, a hammer, and a rusty butter knife that Jonathan kept there for prying things open. Then he went back upstairs as fast as he could.

Now Lewis was sitting at the organ again. He scanned the long wooden panel; seven round black holes stared back at him. There were four screws holding the panel to the organ case, and they came out easily. Lewis stuck his fingers into two of the holes and pulled. The panel was stuck. He thought a bit, then he picked up the butter knife and slid it into a crack. *Skreek!* A little eddy of dust rose and tickled his nostrils. He moved the knife along to the right a bit and pried again. *Skreek!* The panel flopped out onto the keyboard. Ah! Now we would see what was what.

Lewis bent over and put his head close to the hole. He could smell a lot of dust, but he couldn't see a thing in there. Darn it, he had forgotten to bring a flashlight! He reached in and felt around. His arm went in all the way up to the armpit. He groped some more. What was this? Paper? He heard a dry crackling sound. Maybe it was money. He grabbed hold of the bundle and drew it out. His heart sank. It was just an old pile of papers.

Lewis sat there staring at them in disgust. So this was the secret treasure of Izard's castle! Some treasure! Well, there might be something interesting in them, like secret formulas. He flipped through the papers. Hmm . . . hmmm. . . . He flipped some more. The light in the room was very weak, and the old paper had turned practically the same shade as the copper-colored ink Isaac Izard had used. He figured the writing must be Isaac Izard's, since the first sheet said:

CLOUD FORMATIONS

AND

OTHER PHENOMENA

Observed from this Window

by

ISAAC IZARD

Hadn't Mrs. Zimmermann said that she had seen old Isaac taking notes on the sky? There were dates here and entries after them. Lewis read a few entries, and his eyes opened wider. He leafed some more.

A spatter of rain hit the window. Lewis jumped. Outside he could see thick masses of blue clouds piled up in the west. Through them ran a jagged red streak. It looked to Lewis like a hungry mouth. As he watched, the mouth opened and a ray of blood-red light shot into the room. It lit up the page he was holding. On the page were scrawled these words:

Doomsday not come yet! I'll draw it nearer by a perspective, or make a CLOCK *that shall set all the world on fire upon an instant.*

Lewis felt very frightened. He gathered the papers together and started to get up. As he did so, he heard a noise. A very faint noise. Something was fluttering around down inside the organ case.

Lewis stumbled backward, knocking over the bench. The papers slid out of his hand and scattered over the floor. What should he do? Run for his life or save the papers? He gritted his teeth and knelt down. As he gathered up the sheets, he said to himself over and over again, "*Quia tu es Deus fortitudo mea . . . quia tu es Deus fortitudo mea.*"

Now he had all the papers again. He was about to dash for the door when he saw something come floating up out of the darkness inside the organ. A moth. A moth with silver-gray wings. They shone like leaves in the moonlight.

Lewis ran to the door. He rattled the knob but he couldn't get it open. Now he could feel the moth in his hair. Lewis went rigid. His face flushed. He was not scared any more. He was angry. Very angry.

He swatted at the moth and crushed it. Lewis felt a horrible runny stickiness in his hair, and all the fear came rushing back. He wiped his hand frantically on his trouser leg. Now Lewis was out in the hall, running and shouting, "Uncle Jonathan! Mrs. Zimmermann! Come quick! Oh, please come quick, I've found something! Uncle Jonathan!"

A little while later Jonathan, Lewis, and Mrs. Zimmermann were sitting around Mrs. Zimmermann's kitchen table drinking cocoa. The dusty papers lay in a heap on

the table. Jonathan put down his mug and said, "No, Lewis. I tell you again. They're nothing to worry about. Old Isaac was crazy—crazy as a coot. This stuff has nothing to do with that ticking noise in the walls. Or if it does, it can't help us any. It can only frighten us."

"I'd say that was why Isaac left those papers there, wouldn't you, Jonathan? To frighten us to death, I mean."

This was Mrs. Zimmermann speaking. She was standing at the stove with her back to Lewis, and she was making a great show of stirring the cocoa.

"Sure. I'd say that was it, Florence," said Jonathan, nodding. "One last trick for the road and that sort of thing."

Lewis looked from one to the other. He knew they were covering up. But what could he say? One thing would lead to another, and before long he would have to tell about Halloween night. When you are hiding something, you get the feeling that every other secret is connected to your secret. Lewis couldn't challenge anyone for fear of being exposed himself.

Late that same night, Lewis lay awake in his bed listening to Jonathan and Mrs. Zimmermann talking. They were in the study below and, as usual, their voices drifted up the hot-air register. And, as usual, he couldn't quite make out what they were saying. He got out of bed and crawled over to the wooden grating in the floor. A warm breath of heat softly beat at his face. He listened. Even now, he just couldn't hear well enough. There was only one thing to do. He had to use the secret passageway.

Lewis put on his bathrobe and tiptoed down the back stairs. The kitchen was dark. Good. Slowly, carefully, he removed all the china from the shelves of the china cupboard. Then he tripped the hidden spring, and the cupboard swung outward. He walked softly in.

This time Lewis remembered to bring a flashlight. Not that he needed it much. He didn't have far to go, and light shone through many chinks into the cobwebbed passage. Before long he was standing behind the bookcases that lined the wall of Jonathan's study. He peered through a crack in the boards, and there, beyond the books, were Jonathan and Mrs. Zimmermann. Mrs. Zimmermann had just conjured up a match out of thin air, and she was lighting a long twisted cigar with it. She blew smoke out of both corners of her mouth.

"Well, now we know," she said.

"Yes, now we know." Jonathan's voice came from his leather armchair, where he sat slumped. All that Lewis could see of him was one blue-sleeved arm and a set of hairy knuckles grasping the chair arm.

"The question is," Jonathan went on, "can we do anything about it?"

Mrs. Zimmermann began to pace. Cigar smoke trailed off behind her. She scraped the large purple stone of her ring along the whole length of a bookshelf. "Do?" she said. "Do? We fight them. What else?"

Jonathan gave a hoarse laugh. It made Lewis feel very uncomfortable.

"Easier said than done, Florence. They're both stronger than we are, you know. We only fiddle around with magic; they gave their lives to it. As for her, she may have quite literally given her life for it."

"But why would they want to do what they're doing?" said Mrs. Zimmermann, folding her arms and puffing angrily at her cigar. "Why? This beautiful world. End it. Why?"

Jonathan thought a minute. "Well, Florence, I can't really see into the workings of a mind like Isaac Izard's, but I'd say the answer was scientific curiosity. Think of all that's been written about the Last Day: graves opening, bodies rising up fresh and new. Some think there will be a whole new earth, much better than the present one. Wouldn't you like to see it? And another thing occurs to me. Isaac and Selenna Izard didn't enjoy this world very much. Why shouldn't they try for the next one?"

Jonathan puffed on his hookah. There was silence for several minutes.

"And the clock," said Mrs. Zimmermann. "I have to hand it to you. You were dead right. There *is* a real, literal clock in these walls. He calls it a 'device,' but it has to be a clock. He wasn't kind enough to tell us where it is, of course, though it seems to me that he tells practically everything else. He even gives hints about where he hid the key. Not that that matters now." She broke her cigar in two and threw it into the fireplace.

"But there's one thing I'd like to know," she said, turning suddenly to Jonathan. "Why did he need a clock to bring about the End of the World?"

Lewis gasped and put his hand over his mouth. Then it *was* going to be the end of the world, after all!

"Because he lost the moment," Jonathan answered. "The moment he had been seeking all those years. It was quite a search that old Isaac made. That's why he has all those crazy notes about mackerel skies and Last-Judgment skies and clouds that look like chariots and trumpets and masks of doom. That was what he was after. A mask of doom. A sky that would be right for his incantations. Sky magic is old stuff, as you know. The Romans used to——"

"Yes, yes!" cut in Mrs. Zimmermann impatiently. "I know all about sky and bird divination. Who's got the D.Mag.A. around here, anyhow? All right. So the right sky comes along for old Droopy Drawers. Fine. Dandy. So why doesn't he just wave his wand and turn us all into mullygrubs?"

"Because by the time he had made sure it was the right kind of sky, the sky had changed. It doesn't take long for clouds to move and change their patterns, you know.

Or maybe he lacked the heart to do it. It sounds silly, but I keep hoping that was what held him off."

"Him? Lack the heart? Isaac Izard? He was a hard man, Jonathan. He'd have pulled out his mother's teeth one by one, if he had to have them for some devil magic."

Jonathan sighed. "Maybe you're right. I don't know. The important thing is that he did miss his opportunity. That's why he had to build the clock. To bring the time back. The exact time when everything was right and in its place. That's what he means when he talks about 'a device to redeem the time.' Redeem, indeed! He wanted to destroy us all!"

Mrs. Zimmermann was pacing again. "All right," she said. "All right. So he built the clock. Why didn't he just wind it up?"

"He couldn't. Not all the way, at any rate. Didn't you read that passage?" Jonathan got up and went to the library table, where the papers were lying. He picked them up and leafed until he found the page he wanted.

"Ah. Here it is: 'But when the device was completed, I found that I lacked the skill to wind it all the way up. I have tried, but I must conclude that one with greater power than I possess will be needed for the final adjustment. Curse the day she left me! Curse the day she went away! *She* might have done it!' "

Jonathan looked up. "In that last sentence the word 'she' is underlined four times. 'She,' of course, is our friend across the street."

Lewis closed his eyes. Mrs. O'Meagher really was Mrs. Izard then! He had guessed it, of course, but he hadn't been sure. Mrs. Izard! And he had let her out. He felt like the stupidest, most foolish person in the whole world.

"Ah, yes," said Mrs. Zimmermann, smiling wryly. "Well, we shall see in the end who is stronger. But tell me one thing more, oh, sage, since it seems that you have been cast in the role of explicator and annotator of the testament of Isaac Izard."

"Yes? What would you like to know, Florence?"

"Well, he claims that the clock isn't wound all the way up. But it has been making a ticking sound for years now. A magic ticking that seems to be coming from behind every wall of this house. It's hard for me to believe that the clock is just whiling the time away until old Auntie Izard arrives with her key. *What is the clock doing?*"

Jonathan shrugged. "Search me, Florence. Maybe it's trying to drag the house back into the past without the aid of that 'final adjustment.' Maybe he fixed it so the ticking sound would scare away anyone who might be foolish enough to come and live in this house. Isaac didn't want his clock found by accident and destroyed, after all. I don't know why the clock is ticking, Florence. But I do know this. When Mrs. Izard or whoever is over there puts that key in the slot of that clock and finishes the job that Isaac started, then—at that moment—Isaac

Izard will return. You and I and Lewis will be ghosts or something worse, and he will be standing in the turret with power in his right hand. And the End of the World will come to pass."

Lewis clamped both hands over his mouth. He fell to his knees, shuddering and sobbing. For a moment he was on the verge of shouting, "Here I am! Come and get me!" so they could come and take him away and put him in the Detention Home for life. But he didn't shout. He clamped his hands more tightly over his mouth and cried in muffled bursts that shook his whole body. He cried for a long time, and when he was through, he sat staring listlessly at the dark wall of the passageway.

Mrs. Zimmermann and Jonathan left the room. The fire burned low, but still Lewis sat there. His mouth was full of the taste of ammonia, and his eyes burned. He took his handkerchief out of the pocket of his bath-robe and blew his nose. Where was the flashlight? Ah. Here it was. He clicked it on.

Lewis got up slowly and started to pick his way toward the entrance. Even though he was walking upright, he felt as if he were slinking. Now he was running his hand over the splintery back of the china cupboard. He tripped the spring, and the cupboard swung silently outward. Lewis half expected to see Mrs. Zimmermann and Jona-than sitting there with their arms folded, waiting for him. But the kitchen was dark and empty.

Lewis went up to his room. He felt as if he had stayed awake three nights in a row. Without even stopping to take off his bathrobe, he threw himself onto the rumpled bed. Darkness filled his brain, and he fell into a dead dreamless sleep.

CHAPTER NINE

The next day was Saturday, and Lewis woke up in a state of panic. He was like a pressure cooker with the lid clamped on tight and the steam hole clogged up with chewing gum. Thoughts kept bubbling and seething to the surface of his mind, but none of them seemed to make sense. What was he going to do? What *could* he do?

Lewis sat up and looked around the room. Two long panes of sunlight lay on the splintered and paint-stained floor. Over by the fireplace stood a tall mirror with battlements on top that matched the ones on Lewis's bed. Before the mirror lay a beautiful hooked rug. Jonathan claimed that Mrs. Zimmermann's great-grandmother had made it. The pattern of the rug was "Autumn Leaves."

Scallop-edged leaves, bright gold and deep blood-red, with some green ones thrown in for contrast. The rug seemed to float before the mirror, and the leaves swam in the pool of bright sunlight. It was an illusion, of course. This was no magic carpet. But Lewis liked to stand on it in the morning while he was dressing. It made him feel that he was free of the earth, if only for a little while.

He stood on it now as he pulled on his pants and tucked in his shirt. The shimmer of leaves lifted him off the floor. Things seemed clearer now. He had to get hold of Tarby. Tarby would know what to do. It was true that he had been avoiding Lewis, but they weren't exactly enemies. And anyway, Tarby was in this thing as deep as he was. He had held the flashlight while Lewis drew the magic pentacle and chalked in the name, Selenna. That must be Mrs. Izard's first name, Lewis thought. She must have put it in my head. Then, behind those iron doors, she was never really dead. . . .

Lewis bit his lip to cut off this line of thought. He went downstairs, ate breakfast alone, and hurried out the door. Tarby, with his nine brothers and sisters, lived in a huge frame house halfway across town. Lewis had never been invited there and he did not even know the first names of Tarby's mother and father, let alone the names of any of the nine brothers and sisters. He knew that Mr. Corrigan—that was Tarby's last name—ran a hardware store. And that was about all Lewis knew.

It was a bright, windy April day, and the sky was full

of little white clouds that kept tearing apart and merging into each other. Birds were flying about and the lawns were showing that first livid wet green. When Lewis got to the Corrigan house he found a bunch of small children playing in the front yard, which was all chewed up and full of mud holes. One of the younger ones, who looked a lot like Tarby, was hanging by his knees from one of the limbs of a dead tree that had red taillight reflectors nailed all over it. Other kids were making mud castles, beating each other over the head with sand shovels, trying to ride broken tricycles, or just sitting around screaming at the top of their lungs. Lewis picked his way past the toy trucks and inner tubes that littered the front walk. He pushed the doorbell and waited.

After a while a fat, tired-looking woman came to the door. She had a baby in her arms, and it was batting her on the shoulder with a bottle that it held by the nipple.

"Yes?" She sounded crabby, and no wonder.

"Uh . . . Mrs. Corrigan? I wonder if you could tell me where Tarby is."

"Tarby? Gee, I wonder if he's in the house. I'll see."

She threw back her head and bellowed, "Taaar-beeee!" No answer, though it would have been hard to hear one over the racket.

"No, I guess not," she said. She smiled a tired, kind smile. "He's probably out playing ball with the other kids."

Lewis thanked her and was about to turn away when she said, "Say! Aren't you that Barnavelt boy?"

Lewis said that he was.

She gave him a pleading look. "Please don't tell Tarby any more stories about ghosts and graveyards. He had nightmares for a week after last Halloween. It was nice of your uncle to invite him over for a cider-and-doughnut party, and let him stay the night and all, but those stories . . . well, you know how sensitive he is."

Lewis managed to keep a straight face. "Mm . . . sure . . . okay, Mrs. Corrigan, I won't tell him any more ghost stories. See you."

As he picked his way back down the walk, tripping on toys and dodging one or two mud balls that were thrown his way, Lewis had a hard time keeping from laughing right out loud. So that was Tarby's version of last Halloween night! Well, well. And where had Tarby spent the night? Shuddering under the back porch? Sleeping in a tree? And a whole week of nightmares! Of course, he hadn't been scared. It was just the moonlight. Lewis's inner laughter turned into a wry grin.

Lewis stopped at a hitching block to tie his shoelace. Now what was he going to do? Well, there were only two regular baseball diamonds in New Zebedee. The one out behind the school, and the one at the athletic field. He decided to go to the one behind the school.

When he got there, he found Tarby playing ball with

a lot of other kids. He was pitching, and various boys were shouting, "Come on, Tar-babee! Strike him out!" and, "Give 'em the old knuckleball!" or, if they happened to be on the other side, "Yaah! Pitcher's got a rubber arm!"

Tarby wound up with a windmill motion, balked several times—this was allowed, because it was softball, not baseball—and when he had the batter making nervous little half-swings, he fired the ball up to the plate. The batter swung so hard that he fell down.

"Strrrike three! Yerrr—out!" yelled the boy who was the umpire.

Lewis, standing on the sidelines, cupped his hands to his mouth and shouted, "Hey, Tarby! Can I talk to you?"

"Not now, Fatty. I'm in the middle of a game."

Tears filled Lewis's eyes. Tarby had never called him "fatty" before. At least he couldn't remember him doing it. Lewis choked back the tears and stood waiting patiently while Tarby mowed down the next batter with three blazing fastballs. That was the third out, so Tarby's team came in from the field. Carelessly, Tarby threw his glove on the ground and said, "Hi, Lewis. C'n I do f'ya?"

"My Uncle Jonathan's in some awful trouble. We're all in awful trouble. You know that night when we went up to the cemetery?"

To Lewis's complete surprise, Tarby grabbed him

by the collar and yanked him forward till their faces were about two inches apart.

"Look. If they ever find out that you were up there that night, you tell them that you were there by yourself. If you don't, you'll have two broken arms and maybe a broken head."

Lewis tried to shake himself free of Tarby's grip, but he couldn't. He felt blood rushing into his face as he shouted, "Tarby, this is worse than Halloween stuff! This is ghosts and witches and devils and . . . *let go of me, you candle-head!*"

Tarby let go of Lewis. He stared at him with his mouth open. "Candle-head" was just a name someone had called someone in a comic book Lewis was reading. It didn't mean anything.

Tarby's lips drew together. "What did you call me?"

Several of the other boys started to shout, "Fight! Fight!" though they really didn't expect much of one. It was only Lewis, after all.

Lewis stood there red-faced and frightened.

"I . . . I don't know what I called you."

"Well, remember next time." Tarby raised his fist and brought it down hard on Lewis's shoulder. It really hurt.

"C'mon, Tarby," shouted a tall boy named Carl Hola-baugh. "Don't waste your time with Tubbo. You lead off this inning, and we're six runs behind. Get up there and slug it."

Tarby turned back to the game, and Lewis stumbled

off down the street, rubbing his shoulder. He was crying.

With the tears still welling uncontrollably into his eyes, Lewis started to walk. He walked all over town, past rows of houses that stared at him blankly. They had no advice to give him. He walked down Main Street, and stared for a while at the Civil War Monument. But the stone soldiers with their upraised bayonets and cannon swabbers did not have anything to say to him, either. He walked to the other end of Main Street and stared at the fountain that spumed a crystal willow tree from within a circle of marble columns. At night the fountain was lit up and it turned from red to orange and from orange to yellow and from yellow to blue and from blue to green and back to red again. But right now it was clear. Lewis wished his mind were clear too, but it wasn't.

He walked around the fountain three or four times, and then he crossed the street and started to walk up U.S. 9, which took up where Main Street left off, and led out of town. When he got to the square, tin CITY LIMITS sign, he just walked off into some tall grass and sat there, watching the ants crawl and listening to the cars as they whooshed past. His eyes were dry now. He was through crying. It occurred to him that he had been doing a lot of crying lately. That wasn't going to solve anything. Thinking might help, though he wasn't sure it would. He sat and thought, and tried to make up his mind what to do.

It was late in the afternoon when Lewis got up. He almost fell over because his left leg had gone to sleep. After he had stomped around in the weeds for a while to get the circulation going again, he set out for home. His mind was made up. All he could hear in his head was the old church hymn that ran:

> Once to every man and nation
> Comes the moment to decide
> In the strife of truth with falsehood
> For the good or evil side.

He imagined that he was leading a cavalry charge. If he had had one of Jonathan's canes with him, he would have swung it like a sword. Now and then he stopped and felt goose-pimple shivers run in waves through his body. He felt very proud and brave, and very frightened too. It is a hard thing to describe.

That night, long after everyone had gone to sleep, Lewis crawled out of bed and tiptoed down the front stairs. The house was quiet, very quiet, because it was one of those nights when Jonathan had stopped all the clocks —all but the one he couldn't stop. Out in the front hall the mirror on the coat rack was talking to itself amid little bursts of static. Now and then its edges flickered faintly. Maybe it was trying to warn Lewis. If it was, he ignored the warning. His mind was made up. He had started this whole horrible business, and now he was going to try to end it.

His hand rested on the cool lip of the Willoware umbrella stand. He groped among the canes, rattling them a good deal. Ah, here it was. His hand closed on the black wooden rod and—what was this? Lewis pulled his fingers away with a sucked-in gasp. Touching the magic cane was like touching a living human arm. Life pulsed through it. Lewis stood there staring at the cane. Its globe was now faintly lit. In the gray light he saw snow swirling, and there, shadowy but real, was the strange little castle. The magic light cast a pale shaking blotch on the wallpaper. Could he use it, this thing of power? It occurred to him that Jonathan was being very modest when he called himself a parlor magician.

Lewis set his teeth and reached out with a hand that still tingled from the shock it had received. He grasped the rod firmly. He drew it out. The globe sizzled and crackled, and turned from gray to rosy pink and then back to gray again. Now he opened the front door. A wet fresh-smelling breeze blew in and banged the door gently against the wall. The leaves of the chestnut tree drifted and sighed, and white blossoms came sailing down. He looked across the street. Despite the overgrown hedge, he could see that there were lights on in the Hanchett house. Muttering a prayer, he started down the steps.

In the middle of the street he almost turned and ran, but something kept him going. Once he had crossed to the other side it seemed easier to go on. It was like running downhill with the wind pushing you. The hedge parted at the brick walk that led up to the front stoop. Lewis walked in under the overhanging branches. Now he was at the bottom of the steps.

The Hanchett house had an old-fashioned double door of black wood with two frosted panes set in it. The panes had always reminded Lewis of the Ten Commandments, and now he thought: *Thou shalt not enter*. But one door panel stood ajar. Was he expected? His heart was pounding, but he went up.

He stopped just inside the door, under the hall lamp. The corridor was empty. Empty and bare. There wasn't a stick of furniture in it, no chairs or chests or little tables. No umbrellas propped against walls. On the pale, rose-colored wallpaper Lewis saw dark squares. The squares were the color the paper had been when it was new. The Hanchetts had hung pictures in these spaces, but now the pictures were gone. Mrs. O'Meagher had not put up any of her own.

Lewis walked quietly to the wide arch that opened into the living room. No one there. Some furniture, but not much. A few weak-looking little chairs with bow legs and an uncomfortable-looking couch. One low coffee table with two postage-stamp-sized china ash trays. One blow from Jonathan's flat-bottomed pipe would have smashed either one to smithereens. Lewis went from chair to chair, touching polished arms and smooth upholstered backs. He half expected the furniture to pop, like soap bubbles, when he touched it. But everything was solid. The floor was so highly polished that you could see your reflection in it. Over on one wall was a brick fireplace. It was painted bright pink all over, even on its inside walls. There were no soot stains. Apparently the old witch didn't like fires. Two birch logs were balanced neatly on the shiny brass andirons.

On the mantelpiece Lewis saw something that surprised him: an ornament. It was one of those whirligigs with tin cutout angels. You lit the candles in the middle, and the heat made the angels go around. These angels were blowing trumpets. Lewis reached up and touched the little wheel. *Squeee.* It spun tipsily. The sound startled him so much that he whirled around, holding the magic cane up for protection. No one was there.

He looked in the kitchen. A couple of little plaster plaques on the wall and an electric clock. A red formica counter and a tubular steel chair, also upholstered in cherry red. In the corner there was an icebox. He opened it and found one bottle of Coke. Or was it Coke? He turned the bottle over in his hands. It was gritty on the outside. Covered with dirt. Like it had been buried. And the liquid inside—it was lighter than Coke. Sort of a brownish red. Lewis put the bottle back. He shut the icebox door. The house seemed to be filled with a humming noise, and he knew that it was his blood in his ears. Gripping the magic cane with a trembling, sweaty hand, he went to inspect the other rooms.

He checked out the whole first floor, but he found

nothing—nothing but more half-furnished rooms. A chair here, a table there. What lamps there were, were unplugged, but a bare ceiling fixture burned in each room. Now Lewis was at the bottom of the brightly lit staircase. He paused for a moment and then, suddenly, he pounded the cane on the floor and shouted, "I have come to defeat you, Mrs. Izard! Show yourself! Are you afraid of me? You ought to be! I know who you are and what you want to do. I challenge you to a duel by the ancient rules of magic!"

Lewis had expected his challenge to sound grand and majestic, to ring high and clear like a blast on a silver trumpet. Instead, it fell flat. It died away in the heavy stillness of the house. Lewis felt foolish. His cheeks burned. And he began to get worried.

Lewis did not know a blessed thing about "the ancient rules of magic." He had come over here with Jonathan's magic stick in his hand, hoping that the stick would do his work for him. Now he was doubtful. What if the cane wouldn't work for anyone but its master? What if Mrs. Izard's magic was stronger than Jonathan's?

Lewis looked at the burning globe, and he looked up the staircase. He felt like turning around and running home as fast as he could. But then how would he save Mrs. Zimmermann and Jonathan and the world, and make up for what he had done?

The house was very silent. Lewis took a deep breath and started to climb the staircase.

Halfway up the stairs, on the broad landing, Lewis stopped to look at a picture. It was the only picture he had seen in the house. There, in a heavy oval black frame, was a photo of an unpleasant-looking old man. He was sitting or standing—you couldn't tell which—against a wall covered with intricately patterned wallpaper. Lewis looked at the picture for a long time. He took in all the details: the two or three strands of hair combed over the almost-bald head, the deep-set eyes that seemed to be staring right at him, the hawkish nose. He looked at the man's clothing. He was wearing an old-fashioned, stiff cardboard collar with folded-back points. And his left hand rested on the ball of what must be a cane. There appeared to be some writing on the cane, but Lewis couldn't read it.

Lewis stood there wondering who the old man was. Could it be . . . ? He snatched the picture down and looked on the back. No label. Quickly he turned it over and stared at the picture again. Something was familiar. Of course! The wallpaper! It was the wallpaper in the upstairs front hallway. Roman numeral II's hooked together with curlicues. Lewis knew now that he was staring at a picture of Isaac Izard.

Then it was all true. This woman was his wife, come back from the grave to . . . to do what? Lewis felt his heart pounding. He was more scared than he had ever been in his life. He didn't want to fight Mrs. Izard any more. He just wanted to get out. He looked frantically up the stairs toward the dark doorway of the bedroom. No one was coming. He started down the stairs, but Mrs. Izard was in the way.

She stood there smiling. In her hand was an ivory-handled cane. "Well, young man, what is it? What makes you think you can roam around other people's houses at night? What do you want?"

Lewis was afraid he might faint, but he didn't. Instead, he felt himself stiffen. He raised the cane. "I don't know what you want to do to us, Mrs. Izard," he said, "but you're not going to do it. My uncle's magic is stronger than yours."

She laughed a harsh, nasty laugh. "Do you mean that toy cane? He probably got it at the Capharnaum County Fair. Don't be foolish, child."

All through the house the cane had burned with a steady gray light. Now, as Mrs. Izard spoke, the globe began to go dark. Lewis looked down and saw that he was staring at something that looked very much like a burned-out light bulb.

"And now," said Mrs. Izard, stepping forward, "and now, my fine young friend, you will see what it is to bother nice old ladies who just want to be left alone."

She snatched the cane from his numb hand and threw it clattering down the stairs. Now she was bending over him, and the light reflected from her spectacles hurt his eyes. Her voice was angry now, and she talked faster.

"Do you have any idea what it is like to be buried

deep in the earth, dark stone all around, no one to hear you or see you, your only company a dead man? *Do you?*"

"Stop right there, Mrs. Izard. You're not dealing with children now."

There at the bottom of the stairs stood Mrs. Zimmermann. Her face was lit by invisible footlights, and she wore a floor-length purple cape. In the folds, instead of shadows, were deep wells of orange fire. In one hand she held a tall black pole with a clear glass globe on top. Inside the globe a magenta star burned. It grew in brightness when she spoke and dwindled when she was silent.

Mrs. Izard turned around. She faced Mrs. Zimmermann calmly. "So it's you," she said. "Well, my power has not reached its height, but I am still strong enough to deal with you. *Aroint ye!*"

She pointed the ivory cane at Mrs. Zimmermann. Nothing happened. She stopped smiling and dropped her cane.

Now it was Mrs. Zimmermann's turn. She pounded the butt of her staff once on the floor, and the staircase was lit with a flash of ultraviolet lightning. With an awful scraping cry that no human ever made, Mrs. Izard rushed past Lewis and up the stairs. Mrs. Zimmermann started up after her.

"Run back home, Lewis!" she shouted as she dashed past him. "You're a brave boy, but you're no match for that thing. *Run,* I tell you!"

Lewis bounded down the stairs, taking them two at a time. He was terrified, but he was very happy too. As he ran down the front steps of the house he heard strange exploding sounds and sharp cries. Branches grabbed at him as he ran along the well-swept brick walk. One of them actually wrapped itself around his left leg and started to pull. With a scream and a frantic thrashing motion, Lewis tore loose and plunged across the street. He threw open the gate and ran *whump!* into something hard and yet soft. Jonathan.

Lewis broke down. He began to weep hysterically with his face pressed into Jonathan's blue work shirt. Jonathan wrapped his arms around Lewis and held him tight. Though Lewis could not see it, Jonathan was staring over his head at the Hanchett house, and there was a grim smile on his face. A purple flash lit up one of the upstairs windows. Now a cold, blue-white pinpoint was kindled in the adjoining window, as if someone had just lit a strange kind of match. The blue light spread till it filled the window. It spread to the other window and ate up the fading purple light. Now there was a dull powerful explosion like an aerial bomb at a fireworks display. It hurt Jonathan's ears. As he watched, both upstairs windows turned a brilliant purple. The chimney of the house toppled, and its bricks slid down the roof. The overgrown hedge thrashed and swayed as if it had been caught in a hurricane. Several diamond-shaped pieces of glass fell out of their frames and tinkled on the walk below. Then the house was silent and dark.

Lewis had stopped crying, and now he turned around to look. A full minute passed. Then the front door scraped open and Mrs. Zimmermann appeared. She walked calmly down the steps and down the brick walk and out into the street, humming as she went. The orange fires in the creases of her robe had gone out, and so had the magic footlights. In one hand she held an old umbrella. The handle of the umbrella was a crystal knob, and a tiny seed of violet fire still burned in it. In her other hand Mrs. Zimmermann held Jonathan's cane; its globe was still dark.

"Hi, Florence," said Jonathan, as if he were meeting her on the street on a Sunday afternoon. "How did it go?"

"Well enough," she said, handing him his cane. "Here's your magic wand. It's had quite a shock, but I think it'll recover. As for Mrs. Izard, I just don't know. I may have destroyed her, or I may have just put her out of action for a while. In any case, let's take the time that has been given to us and *find that clock!*"

CHAPTER TEN

When the three of them got back to the house, they had
a shock. The ticking was very loud now, louder than it
had ever been. It was like standing inside the works of
Big Ben.

Jonathan turned pale. "It looks," he said, "as if things
are drawing to some conclusion. Mrs. Izard may not be
as dead as we could wish."

Mrs. Zimmermann began to pace back and forth. She
rubbed the purple stone of her ring against her chin.
"She may be, or she may not be. Either way, having her
out of the way is no guarantee that the bomb won't blow
up in our faces," she said. "But let's assume the worst.
Let's assume that she's still in the game. All right." She

took a deep breath and let it out. "It has been my theory, ever since yesterday, that the old hag is just waiting for the proper *time* to use that wretched key. The proper action at the proper time to achieve the proper effect. That would be like her. And like her old husband too. His magic is logical. It proceeds from A to B to C in nice, neat steps. As logical and neat as the movement of a hand around the face of a clock."

"Then there's no point in our being logical, is there?" said Jonathan. He was smiling very strangely and clicking the paper clips on his watch chain. This was always a sign that he was thinking.

"What do you mean?" said Lewis and Mrs. Zimmermann at the same time.

"I mean," he said patiently, "that we're no good at that sort of game. Our game is wild swoops, sudden inexplicable discoveries, cloudy thinking. Knights' jumps instead of files of rooks plowing across the board. So we'd better play our way if we expect to win."

Mrs. Zimmermann folded her arms and looked grumpy. "I see," she said. "It sounds very reasonable. If you're in a chess game, draw to an inside straight. If you're playing tennis, try to hit a home run. Very intelligent."

Jonathan seemed unruffled. "Why not?" he said. "It all seems clear enough to me. Lewis, what I want you to do is this. Get a pencil and paper, and dream up the silliest set of instructions you can think of."

Lewis looked puzzled. "Instructions for what?"

"For a ceremony. A ritual. A magic show for getting the clock out of its hiding place. Make it as goofy as you can."

Lewis felt very excited and happy. "Okay," he said. "If that's what you want, here we go!"

He ran to the sideboard and dug out a yellow Ticonderoga NO. 2 pencil and a five-cent pad of writing paper. Then he ran into the study and slammed the doors. Jonathan and Mrs. Zimmermann paced nervously outside, and the gigantic ticking continued.

Fifteen minutes later Lewis slid back the doors of the study. He handed Jonathan a blue-lined sheet of paper with writing on both sides. The first line that Jonathan read made him throw back his head and laugh loudly. He mumbled rapidly through the rest of the list, chuckling all the while. Mrs. Zimmermann kept trying to read it over his shoulder, but finally she lost her temper and snatched it out of his hand. She laughed even harder than Jonathan had. She snortled and cackled and giggled. Finally, she handed the paper back to Jonathan.

"Okay," she said. "So be it. First we put lighted candles in all the windows. Real candles, that is."

"Yes," said Jonathan, wrinkling up his nose. "I see Lewis has the poor taste to prefer real candles. Ah, well . . . let's get going. There are several boxes of candle ends in the sideboard."

Jonathan took the first floor, Mrs. Zimmermann took

the second floor, and Lewis took the third floor and the stained-glass windows, wherever they might be. Before long, the whole house was lit up for Christmas in April.

Lewis paused outside the door of the room that had Isaac Izard's organ in it. He looked into the shoe box that had been full of candle stubs. Only one left. Should he put it in there? No, there was a better place.

With a fat red candle in his hand, Lewis climbed the dusty spiral staircase that led to the cupola room. He shoved open the narrow door. The room was dark except for streaks of moonlight on the floor. Lewis moved over to the window. He knelt down and leaned forward into the deep embrasure.

The oval window gave him a bird's-eye view of the Hanchett house. Or would have, if he had been able to see it. Brilliant moonlight bathed the hill, but the Hanchett house lay in a mass of shadow. Only the dark point of its roof could be seen.

Lewis stared, fascinated. Then, suddenly, he began to hear the ticking, faint but audible, that filled even this room in the house at 100 High Street. He shook his head, got out his matches, and quickly lit the candle.

When he got back downstairs, he found that his second instruction was being obeyed. Mrs. Zimmermann was playing "Chopsticks" on the organ in the front parlor. When she got up and went back to the dining room, the organ kept on playing "Chopsticks," since it was a player organ, and she had set it on "Infinite Replay." The silly monotonous music almost drowned out the steady ticking—almost, but not quite.

Jonathan came bouncing in from the back bedrooms. His face was red, and he was breathing hard. "Okay," he said. "What's next?"

Mrs. Zimmermann picked up the paper and read in a solemn voice. "We are to play a game of Bon-Sour-One-Frank until the Ace of Nitwits appears."

As unlikely as it may seem, Jonathan knew what Bon-Sour-One-Frank was. It was Lewis's name for poker. The three of them had played a lot of poker since that first August evening, and Lewis had named the game for the inscription he thought he saw on the shiny brass one-franc pieces. When you called someone, you had to shout, "Bon Sour One Frank!" very loudly.

But Jonathan was puzzled about one detail. He turned to Lewis with a quizzical look on his face. "And what, may I ask, is the Ace of Nitwits?"

"I don't know. It just came to me. I guess we'll know when we find it."

Out came the red box of coins. Out came the blue and gold cards. Jonathan lit his pipe and unbuttoned his vest till it was only held together by the chain of paper clips. He got his dusty old gray fedora out of the closet and parked it on the back of his head. This, he explained, was the proper poker-playing costume.

Jonathan shuffled and dealt. Shekels and guilders, ducats and florins, drachmas and didrachmas clattered over the table. At first the hands were ordinary. Pair of eights, nothing, kings and tens. Then people started getting six of a kind and cards with square-root signs and question marks all over them. Jonathan and Mrs. Zimmermann were not pulling any tricks. The strange cards appeared all by themselves. On they played, while the giant clock ticked and the organ played "Chopsticks" and the candles threw fruit and flower patterns or plain yellow splotches onto the gray moonlit grass outside.

It was after a half hour of playing that Lewis picked up a card and found that he was staring at the Ace of Nitwits. There it was. Instead of clubs or hearts, it had ears of corn and green peppers all over it. In the center was a dopey-looking man in a flat black hat called a mortarboard, the kind of hat that college professors wear to graduations. Ice cream was heaped up on the hat, and the professor was tasting it with his index finger.

Lewis showed the card around.

"Why so it is!" cried Jonathan. "The Ace of Nitwits! I'd recognize it anywhere. Now just what does *that* mean, Lewis?"

"It means you have to wear it stuck to your forehead with a piece of bubble gum. Here." Lewis took out the piece he had been chewing and handed it to Uncle Jonathan.

"Thanks awfully," said Jonathan. He squashed the card against his forehead. "Now what?"

"You get all done up and come down with the eight ball, like it says in the instructions."

"Hm. Yes. Righty-ho, and all that sort of thing. See you, folks."

Jonathan went upstairs. He stayed up there a long time, so long that the parlor organ broke into "Stars and Stripes Forever" out of pure boredom. Mrs. Zimmermann sat tapping her fingers on the table, while Lewis did what he always did when he was nervously waiting for somebody. He slapped the sides of his chair, rocked back and forth, and wiggled his right leg.

"Well, here I am!"

Mrs. Zimmermann and Lewis looked up. There at the head of the stairs stood Jonathan. He was wearing a cape made from a crazy quilt, and on his head was a flowered toaster cover Mrs. Zimmermann had made. The Ace of Nitwits was still glued to his forehead, and he bore in his hands a small, round, black object. As he started down the stairs, the organ played "Pomp and Circumstance," but it soon got tired of that and switched to radio commercials:

> Call for Cuticura
> It's fragrant, and pura
> It's mildly medicated too
> It's grand for you and yoo-hooo!

Clark's Super One Hundred Gasoline
Thousands say it's best!
The largest-selling, independent gasoline
In the Middle West!

Super Suds, Super Suds
Lots more suds from Super Su-u-uds
Richer longer lasting too
They're the ones with Super Doo-oo-oooo.

To this solemn accompaniment, Jonathan advanced to
the dining-room table and set down the black ball. It was
one of those fortune-telling eight-balls, the kind you buy
in dime stores. The ball was full of fluid, and when you
shook it, ghostly white cards came floating up to the little
window. There were only three of them: YES, NO, and
MAYBE.

"Now what?" asked Jonathan.

"Ask it," said Lewis.

"Ask it what?" Jonathan looked blank.

"The circumference of the moon, you bearded
booby!" screamed Mrs. Zimmermann. "Where I left my
hat after the Chicago World's Fair! Now *think* a minute,
Jonathan. What would you *want* to ask it?"

"Where the clock is?" asked Jonathan in a small voice.

A burst of rather mechanical applause came from the
front room. It was the organ, smarting off as usual. Jonathan stuck his tongue out at it over his shoulder. Then
he turned back to the table where the eight-ball lay.

Carefully, reverently, he picked it up. He held it like a microphone and talked into it.

"Where is the clock?"

The dark window stayed dark. Jonathan shook the ball till the liquid inside it foamed. *"Where is the clock?"* he shouted, and he repeated this question in Greek, Latin, French, German, and Middle-Kingdom Egyptian. Still no answer.

"Your French is terrible," said Mrs. Zimmermann, grabbing the ball out of his hand. "Here . . . let me try."

Holding the ball under a corner of her cloak as if she were protecting it from rain, Mrs. Zimmermann jabbered at it in Bengali, Finno-Ugric, Basque, Old High Norse, and Geez. She used all the commands for unlocking the secrets of specular stones that are favored by Regiomontanus, Albertus Magnus, and Count Cagliostro. Still nothing.

"Can I try?" asked Lewis. His voice was timid and weak.

Mrs. Zimmermann looked down at him. Perspiration was pouring along all the wrinkles of her face. Her eyes looked wild. "What did you say?"

"I wonder if I might try. I know I'm not a wizard or anything, but it *is* my ball. I bought it in Chicago and . . ."

"Of course!" cried Mrs. Zimmermann, pounding the table with her fist. "Of *course!* What fools we are! Like any magic object, it only responds to its owner. Here. But hurry!" She shoved the ball into his hands.

The ticking of the clock got softer, but it was faster now.

Lewis held the magic toy up before his face. His voice was calm and quiet. "Please tell us where the clock is," he whispered.

There was motion inside the ball. YES drifted out of the void like a ghostly newspaper in a black wind. It passed by. So did NO and MAYBE. Finally, after several tense minutes, a card appeared bearing the words: COAL PIT.

"It says coal pit." Lewis's voice was dull and lifeless now. He hung his head.

"May I see the ball?" said Jonathan softly. Lewis handed it to him.

Jonathan held the ball up to the light. He wrinkled his forehead, and the Ace of Nitwits fluttered away to the floor. "Yes, it certainly says 'coal pit.' Coal pit? *Coal pit?* What the devil does it mean by saying *that?*" Jonathan glowered at the shiny little ball. He was beginning to think it might be nice to dash the wretched thing against the mantelpiece.

Suddenly the ball hiccuped. Jonathan glanced quickly down at it, and saw that the little window was filled with bubbles.

"Oh, good grief! Look at this, Florence. Now it thinks it's a Bendix washer. Shall we get out the ouija board?"

"Wait a minute," said Mrs. Zimmermann. "It looks like the bubbles are starting to break up."

Lewis, Jonathan, and Mrs. Zimmermann watched breathlessly as the little bubbles popped, one by one. Pop, pop, pop. It seemed to take forever. Meanwhile, the clock ticked.

At last the window was clear. Now the sign said: COAL BIN.

"Oh, great!" said Jonathan. "Just great! Now it says coal *bin!* That's a big improvement."

"Don't you have a coal bin?" asked Mrs. Zimmermann.

Jonathan gave her an irritated look. "Of course not, Florence! You ought to know that. Remember, I switched to oil when I bought this . . . oh! *Oh!*" Jonathan clapped his hands over his mouth. "Oh! I think I see! Come on, everybody. We're going to the basement."

Lewis and Mrs. Zimmermann followed Jonathan to the kitchen. He opened the cellar door, and jumped back as if he had been hit in the face. The ticking down there was thunderous.

Jonathan looked at Mrs. Zimmermann. His face was haggard, and his eyes were wide with fear. "Got your umbrella, Florence? Good. Then down we go."

Over in a black sooty corner of the basement was the old coal bin. Two of its walls were formed by gray slats nailed to worm-eaten wooden pillars. The other two walls were whitewashed stone, and up against one of these lay a high rampart of coal. It had been there when Jonathan moved in, and he had always meant to have it hauled away.

"I certainly get the idiot prize," he said quietly. Jonathan took a long backswing and started shoveling. Lewis and Mrs. Zimmermann helped with their hands. Before long they had cleared all the coal away from the wall.

"Doesn't *look* like there's any secret panel," said Jonathan, feeling around for springs and hidden levers. "But then, if it looked that way, it wouldn't be secret, would it? Hmm . . . no . . . nothing. I'm afraid we'll have to use the pick. Stand back, everybody."

Lewis and Mrs. Zimmermann got well away from the wall, and Jonathan started swinging. By now the ticking was hurried and staccato, and the blows of the pick were like heavy beats in the rhythm. Every stroke sent whitish-gray chips flying in all directions. But it was an easier job than anyone would have thought. The wall began to shake and crumble at Jonathan's first stroke, and the whole solid-looking mass was soon lying in pieces on the hard dirt floor of the cellar. For it had not been a real wall, but merely a plaster mock-up. What lay behind was a weathered, old wooden door with a black china knob. There was a lock plate, but there was no keyhole.

Jonathan leaned his pick up against a pillar and stepped back.

"Don't dawdle!" said Mrs. Zimmermann nervously. "Get that door open! I have a feeling that we are on the very edge of disaster."

Jonathan stood there rubbing his chin. Exasperated, Mrs. Zimmermann grabbed his arm and started to shake it. "Hurry, Jonathan! What on earth are you waiting for?"

"I'm trying to think of door-opening spells. Know any?"

"Why not pull at it?" said Lewis. "It may not be locked."

Jonathan was about to say that he had never heard of anything so stupid in all his life. But he never got a chance to say this. The door opened all by itself.

Jonathan, Mrs. Zimmermann, and Lewis stared. They were looking down a long corridor—more like a mine shaft it was, really, with square wooden arches diminishing into the dark distance. Something vague and gray was moving at the far end of the tunnel. It seemed to be getting closer.

"Look!" cried Lewis.

He was not pointing at the gray shape. He was pointing at something that was sitting on the floor of the tunnel, right there at their feet.

A clock. A plain, old, Waterbury eight-day clock.

Its pendulum oscillated madly behind a little glass door, and it was making a sound like a Geiger counter gone crazy.

"I'm so glad you've done my work for me," said a voice behind them. Jonathan and Mrs. Zimmermann spun around and froze. Really froze. They could not move their hands or feet or heads. They couldn't even wiggle their ears. They were completely paralyzed, though they could still see and hear.

There stood Mrs. Izard. Or Mrs. O'Meagher, or whatever name you choose. She was wearing a black-velvet cloak with an ivory brooch at her neck. The brooch bore a raised Greek omega. In her right hand was a plain black rod, and in her left she carried what looked like a severed hand with a lighted candle growing out of its back. Concentric rings of yellow light spread outward from the hand, and through them Jonathan and Mrs. Zimmermann could see Mrs. Izard's glasses, which looked like tablets of gray slate.

"I do hope you haven't tired yourselves, my dears," said the old woman in a nasty, sneering voice. "I do hope you haven't. But if you have, it's all been in a good cause. I couldn't have done anything without you. Not a thing. Because, you see, since I was set free, I've been able to pass through walls and doors, but these poor old hands of mine just haven't been able to wield tools. I even had to get Mr. Hammerhandle to find this for me."

She let go of her wand—it stood up by itself—and reached deep into the folds of her cloak. What she brought out was a greenish copper key. She held it up and turned it around. "Pretty, isn't it? I told him where to look, but he had to do the work. He's really been very good at following directions, and he made it quite easy for me to set up light housekeeping across the street. But, alas, that is all over and done with. You played right into my hands as I thought you would. Did you *really* think you had defeated me, you foolish old biddy? You merely hastened the Day of Judgment. And it is at hand. My Lord and master is coming to meet us. And when he arrives it will be a very different world. *Very* different, I assure you. Let me see . . . you two will change first, I think." She pointed at Jonathan and then at Mrs. Zimmermann. "Yes, that's the way it will be. You two first, so Sonny here can watch. You'll want to watch, won't you, Lewis?"

Lewis stood with his back to Mrs. Izard. He was as still as a clothes-store dummy.

"Turn around, Lewis," said Mrs. Izard, in that nasty-sweet voice she had used from the beginning. "Don't you want to kiss your old Auntie Izard?"

He didn't move.

"Come now, Lewis. I command you. Don't be foolish. It'll just make things worse for you in the end. Turn around, I say!"

Lewis's body grew tense, and then he rushed forward into the tunnel. He picked up the clock, which had just begun to make that whirring sound clocks make when they are going to strike the hour.

"Stop, boy!" shouted Mrs. Izard. "Stop, you filthy fat

pig! I'll turn you into something that your own mother wouldn't—don't you dare! Don't . . . ."

Lewis threw the clock down. There was a sproinging of uncoiled springs and a clatter of cogs and a splintering of wood and a tinkle of broken glass. He reached down into the wreckage and ripped the pendulum free of the works, which were still buzzing furiously. At that moment, a figure which stood only a few yards from Lewis, the figure of an elderly man in a rotting black Sunday suit, vanished. Then there was an awful shriek, a loud, inhuman sound like a siren at the top of its wail. It filled the air and seemed to turn it red. Lewis covered his ears, but the sound was inside his head and in the marrow of his bones. And then it was gone.

He turned around. There stood Jonathan, smiling and trying to blink away the tears in his eyes. There stood Mrs. Zimmermann, smiling even more broadly. And behind them, on the cellar floor, under a swaying bare bulb, lay a crumpled pile of black cloth. A yellow skull was staring up out of it, staring up in gap-jawed amazement. A few wisps of gray hair clung to the crevices in the smooth dome, and over the empty eyeholes a pair of rimless glasses was perched. The glasses were shattered.

CHAPTER ELEVEN

Three days after the destruction of Mrs. Izard and her magic clock, Jonathan, Mrs. Zimmermann, and Lewis were sitting around a bonfire in the driveway of the house at 100 High Street. It was a chilly night, and the stars were cold overhead, but the fire burned a warm, bright orange. Mrs. Zimmermann had a steaming earthenware pot of cocoa by her side. She kept it close to the fire so it would stay warm. Jonathan and Lewis stared at the fire and sipped cocoa from their mugs. It tasted very good.

There was a pile of Isaac Izard's dusty papers in Jonathan's lap. Every now and then he would pick one up and throw it into the fire. Lewis watched each sheet as the fire licked at its corners, then blackened it, then wadded it into a fluffy ball of ashes.

After a while Lewis said, "Uncle Jonathan?"

"Yes, Lewis?"

"Was Mrs. Izard really trying to make the world end?"

"As far as I can tell, she was," said Jonathan. "And she would have done it, too, if you hadn't fixed her clock for her. But tell me, Lewis. Why didn't you turn around when we did?"

Lewis smiled broadly. "I looked at the glass door on the clock and I saw the reflection of what Mrs. Izard was holding, and I knew it was a Hand of Glory. John L. Stoddard tells you all about Hands of Glory."

"I'm glad he does," said Mrs. Zimmermann. "One look at that hand and you'd have been as numb as we were. But still, it took a great deal of courage for you to rush in and smash the clock. After all, you didn't know what would happen to you when you did that."

Lewis was silent. He had always thought that courage had something to do with riding your bicycle through bonfires and hanging by your knees from the limbs of trees.

Mrs. Zimmermann picked up a plate of chocolate-chip cookies and passed them around. Jonathan took two and Lewis took several. There was another silence while everyone munched and sipped for a while. Jonathan threw more papers into the fire.

Lewis squirmed around and stared at the dark house across the street.

"Do you think Mrs. Izard could ever . . . come back?" he said in a faltering voice.

"No," said Jonathan, shaking his head gravely. "No, Lewis, I think that when you smashed the clock in the walls, you destroyed any power she might have in this world. Just to be on the safe side, though, I put what was left of her back in the mausoleum and locked the doors with a nice shiny new lock. A lock that has had spells said over it. That ought to hold her for a while."

"What about the Hanchetts?" said Lewis. "I mean, are they going to come back to live in their house?"

Jonathan paused for a minute before speaking. He clicked the paper clips on his watch chain. "I think they are," he said at last. "But certain rites will have to be performed before they return. When an unclean spirit inhabits a house, it leaves behind a bad aura."

"Speaking of bad auras and unclean spirits," said Mrs. Zimmermann, "do you have any idea of what happened to Hammerhandle?"

Jonathan's face grew grim for an instant. He had made a few guesses about Hammerhandle's fate, but he had kept them to himself. For one thing, he knew that the blood of a hanged man went into the making of a Hand of Glory.

"No idea at all," said Jonathan, shaking his head. "He seems to have vanished from the face of the earth."

Suddenly Lewis began to squirm and scrunch around in his seat again. He was on the brink of saying something.

"Uncle . . . Jonathan?" Lewis's voice was dry and throaty.

"Yes, Lewis? What is it?"

"I . . . I let Mrs. Izard out of her tomb."

Jonathan smiled calmly. "Yes," he said. "I knew you did."

Lewis's mouth dropped open. "How did you know?"

"You left your flashlight up at the cemetery. I found it in a pile of leaves when I went up to put Mrs. Izard back in her tomb."

"Are you going to send me to the Detention Home?" asked Lewis in a tiny, frightened voice.

"Am I going to *what?*" said Jonathan, staring at him in disbelief. "Lewis, what kind of ogre do you think I am?

"And besides," Jonathan added with a sudden smile, "why should I punish you for doing what I tried to do myself when I was a boy? Like you, I was interested in magic at an early age. It runs in our family, I guess. I was trying to impress a girl. You wanted to keep Tarby for a friend. Isn't that right?"

Lewis nodded sadly.

"By the way, Lewis," said Mrs. Zimmermann. "How are things between you and Tarby these days?"

"Not so good," said Lewis. "I don't think Tarby and

I were meant to be friends. We're not the same type. But it doesn't matter."

"Doesn't matter?" said Jonathan. "Well, it certainly *does* matter! If he's such a stuck-up little . . ." He stopped because he saw that Lewis was smiling smugly.

Jonathan wrinkled up his eyebrows so that they looked like two mating auburn caterpillars. "Lewis Barnavelt!" he roared. "Are you hiding something from me?"

Lewis was trying very hard to keep from giggling. "Oh, nothing much, Uncle Jonathan," he said. "Except that I have a new friend."

"*Whaaat?* You *dooo?*" said Jonathan and Mrs. Zimmermann in unison.

"Yes. Her name is Rose Rita Pottinger, and she lives down on Mansion Street. She knows the names of all the different kinds of cannon. Want to hear them? Saker, minion, falconet, demi-culverin . . ."

"Aaaaah!" screamed Jonathan. He threw two fistfuls of paper into the fire. "That's all I need. An expert in Elizabethan ordnance. Promise me one thing, Lewis."

"What's that?"

"If you and tiny Rosie decide to start a cannon foundry in our basement, let Mrs. Zimmermann and me know so we can go visit my relatives in Osee Five Hills, Okay?"

Lewis giggled. "Sure, Uncle Jonathan. I'll let you know."

Jonathan waved his pipe at the bonfire. The leaves stirred uneasily, and then they gathered into a large black ball. The bonfire turned into a jack-o'-lantern. Now the three of them took turns pitching chestnuts into the eyes, nose, and mouth of the ferocious lantern. *Pop! Pop! Pop!* The chestnuts went off in a ripping string, like a fusillade of musket fire.

Jonathan, Lewis, and Mrs. Zimmermann sat around the fire talking until the scowling orange face fell in with an airy *whoosh*. Then they got up, stretched, and went wearily off to bed.

About the Author

John Bellairs was the critically acclaimed, best-selling author of many Gothic novels: *The Curse of the Blue Figurine*, *The Mummy, the Will, and the Crypt*, *The Lamp from the Warlock's Tomb*, *The Spell of the Sorcerer's Skull*, *The Revenge of the Wizard's Ghost*, *The Chessmen of Doom*, *The Eyes of the Killer Robot*, and the novels starring Lewis Barnavelt, Rose Rita Pottinger, and Mrs. Zimmermann — *The House with a Clock in Its Walls*, *The Figure in the Shadows*, *The Letter, the Witch, and the Ring*, and *The Ghost in the Mirror* (completed by Brad Strickland).

John Bellairs died in 1991. However, there are several more books that Mr. Bellairs left that Puffin will be publishing. Brad Strickland, a longtime Bellairs fan, will be completing them, just as he did *The Ghost in the Mirror*.

About the Artist

Edward Gorey is the well-known illustrator of many books, including *The Shrinking of Treehorn* and *Sam and Emma*, both selected for the 1972 Children's Book Showcase, and *Red Riding Hood*. He lives in New York City.

The text of this book was set in Janson, a Linotype face
based on the original design of Antonius Janson, a Dutch
punchcutter and typefounder who worked in Frankfurt
and Leipzig from 1651 to 1687. The Linotype rendition of
Janson, introduced in 1932, was cut by the Mergenthaler
Linotype Company under the direction of C. H. Griffith.
Janson is an old style book face characterized by narrow
characters and a marked contrast between thick and thin
strokes.

Composition by Connecticut Printers, Inc.

Typography by Atha Tehon

"A compelling read."

—FOREIGN AFFAIRS

"The images are searing."

—CHRISTIAN SCIENCE MONITOR

"A pained, personal testament and a prophetic warning.... Crucially important."

—THE NEW LEADER

"Timely and powerful."

—TIMES LITERARY SUPPLEMENT

"Splendid....
His understanding is profound."

—MOLLY·IVINS, FORT WORTH STAR-TELEGRAM

"Insightful, provocative."

—THE NATION

"Unusual and searing, deeply researched."
—*TORONTO STAR*

"[A] searching indictment of
international violence."
—*NATIONAL CATHOLIC REPORTER*

"Written with extreme
thoughtfulness and grace."
—DOUGLAS BRINKLEY

"[Hedges] escorts us through the
streets made slick with the blood and
guts of innocents."
—*DALLAS MORNING NEWS*

"[P]owerful and highly
significant.... [A] wake-up call."
—GENERAL WESLEY K. CLARK

"A refreshing jolt of cerebral
and emotional clarity."
—*WILLAMETTE WEEK*

"[A] searching indictment of international violence. . . . What makes this more than just another treatise on the futility of war is the personal witness Hedges brings to the subject."

—*National Catholic Reporter*

"A profound meditation on the dangers of mindless jingoism and patriotic overkill which too often constitute policy in the Modern World. Written with extreme thoughtfulness and grace."   —Douglas Brinkley,
Director of the Eisenhower Center and
Professor of History at the University of New Orleans

"An angry, articulate book. . . . A compelling read and a valuable counterweight to the more antiseptic discussions common among strategic analysts."   —*Foreign Affairs*

"What separates [Hedges's] account . . . is that he has been there, repeatedly. Page after page, the author shows the good reporter's gift for putting faces on the dead and the maimed who might otherwise remain undifferentiated 'casualties.' "

—*Dallas Morning News*

CHRIS HEDGES

WAR IS A FORCE THAT

GIVES US MEANING

Chris Hedges has been a foreign correspondent for fifteen
years. He joined the staff of *The New York Times* in 1990 and
previously worked for *The Dallas Morning News, The Christian
Science Monitor,* and National Public Radio. He holds a B.A. in
English literature from Colgate University and a master of
divinity from Harvard University. He is Lecturer in the Council of the Humanities and Ferris Professor of Journalism at
Princeton University. Hedges was a member of the *New York
Times* team that won the 2002 Pulitzer Prize for Explanatory
Reporting for the paper's coverage of global terrorism, and
he received the 2002 Amnesty International Global Award
for Human Rights Journalism. He lives in New York City.

WAR

IS A FORCE THAT
GIVES US MEANING

CHRIS HEDGES

PUBLICAFFAIRS

New York

Published in 2014 in the United States by PublicAffairs™, a Member of the Perseus Books Group
Paperback first published in 2003 by Anchor Books, a Division of Random House, Inc.
Hardcover first published in 2002 by PublicAffairs

PublicAffairs books are available at special discounts for bulk purchases in the U.S. by corporations, institutions, and other organizations. For more information, please contact the Special Markets Department at the Perseus Books Group, 2300 Chestnut Street, Suite 200, Philadelphia, PA 19103, call (800) 810-4145, ext. 5000, or e-mail special.markets@perseus books.com.

From Homer, *Odyssey,* trans. Stanley Lombardo, copyright © 2000, reprinted by permission of Hackett Publishing Company, Inc. All rights reserved. "Epitaph on a Tyrant," copyright © 1940 and renewed 1968 by W. H. Auden, from *W.H. Auden: The Collected Poems* by W. H. Auden. Used by permission of Random House, Inc. "Wants" from *Collected Poems* by Philip Larkin, copyright © 1988, 1989 by the Estate of Philip Larkin. Reprinted by permission of Farrar, Straus and Giroux, LLC. "Catullus, CI" translated by Robert Fitzgerald, from *In the Rose of Time,* copyright © 1956 by Robert Fitzgerald. Reprinted by permission of New Directions Publishing Corp. From *Goodbye Darkness* by William Manchester, published by Little, Brown and Company (Back Bay Books), copyright © 1979, 1980 by William Manchester. Reprinted by permission of Don Congdon Associates, Inc.

The Library of Congress has cataloged the hardcover edition as follows:
  Hedges, Chris.
  War is a force that gives us meaning / Chris Hedges.—1st ed.
    p.cm.
  Includes index.
  · ISBN 1-58648-049-9
  1. War (Philosophy) 2. Hedges, Chris. 3. Military history, Modern—20th century. I. Title.

U21.2 .H43 2002
355.02—dc21

2002068136

ISBN 978-1-61039-359-1 (PublicAffairs paperback)
ISBN 978-0-7867-4185-4 (original e-book)
ISBN 978-1-61039-510-6 (revised e-book)

LSC-C

10 9 8 7 6

For my father, the Rev. Thomas Hedges,

who taught me that compassion was the highest virtue,

and for the Rev. Coleman Brown,

who has never let me forget it.

CONTENTS

INTRODUCTION 1

1 The Myth of War 19

2 The Plague of Nationalism 43

3 The Destruction of Culture 62

4 The Seduction of Battle and
the Perversion of War 83

5 The Hijacking and
Recovery of Memory 122

6 The Cause 142

7 Eros and Thanatos 157

NOTES 187

BIBLIOGRAPHY 192

ACKNOWLEDGMENTS 196

INDEX 200

If in smothering dreams you too could pace
Behind the wagon that we flung him in,
And watch the white eyes writhing in his face,
His hanging face, like a devil's sick of sin;
If you could hear, at every jolt, the blood
Come gargling from the froth-corrupted lungs,
Obscene as cancer, bitter as the cud
Of vile, incurable sores on innocent tongues, —
My friend, you would not tell with such high zest
To children ardent for some desperate glory,
The old Lie: Dulce et decorum est
Pro Patria mori.

WILFRED OWEN
Dulce et decorum est

WAR IS A FORCE THAT
GIVES US MEANING

INTRODUCTION

Only the dead have seen the end of war.

•

PLATO

S ARAJEVO IN THE SUMMER OF 1995 CAME CLOSE TO
Dante's inner circle of hell. The city, surrounded by Serb
gunners on the heights above, was subjected to hundreds of
shells a day, all crashing into an area twice the size of Central
Park. Ninety-millimeter tank rounds and blasts fired from huge
155-millimeter howitzers set up a deadly rhythm of detonations.
Multiple Katyusha rockets—whooshing overhead—burst in
rapid succession; they could take down a four- or five-story
apartment building in seconds, killing or wounding everyone
inside. There was no running water or electricity and little to eat;
most people were subsisting on a bowl of soup a day. It was
possible to enter the besieged city only by driving down a dirt
track on Mount Igman, one stretch directly in the line of Serb
fire. The vehicles that had failed to make it lay twisted and
upended in the ravine below, at times with the charred remains
of their human cargo inside.

Families lived huddled in basements, and mothers, who had
to make a mad dash to the common water taps set up by the
United Nations, faced an excruciating choice—whether to run
through the streets with their children or leave them in a building that might be rubble when they returned.

The hurling bits of iron fragmentation from exploding shells left bodies mangled, dismembered, decapitated. The other reporters and I slipped and slid in the blood and entrails thrown out by the shell blasts, heard the groans of anguish, and were, for our pains, in the sights of Serb snipers, often just a few hundred yards away. The latest victims lay with gaping wounds untended in the corridors of the hospitals that lacked antibiotics and painkillers.

When the cease-fires broke down, there would be four to five dead a day, and a dozen wounded. It was a roulette wheel of death, a wheel of fire that knew no distinctions of rank or nationality. By that summer, after nearly four years of fighting, forty-five foreign reporters had been killed, scores wounded. I lived—sheltered in a side room in the Holiday Inn, its front smashed and battered by shellfire—in a world bent on self-destruction, a world where lives were snuffed out at random.

War and conflict have marked most of my adult life. I began covering insurgencies in El Salvador, where I spent five years, then went on to Guatemala and Nicaragua and Colombia, through the first *intifada* in the West Bank and Gaza, the civil war in the Sudan and Yemen, the uprisings in Algeria and the Punjab, the fall of the Romanian dictator Nicolae Ceauşescu, the Gulf War, the Kurdish rebellion in southeast Turkey and northern Iraq, the war in Bosnia, and finally to Kosova. I have been in ambushes on desolate stretches of Central American roads, shot at in the marshes of southern Iraq, imprisoned in the Sudan, beaten by Saudi military police, deported from Libya and Iran, captured and held for a week by Iraqi Republican Guard during the Shiite rebellion following the Gulf War, strafed by Russian Mig-21s in Bosnia, fired upon by Serb snipers, and shelled for days in Sarajevo with deafening rounds of heavy artillery that threw out thousands of deadly bits of iron fragments. I have seen too much of violent death. I have tasted too much of my own fear. I have painful memories that lie buried and untouched most of the time. It is never easy when they surface.

I learned early on that war forms its own culture. The rush of battle is a potent and often lethal addiction, for war is a drug, one I ingested for many years. It is peddled by mythmakers—historians, war correspondents, filmmakers, novelists, and the state—all of whom endow it with qualities it often does possess: excitement, exoticism, power, chances to rise above our small stations in life, and a bizarre and fantastic universe that has a grotesque and dark beauty. It dominates culture, distorts memory, corrupts language, and infects everything around it, even humor, which becomes preoccupied with the grim perversities of smut and death. Fundamental questions about the meaning, or meaninglessness, of our place on the planet are laid bare when we watch those around us sink to the lowest depths. War exposes the capacity for evil that lurks not far below the surface within all of us. And this is why for many war is so hard to discuss once it is over.

The enduring attraction of war is this: Even with its destruction and carnage it can give us what we long for in life. It can give us purpose, meaning, a reason for living. Only when we are in the midst of conflict does the shallowness and vapidness of much of our lives become apparent. Trivia dominates our conversations and increasingly our airwaves. And war is an enticing elixir. It gives us resolve, a cause. It allows us to be noble. And those who have the least meaning in their lives, the impoverished refugees in Gaza, the disenfranchised North African immigrants in France, even the legions of young who live in the splendid indolence and safety of the industrialized world, are all susceptible to war's appeal.

Those who make war do so for many reasons, although many of these motives are never acknowledged publicly.

The Palestinian uprising was not just about throwing the Israelis out of Gaza and the West Bank, but also about crushing the urban elite, the shop owners and businessmen, in East Jerusalem and Gaza City. The "strikes" organized by the *shabab*, the young men who fueled the uprising from the refugee camps, hurt the Palestinian community far more than they hurt the Israelis. In Bosnia it was the same, the anger turned against a Communist hierarchy that kept for itself the privileges and perks of power even as power slipped from their hands in the decaying state. There is little that angers the disenfranchised more than those who fail to exercise power yet reap powerful rewards. Despots can be understood, even tolerated, but parasites rarely last long.

War is a crusade. President George W. Bush is not shy about warning other nations that they stand with the United States in the war on terrorism or will be counted with those that defy us. This too is a *jihad*. Yet we Americans find ourselves in the dangerous position of going to war not against a state but against a phantom. The *jihad* we have embarked upon is targeting an elusive and protean enemy. The battle we have begun is never-ending. But it may be too late to wind back the heady rhetoric. We have embarked on a campaign as quixotic as the one mounted to destroy us.

"We go forward," President Bush assures us, "to defend freedom and all that is good and just in the world."

The patriotic bunting and American flags that proliferated in the wake of the attacks on the World Trade Center and the Pentagon were our support for the war mounted against the "axis of evil." Elected officials, celebrities and news anchors lined up to be counted. On Friday, September 14, three days after the attacks, Congress granted the President the right to "use all necessary and appropriate force against those nations, organizations, or persons he determines planned, authorized, committed, or aided the terrorist attacks." The resolution was passed unanimously by the Senate. There was in the House only one dissenting vote, from Barbara J. Lee, a Democrat from California, who warned that military action could not guarantee the safety of the country and that "as we act, let us not become the evil we deplore."

When we ingest the anodyne of war we feel what those we strive to destroy feel, including the Islamic fundamentalists who are painted as alien, barbaric, and uncivilized. It is the same narcotic. I partook of it for many years. And like every recovering addict there is a part of me that remains nostalgic for war's simplicity and high, even as I cope with the scars it has left behind, mourn the deaths of those I worked with, and struggle with the bestiality I would have been better off not witnessing. There is a part of me—maybe it is a part of many of us—that decided at certain moments that I would rather die like this than go back to the routine of life. The chance to exist for an intense and overpowering moment, even if it meant certain oblivion, seemed worth it in the midst of war—and very stupid once the war ended.

I covered the war in El Salvador from 1983 to 1988. By the end I had a nervous twitch in my face. I was evacuated three times by the U.S. embassy because of tips that the death squads planned to kill me. Yet each time I came back. I accepted with a grim fatalism that I would be killed in El Salvador. I could not articulate why I should accept my own destruction and cannot now. When I finally did leave, my last act was, in a frenzy of rage and anguish, to leap over the KLM counter in the airport in Costa Rica because of a perceived slight by a hapless airline clerk. I beat him to the floor as his bewildered colleagues locked themselves in the room behind the counter. Blood streamed down his face and mine. I refused to wipe the dried stains off my cheeks on the flight to Madrid, and I carry a scar on my face from where he thrust his pen into my cheek. War's sickness had become mine.

In the fall of 1995, a few weeks after the war in Bosnia ended, I sat with friends who had suffered horribly. A young woman, Ljiljana, had lost her father, a Serb who refused to join the besieging Serb forces around the city. She had been forced a few days earlier to identify his corpse. The body was lifted, the water running out of the sides of a rotting coffin, from a small park for reburial in the central cemetery. She was emigrating to Australia soon—where, she told me, "I will marry a man who has never heard of this war and raise children who will be told nothing about it, nothing about the country I am from."

Ljiljana was beautiful and young, but the war had exacted a toll. Her cheeks were hollow, her hair dry and brittle. Her teeth were decayed and some had broken into jagged bits. She had no money for a dentist. She hoped to fix them in Australia.

Yet all she and her friends did that afternoon was lament the days when they lived in fear and hunger, emaciated, targeted by Serbian gunners on the heights above. They did not wish back the suffering, and yet, they admitted, those days may have been the fullest of their lives. They looked at me in despair. I knew them when they were being stonked by hundreds of shells a day, when they had no water to bathe in or to wash their clothes, when they huddled in unheated, darkened apartments with plas- tic sheeting for windows. But what they expressed was real. It was the disillusionment with a sterile, futile, empty present. Peace had again exposed the void that the rush of war, of bat- tle, had filled. Once again they were, as perhaps we all are, alone, no longer bound by that common sense of struggle, no longer given the opportunity to be noble, heroic, no longer sure what life was about or what it meant.

The old comradeship, however false, that allowed them to love men and women they hardly knew, indeed, whom they may not have liked before the war, had vanished. Moreover, they had seen that all the sacrifice had been for naught. They had been betrayed. The corrupt old Communist Party bosses, who became nationalists overnight and got my friends into the mess in the first place, those who had grown rich off their suffering, were still in power. There was a 70 percent unemployment rate. They depended on handouts from the international community. They knew the lie of war, the mockery of their idealism and struggled with their shattered illusions. They had seen the grin- ning skull of death that speaks in the end for war. They under- stood that their cause, once as fashionable in certain intellectual circles as they were themselves, lay forgotten. No longer did actors, politicians, and artists scramble to visit, acts that were almost always ones of gross self-promotion. And yet they wished it all back. I did too.

A year later I received a Christmas card. It was signed "Ljil- jana from Australia." It had no return address. I never heard from her again.

Many of us, restless and unfulfilled, see no supreme worth in our lives. We want more out of life. And war, at least, gives a sense that we can rise above our smallness and divisiveness.

The weeks after the September 11 attacks saw New York City, with some reluctance, slip back to normal. One felt the same nostalgia.

The attacks on the World Trade Center illustrate that those who oppose us, rather than coming from another moral universe, have been schooled well in modern warfare. The dramatic explosions, the fireballs, the victims plummeting to their deaths, the collapse of the towers in Manhattan, were straight out of Hollywood. Where else, but from the industrialized world, did the suicide hijackers learn that huge explosions and death above a city skyline are a peculiar and effective form of communication? They have mastered the language. They understand that the use of disproportionate violence against innocents is a way to make a statement. We leave the same calling cards.

Corpses in wartime often deliver messages. The death squads in El Salvador dumped three bodies in the parking lot of the Camino Real Hotel in San Salvador, where the journalists were based, early one morning. Death threats against us were stuffed in the mouths of the bodies. And, on a larger scale, Washington uses murder and corpses to transmit its wrath. We delivered such incendiary messages in Vietnam, Iraq, Serbia, and Afghanistan. Osama bin Laden has learned to speak the language of modern industrial warfare. It was Robert McNamara, the American Secretary of Defense in the summer of 1965, who defined the bombing raids that would eventually leave hundreds of thousands of civilians north of Saigon dead as a means of communication to the Communist regime in Hanoi.

It is part of war's perversity that we lionize those who make great warriors and excuse their excesses in the name of self-defense. We have built or bolstered alliances with Israel and

Russia, forming a dubious global troika against terrorism, a troika that taints us in the eyes of much of the rest of the world, especially among Muslims. Suddenly all who oppose our allies and us—Palestinians, Chechens, and Afghans—are lumped into one indistinguishable mass. They are as faceless as we are for our enemies.

As the battle against terrorism continues, as terrorist attacks intrude on our lives, as we feel less and less secure, the acceptance of all methods to lash out at real and perceived enemies will distort and deform our democracy. For even as war gives meaning to sterile lives, it also promotes killers and racists.

Organized killing is done best by a disciplined, professional army. But war also empowers those with a predilection for murder. Petty gangsters, reviled in pre-war Sarajevo, were transformed overnight at the start of the conflict into war heroes. What they did was no different. They still pillaged, looted, tortured, raped, and killed; only then they did it to Serbs, and with an ideological veneer. Slobodan Milošević went one further. He opened up the country's prisons and armed his criminal class to fight in Bosnia. Once we sign on for war's crusade, once we see ourselves on the side of the angels, once we embrace a theological or ideological belief system that defines itself as the embodiment of goodness and light, it is only a matter of how we will carry out murder.

The eruption of conflict instantly reduces the headache and trivia of daily life. The communal march against an enemy generates a warm, unfamiliar bond with our neighbors, our community, our nation, wiping out unsettling undercurrents of alienation and dislocation. War, in times of malaise and desperation, is a potent distraction.

George Orwell in *1984* wrote of the necessity of constant

wars against the Other to forge a false unity among the proles:
"War had been literally continuous, though strictly speaking it
had not always been the same war. . . . The enemy of the
moment always represented absolute evil."[1]

Patriotism, often a thinly veiled form of collective self-
worship, celebrates our goodness, our ideals, our mercy and
bemoans the perfidiousness of those who hate us. Never mind
the murder and repression done in our name by bloody surro-
gates from the Shah of Iran to the Congolese dictator Joseph-
Désiré Mobutu, who received from Washington well over a
billion dollars in civilian and military aid during the three
decades of his rule. And European states—especially France—
gave Mobutu even more as he bled dry one of the richest countries in Africa. We define ourselves. All other definitions do not
count.

War makes the world understandable, a black and white
tableau of them and us. It suspends thought, especially self-
critical thought. All bow before the supreme effort. We are one.
Most of us willingly accept war as long as we can fold it into a
belief system that paints the ensuing suffering as necessary for a
higher good, for human beings seek not only happiness but also
meaning. And tragically war is sometimes the most powerful
way in human society to achieve meaning.

But war is a god, as the ancient Greeks and Romans knew,
and its worship demands human sacrifice. We urge young men
to war, making the slaughter they are asked to carry out a rite of
passage. And this rite has changed little over the centuries, centuries in which there has almost continuously been a war raging
somewhere on the planet. The historian Will Durant calculated
that there have only been twenty-nine years in all of human history during which a war was not underway somewhere. We call

on the warrior to exemplify the qualities necessary to prosecute war—courage, loyalty, and self-sacrifice. The soldier, neglected and even shunned during peacetime, is suddenly held up as the exemplar of our highest ideals, the savior of the state. The soldier is often whom we want to become, although secretly many of us, including most soldiers, know that we can never match the ideal held out before us. And we all become like Nestor in *The Iliad*, reciting the litany of fallen heroes that went before to spur on a new generation. That the myths are lies, that those who went before us were no more able to match the ideal than we are, is carefully hidden from public view. The tension between those who know combat, and thus know the public lie, and those who propagate the myth, usually ends with the mythmakers working to silence the witnesses of war.

John Wheeler, who graduated from West Point in 1966, went to Vietnam, where he watched his class take the highest number of dead and wounded of all the classes that fought there. "I was a witness in Vietnam," he told me. "I spent half my time in a helicopter traveling around the country. I was a witness to the decimation of my West Point class. And I knew we were decimated for a lie." He left the army as a captain in 1971, went to Yale Law School, and became an activist. He was the driving force behind the Vietnam Veterans Memorial wall in Washington. "When I left law school the full impact of the lies hit me," he said. "I have been thinking about these lies, meditating on them and acting on them ever since. The honor system at West Point failed grotesquely within the chain of command. The most senior officers went along with McNamara and Johnson and were guilty. It was an abomination. If in order to do your duty as an Admiral or a General you have to lie, West Point should tell the new plebes."

The Iliad is about power and force. Those who inhabit its space abide by the warrior's code. Its heroes are vain, brave, and consumed by the heady elixir of violence and the bitterness of bereavement. The story is primarily that of one man, Achilles, who returns to the battlefield at Troy to attain *kleos*, the ever-lasting fame that will be denied to him without heroic death. *The Iliad* could have been written about Bosnia, with its competing warlords and its commanders willing to sacrifice men and villages to their egos and ambition.

The Odyssey is different. It is also built around one character, Odysseus. In *The Odyssey* the hubris and inflexibility of the warrior fail to ward off the capriciousness of fate, the indifference of nature. Odysseus has trouble coping with the conventions of civilized life. When he takes umbrage at more powerful forces and cannot resist revealing his name to the Cyclops, he condemns his men to death and himself to prolonged suffering. As the sailors beat the sea to white froth with their oars, Odysseus calls out to Cyclops: "With my men / hanging all over me and begging me not to," but they "didn't persuade my hero's heart."[2]

It is his hero's heart that Odysseus must learn to curb before he can return to the domestic life he left twenty years earlier. The very qualities that served him in battle defeat him in peace. These dual codes have existed, perhaps, since human societies were formed, and every recruit headed into war would be well-advised to read *The Iliad*, just as every soldier returning home would be served by reading *The Odyssey*. No two works have come closer to chronicling the rage and consumption of war and the struggle to recover. The name Odysseus is tied to the Greek verb *odussomai*, which means "to suffer pain."

War exposes a side of human nature that is usually masked by the unacknowledged coercion and social constraints that glue us together. Our cultivated conventions and little lies of civility lull us into a refined and idealistic view of ourselves. But modern industrial warfare may well be leading us, with each technological advance, a step closer to our own annihilation. We too are strapping explosives around our waists. Do we also have a suicide pact?

Look just at the 1990s: 2 million dead in Afghanistan; 1.5 million dead in the Sudan; some 800,000 butchered in ninety days in Rwanda; a half-million dead in Angola; a quarter of a million dead in Bosnia; 200,000 dead in Guatemala; 150,000 dead in Liberia; a quarter of a million dead in Burundi; 75,000 dead in Algeria; and untold tens of thousands lost in the border conflict between Ethiopia and Eritrea, the fighting in Colombia, the Israeli-Palestinian conflict, Chechnya, Sri Lanka, southeastern Turkey, Sierra Leone, Northern Ireland, Kosova, and the Persian Gulf War (where perhaps as many as 35,000 Iraqi citizens were killed). In the wars of the twentieth century not less than 62 million civilians have perished, nearly 20 million more than the 43 million military personnel killed.

Civil war, brutality, ideological intolerance, conspiracy, and murderous repression are part of the human condition—indeed almost the daily fare for many but a privileged minority.

War is not a uniform experience or event. My time in the insurgencies in Central America, the Persian Gulf War—where two large armies clashed in the desert—and the Balkans, where warlords and gangsters tried to pass themselves off as professional soldiers, illustrated the wide differences that make up modern warfare. But war usually demands, by its very logic, the disabling of the enemy, often broadly defined to include civilians who may have little love for the Taliban or Saddam Hussein or Somali warlords. While we venerate and mourn our own dead we are curiously indifferent about those we kill. Thus killing is done in our name, killing that concerns us little, while those who kill our own are seen as having crawled out of the deepest recesses of the earth, lacking our own humanity and goodness. Our dead. Their dead. They are not the same. Our dead matter, theirs do not. Many Israelis defend the killing of Palestinian children whose only crime was to throw rocks at armored patrols, while many Palestinians applaud the murder of Israeli children by suicide bombers.

Armed movements seek divine sanction and the messianic certitude of absolute truth. They do not need to get this from religions, as we usually think of religion, but a type of religion: Patriotism provides the blessing. Soldiers want at least the consolation of knowing that they risk being blown up by land mines for a greater glory, for a New World. Dissension, questioning of purpose, the exposure of war crimes carried out by those fighting on our behalf are dangerous to such beliefs. Dissidents who challenge the goodness of our cause, who question the gods of war, who pull back the curtains to expose the lie are usually silenced or ignored.

We speak of those we fight only in the abstract; we strip them of their human qualities. It is a familiar linguistic corruption. During the war in Bosnia, many Muslims called the Serbs "Chetniks," the Serbian irregulars in World War II, who slaughtered many Muslims. Muslims, for many Serbs in Bosnia, were painted as Islamic fundamentalists. The Croats, to the Serbs and Muslims, were branded "Ustashe," the fascist quislings who ruled Croatia during World War II. And there were times when, in interviews, it was hard to know if people were talking about what happened a few months ago or a few decades ago. It all merged into one huge mythic campaign. It was as if Josip Broz

Tito, who had held Yugoslavia together for most of the Cold War era, had put the conflicted country into a deep freeze in 1945.

The goal of such nationalist rhetoric is to invoke pity for one's own. The goal is to show the community that what they hold sacred is under threat. The enemy, we are told, seeks to destroy religious and cultural life, the very identity of the group or state. Nationalist songs, epic poems, twisted accounts of history take the place of scholarship and art.

America is not immune. We mourn the victims of the World Trade Center attack. Their pictures cover subway walls. We mourn the firefighters, as well we should. But we are blind to those whom we and our allies in the Middle East have crushed or whose rights have been ignored for decades. They seem not to count.

"The principle of the movement is whoever is not included is excluded, whoever is not with me is against me, so the world loses all the nuances and pluralistic aspects that have become too confusing for the masses," wrote Hannah Arendt in *The Origins of Totalitarianism.*[3]

Before conflicts begin, the first people silenced—often with violence—are not the nationalist leaders of the opposing ethnic or religious group, who are useful in that they serve to dump gasoline on the evolving conflict. Those voices within the ethnic group or the nation that question the state's lust and need for war are targeted. These dissidents are the most dangerous. They give us an alternative language, one that refuses to define the other as "barbarian" or "evil," one that recognizes the humanity of the enemy, one that does not condone violence as a form of communication. Such voices are rarely heeded. And until we learn once again to speak in our own voice and reject that handed to us by the state in times of war, we flirt with our own destruction.

And yet, despite all this, I am not a pacifist. I respect and admire the qualities of professional soldiers. Without the determination and leadership of soldiers like General Wesley K. Clark we might not have intervened in Kosova or Bosnia. It was, in the end, a general, Ulysses S. Grant who saved the union. Even as I detest the pestilence that is war and fear its deadly addiction, even as I see it lead states and groups towards self-immolation, even as I concede that it is war that has left millions of dead and maimed across the planet, I, like most reporters in Sarajevo and Kosova, desperately hoped for armed intervention. The poison that is war does not free us from the ethics of responsibility. There are times when we must take this poison—just as a person with cancer accepts chemotherapy to live. We can not succumb to despair. Force is and I suspect always will be part of the human condition. There are times when the force wielded by one immoral faction must be countered by a faction that, while never moral, is perhaps less immoral.

We in the industrialized world bear responsibility for the world's genocides because we had the power to intervene and did not. We stood by and watched the slaughter in Chechnya, Sri Lanka, Sierra Leone, Liberia, and Rwanda where a million people died. The blood of the victims of Srebrenica—a designated U.N. safe area in Bosnia—is on our hands. The generation before mine watched, with much the same passivity, the genocides of Germany, Poland, Hungary, Greece, and the Ukraine. These slaughters were, as in Gabriel García Márquez's book *Chronicle of a Death Foretold*, often announced in advance.[4] Hutu radio broadcasts from Kigali called on the Interahamwe in Rwanda to carry out genocide. The U.N. Belgian detachment, however, like the Dutch peacekeepers in Srebrenica, stood by and watched. The radio in Kigali was never shut down. The rampages began. There was never any secret about Milošević's plans for a greater Serbia or his intent to use force and ethnic cleansing to create it.

I wrote this book not to dissuade us from war but to understand it. It is especially important that we, who wield such massive force across the globe, see within ourselves the seeds of our own obliteration. We must guard against the myth of war and the drug of war that can, together, render us as blind and callous as some of those we battle.

We were humbled in Vietnam, purged, for a while, of a dangerous hubris, offered in our understanding and reflection about the war, a moment of grace. We became a better country. But once again the message is slipping away from us, even as we confront the possibility of devastating biological or nuclear terrorist attacks in Washington or New York. If the humility we gained from our defeat in Vietnam is not the engine that drives our response to future terrorist strikes, even those that are cataclysmic, we are lost.

The only antidote to ward off self-destruction and the indiscriminate use of force is humility and, ultimately, compassion. Reinhold Niebuhr aptly reminded us that we must all act and then ask for forgiveness. This book is not a call for inaction. It is a call for repentance.

1

THE MYTH OF WAR

When our own nation is at war with any other, we detest them under the character of cruel, perfidious, unjust and violent: But always esteem ourselves and allies equitable, moderate, and merciful. If the general of our enemies be successful, 'tis with difficulty we allow him the figure and character of a man. He is a sorcerer: He has a communication with daemons; as is reported of Oliver Cromwell, and the Duke of Luxembourg: He is bloody-minded, and takes a pleasure in death and destruction. But if the success be on our side, our commander has all the opposite good qualities, and is a pattern of virtue, as well as of courage and conduct. His treachery we call policy: His cruelty is an evil inseparable from war. In short, every one of his faults we either endeavour to extenuate, or dignify it with the name of that virtue, which approaches it. It is evident the same method of thinking runs thro' common life.

•

DAVID HUME
A Treatise on Human Nature, 1740

THE ETHNIC CONFLICTS AND INSURGENCIES OF OUR TIME, whether between Serbs and Muslims or Hutus and Tutsis, are not religious wars. They are not clashes between cultures or civilizations, nor are they the result of ancient ethnic hatreds. They are manufactured wars, born out of the collapse of civil societies, perpetuated by fear, greed, and paranoia, and they are run by gangsters, who rise up from the bottom of their own societies and terrorize all, including those they purport to protect.

Often, none of this is apparent from the outside. We are quick to accept the facile and mendacious ideological veneer that is wrapped like a mantle around the shoulders of those who prosecute the war. In part we do this to avoid intervention, to give this kind of slaughter an historical inevitability it does not have, but also because the media and most of the politicians often lack the perspective and analysis to debunk the myths served up by the opposing sides.

The United States and the West based our responses in Bosnia, or perhaps it is better to say our arguments not to respond, on such myths: the myth of the Serbian warrior who would fight to the death against overwhelming odds; the myth that the Croats, Muslims, and Serbs, who speak the same language and are nearly indistinguishable, were different people; the myth that Yugoslavia, a country that Josip Broz Tito made an important player in international affairs, had failed to give its citizens a national identity. These myths, swallowed whole, permitted us to stand by as 250,000 human beings were killed and Sarajevo spent three and a half years under siege. Although the United States finally intervened, we did so because the United Nations mission collapsed in the summer of 1995, not because of any foresight or courage on the part of the administration of President Bill Clinton.

Look not to religion and mythology and warped versions of history to find the roots of these conflicts, but to the warlords who dominated the Balkans. It took Milošević four years of hate propaganda and lies, pumped forth daily over the airways from Belgrade, before he got one Serb to cross the border into Bosnia and begin the murderous rampage that triggered the war. And although the war was painted from afar as a clash of rival civilizations, the primary task of Milošević in Serbia, Franjo Tudjman in Croatia, and the other ethnic leaderships was to dismantle and silence their own intellectuals and writers of stature and replace them with second-rate, mediocre pawns willing to turn every intellectual and artistic endeavor into a piece of ethnic triumphalism and myth.

Lawrence LeShan in *The Psychology of War* differentiates between "mythic reality" and "sensory reality" in wartime.[1] In sensory reality we see events for what they are. Most of those who are thrust into combat soon find it impossible to maintain the mythic perception of war. They would not survive if they did. Wars that lose their mythic stature for the public, such as Korea or Vietnam, are doomed to failure, for war is exposed for what it is—organized murder.

But in mythic war we imbue events with meanings they do not have. We see defeats as signposts on the road to ultimate victory. We demonize the enemy so that our opponent is no longer human. We view ourselves, our people, as the embodiment of absolute goodness. Our enemies invert our view of the world to justify their own cruelty. In most mythic wars this is the case. Each side reduces the other to objects—eventually in the form of corpses.

"Force," Simone Weil wrote, "is as pitiless to the man who possesses it, or thinks he does, as it is to its victims; the second it crushes, the first it intoxicates."[2]

When we allow mythic reality to rule, as it almost always does in war, then there is only one solution—force. In mythic war we fight absolutes. We must vanquish darkness. It is imperative and inevitable for civilization, for the free world, that good triumph, just as Islamic militants see us as infidels whose existence corrupts the pure Islamic society they hope to build.

But the goal we seek when we embrace myth is impossible to achieve. War never creates the security or the harmony we desire, especially the harmony we briefly attain during wartime. And campaigns, such as the one in Afghanistan, become starting points for further conflicts, especially as we find that we are unable to root out terrorism or maintain the kind of solidarity that comes in the days just after a terrorist attack.

The chief institutions that disseminate the myth are the press and the state. The press has been culpable since the telegraph made possible the modern war correspondent. And starting with the Crimean War, when the first dispatches were fed by newly minted war correspondents in real time, nearly every reporter has seen his or her mission as sustaining civilian and army morale. The advent of photography and film did little to alter the incentive to boost morale, for the lie in war is almost always the lie of omission. The blunders and senseless slaughter by our generals, the execution of prisoners and innocents, and the horror of wounds are rarely disclosed, at least during a mythic war, to the public. Only when the myth is punctured, as it eventually was in Vietnam, does the press begin to report in a sensory rather than a mythic manner. But even then it is it reacting to a public that has changed its perception of war. The press usually does not lead.

Mythic war reporting sells papers and boosts ratings. Real reporting, sensory reporting, does not, at least not in comparison with the boosterism we witnessed during the Persian Gulf War and the war in Afghanistan. The coverage in the Persian Gulf War was typical. The international press willingly administered a restrictive pool system on behalf of the military under which carefully controlled groups of reporters were guided around the front lines by officers. It could have never functioned without the cooperation of the press. The press was as eager to be of service to the state during the war as most everyone else.

Such docility on the part of the press made it easier to do what governments do in wartime, indeed what governments do much of the time, and that is lie. When Iraqi troops seized the Saudi border town of Khafji, sending Saudi troops fleeing in panic, the headlong retreat was never mentioned. Two French photographers and I watched as frantic Saudi soldiers raced away from the fighting, dozens crowded on a fire truck that tore down the road. U.S. Marines were called in to push the Iraqis back. We stood on rooftops with young Marine radio operators who called in air strikes as Marine units battled Iraqi troops in the streets.

Yet back in Riyadh and Dhahran military press officers spoke about our Saudi allies defending their homeland.

The potency of myth is that it allows us to make sense of mayhem and violent death. It gives a justification to what is often nothing more than gross human cruelty and stupidity. It allows us to believe we have achieved our place in human society because of a long chain of heroic endeavors, rather than accept the sad reality that we stumble along a dimly lit corridor of disasters. It disguises our powerlessness. It hides from view our own impotence and the ordinariness of our own leaders. By turning history into myth we transform random events into a chain of events directed by a will greater than our own,

one that is determined and preordained. We are elevated above
the multitude. We march toward nobility. And no society is
immune.

Most national myths, at their core, are racist. They are fed by
ignorance. Those individuals who understand other cultures,
speak other languages, and find richness in diversity are shunted
aside. Science, history, and psychology are often twisted to serve
myth. And many intellectuals are willing to champion and
defend absurd theories for nationalist ends.

By finding our identity and meaning in separateness the myth
serves another important function: It makes communication
with our opponents impossible. When the Palestinian leader
Yasir Arafat makes statements that call for moderation and
peace he is accused by the Israelis of using words to conceal his
intention to wipe out Israel. The Palestinians react in the same
manner to statements by most Israeli leaders. It does not matter
what they say, just as it did not matter what the Serb or Croat
nationalists said to each other; the intentions of the other were
predetermined by nationalist myth.

We often become as deaf and dumb as those we condemn.
We too have our terrorists. The Contras in Nicaragua carried
out, with funding from Washington, some of the most egre-
gious human rights violations in Central America, yet were
lauded as "freedom fighters." Jonas Savimbi, the rebel leader the
United States backed in Angola's civil war, murdered and tortured with a barbarity that far outstripped the Taliban. The
rebellion Savimbi began in 1975 resulted in more than 500,000
dead. President Ronald Reagan called Savimbi the Abraham
Lincoln of Angola, although he littered the country with land
mines, once bombed a Red Cross–run factory making artificial
legs for victims of those mines, and pummeled a rival's wife and

children to death. The mayhem and blood-letting we backed in
Angola were copied in many parts of Africa, including Zaire
and Liberia.

The myth of war sells and legitimizes the drug of war. Once
we begin to take war's heady narcotic, it creates an addiction that
slowly lowers us to the moral depravity of all addicts. War's utter
depravity was captured in Shakespeare's play *Troilus and Cressida*,
a work that as far as is known was never performed in Shakespeare's lifetime, perhaps due to its savage indictment of war
and human society. Nearly every figure in the play, including
Ulysses, lies to and tries to manipulate those around him: that
is the trait of most leaders, no matter what political agenda they
espouse. Here, unlike *Henry V*, Shakespeare excoriates the
established order; the play is one that debunks national myth.
There are only three characters who speak about war with any
sanity or truth: Pandarus, who is a lecher and a coward; Cassandra, who is deranged; and Thersites, as described by Shakespeare, "a deformed and scurrilous Greek."[3] Yet Thersites'
bleak view of human nature and human folly is borne out by
the play's end. We are left with the realization that characters
who are, by the standards of civil society, the most retrograde
stand above the baseness of those who prosecute war, if only
because they speak the truth.

"Lechery, lechery, still wars and lechery, nothing else holds
fashion," Thersites rails.[4]

War can be the natural outcome of brutal repression; witness
Kosova or El Salvador. Or it can be manufactured by warlords
intent on enrichment, as in Bosnia. It can also, although less and
less, be the result of vying interests between nation-states, such
as the Gulf War, fought over control of the oil fields in Kuwait.
War, at times inevitable and unavoidable, is part of human

society. It has been since the dawn of time—and probably will be until we are snuffed out by our own foolishness.

"We believed we were there for a high moral purpose," wrote Philip Caputo in his book on Vietnam, *Rumor of War*. "But somehow our idealism was lost, our morals corrupted, and the purpose forgotten."[5]

The employment of organized violence means one must, in fact, abandon fixed and established values. This is a truth made apparent in *Troilus and Cressida*. It is a truth *Henry V* ignores. Once war, and especially the total war that marked both the ancient and the modern way of battle, erupts, all is sacrificed before it. The myth of war is essential to justify the horrible sacrifices required in war, the destruction and the death of innocents. It can be formed only by denying the reality of war, by turning the lies, the manipulation, the inhumanness of war into the heroic ideal. Homer did this for the Greeks, Virgil for the Augustan age, and Shakespeare for the English in his history plays. But these great writers also understood what they were doing, and thus in the canon of their works come moments when war is laid bare.

Troilus, at the start of the play, states that he will not fight for Helen, a woman portrayed by Shakespeare as a mindless paramour. "It is," he says, "too starved a subject for my sword."[6] Dying for this Helen, who has neither morals nor wit, is absurd. Yet I have seen men fight for even more ridiculous reasons. There was no reason for the war in Bosnia. The warring sides invented national myths and histories designed to mask the fact that Croats, Muslims, and Serbs are nearly indistinguishable. It was absurd nuances that propelled the war, invented historical wrongs, which, as in the Middle East, stretched back to dubious accounts of ancient history. I have heard Israeli settlers on the

West Bank, for example, argue that Palestinian towns, towns that have been Muslim since the seventh century, belong to them because it says so in the Bible, a reminder that this sophistry extends beyond the Balkans.

The competing nationalist propaganda in Yugoslavia created a conflict in the country best equipped of all the Eastern European states to integrate with the West after the collapse of communism. Because there was no real reason to fight, there was an urgent need to swiftly turn a senseless fratricide, one organized by criminals and third-rate political leaders for power and wealth, into an orgy of killing, torture, and mass execution. This indiscriminate murder, these campaigns of ethnic cleansing, were used to create facts, as it were. The slaughter was carried out to give to these wars the justifications they lacked when they began, to fuel mutual hatred and paranoia, as well as to enrich the militias and paramilitary groups that stole and looted from their victims. Ethnic warfare is a business, and the Mercedes and mansions of the warlords in Belgrade prove it. Fighting for a Helen who is a strumpet, or Don Quixote's Dulcinea, looks noble by comparison.

The cast of warlords in the former Yugoslavia was made up of the dregs of Yugoslav society. These thieves, embezzlers, petty thugs, and even professional killers swiftly became war heroes. They were, at least, colorful, with Captain Dragan, a Serbian soldier of fortune who was allegedly an ex-convict from Australia; the fascist demagogue Vojislav Šešelj; and Zeljko Ražnjatović, known as Arkan, who had a criminal record in several Western European countries. The Croats had their own collection of gangsters, including Branimir Glavaš, who stormed into Serbian villages with his militias and executed the Serbian civilians and the Croatian policemen who had tried to keep the nationalist mobs from killing them. The gangsters who took over Sarajevo at the start of the war to battle the Serbs were no different. Loot and power were always their primary objectives.

The conclusion of *Troilus and Cressida*—like *Macbeth* and *King Lear*—produces no catharsis. There is nothing redeeming about the Trojan War, in both Euripides and Shakespeare, just as there is nothing redeeming about any war, including the supposed good wars that we might all agree had to be fought. The Allied incendiary bombs that spread fires through Dresden and Tokyo left some 150,000 people dead. Talk not of the good war to those in Hiroshima or Nagasaki. It does not mean the bombing of Dresden or the dropping of the atomic bombs was wrong, given the concept of total war—a concept that would not be alien to the victorious Greeks in Troy. It means that we are naïve to ignore these and countless other events, to ennoble indiscriminate slaughter and industrial killing on so vast a scale. Modern war is directed primarily against civilians. Look at Kosova, Bosnia, Rwanda, Vietnam, or World War II. And nuclear terrorism is the logical outcome of modern industrial warfare.

"Let it be said then that I wrote this book in the absolute conviction that there never has been, nor ever can be, a 'good' or worthwhile war," wrote the Canadian World War II veteran Farley Mowat. "Mine was one of the better ones (as such calamities are measured), but still, a bloody awful thing it was. So awful that through three decades I kept the deeper agonies of it wrapped in the cotton-wool of protective forgetfulness, and would have been well content to leave them buried forever . . . but could not, because the Old Lie—temporarily discredited by the Vietnam debacle—is once more gaining credence; a whisper which soon may become another strident shout urging us on to mayhem."[7]

In Homer it is the malice of the gods that propels both sides to destruction. In Shakespeare, it is the capriciousness of men. There is, at the end of *Troilus and Cressida*, one of the great scenes of war set down in literature. It is the moment when Achilles, roused to fury over the death of his companion Patroclus on the battlefield, finds Hector, unarmed, stripping the armor off the body of a Greek soldier whom he had struck down as he was fleeing the battlefield.

Shakespeare turns the scene into butchery, with the helpless Hector begging Achilles not to strike him while he has no weapon. Achilles has no chivalry. Rather than a fight between equals, it is murder, with Hector being surrounded and struck by a swarm of Achilles' Myrmidon soldiers.

ACHILLES:
> Look, Hector, how the sun begins to set,
> How ugly night comes breathing at his heels;
> Even with the vail and dark'ning of the sun,
> To close the day up. Hector's life is done.

HECTOR:
> I am unarm'd, forgo this vantage.

ACHILLES:
> Strike, fellows, strike, this is the man I seek.
> So, Ilion, fall thou next! Come, Troy, sink down!
> Here lies thy heart, thy sinews, and thy bone.
> On Myrmidons, and cry you all amain,
> "Achilles hath the mighty Hector slain!"[8]

Moments after Hector's death dozens of heavily armed men thrust spears into Hector's corpse. Achilles commands his Myrmidons to cry out to the Greeks that he "hath the mighty Hector slain." Here is the lie of the heroic ideal, an ideal we nurture, despite centuries of war. Here is the instant creation of heroic myth, out of murder. Here also we see the mutilation of the dead that has been part of military behavior since there were men in arms. If you kill your enemy his body becomes your trophy, your possession, and this has been a fundamental part of warfare since before the Philistines beheaded Saul.

In Bosnia there was a local Croat warlord who rode around his village with the skull of the local imam for a hood ornament. In El Salvador government soldiers sometimes carried photos of themselves squatted around the body of a rebel killed in a firefight.

History for Shakespeare was not the example of the inner workings of the divine or the fodder for some generalized principle. It was merely itself. It moved toward no goal. Shakespeare understood the monstrous, deadly neutrality of nature.

"Those who believe that God himself, once he became man, could not face the harshness of destiny without a long tremor of anguish," Simone Weil writes, "should have understood that the only people who can give the impression of having risen to a higher plane, who seem superior to ordinary human misery, are the people who resort to the aids of illusion, exaltation, fanaticism, to conceal the harshness of destiny from their own eyes. The man who does not wear the armor of the lie cannot experience force without being touched by it to the very soul."[9]

And when the rhetoric of war is long forgot, what happens to the heroic dead, the bereaved mothers, fathers, husbands, wives, and children of those killed and lost? What comes of those who made, in the glib term of politicians, the supreme sacrifice?

A passage from the November 18, 1822, *London Observer* caught the aftermath of war:

It is estimated that more than a million bushels of human and inhuman bones were imported last year from the continent of Europe into the port of Hull. The neighborhood of Leipzig, Austerlitz, Waterloo, and of all the places where, during the late bloody war, the principal battles were fought, have been swept alike of the bones of the hero and the horse which he rode. Thus collected from every quarter, they have been shipped to the port of Hull and thence forwarded to the Yorkshire bone grinders who have erected steam-engines and powerful machinery for the purpose of reducing them to a granularly state. In this condition they are sold to the farmers to manure their lands.[10]

In World War I, on the Western Front, the putrifying and decomposed dead lay draped on the barbed wire and rotting in gaping shell holes. Half a million British dead in World War I were never found, and this number was dwarfed by the missing Russians, Germans, Austrians, and French. The earth consumed them, just as at Waterloo, as in all battles. They vanished as swiftly as the eternal causes for which they were sacrificed. They were replaced by a new generation and new causes. In the light of time, what looked so momentous then now looks like folly.

In *Life in the Tomb*, the Greek author Stratis Myrivilis, who fought in the Balkans in World War I, writes,

A few years from now, I told him, perhaps others would be killing each other for anti-nationalist ideals. Then they would laugh at our own killings just as we had laughed at those of the Byzantines. These others would indulge in mutual slaughter with the same enthusiasm, though their ideals were new. Warfare under the entirely fresh banners would be just as disgraceful as always. They might even rip out each other's guts then with religious zeal, claiming that they were "fighting to end all fighting." But they too would be followed by still others who would laugh at them with the same gusto.[11]

Nationalist and ethnic conflicts are fratricides that turn on absurdities. They can only be sustained by myth. The arguments and bloody disputes take place over tiny, almost imperceptible nuances within the society—what Sigmund Freud calls the "narcissism of minor differences."[12] In the Balkans, for example, there were heated debates over the origin of gingerbread hearts—cookies in the shape of hearts. The Croats insisted that the cookies were Croatian. The Serbs angrily countered that the cookies were Serbian. The suggestion to one ethnic group that gingerbread hearts were invented by the other ethnic group could start a fight. To those of us on the outside it had a Gilbert and Sullivan lunacy to it, but to the participants it was deadly serious. It had to be. For the nationalist myths stand on such minuscule differences. These myths give neighbors the justification to kill those they had gone to school and grown up with.

The Serbs, Muslims, and Croats struggled, like ants on a small hill, to carve out separate, antagonistic identities. But it was all negative space. One defined oneself mostly by what the other was not.

The term Serbo-Croatian, for example, caused great umbrage to anyone who was not a Serb. Suddenly, instead of one language called Serbo-Croatian, there were three languages in Bosnia—Bosnian, Serbian, and Croatian. And the United Nations, pandering to nationalist cant, printed public reports in all three, although the reports were nearly identical.

Spoken Serbian, Bosnian, and Croatian are of Slavic origin and have minor differences in syntax, pronunciation, and slang. The Croats and Bosnian Muslims use the Roman alphabet. The Serbs use the Cyrillic alphabet. Otherwise the tongue they all speak is nearly the same.

Since there was, in essence, one language, the Serbs, Muslims and Croats each began to distort their own tongue to accommodate the myth of separateness. The Bosnian Muslims introduced Arabic words and Koranic expressions into the language. The Muslims during the war adopted words like *shahid*, or martyr, from Arabic, dropping the Serbian word *junak*. They begun using Arabic expressions, like *inshallah* (God willing), *marhaba* (hello) and *salam alekhum* (peace be upon you).

Just as energetically the Croats swung the other way, dusting off words from the fifteenth century. The Croatian president at the time, Franjo Tudjman, took delight in inventing new terms. Croatian parliamentarians proposed passing a law that would levy fines and prison terms for those who use "words of foreign origin."

In Zagreb, the capital of Croatia, waiters and shop clerks would turn up their noses at patrons who used old "Serbian" phrases. The Education Ministry in Croatia told teachers to mark "non-Croatian" words on student papers as incorrect. The stampede to establish a "pure" Croatian language, led by a host of amateurs and politicians, resulted in chaos and rather bizarre linguistic twists.

There are two words in Serbo-Croatian, for example, for "one thousand." One of the words, *tisuca*, was not used by the Communist government that ruled the old Yugoslavia, which preferred *hiljada*, paradoxically, an archaic Croatian word. *Hiljada*, although more authentically Croatian, was discarded by

Croatian nationalists; *tisuca*, perhaps because it was banned by the Communists, was in fashion.

The movement, done in the name of authenticity, was patently artificial. It was a linguistic version of gingerbread hearts. It was a way in which a nation could find tiny specks over which to argue and establish an identity and go to war.

The campaign soon included efforts to eradicate words borrowed from English, German, and French. President Tudjman dreamed up new tennis terms to replace English ones. International judges, forced to use the president's strange sports vocabulary at tennis tournaments, stumbled over the unfamiliar words, like the unwieldy word *pripetavanje*, difficult even for Croatians, which had to be used instead of "tiebreaker."

It reached a point of such confusion that Tudjman began to slip up. When he greeted President Clinton in Zagreb he used the Serbian version of the word happy, *srecan*, rather than *sretan*, deemed to be Croatian. The gaffe, broadcast live, was quickly edited out of later news reports on the state-controlled television.

Off-duty Croatian policemen in a nightclub beat up members of a Sarajevo rock band, No Smoking, after they sang a tune with Serbian lyrics. The police, who punched and kicked the musicians, had taken offense at the Serbian word *delija*, which means "a cool dude."

It was not the first time that the Croatian authorities tried to create a politically appropriate lexicon. In 1941, the fascist war leader in Zagreb, Ante Pavelić, also banned all words he deemed not to be of Croatian origin. Nor was this unique to the former Yugoslavia. The hijacking of language is fundamental to war. It becomes difficult to express contrary opinions. There are simply not the words or phrases to do it. We all speak with the same clichés and euphemisms.

The myth of war creates a new, artificial reality. Moral precepts—ones we have spent a lifetime honoring—are jettisoned. We accept, if not condone, the maiming and killing of others as the regrettable cost of war. We operate under a new moral code.

The political left in America and Europe, the intellectuals and artists, those who spent a lifetime outside of the mainstream, are equally susceptible. Many were rarely content with simply denouncing American foreign policy in places like Central America or the Middle East—a stance for which I have some sympathy—but had to embrace opposition forces with stunning credulity.

During the Spanish Civil War George Orwell observed that "The thing that was truly frightening about the war in Spain was . . . the immediate reappearance in left-wing circles of the mental atmosphere of the Great War. The very people who for 20 years sniggered over their own superiority to war hysteria were the ones who rushed straight back into the mental slum of 1915."[13]

By supporting "revolutionary" movements in El Salvador or Nicaragua these social critics found a balm for their alienation. They were able to revel in the intoxication of force and still express an antagonism towards American policy. These groups, like fellow travelers before them in the Soviet Union or Cuba, swallowed whole the utopian vision of opposition or revolutionary movements, ignoring the messier realities of internal repression and war crimes. It was not unusual to find political pilgrims who had toured Nicaragua or Gaza overwhelmed with emotion. They poured superlatives on the oppressed people they championed, although once the conflicts ended the lionized peoples of Bosnia, Nicaragua, or El Salvador were usually forgotten.

During the height of the war in Nicaragua these groups

descended frequently on the country. They were nicknamed
"the sandalistas" by critics because of their penchant for dressing in ratty attire and sandals. I spent a day with one group that,
the first day they arrived, headed straight to the U.S. Embassy
for a protest rally.

"For me," said one of the participants, "a demonstration at
the embassy will be my liturgy for the morning."

"Amen," said one of her fifteen companions.

The group was part of a religious organization from Dayton,
Ohio, known as Pledge of Resistance. They would return to
Ohio to speak in church basements and at small gatherings
about their experiences in Nicaragua. The trip, organized by a
group known as Witness for Peace, took the members to a
model prison farm, arranged interviews with Sandinista sup-
porters, and threw in several moderate critics.

Alvaro José Baldizón, the former chief investigator of the
Special Investigations Commission of the Ministry of Interior,
told me after he had fled to the United States that before one of
the solidarity groups arrived in a town, critics were warned by
police to stay away from the foreigners. He said that government employees often posed as local residents or relatives of
local residents and spoke about atrocities carried out by the
Contras as well as the benefits of the Sandinista revolution. The
two-week visits saw most groups live for a few days in a village.
They held prayer vigils, did work projects, and collected testi-
mony from alleged victims of the war.

I went with the group to a model prison farm. It had pleasant
gardens and spotless sleeping quarters. The farm housed forty-
two inmates. The group was told that there were only two
unarmed guards on the farm, prisoners were given a one-week
vacation, and no one had ever tried to escape.

A prisoner, Hernán Lozano, who said he was once a body-guard for the former dictator Anastasio Somoza, spoke to the delegation. I would hear a version of this talk from dozens of other prisoners. The stocky Lozano grinned lavishly and heaped praise on the Sandinistas.

"You appear happy to be here," said one of the Americans. "Are you truly happy or is this an appearance?"

Lozano assured the delegation he was happy on the prison farm. He told them he was telling the truth because "the revolution has brought the loss of fear, especially the fear of telling the truth."

The Potemkin quality of the farm seemed hard to miss even for the delegates.

"Even if this is a showpiece, the cream of the crop, it is here," another participant told me. "It does seem to be more than good intentions. In reality it is a lot better than in our own country."

The group, often praised by Sandinista officials for their courage and dedication, became openly moved at the end of the day. There was an electric current of self-satisfaction and moral outrage that ran concurrently through the conversation.

"To me, the process of the revolution is a religious experience. It's not a political movement," said another American in the group. "It comes from a deep-faith commitment by the Nicaraguan people."

The social critic Christopher Lasch has argued that such radical politics fills empty lives and provides a potent sense of meaning and purpose. It is "a refuge from the terrors of inner life," he observed in *The Culture of Narcissism*.[14]

But it is a refuge for all, for lower classes as well as privileged elite. None of us is immune. All find emotional sustenance in war's myth. That myth can take many forms. It can lead people to celebrate power among those who are America's enemies, those who lead "revolutionary" regimes in Cuba or Vietnam, or it can lead us to celebrate our own power, but the process is the same. It is still myth. It still blinds those who swallow it.

The myth of war rarely endures for those who experience combat. War is messy, confusing, sullied by raw brutality and an elephantine fear that grabs us like a massive bouncer who comes up from behind. Soldiers in the moments before real battles weep, vomit, and write last letters home, although these are done more as a precaution than from belief. All are nearly paralyzed with fright. There is a morbid silence that grips a battlefield in the final moments before the shooting starts, one that sets the back of my own head pounding in pain, wipes away all appetite, and makes my fingers tremble as I ready myself to go forward against logic. You do not think of home or family, for to do so is to be overcome by a wave of nostalgia and emotion that can impair your ability to survive. One thinks, so far as it is possible, of cleaning weapons, of readying for the business of killing. No one ever charges into battle for God and country.

"Just remember," a Marine Corps lieutenant colonel told me as he strapped his pistol belt under his arm before we crossed into Kuwait, "that none of these boys is fighting for home, for the flag, for all that crap the politicians feed the public. They are fighting for each other, just for each other."

It may be that Falstaff, rather than Henry V, is a much more accurate picture of the common soldier, who finds little in the rhetoric of officers who urge him into danger. The average soldier probably sympathizes more than we might suspect with Falstaff's stratagems to save his own hide. Falstaff embodies the carnal yearnings we all have for food, drink, companionship, a few sexual adventures, and safety. He may lack the essential comradeship of soldiering, but he clings to life in a way a soldier under fire can sympathize with. It is to the pubs and taverns, not to the grand palaces, that these soldiers return when the war is done. And Falstaff's selfish lust for pleasure hurts few. Henry's selfish lust for power leaves corpses strewn across muddy battlefields.[15]

The imagined heroism, the vision of a dash to rescue a wounded comrade, the clear lines we thought were drawn in battle, the images we have of our own reaction under gunfire, usually wilt in combat. This is a sober and unsettling realization. We may not be who we thought we would be. One of the most difficult realizations of war is how deeply we betray ourselves, how far we are from the image of gallantry and courage we desire, how instinctual and primordial fear is. We do not meditate on action. Our movements are usually motivated by a numbing and overpowering desire for safety. And yet there are heroes, those who somehow rise above it all, maybe only once, to expose themselves to risk to save their comrades. I have seen such soldiers. I nearly always found them afterward to be embarrassed about what they did, unable to explain it, reticent to talk. Many are not sure they could do it again.

I was in Khartoum in 1989 during one of the attempts to overthrow Sadek Mahdi, who was then the prime minister. The city had fallen into decay, with lines of destitute Sudanese curled up in blankets and with holes in the pitted roads so huge that men fell into them. Electricity and water service were sporadic. The phones did not work. The only thing that seemed to function was the rampant corruption. The coup attempt had been fought off, but the army was still nervous. At dusk another reporter and I took a walk through the streets. Inadvertently, we turned down the road past the Presidential Palace. In the half-light the palace guards, who had ordered the road closed to all traffic and pedestrians, noisly unlocked the safeties on their assault rifles and pointed their weapons toward us. We yelled out in Arabic, "Foreigners! Foreigners!" I deftly, without hesitation or forethought, sidestepped behind my friend. Better to let any bullets pass through him first. It was a disconcerting decision, one made swiftly and instinctually. To this day I have not had the heart to tell him.

We are humiliated in combat. The lofty words that inspire people to war—duty, honor, glory—swiftly become repugnant and hollow. They are replaced by the hard, specific images of war, by the prosaic names of villages and roads. The abstract rhetoric of patriotism is obliterated, exposed as the empty handmaiden of myth. Fear brings us all back down to earth.

Once in a conflict, we are moved from the abstract to the real, from the mythic to the sensory. When this move takes place we have nothing to do with a world not at war. When we return home we view the society around us from the end of a very long tunnel. There they still believe. In combat such belief is shattered, replaced not with a better understanding, but with a disconcerting confusion and a taste of war's potent and addictive narcotic. Combatants live only for their herd, those hapless soldiers who are bound into their unit to ward off death. There is no world outside the unit. It alone endows worth and meaning. Soldiers will rather die than betray this bond. And there is—as many combat veterans will tell you—a kind of love in this.

The Salvadoran town of Suchitoto was a dreary peasant outpost made up of stucco and mud and wattle huts. It was off the main road. The town was surrounded by the Farabundo Marti National Liberation Front (FMLN) rebels, who, when I first arrived in El Salvador in 1982, were winning the war. The government forces kept a small garrison in the town, although its relief columns were regularly ambushed as they ambled down the small strip of asphalt, surrounded by high grass. It was one of the most dangerous spots in El Salvador and had taken the lives of a few reporters.

The rebels launched an attack to take the town. A convoy of reporters in cars marked with "TV" in masking tape on the windshields hightailed it to the small bridge that led to the lonely stretch of road into Suchitoto. We stopped for the familiar ritual of getting high, something as a print reporter who could scramble to safety I did not do, but something many photographers, who would stand and take pictures in the midst of combat, found a necessary salve to their nerves.

Then we moved slowly down the road, the odd round fired ahead or behind us. We made it to the edge of town. We ran into rebel units, now accustomed to the follies of the press. On foot we moved through the deserted streets, the firing from the garrison becoming louder as we weaved our way with rebel fighters to the front line. And then, as we rounded a corner, several full bursts of automatic fire rent the air. We dove head-first onto the dirt. The rebels began to fire noisy bursts from their M–16 assault rifles. The acrid scent of cordite filled the air. Dust was in my eyes. I did not move. I began to pray.

"God," I thought, "if you get me out of here I will never do this again."

I felt powerless, humiliated, weak. I dared not move. I could see the little sprays of dust the bullets threw up from the road. Rebels around me were wounded and crying out in pain. One died yelling out in a sad cadence for his mother. His desperate and final plea seemed to cut through the absurd posturing of soldiering. At first it haunted me. Soon I wished he would be quiet.

"Mama!" . . . "Mama!" . . . "Mama!"

The firefight seemed to go on for an eternity. I cannot say how long I lay there. It could have been a few minutes. It could have been an hour. Here was war, real war, sensory war, not the war of the movies and books I had consumed in my youth. It was disconcerting, frightening, and disorganized, and nothing like the myth I had been peddled. There was nothing gallant or heroic, nothing redeeming. It controlled me. I would never control it.

During a lull I dashed across an empty square and found shelter behind a house. My heart was racing. Adrenaline coursed through my bloodstream. I was safe. I made it back to the capital. And, like most war correspondents, I soon considered the experience a great cosmic joke. I drank away the fear and excitement in a seedy bar in downtown San Salvador. Most people after such an experience would learn to stay away. I was hooked.

2

THE PLAGUE
OF NATIONALISM

War is the health of the state.

•

RANDOLPH BOURNE

THE MILITARY JUNTA THAT RULED ARGENTINA, AND WAS
responsible for killing 20,000 of its own citizens during the
"Dirty War," in 1982 invaded the Falkland Islands, which the
Argentines called the Malvinas. The junta, which had been on
the verge of collapse and beset by violent street demonstrations
and nationwide strikes in the weeks before the war, instantly
became the saviors of the country. Labor union and opposition
leaders, some of whom were still visibly bruised from beatings,
were hauled out of jail cells before cameras to repeat what was
a collective mantra: "Las Malvinas son Argentinas."

The invasion transformed the country. Reality was replaced
with a wild and self-serving fiction, a legitimization of the worst
prejudices of the masses and paranoia of the outside world.
The secret interior world arrayed against Argentina became one

of strange cabals, worldwide Jewry trotted out again to be beaten like an old horse, vast subterranean webs that had as their focus the destruction of the Argentine people. The exterior world was exemplified by the nation. All that was noble and good was embodied, like some unique gene, in the Argentine people. Stories of the heroism of the Argentine military—whose singular recent accomplishment was the savage repression of its own people—filled the airwaves.

Friends of mine, who a few days earlier had excoriated the dictatorship, now bragged about the prowess of Argentine commanders. One general, during a dispute with Chile, flew his helicopter over the Chilean border in order to piss on Chilean soil. This story was repeated with evident pride. Cars raced through the city streets honking horns and waving the blue and white Argentine flag. Argentines burst into the national anthem and ecstatic cheering at sporting events. The large Anglo-Argentine community sent delegations to Britain to lobby for the junta.

I had spent nights with Argentine friends talking of a new Argentina, one that would respect human rights, allow basic freedoms, and perhaps put on trial the generals responsible for the Dirty War. Now such talk was an anathema, even treasonous. On the street any dissent, especially from a foreigner, could mean physical violence. Any suggestion that the invasion was not just and correct and glorious was unpalatable. One never referred to the islands by their English name. Overweening pride and a sense of national solidarity swept through the city like an electric current. It was as if I had woken up, like one of Kafka's characters, and found myself transformed into a huge bug. I would come to feel this way in every nation at war, including in the United States after the attacks of September 11.

This was my first taste of nationalist triumphalism in wartime. There was almost no one I could speak with. A populace that had agitated for change now outdid itself to lionize uniformed killers. All bowed before the state. It taught me a crucial lesson that I would carry into every other conflict. Lurking beneath the surface of every society, including ours, is the passionate yearning for a nationalist cause that exalts us, the kind that war alone is able to deliver. It reduces and at times erases the anxiety of individual consciousness. We abandon individual responsibility for a shared, unquestioned communal enterprise, however morally dubious.

There is little that logic or fact or truth can do to alter the experience. Moreover, once this crusade is embraced by the nation, the myth predetermines how the world is perceived. It is only after the myth implodes, often as suddenly as it descended, that one can again question the motives and the actions of the state. Once the lights are flicked on again there is a *Midsummer Night's Dream* quality to the war experience, as if no one can quite remember what happened.

"The nationalist is by definition an ignoramus," wrote Danilo Kiš, the Yugoslav writer. "Nationalism is the line of least resistance, the easy way. The nationalist is untroubled, he knows or thinks he knows what his values are, his, that's to say national, that's to say the values of the nations he belongs to, ethical and political; he is not interested in others, *they are of no concern of his,* hell—it's other people (other nations, another tribe). They don't even need investigating. The nationalist sees other people in his own image—as nationalists."[1]

Every society, ethnic group or religion nurtures certain myths, often centered around the creation of the nation or the movement itself. These myths lie unseen beneath the surface,

waiting for the moment to rise ascendant, to define and glorify
followers or members in times of crisis. National myths are
largely benign in times of peace. They are stoked by the entertainment industry, in school lessons, stories, and quasi-historical
ballads, preached in mosques, or championed in absurd historical dramas that are always wildly popular during war. They do
not pose a major challenge to real historical study or a studied
tolerance of others in peacetime. But national myths ignite a
collective amnesia in war. They give past generations a nobility
and greatness they never possessed. Almost every group, and
especially every nation, has such myths. These myths are the
kindling nationalists use to light a conflict.

In the former Yugoslavia, it was the nationalist propaganda
pumped out over television, far more than ancient hatreds, that
did the most to provoke rivalry and finally war between ethnic
groups. The nationalist governments, rather than allow for the
discussion of competing ideas and viewpoints, used the
absolute power they wielded over the broadcast media to play
and replay images that provoked outrage and anger. They told
stories, many of them fabricated, about alleged atrocities committed by the enemy. Impartial information disappeared. Television became the emotional crutch used to justify violence and
rally ethnic groups around nationalist leaders. Those who advo-
cated violence were affirmed, night after night, in their righteous anger. The principal religious institutions—the Serbian
Orthodox Church and the Catholic Church in Croatia—were
willing accomplices. They were national churches and worked as
propagandists for the state. The clerics, on all three sides, were a
disgrace. U.N. mediators in Sarajevo wearily complained that it
was easier to get Serb and Muslim commanders to the table for
talks than opposing clerics.

Archeology, folklore, and the search for what is defined as

authenticity are the tools used by nationalists to assail others and promote themselves. They dress it up as history, but it is myth. Real historical inquiry, in the process, is corrupted, assaulted, and often destroyed. Facts become as interchangeable as opinions. Those facts that are inconvenient are discarded or denied. The obvious inconsistencies are ignored by those intoxicated by a newly found sense of national pride and the exciting prospect of war.

To speak of the Israeli war of independence with many Israelis, in which stateless European Jews established a country in a land that had been primarily Muslim since the seventh century, is to shout into a vast black hole. There is an emotional barrier, a desire not to tarnish the creation myth, which makes it difficult for many Israeli Jews, including some of the most liberal and progressive, to acknowledge the profound injustice the creation of the state of Israel meant for Palestinians. As Americans we struggle with these myths as well, only grudgingly conceding that many of our founding fathers were slave owners and much of our nation acquired after a genocidal campaign against Native Americans.

In peacetime this collective amnesia is challenged by a few intrepid scholars. Indeed, some of the best scholarly work on the 1948 war and what it meant for the Palestinians has come from Israeli historians—but their voices are muted or silenced in times of crisis. Our own nation is no different. We embrace gross and overtly racist notions of Islam that paint all Muslims as having a tendency to violence, anger, antimodernism, and close-mindedness. Questioning of the nationalist line, or an attempt to address historical injustices committed by us against our foes, is branded unpatriotic, intellectual treason, just as it was in Argentina in 1982.

Intellectuals and social critics are as susceptible to the plague

of nationalism as the masses. They often find in it an answer to
their own feelings of ostracism. In the nationalist cause they are
given a chance to be exalted by a nation that has ignored them.
They too enjoy intoxication. There are no shortages of intellectuals willing to line up behind leaders they despise in times of
national crisis, an act that negates the moral posturing they
often make from within the confines of academia during peacetime. These enthusiastic intellectuals can become dangerous in
wartime. Many hold messianic and uncompromising beliefs that
they have never had to put into practice. All nationalist movements have such pernicious mentors willing to justify the use of
force for a utopian and unworkable vision. Among the Serbs
Dobrica Ćosić, whose sentimental novels about Serbian heroism during World War I found a wide following, including
Milošević, was able to replace real history with Serbian nationalist myth, which was used to fuel the war.

Those who do defy the nationalist agenda in war are usually
reviled during the conflict and shunned afterward. They are, at
least by the labels placed upon them by the world, often rather
humble, sometimes simple, and not always well educated. The
acts defy the collective psychosis.

A friend of mine in Serbia, Slavica, had a former Muslim
classmate who lived in Mostar, a Bosnian city that was devas-
tated in the war by Serbian and later Croatian troops. She sent
her two small children to live with Slavica, her husband, and
young daughter in a town in northern Serbia. The arrival of the
Muslim children caused a furor. The school did not want them
to attend classes. Neighbors spat at Slavica and the children in
the street. Her windows were broken. Crude graffiti was spray-
painted on the walls of her home. Yet she persisted. She cared
for the children as her own. After a year she got them into the
school, although they endured taunts and harassment.

After the war the townspeople preferred to forget. No one apologized. Slavica was allowed to be a nominal member of the community. She told me that people were uncomfortable around her. She was a reminder of the collective cowardice and indifference by many in her town now. She, I believe, shamed those around her.

"I will never again feel a part of the country where I was born and raised," she said.

Yet Slavica also felt guilt and shame for the way her nation had reacted, although she had chosen a different response. She insisted that she and her husband had done too little, that the sheltering of the children was insignificant given the magnitude of the crimes committed in the name of the Serbs. The Muslim children, whom she eventually sent to their mother when the mother managed to get political asylum in Canada, called infrequently. They may not have wanted to remember the pain and powerlessness of such dislocation. Slavica was profoundly alone.

Many of those who defy the collective psychosis of the nation are solitary figures once the wars end. Yet these acts of compassion were usually the best antidotes to the myths peddled by nationalists. Those who reached across lines to assist the "enemy" freed themselves from nationalist abstractions that dehumanized others. They were vaccinated against the cult of death that dominates societies in wartime. They reduced their moral universe to caring for another human being. And in this they were able to reject the messianic pretensions that come with the nationalist agenda. By accepting that they could only affect a few lives they also accepted their small place in the universe. This daily lesson in humility protected them. They were saved not by what they could accomplish but by faith. Such people are, however, very rare.

"The survivors all suffer from the same certainty: they know that if similar acts of persecution were to begin tomorrow, despite all the official demonstrations of sympathy for the victims and condemnation of the oppressors, the rescuers would be as rare as they were before," wrote Tzvetan Todorov in *Facing the Extreme: Moral Life in the Concentration Camps.* "Their good neighbors who now greet them every morning would once again turn away."[2]

I sat one afternoon with a Bosnian Serb couple, Rosa and Drago Sorak, outside of the Muslim enclave of Goražde where they had once lived. They poured out the usual scorn on the Muslims, but then stopped at the end of the rant and told me that not all Muslims were bad. This, they said, it was their duty to admit.

During the fighting in the bleak, bombed-out shell of a city that was Goražde, where bands of children had become street urchins and hundreds of war-dead lay in hastily dug graves, a glimmer of humanity arrived for the Soraks in the shape of Fadil Fejzić's cow. The cow forged an unusual bond between Fejzić, a Muslim, and his Serbian neighbors, the Soraks.

When the Serbs began the siege of Goražde in 1992, the Soraks lived in the city with their older son, Zoran, and his wife. They were indifferent, although they were Serbs, to the nationalist propaganda of Bosnian Serb leaders like Radovan Karadžić.

After Serbian forces began to shell the city and cut off the electricity, gas, and water, the family refused to move out. They threw their lot in with the Bosnian government and were branded by the Bosnian Serbs, who pounded them each day from the mountains above the town, as traitors.

On the night of June 14, 1992, the Bosnian police came to

the door for Zoran, who until the war was on Yugoslavia's national handball team.

"The Muslim police said they were taking him away for interrogation," said Drago Sorak, "but he never came back. We went nearly every day to the police station, until we left Goražde, to beg for information. They told us nothing. We assume he is dead."

Soon afterward, their second son, who fought with the Bosnian Serbs, was struck by a car and killed. The Soraks were childless.

The couple, harassed by some Muslims in the town, began to consider fleeing, although it would be months before they could get out. Drago Sorak was increasingly pressed into digging trenches and chopping firewood for the Bosnian Army. The couple had little to eat.

"As things deteriorated it got worse and worse," he said. "Some of the Muslims wanted to kill us and others defended us. There were only 200 Serbs left in the city. On some nights, groups of Muslims came to the apartment looking for us. We had to hide until they left. We were frightened."

The difficulties, the harassment, and the disappearance of Zoran all helped turn the couple against a Muslim-led government that they had been willing to accept at the start of the war.

"I would live in Albania before I would go back to living with the Muslims here," Rosa Sorak said. "How can you expect us to live with those who murdered my son?"

Five months after Zoran's disappearance, his wife gave birth to a girl. The mother was unable to nurse the child. The city was being shelled continuously. There were severe food shortages. Infants, like the infirm and the elderly, were dying in droves. The family gave the baby tea for five days, but she began to fade.

"She was dying," Rosa Sorak said. "It was breaking our hearts."

Fejzić, meanwhile, was keeping his cow in a field on the eastern edge of Goražde, milking it at night to avoid being hit by Serbian snipers.

"On the fifth day, just before dawn, we heard someone at the door," said Rosa Sorak. "It was Fadil Fejzić in his black rubber boots. He handed up half a liter of milk. He came the next morning, and the morning after that, and after that. Other families on the street began to insult him. They told him to give his milk to Muslims, to let the Chetnik children die. He never said a word. He refused our money. He came for 442 days, until my daughter-in-law and granddaughter left Goražde for Serbia."

The Soraks eventually left and took over a house that once belonged to a Muslim family in the Serbian-held town of Kopaci, two miles to the east. They could no longer communicate with Fejzić.

The couple said they grieved daily for their sons. They missed their home. They said they could never forgive those who took Zoran from them. But they also said that despite their anger and loss, they could not listen to other Serbs talking about Muslims, or even recite their own sufferings, without telling of Fejzić and his cow. Here was the power of love. What this illiterate farmer did would color the life of another human being, who might never meet him, long after he was gone. In his act lay an ocean of hope.

"It is our duty to always tell this story," Drago Sorak said. "Salt, in those days, cost $80 a kilo. The milk he had was precious, all the more so because it was hard to keep animals. He gave us 221 liters. And every year at this time, when it is cold and dark, when we close our eyes, we can hear the boom of the heavy guns and the sound of Fadil Fejzić's footsteps on the stairs."

Fejzić fell on hard times after the war. I found him selling small piles of worm-eaten apples picked from abandoned orchards outside the shattered remains of an apartment block. His apartment block had been destroyed by artillery shells, leaving him to share the floor of an unheated room with several other men. His great brown-and-white milk cow, the one the Soraks told me about, did not survive the war. It was slaughtered for the meat more than a year before as the Serbian forces tightened the siege. He had only a thin, worn coat to protect him from the winter cold. When we spoke he sat huddled in the corner of a dank, concrete-walled room rubbing his pathetic collection of small apples, many with brown holes in them, against his sleeve.

When I told him I had seen the Soraks, his eyes brightened.

"And the baby?" he asked. "How is she?"

The small acts of decency by people such as Slavica, a Serb, or Fejzić, a Muslim, in wartime ripple outwards like concentric circles. These acts, unrecognized at the time, make it impossible to condemn, legally or morally, an entire people. They serve as reminders that we all have a will of our own, a will that is independent of the state or the nationalist cause. Most important, once the war is over, these people make it hard to brand an entire nation or an entire people as guilty.

"I do not understand," wrote Primo Levi. "I cannot tolerate the fact that a man should be judged not for what he is but because of the group to which he happens to belong."[3]

But these acts also remind us that in wartime most people are unwilling to risk discomfort, censure, or violence to help neighbors. There is a frightening indifference and willful blindness, a

desire to believe the nationalist myth because it brands those
outside a nation or ethnic group with traits and vices that cannot be eradicated. Because they are the other, because they are
not us, they are guilty. Such indifference, such acceptance of
nationalist self-glorification, turns many into silent accomplices.

To those who swallow the nationalist myth, life is transformed. The collective glorification permits people to abandon
their usual preoccupation with the petty concerns of daily life.
They can abandon even self-preservation in the desire to see
themselves as players in a momentous historical drama. This
vision is accepted even at the expense of self-annihilation. Life
in wartime becomes theater. All are actors. Leaders, against the
backdrop of war, look heroic, noble. Pilots who bail out of
planes shot down by the enemy and who make their way back
home play cameo roles. The state, as we saw in the Persian Gulf
War or Afghanistan, transforms war into a nightly television
show. The generals, who are no more interested in candor than
they were in Vietnam, have at least perfected the appearance of
candor. And the press has usually been more than willing to
play the dupe as long as the ratings are good.

The daily wartime episodes are central to the nationalist
vision. The carefully choreographed performances come to
define and make up the body politic. The lines between real
entertainment and political entertainment blur and finally vanish. The world, as we see it in wartime, becomes high drama. It
is romanticized. A moral purpose is infused into the trivial and
the commonplace. And we, who yesterday felt maligned, alienated, and ignored, are part of a nation of self-appointed agents
of the divine will. We await our chance to walk on stage.

During the first protest movement against Milošević in the
winter of 1998, a time when nationalism should have been dis-

credited, I visited one of the faculties occupied by the students who sought Milošević's removal. I arrived at the front door of the Philosophy Department at Belgrade University to be stopped by several curt young men with tags on their jackets identifying them as "security."

Students inside who attempted to speak to me were told by the security detail that only "the committee" had the right to make statements. And when Jack Lang, former minister of culture in France, arrived at the building to express his support for the student protesters, he was escorted by young men in green fatigue jackets to a room where he was declared "an enemy of the Serbs" and ordered to leave.

Lang had stumbled unwittingly on the virulent Serbian nationalism that colored the anti-government protests. The incident highlighted the problem that changing Serbian society did not lie in overturning the rule of one man, but in transforming a country that had come to see racist remarks as acceptable and had learned to express itself in the language of hate and nationalist crusades. The opposition to Milošević came from those who felt he had sold out the Serbs in Croatia and Bosnia. There was no repentance.

"Students, professors, and many Serbs have simply switched their ideological iconography," Obrad Savic, the head of the Belgrade Circle, a dissident group, told me. "They have shifted from a Marxist paradigm to Serbian nationalism. We have failed to build an intellectual tradition where people think for themselves. We operate only in the collective. We speak in the plural as the Serbian people. It's frightening, especially in the young. It will take years for us to rid ourselves of this virus."

As fervently as Western reporters sought, as they often do, to recreate the students in their own image as democratic reformers, the student organizers mocked them. This was no democratic movement, just as the Muslim-dominated government in Sarajevo had no interest in recreating a multi-ethnic city. Serbian flags proliferated in the crowd and many sang "God Give Us Justice," the anthem of the old Kingdom of Yugoslavia. The students requested an audience with Patriarch Pavle, the head of the Serbian Orthodox Church, the institution that had helped give birth to the modern Serbian nationalist movement. They rejected a suggestion that they also see Belgrade's Catholic cardinal and the mufti, the leader of the tiny Islamic community.

The nationalist virus was the logical outcome of the destruction of the country's educational system that began in the 1950s under Tito's rule. Departments were purged of professors who refused to teach subjects like "Marx and Biology" and to adhere to party doctrine. Many of the best academics were blacklisted or left the country.

Following Tito's death in 1980, academics, freed from party dogma, reached out to Western intellectual traditions. But this was swiftly terminated with the rise of Serbian nationalism, an ideology that replaced the rigidity of dogmatic Marxism. By the mid–1980s the History Department, flush with the new orthodoxy, was exalting Byzantine culture and using it, instead of Marx, as a tool to bash Western liberal democracy. The works of Serbian nationalist writers were taught in literature classes, and Serbian philosophers, who espoused theories of racial superiority, including the idea that the Serbs were the oldest human race, dominated university classrooms.

The war only accelerated the decline in the educational system. More than 400,000 Serbs, many of them young and talented, left the country in the first few years of the war.

Academic standards fell as Milošević put party hacks in charge of schools and departments and sliced government spending for education.

I developed a close friendship in Belgrade with Miladin Zivotić, a leading dissident during the Communist era in Yugoslavia and one of the most prominent domestic critics of Serbian involvement in the Balkan wars. He was the leader of the Belgrade Circle, a small group of intellectuals and artists who condemned the Serbian role in the wars in Bosnia and Croatia. The groups, which he helped found in 1992 and which included Yugoslavia's best-known dissident, Milovan Djilas, tried to reach out to Muslims and Croats to create a common front against nationalist movements in the Balkans. It was often denounced by the authorities as being a tool of Serbia's enemies.

To register his disapproval of the siege of Sarajevo by the Bosnian Serbs, Zivotić visited the city in 1993 to express his solidarity with those besieged by Serb forces. He was an outspoken critic of Serbia's treatment of its ethnic minorities, especially the two million Albanians in the Kosova region. And when nationalists began to threaten Muslims in the Sanjak region of Serbia early in the Bosnian war, he went to live with Muslim families.

"The first act any new president of this country must do is travel to Sarejevo and beg for forgiveness, just as Willy Brandt did when he traveled to Warsaw," Zivotić told me, referring to the West German chancellor who pursued a policy of reconciliation with the victims of German Nazism. "This is the only way we can heal ourselves."

Zivotić first came to prominence in 1968, when Yugoslav university students staged anti-Communist protests at the time of the Soviet-led invasion of Czechoslovakia. For their support of the students he and seven other philosophy professors were dismissed. He started the Free Belgrade University, which met secretly in houses and whose classes were often broken up by the police. He did not return to his University of Belgrade post until 1987, seven years after the death of Tito.

Soon after he regained his old position, he found himself ostracized again because of his condemnation of growing Serbian nationalism. He was attacked by students and professors for being a "traitor to the Serbian people." He retired in 1994.

"I could not stand to go to work," he said. "I had to listen to professors and students voice support and solidarity for these Bosnian fascists, Radovan Karadžić and Ratko Mladić, in the so-called Republika Srpska. It is worse now than it was under Communism. The intellectual corruption is more pervasive and profound."

He was a lonely and distraught figure. He spent his days in the offices of the Belgrade Circle headquarters, where he drank too much coffee and smoked too many cigarettes. His was a one-man crusade against nationalist madness. He was pointedly ignored by the Serbian media, who usually only quoted him after his comments appeared in my articles in *The New York Times*. The student protesters who mounted demonstrations against the Milošević government never invited him to speak, preferring to listen to rants by Serbian nationalists, who fomented the war in the first place. These speakers condemned Milošević for betraying the nationalist cause. The callous indifference of the university students hurt Zivotić tremendously.

He died of a heart attack in 1997, a year before I left the Balkans. His loss for Serbia was tremendous, for with him went one of the few remaining moral voices in the region.

The nationalist myth often implodes with a startling ferocity. It does so after the lies and absurdities that surround it become too hard to sustain. They collapse under their own weight. The contradictions and torturous refusal to acknowledge the obvious becomes more than a society is able to bear. The collapse is usually followed by a blanket refusal, caused by shame and discomfort, to examine or acknowledge the crimes carried out in the name of nationalist cause.

By the time British forces had landed on the Falklands and were rolling over the poorly supplied and ill-clad Argentine soldiers, the Argentine public had retreated into a mythic world that was not unfamiliar to Germans in the last days of the Third Reich. There was no hint in the national press that the Argentine forces were being defeated. It appeared that the British were losing the war. When the Argentine forces surrendered it hit the country like a tidal wave.

Curiously, it was not that Argentines believed their own propaganda. Many told me that they understood that much what they saw and heard in their own press was a lie. They could tune in the BBC broadcasts. They knew what the British were saying about the war. But they assumed, with a mixture of gullibility and cynicism, that each side was lying. They preferred to pick and choose. They regularly dismissed some of their own propaganda, but not the central message—that Argentina was triumphant.

The fall of the islands sent hundreds of thousands of enraged Argentines to the Plaza de Mayo in front of the Casa Rosada in Buenos Aires to demand weapons to fight. Foreign reporters were attacked, their cars overturned and burned. When a group of toughs cornered me in an alley, I was spared when I told them I was German, a fabrication they bought—convinced, I suspect, by my blond hair.

All of that rage should have been directed against the government, but instead it was turned on the foreign conspirators who were arrayed against the Argentine nation. Even in defeat, the Argentines could not let go of the nationalist myth. The next morning the government-controlled press began to explain what happened. What happened, it said, was that Argentina had been betrayed by the United States. "We can defeat one superpower," a front-page article read, "but we can not defeat two."

And then, in the days after the defeat, the myth suddenly vanished. My Argentine friends picked up where they had left off, as if there never had been a war, as if the collective intoxication was nothing more than a bad dream, a drunken night of debauchery best forgotten and impolitic to mention. One felt dirty to bring it up. I woke up one morning after the surrender and I was no longer a freak. Argentines were again able to grasp reality and respond to it. The junta, whose members should have been imprisoned, especially given the downward spiral that soon beset the economy, was allowed to fade away. No one really wanted to be reminded of the whole affair.

The novelist Marguerite Duras, who as a member of the French resistance during World War II took part in the torture of collaborators, wrote of such a moment. "Peace is visible already," she wrote. "It's like a great darkness falling, it's the beginning of forgetting. You can see already . . . I went out, peace seemed imminent. I hurried back home, pursued by peace. It had suddenly struck me that there might be a future, that a foreign land was going to emerge out of this chaos where no one would wait any more."[4]

This blanket amnesia is often part of the aftermath of war. The puncturing of the nationalist myth, an event that saw the Serbs turn their back on Milošević once Kosova was lost, does not mean, however, that the nationalist virus has been conquered. While the excesses carried out in the name of the nationalist cause are forgotten or ignored, the myth of the nation has a disturbing longevity. It lies dormant, festering in the society, nurtured by boys' adventure stories of heroism in service to the nation, the monuments we erect to the fallen, and carefully scripted remembrances until it slowly slouches back into respectability.

Nationalist triumphalism was shunned and discredited in America after Vietnam. We were forced to see ourselves as others saw us, and it was not always pleasant. We understood, at least for a moment, the lie. But the plague of nationalism was resurrected during the Reagan years. It became ascendant with the Persian Gulf War, when we embraced the mythic and unachievable goal of a "New World Order." The infection of nationalism now lies unchecked and blindly accepted in the march we make as a nation towards another war, one as ill conceived as the war we lost in southeast Asia.

3

THE DESTRUCTION
OF CULTURE

The first casualty when war comes is truth.

•

SENATOR HIRAM JOHNSON

1917

I N WARTIME THE STATE SEEKS TO DESTROY ITS OWN
culture. It is only when this destruction has been completed
that the state can begin to exterminate the culture of its opponents. In times of conflict authentic culture is subversive. As the
cause championed by the state comes to define national identity,
as the myth of war entices a nation to glory and sacrifice, those
who question the value of the cause and the veracity of the
myths are branded internal enemies.

Art takes on a whole new significance in wartime. War and
the nationalist myth that fuels it are the purveyors of low culture—folklore, quasi-historical dramas, kitsch, sentimental dog-
gerel, and theater and film that portray the glory of soldiers in
past wars or current wars dying nobly for the homeland. This
is why so little of what moves us during wartime has any cur-

rency once war is over. The songs, books, poems, and films that arouse us in war are awkward and embarrassing when the conflict ends, useful only to summon up the nostalgia of war's comradeship.

States at war silence their own authentic and humane culture. When this destruction is well advanced they find the lack of critical and moral restraint useful in the campaign to exterminate the culture of their opponents. By destroying authentic culture—that which allows us to question and examine ourselves and our society—the state erodes the moral fabric. It is replaced with a warped version of reality. The enemy is dehumanized; the universe starkly divided between the forces of light and the forces of darkness. The cause is celebrated, often in overt religious forms, as a manifestation of divine or historical will. All is dedicated to promoting and glorifying the myth, the nation, the cause.

The works of the writers in Serbia, such as Danilo Kiš and Milovan Djilas, were mostly unavailable during the war. It remains hard even now to find their books. In Croatia the biting satires of Miroslav Krleža, who wrote one of the most searing portraits of Balkan despots, were forgotten. Writers and artists were inconvenient. They wrote about social undercurrents that were ignored by a new crop of self-appointed nationalist historians, political scientists, and economists.

National symbols—flags, patriotic songs, sentimental dedications—invade and take over cultural space. Art becomes infected with the platitudes of patriotism. More important, the use of a nation's cultural resources to back up the war effort is essential to mask the contradictions and lies that mount over time in the drive to sustain war. Cultural or national symbols that do not support the crusade are often ruthlessly removed.

In Bosnia the ethnic warlords worked hard to wipe out all the records of cohabitation between ethnic groups. The symbols of the old communist regime—one whose slogan was "Brotherhood and Unity"—were defaced or torn down. The monuments to partisan fighters who died fighting the Germans in World War II, the lists of names clearly showing a mix of ethnic groups, were blown up in Croatia. The works of Ivo Andrić, who wrote some of the most lyrical passages about a multiethnic Bosnia, were edited by the Bosnian Serbs and selectively quoted to support ethnic cleansing.

All groups looked at themselves as victims—the Croats, the Muslims, and the Serbs. They ignored the excesses of their own and highlighted the excesses of the other in gross distortions that fueled the war. The cultivation of victimhood is essential fodder for any conflict. It is studiously crafted by the state. All cultural life is directed to broadcast the injustices carried out against us. Cultural life soon becomes little more than the drivel of agitprop. The message that the nation is good, the cause just, and the war noble is pounded into the heads of citizens in everything from late-night talk shows to morning news programs to films and popular novels. The nation is soon thrown into a trance from which it does not awake until the conflict ends. In parts of the world where the conflict remains unresolved, this trance can last for generations.

I walked one morning a few years ago down the deserted asphalt tract that slices through the center of the world's last divided capital, Nicosia, on the island of Cyprus. At one spot on the asphalt dividing line was a small painted triangle. For fifteen minutes each hour, Turkish troops, who control the northern part of the island, were allowed to move from their border posts and stand inside the white triangular lines. The arrangement was part of a deal laboriously negotiated by the United

Nations to give Greek Cypriots and Turkish Cypriots access to several disputed areas along the 110-mile border that separates the north from the south. The triangle was a potent reminder that once the folly of war is over, folly itself is often all that remains.

"It's really a game of hopscotch," said Major Richard Nixon-Eckersall, a British peacekeeper who was escorting me. "You see, the Greek sentries, over there, can't see the lines. Are the Turks inside the lines or not? A lot of rock-throwing and insults are generated over this triangle. Last year the Greeks fired off five rounds at the Turks. This is considered one of the most volatile areas along the Green Line."

A buffer zone along the Green Line, set up after the Turkish invasion of Cyprus in 1974 and patrolled by United Nations soldiers, has prevented the resumption of a civil war that began in 1963. The zone—four miles wide in spots, narrowing to just a few yards in others—cuts through farmland, mountain passes, and Nicosia itself. Many of the houses and shops in the no-man's-land have dusty and decaying furniture and goods still stacked inside. Some doors have signs warning of booby traps. The deserted Nicosia International Airport with its gutted terminals, the seaside resort of Varosha swallowed up in thick vegetation, and the whitewashed Olympus Hotel were crumbling from neglect and inhabited by stray dogs and cats.

The buffer zone was lined with earthworks, barbed wire, trenches, bunkers, and watchtowers manned by troops with automatic weapons. There were about 43,000 Turkish and Greek Cypriot troops, including 30,000 Turkish soldiers sent by Ankara to the island, stationed along it.

On one side is Northern Cyprus, with one-fifth of the island's 650,000 people and a government recognized only by

Turkey. It is a dreary collection of towns and villages that look like working-class districts in Ankara or Istanbul. It suffers from constant shortages and high rates of unemployment. It is propped up by the Ankara government with an estimated $200 million a year.

The south, by contrast, has a per capita income of $12,000 a year, equal to those of Ireland or Spain. Luxury hotels and shops selling designer clothes, bone china, and computer software nestle along tree-lined avenues.

As if the war had ended only a few days ago, the Greek Cypriots and the Turkish Cypriots denounce each other in repetitive weekly editorials and political rallies. The Ayios Demetrios Church in Nicosia, in one of the stream of Greek exhibitions portraying Turkish perfidy, had just mounted a photo display of the desecration of more than 200 Greek churches in the northern part of the island. The island is hostage to its own hatred.

"For over twenty years our young men have been trained in the art of war," the Greek Cypriot president, Glafkos Clerides, told me as we chatted in his hilltop palace. "They are trained not to fight an external foe, but an internal enemy. This has had a devastating effect on the younger generation."

The war between the Orthodox Serbs and the Muslims in the Balkans was viewed by many on the island as an extension of the global religious clash that grips Cyprus. The mayor in northern Nicosia, whose father disappeared in the violence in 1963, had a poster denouncing the siege of Sarajevo on his office door.

United Nations officials, along with Greek Cypriot and Turkish Cypriot leaders, warned it would take little to trigger the conflict again.

"The two peoples cannot be put back together," said Rauf Denktash, the leader of the Turkish Cypriots, when I crossed the Green Line to see him. "One single incident, one crime involving a Turk and a Greek, would ignite the whole thing. We can't play with the fears of the people."

The white glare of the Mediterranean sun beat down on the Ledra Palace Hotel checkpoint. Only foreign visitors who do not have Turkish or Greek names can cross. At the checkpoint the Greek Cypriots and the Turkish Cypriots had set up competing billboards. Each side displayed gruesome photos of the atrocities they had allegedly endured. It was, once again, the struggle by opposing sides to wrap themselves in the mantle of victimhood. For once a group or a nation establishes that it alone suffers, then all other competing claims to injustice are canceled out. The nation or the group falls into a collective "autism," to use a phrase coined by Hans Magnus Enzensberger, and does not listen to those outside the inner circle. Communication is impossible.

"Enjoy yourself in this land of racial purity and true apartheid," read a billboard directed at those headed to the north. "Enjoy the sight of our desecrated churches. Enjoy what remains of our looted heritage and homes."

The red and white star-and-crescent flags flapped over the Turkish Cypriot guard posts, about 400 yards away, and a sign welcomed me to the Turkish Republic of Northern Cyprus.

An enlarged photo showed the bloody bodies of a Turkish Cypriot mother and her three children in a bathtub. Another showed a priest firing a rifle with the awkward English caption "A Greek Cypriot priest who forgot his religious duties and joined to the hunting of Turks."

Like the Cypriots, the Palestinians have been nurtured on bit-

ter accounts of abuse, despair, and injustice. Families tell and
retell stories of being thrown off their land and of relatives
killed or exiled. All can tick off the names of martyrs within
their own clan who died for the elusive Palestinian state. The
only framed paper in many Palestinians' homes is a sepia land
deed from the time of the British mandate. Some elderly men
still keep the keys to houses that have long since vanished.
From infancy, Palestinians are inculcated with myopic nationalism and the burden of revenge. As in Bosnia, such resentment
seeps into the roots of society. Private histories of despair over-
whelm the present. Each generation is raised to exact revenge
for the injustices visited on the last, real or imagined.

"Tell the man what you want to be," said Hyam Temraz to
her two-year-old son, Abed, as she peeped out of the slit of a
black veil one afternoon in Gaza.

"A martyr," the child told me.

"We were in Jordan when my son Baraa was four," she said.
"He saw a Jordanian soldier and ran and hugged him. He asked
him if it was he who would liberate Palestine. He has always
told me that he would be a martyr and that one day I would dig
his grave."

Nezar Rayyan, her husband, was a theology professor at
Islamic University in Gaza. He was a large man with a thick
black beard and the quiet, soft-spoken manner of someone
who has spent much of his life reading. On the walls of his
office, black and white photographs illustrated the history of
Palestinians over the last five decades. They showed lines of
trucks carrying refugees from their villages in 1948, after the
United Nations created Israel and its Arab neighbors attacked
the new state. They showed the hovels of new refugee camps
built after the 1967 war. And they showed the gutted remains of
Palestinian villages in what is now Israel.

Rayyan's grandfather and great-uncle were killed in the 1948 war. His grandmother died shortly after she and her son, Rayyan's father, were forced from their village. His father was passed among relatives and grew up with the bitterness of the dispossessed—a bitterness the father passed on to the son and the son has passed on to the grandchildren.

"There was not a single night that we did not think and talk about Palestine," Rayyan said, his eyes growing moist. "We were taught that our lives must be devoted to reclaiming our land."

Rayyan spent twelve years in an Israeli jail. His brother-in-law blew himself up in a suicide-bomb attack on an Israeli bus in 1998. One of his brothers had been shot dead by Israelis in street protests five years earlier. Another brother was expelled to Lebanon and several more were wounded in clashes.

He gave two of his sons—ages fifteen and sixteen—money to join the youths who throw rocks at Israeli checkpoints. His youngest, Mohammed, twelve, was crippled by an Israeli bullet. All three, according to their father, strive to be one thing: martyrs for Palestine.

"I pray only that God will choose them," he said.

The rewriting and distortion of history—as in all wartime regimes—is crucial. Many of those who went on to prosecute the war in the Balkans, such as the Bosnian Serb leader Radovan Karadžić, who fancied himself a poet, and Croatian president Franjo Tudjman, who after a lifetime in the Yugoslav army began writing nationalist tracts about Croatia, looked at themselves as academics or intellectuals. They believed they were unearthing or championing a true version of history, but what they were doing was tearing down one national identity and replacing it with another. For Tudjman and his Serbian counterparts, the new identity glorified Croatian or Serbian cultural heritage and denigrated the heritage of others. And, for all my sympathy for the plight of the Palestinians, most Palestinians have done the same thing.

Tudjman was part of a long line of mediocre writers and artists who found their voice and a route to power in national chauvinism. In 1963, after a career as an army general, he managed to be appointed professor of history at Zagreb University, even though he lacked a doctoral degree and his dissertation was rejected. He was part of the nationalist campaign for the linguistic separation of the Serbo-Croatian language, which had also been championed by the Nazi puppet state in Croatia run by the Ustashe. His turgid nationalist historical tracts were in the service of one idea—Croatian nationalism. In his book *Impasses of Historical Reality*, he challenged the numbers of victims of World War II genocide by the Germans and the Ustashe. He reduced the number of Jews killed in the Holocaust to one million instead of six million—as well as the number killed in Croatia's main death camp, at Jasenovac, from more than 500,000 to 59,639.

"A Jew is still a Jew," he wrote, "even in the camps they retained their bad characteristics: selfishness, perfidy, meanness, slyness and treachery."

During the 1990 election campaign that saw him ascend to the presidency and lead Croatia's bloody secession from Yugoslavia, he said, "Thank God, my wife is neither a Serb nor a Jew."

In 1992, he said his comments in his books had been "misinterpreted" and in 1994 he offered "an apology" in a letter to B'nai B'rith, saying that he intended to delete "controversial portions" from later editions, which he did. But by then the Croatian state, which carried out the forced expulsion of nearly all the ethnic Serbs—there were 600,000 of them, 12 percent of the population—was complete. Croatia had become the most ethnically cleansed state in the former Yugoslavia.

Tudjman declared Croatia "the national state of the Croatian nation" when he assumed power. And when his government began wholesale dismissals of Serbs from civil service jobs, Serbian communities began arming themselves. The civil society broke down. As Michael Ignatieff wrote in *The Warrior's Honor: Ethnic War and the Modern Conscience*, it is this fear of the other, perhaps more than anything else, that triggers war.

> It is fear that turns minor difference into major, that makes the gulf between ethnicities into a distinction between species, between human and inhuman. And not just fear, but guilt as well. For if you have shared a common life with another group and then suddenly begin to fear them, because they suddenly have power over you, you have to overcome the weight of happy memory; you have to project onto *them* the blame for destroying a common life.[1]

The fervent drive for "authenticity" leads nationalist leaders to use a variety of disciplines to promote and legitimize the cause. In Israel the mania for archeology, for excavating ancient Jewish ruins, is a way of legitimizing the presence of Jews in what was once Palestine. These sites are given a prominence out of proportion to the multitude of other ruins that are not Jewish in character. Sociologists, historians, and writers all seek to find that within the culture that champions the myth and the state, ignoring that which challenges their own supremacy.

No nation is free from this distortion. After the September attacks in the United States a document entitled "Defending Civilization" was compiled by a conservative organization called the American Council of Trustees and Alumni. It set out to show that the American universities did not respond to the September attacks with a proper degree of "anger, patriotism, and support of military intervention." The report offered a list of 115 subversive remarks taken from college newspapers or made on college campuses.

What is at work in this report is the reduction of language to code. Clichés, coined by the state, become the only acceptable vocabulary. Everyone knows what to say and how to respond. It is scripted. Vocabulary shrinks so that the tyranny of nationalist rhetoric leaves people sputtering state-sanctioned slogans. There is a scene in *Othello* when Othello is so consumed by jealousy and rage that he has lost the eloquence and poetry that won him Desdemona. He turns to the audience in Act IV and mutters, "Goats and monkeys!"[2] Nationalist cant, to me, always ends up sounding just as absurd.

The destruction of culture in wartime is also physical. There is an effort to eradicate the monuments and buildings that challenge the myth of the nation. There are thousands of Armenian villages in Turkey, Kurdish villages in Iraq, and Palestinian villages in Israel that have been razed in this process of state-sponsored forgetting. Along with their destruction has been a ferocious campaign to deny the displaced the right to remember where they once belonged.

Those displaced from their homes, those who have seen an assault on their culture, nurture an anger and alienation they assiduously pass on to their children. In many Palestinian refugee camps in Gaza the camps are divided according to villages left behind in 1948. Many of these villages no longer exist. Most of those in the camps never lived in these villages. Yet when you ask where someone is from, the name of the village is the first thing out of his or her mouth. Each side creates a narrative. Each side insists they are the true victims. And each side works overtime to bend their culture to support this narrative.

The city of Mostar in Bosnia was the scene of some of the most savage fighting of the war. The eastern Muslim section was surrounded and heavily shelled by the Bosnian Croats. The town owed its name, "Bridge-keeper," to an elegant, arched Ottoman bridge built in 1566 to join the banks of the Neretva River. The city, a quaint example of Ottoman architecture, was dotted with cobblestone alleys, stone houses, spindly minarets, the Catholic campanile, and Orthodox steeples.

But Croatian commanders, intent on wiping out what was the heart of the city, blasted the bridge for two days in November 1993 until it tumbled into the river. It, like the Moorish-revival library in Sarajevo, which was bombarded for three days by Serbian incendiary bombs in the summer of 1992, was a cultural symbol that did not fit with the narrative of Serbian or Croatian nationalists. It was part of the assault against all cultural icons that spoke of the plurality of peoples in Mostar and Sarajevo.

War, just as it tears down old monuments, demands new ones. These new monuments glorify the state's uniform and unwavering call for self-sacrifice and ultimately self-annihilation. Those who find meaning in the particular, who embrace affirmation not through the collective of the nation but through the love of another individual regardless of ethnic or national identity, are dangerous to the emotional and physical domination demanded by the state. Only one message is acceptable.

A soldier who is able to see the humanity of the enemy makes a troubled and ineffective killer. To achieve corporate

action, self-awareness and especially self-criticism must be obliterated. We must be transformed into agents of a divinely
inspired will, as defined by the state, just as those we fight must
be transformed into the personification of unmitigated evil.
There is little room for individuality in war.

The effectiveness of the myths peddled in war is powerful.
We often come to doubt our own perceptions. We hide these
doubts, like troubled believers, sure that no one else feels them.
We feel guilty. The myths have determined not only how we
should speak but how we should think. The doubts we carry,
the scenes we see that do not conform to the myth are hazy, difficult to express, unsettling. And as the atrocities mount, as civil
liberties are stripped away (something, with the "War on Terror," already happening to hundreds of thousands of immigrants in the United States), we struggle uncomfortably with the
jargon and clichés. But we have trouble expressing our discomfort because the collective shout has made it hard for us to give
words to our thoughts.

This self-doubt is aided by the monstrosity of war. We gape
and wonder at the collapsing towers of the World Trade Center.
They crumble before us, and yet we cannot quite comprehend
it. What, really, did we see? In wartime an attack on a village
where women and children are killed, an attack that does not
conform to the myth peddled by our side, is hard to fathom and
articulate. We live in wartime with a permanent discomfort, for
in wartime we see things so grotesque and fantastic that they
seem beyond human comprehension. War turns human reality
into a bizarre carnival that does not seem part of our experience. It knocks us off balance.

On a chilly, rainy day in March 1998 I was in a small Albanian
village in Kosova, twenty-five miles west of the provincial cap-

ital of Pristina. I was waiting with a few thousand Kosovar Albanian mourners for a red Mercedes truck to rumble down the dirt road and unload a cargo of fourteen bodies. A group of distraught women, seated on wooden planks set up on concrete blocks, was in the dirt yard.

When the truck pulled into the yard I climbed into the back. Before each corpse, wrapped in bloodstained blankets and rugs, was lifted out for washing and burial I checked to see if the body was mutilated. I pulled back the cloth to uncover the faces. The gouged-out eyes, the shattered skulls, the gaping rows of broken teeth, and the sinewy strands of flayed flesh greeted me. When I could not see clearly in the fading light I flicked on my Maglite. I jotted each disfigurement in my notebook.

The bodies were passed silently out of the truck. They were laid on crude wooden coffin lids placed on the floor of the shed. The corpses were wound in white shrouds by a Muslim cleric in a red turban. The shed was lit by a lone kerosene lamp. It threw out a ghastly, uneven, yellowish light. In the hasty effort to confer some dignity on the dead, family members, often weeping, tried to wash away the bloodstains from the faces. Most could not do it and had to be helped away.

It was not an uncommon event for me. I have seen many such dead. Several weeks later it would be worse. I would be in a warehouse with fifty-one bodies, including children, even infants, women, and the elderly from the town of Prekaz. I had spent time with many of them. I stared into their lifeless faces. I was again in the twilight zone of war. I could not wholly believe what I saw in front of me.

This sense that we cannot trust what we see in wartime spreads throughout the society. The lies about the past, the eradication of cultural, historical, and religious monuments that have been part of a landscape for centuries, all serve to shift the ground under which we stand. We lose our grip. Whole worlds vanish or change in ways we can not fully comprehend. A catastrophic terrorist strike will have the same effect.

In Bosnia the Serbs, desperately trying to deny the Muslim character of Bosnia, dynamited or plowed over libraries, museums, universities, historic monuments, and cemeteries, but most of all mosques. The Serbs, like the Croats, also got rid of monuments built to honor their own Serb or Croat heroes during the communist era. These monuments championed another narrative, a narrative of unity among ethnic groups that ran contrary to the notion of ancient ethnic hatreds. The partisan monuments that honored Serb and Croat fighters against the Nazis honored, in the new narrative, the wrong Serbs and Croats. For this they had to be erased.

This physical eradication, coupled with intolerance toward any artistic endeavor that does not champion the myth, formed a new identity. The Serbs, standing in flattened mud fields, were able to deny that there were ever churches or mosques on the spot because they had been removed. The town of Zvornik in Serb-held Bosnia once had a dozen mosques. The 1991 census listed 60 percent of its residents as Muslim Slavs. By the end of the war the town was 100 percent Serb. Branko Grujić, the Serb-appointed mayor, informed us: "There never were any mosques in Zvornik."

No doubt he did not believe it. He knew that there had been mosques in Zvornik. But his children and grandchildren would come to be taught the lie. Serbs leaders would turn it into accepted historical fact. There are no shortage of villages in Russia or Germany or Poland where all memory of the Jewish community is gone because the physical culture has been destroyed.

And, when mixed with the strange nightmarish quality of war, it is hard to be completely sure of your own memories.

The destruction of culture sees the state or the group prosecuting the war take control of the two most important mediums that transmit information to the nation—the media and the schools. The alleged "war crimes" of the enemy, real and imagined, are played and replayed night after night, rousing a nation to fury. In the Middle East and the Balkans, along with many other parts of the world, children are taught to hate. In Egypt pupils are told Jews are interlopers on Arab land. Israel does not appear on schoolroom maps. In Jordan, children learn that Christians are "infidels" who "must be forced into submission," that the Jewish Torah is "perverted," and that Jews have only "their own evil practices" to blame for the Holocaust. Syrian schoolbooks exhort students to "holy war" and paint pictures of Israelis "perpetrating beastly crimes and horrendous massacres," burying people alive in battle and dancing drunk in Islamic holy places in Jerusalem. And Israel, despite efforts in secular state schools to present a more balanced view of Arab history, allows state-funded religious schools to preach that Jewish rule should extend from the Nile in Egypt to the Euphrates in Iraq and that the kingdom of Jordan is occupied Jewish land.[3]

The reinterpretation of history and culture is dizzying and dangerous. But it is the bedrock of the hatred and intolerance that leads to war.

On June 28, 1914, Gavrilo Princip shot and killed Archduke Franz Ferdinand of Austria in a Sarajevo street, an act that set off World War I. But what that makes him in Bosnia depends on which lesson plan you pick up.

"A hero and a poet," says a textbook handed to high school students in the Serb-controlled region of this divided country.

An "assassin trained and instructed by the Serbs to commit this act of terrorism," says a text written for Croatian students. "A nationalist whose deed sparked anti-Serbian rioting that was only stopped by the police from all three ethnic groups," reads the Muslim version of the event.

In communist Yugoslavia, Princip was a hero. But with the partition of Bosnia along ethnic lines, huge swathes of history are reinterpreted. The Muslim books, for example, portray the Ottoman Empire's rule over Bosnia, which lasted 500 years, as a golden age of enlightenment; the Serbs and Croats condemn it as an age of "brutal occupation."

These texts have at least one thing in common: a distaste for Tito, the Communist leader who ruled the country from 1945 to 1980 and was a staunch opponent of the nationalist movements that now hold power. And Tito's state pioneered the replacement of history with myth, forcing schoolchildren to memorize mythical stories about Tito's life and aphorisms.

By the time today's books in the Balkans reach recent history, the divergence takes on ludicrous proportions; each side blames the others for the Bosnian war and makes no reference to crimes or mistakes committed by its own leaders or fighters.

The Muslims are taught that the Serbs "attacked our country" and started the war. The Serbs are told that "Muslims, with the help of mujahadeen fighters from Pakistan, Iraq and Iran, launched a campaign of genocide against the Serbs that almost succeeded."

The Croatian students learn that Croatian forces in "the homeland war" fought off "Serbian and Muslim aggressors."

Even the classics get twisted into a political diatribe. I saw a pro-Milošević production of *Hamlet* in Belgrade that was scripted to convey the message that usurping authority, even illegitimate authority, only brings chaos and ruin. Hamlet was portrayed as a bold and decisive man, constantly training for battle. He was not consumed by questions about the meaning of existence or a desire to withdraw from society, but the steely drive to seize power, even if it plunged the kingdom into chaos. Horatio, usually portrayed as a thoughtful and humane scholar, was the incarnation of evil.

Hamlet's treachery was illustrated at the conclusion of the play when Prince Fortinbras of Norway entered Elsinore to view the carnage. Fortinbras, dressed to look like the chief European representative at the time in Bosnia, Carl Bildt, walked onstage with a Nazi marching song as his entrance music. He unfolded maps showing how, with the collapse of authority, he had now carved up Serbian territory among foreign powers.

"Here is a *Hamlet* for our time," the director, Dejan Krstović, told me. "We want to show audiences what happens when individuals tamper with power and refuse to sublimate their own ambitions for the benefit of the community.

"Because of Hamlet, the bodies pile up on the altar of authority and the system collapses. Because of Hamlet, the foreign prince, Fortinbras, who for us represents the new world order, comes in from the outside and seizes control, as has happened to the Serbs throughout their history."

Every reporter struggles with how malleable and inaccurate memory can be when faced with trauma or stress. Witnesses to war, even moments after a killing or an atrocity, often cannot remember what took place in front of them. They struggle to connect disparate images. And those who see events with some

coherency find there is an irreversible pull to twist the facts to
conform to the myth. Truth, in such moments, is too nuanced
and contradictory for most to swallow. It is best left untouched.

I went one rainy afternoon to the Imperial War Museum in
Vienna, mostly to see the rooms dedicated to the 1878 Bosnian
rebellion and the assassination of Archduke Franz Ferdinand.
His car, peppered with bullet holes, and the bloodstained couch
on which he died are on display. But I also wandered through
the other rooms designed to honor the bloodlust and forgotten skirmishes of the Austro-Hungarian Empire. When I finished with the World War I exhibit I looked for the room
dedicated to World War II. There wasn't one. And when I
inquired at the desk, I was told there was no such exhibit in the
city. World War II, at least in terms of the collective memory of
the Austrian nation, unlike in Germany, might as well have not
existed. Indeed, in one of the great European perversions of
memory, many Austrians had come to think of themselves as
victims of that war.

The destruction of culture plays a crucial role in the solidifi-
cation of a wartime narrative. When the visible and tangible
symbols of one's past are destroyed or denied, the past can be
recreated to fit the myth. It is left only to those on the margins
to keep the flame of introspection alive, although the destruction of culture is often so great that full recovery is impossible.
Yugoslavia, a country that had a vibrant theater and cinema, has
seen its cultural life wither, with many of its best talents living in
exile or drinking themselves to death in bars in Belgrade or
Vienna.

Most societies never recover from the self-inflicted wounds
made to their own culture during wartime. War leaves behind

not memory but amnesia. Once wars end, people reach back to the time before the catastrophe. The books, plays, cinema take up the established cultural topics; authors and themes are often based on issues and ideas that predated the war. In post-war Germany it was as if Weimar had never ended, as if the war was just some bad, horrible dream from which everyone had just awoken and no one wanted to discuss.

This is why the wall of names that is the Vietnam Veterans Memorial is so important. It was not a project funded or organized by the state but by those who survived and insisted we not forget. It was part of America's battle back to truth, part of our desire for forgiveness. It ultimately held out to us as a nation the opportunity for redemption, although the state has prodded us back towards the triumphalism that led us into Vietnam.

But just as the oppressors engage in selective memory and myth, so do the victims, building unassailable monuments to their own suffering. It becomes impossible to examine, to dispute, or to criticize the myths that have grown up around past suffering of nearly all in war. The oppressors are painted by the survivors as monsters, the victims paint themselves as holy innocents. The oppressors work hard to bury inconvenient facts and brand all in wartime with the pitch of atrocity. They strive to reduce victims to their moral level. Each side creates its own narrative. Neither is fully true.

Until there is a common vocabulary and a shared historical memory there is no peace in any society, only an absence of war. The fighting may have stopped in Bosnia or Cyprus but this does not mean the war is over. The search for a common narrative must, at times, be forced upon a society. Few societies seem able to do this willingly. The temptation, as with the Turks and the Armenian genocide, is to forget or ignore, to wallow in the lie. But reconciliation, self-awareness, and finally the humility that makes peace possible come only when culture no longer serves a cause or a myth but the most precious and elusive of all human narratives—truth.

4

THE SEDUCTION OF
BATTLE AND THE
PERVERSION OF WAR

Let me have a war, say I: It exceeds peace as far as day
Does night; it's spritely, waking, audible, full of vent.
Peace is a very apoplexy, lethargy, mull'd, deaf, sleepy,
Insensible; a getter of more bastard children than war is a
Destroyer of men.

.

WILLIAM SHAKESPEARE
Coriolanus, Act IV, SCENE V

THE MYTH OF WAR ENTICES US WITH THE ALLURE OF heroism. But the images of war handed to us, even when they are graphic, leave out the one essential element of war—fear. There is, until the actual moment of confrontation, no cost to imagining glory. The visual and audio effects of films, the battlefield descriptions in books, make the experience appear real. In fact the experience is sterile. We are safe. We do not smell rotting flesh, hear the cries of agony, or see before us

blood and entrails seeping out of bodies. We view, from a distance, the rush, the excitement, but feel none of the awful gut-
wrenching anxiety and humiliation that come with mortal
danger. It takes the experience of fear and the chaos of battle,
the deafening and disturbing noise, to wake us up, to make us
realize that we are not who we imagined we were, that war as
displayed by the entertainment industry might, in most cases,
as well be ballet. But even with this I have seen soldiers in war
try to recreate the fiction of war, especially when a television
camera is around to record the attempted heroics. The result is
usually pathetic.

The prospect of war is exciting. Many young men, schooled
in the notion that war is the ultimate definition of manhood, that
only in war will they be tested and proven, that they can discover
their worth as human beings in battle, willingly join the great
enterprise. The admiration of the crowd, the high-blown rhetoric, the chance to achieve the glory of the previous generation,
the ideal of nobility beckon us forward. And people, ironically,
enjoy righteous indignation and an object upon which to unleash
their anger. War usually starts with collective euphoria.

It is all the more startling that such fantasy is believed, given
the impersonal slaughter of modern industrial warfare. I saw
high explosives fired from huge distances in the Gulf War
reduce battalions of Iraqis to scattered corpses. Iraqi soldiers
were nothing more on the screens of sophisticated artillery
pieces than little dots scurrying around like ants—that is, until
they were blasted away. Bombers dumped tons of iron fragmentation bombs on them. Our tanks, which could outdistance
their Soviet-built counterparts, blew Iraqi armored units to a
standstill. Helicopters hovered above units like angels of death
in the sky. Here there was no pillage, no warlords, no collapse of
unit discipline, but the cold and brutal efficiency of industrial

warfare waged by well-trained and highly organized professional soldiers. It was a potent reminder why most European states and America live in such opulence and determine the fate of so many others. We equip and train the most efficient killers on the planet.

I drove my Land Rover down the highway north of Kuwait City a day or two following the liberation. For seven miles there was a line of burned-out cars, trucks, and tanks, many with the charred remains of Iraqi soldiers inside. The retreating convoy had been strafed by F-16 fighter jets. Some of the 1,500 vehicles were turned in an apparent attempt to flee back towards the city. They had caused a massive traffic jam. The only escape was on foot. The air was pungent with the stench of rotting bodies. In the cab of one truck were the blackened remains of a soldier curled up over the steering wheel. Bits of legs and arms stuck out in strange positions from the burned metal. Cobra helicopters hovered noisily above me.

Millions of men watched mass death in World War I. They understood the power of modern weaponry. They struggled after the war to fit back into European society. But the world, from World War I onward, had changed. Writers such as Joseph Roth or Ernst Jünger understood that we had entered into a new era, one in which we would always flirt with death and self-destruction on a hitherto unknown scale. Redemption, since World War I, comes to us only through apocalypse. The old world order, captured in works such as the 1937 French film *Grand Illusion*, died with the end of the spontaneous 1914 Christmas truce. The accepted principles of humanity, the archaic code of the warrior, became quaint and obsolete. The technological and depersonalized levels of organized killing begun in World War I have defined warfare ever since.

"Having torn out of its midst millions upon millions of its

own people, inverted and perverted every value and belief, exploited to the limit humanity's willingness to sacrifice itself for a higher cause in order to perpetuate the most heinous crimes, the war has left us with a legacy of gaping absences of memory and identity, culture and biography," wrote the Israeli historian Omer Bartov.[1]

But even in the new age of warfare we cling to the outdated notion of the single hero able to carry out daring feats of courage on the battlefield. Such heroism is about as relevant as mounting bayonet or cavalry charges. But peddling the myth of heroism is essential, maybe even more so now, to entice soldiers into war. Men in modern warfare are in service to technology. Many combat veterans never actually see the people they are firing at nor those firing at them, and this is true even in low-intensity insurgencies.

To be sure, soldiers who kill innocents pay a tremendous personal emotional and spiritual price. But within the universe of total war, equipped with weapons that can kill hundreds or thousands of people in seconds, soldiers only have time to reflect later. By then these soldiers often have been discarded, left as broken men in a civilian society that does not understand them and does not want to understand them. Once violence on this scale is unleashed it usually continues to plague societies. The civil war in El Salvador, as in many African states, has left the country beset by violent crime and dominated by armed militias and gangs. We are hostage to a vast and powerful military-industrial complex that exports more weapons than all other nations combined.

I knew a Muslim soldier, a father, who fought on the front lines around Sarajveo. His unit, in one of the rare attempts to take back a few streets controlled by the Serbs, pushed across

Serb lines. They did not get very far. The fighting was intense. As he moved down the street he heard a door swing open. He fired a burst from his AK-47 assault rifle. A twelve-year-old girl dropped dead. He saw in the body of the unknown girl lying prostrate in front of him the image of his own twelve-year-old daughter. He broke down. He had to be helped back to the city. He was lost for the rest of the war, shuttered inside his apartment, nervous, morose, and broken. This experience is far more typical of warfare than the Rambo heroics we are fed by the state and the entertainment industry. The cost of killing is all the more bitter because of the deep disillusionment that war usually brings.

It takes little in wartime to turn ordinary men into killers. Most give themselves willingly to the seduction of unlimited power to destroy and all feel the heavy weight of peer pressure. Few, once in battle, can find the strength to resist.

The German veteran of World War I Erich Maria Remarque, in *All Quiet on the Western Front*, wrote of the narcotic of war that quickly transformed men into beasts. He knew the ecstatic high of violence and the debilitating mental and physical destruction that comes with prolonged exposure to war's addiction.

"We run on," he wrote, "overwhelmed by this wave that bears us along, that fills us with ferocity, turns us into thugs, into murderers, into God knows what devils; this wave that multiplies our strength with fear and madness and greed of life, seeking and fighting for nothing but our deliverance."[2]

The historian Christopher Browning noted the willingness to kill in *Ordinary Men,* his study of Reserve Police Battalion 101 in Poland during World War II. The battalion was ordered to shoot 1,800 Jews in the Polish village of Jozefow in a day-long action. The men in the unit had to round up the Jews, march

them into the forest, and one by one order them to lie down in
a row. The victims, including women, infants, children, and the
elderly, were shot dead at close range.

The battalion was ordered to do the killing on the morning
of July 12, 1942. They were offered the option to refuse, an
option only about a dozen men took, although more asked to
be relieved once the killing began. Those who did not want to
continue, Browning says, were disgusted rather than plagued by
conscience. When the men returned to the barracks they "were
depressed, angered, embittered and shaken."[3] They drank heavily. They were told not to talk about the event, "but they needed
no encouragement in that direction."[4]

In the massacres that followed, the killings by the battalion
became less personal. The executioners drank now, as executioners did in Bosnia and Kosova, before their work. Having
killed once, Browning wrote, the men "did not experience such
a traumatic shock the second time."[5] It no longer became hard
to find volunteers, and the killing escalated. In a massacre that
became known as the "Harvest Festival" some 500 men killed
30,500 Jewish inhabitants of the work camps Trawniki, Poniatowa, and Majdanek in a matter of days.

The men in the battalion, aged thirty-seven to forty-two,
were not elite troops. They were not highly trained nor had they
been specially picked for the job. They were of middle- or
lower-class origin. And their behavior, given the savagery of
modern warfare, has been widely replicated. There are no
shortages of former soldiers and militiamen in Algeria, Argentina, Rwanda, El Salvador, Iraq, or Bosnia who have done the
same. There are always people willing to commit unspeakable
human atrocity in exchange for a little power and privilege.

The task of carrying out violence, of killing, leads to perversion. The seductiveness of violence, the fascination with the grotesque—the Bible calls it "the lust of the eye"—the god-like empowerment over other human lives and the drug of war combine, like the ecstasy of erotic love, to let our senses command our bodies. Killing unleashes within us dark undercurrents that see us desecrate and whip ourselves into greater orgies of destruction. The dead, treated with respect in peacetime, are abused in wartime. They become pieces of performance art. Corpses were impaled in Bosnia on the sides of barn doors, decapitated, or draped like discarded clothing over fences. They were dumped into rivers, burned alive in homes, herded into warehouses and shot and mutilated, or left on roadsides. Children could pass them on the street, gape at them and walk on.

There are few anti-war movies or novels that successfully portray war, for amidst the horror is also the seduction of the machine of war, all-powerful, all-absorbing. Most of the effective anti-war novels—such as Elsa Morante's *History: A Novel*— focus on the effects of war, on those who bear the brunt of war's brutality. Morante, who spent a year hiding among remote farming villages south of Rome at the end of World War II, set out to write a novel about those whom history ignores and forgets. Her world was that of victims. It is was a world not of heroics and glory but of rape, bombing raids, crime, cattle cars filled with human beings being taken to slaughter, soldiers dying of frostbite, and the fear of secret police and the military. In her world, no one had control.[6]

Pity is often banished in war. And the desperate struggle of the weak to survive, so fundamental to what war is about, rarely seems able to achieve the centrality it deserves.

Following the Gulf War, during the Shiite uprising in Basra,

I was captured by the Iraqi Republican Guard. The soldiers threw me onto the floor in the back of my jeep, pressed the barrel of an AK–47 assault rifle to my forehead, and drove into the desert. They stripped me of my M–65 jacket, useful to them in the cold desert night. In the pocket were three books: *Antony and Cleopatra*, *The Iliad*, and Joseph Conrad's *Outcast of the Islands*. I was bereft of reading material, left to cling to those lines of Shakespeare and poems by W. H. Auden, T. S. Eliot, and William Butler Yeats I had memorized in my youth. Over and over during my captivity I pieced them back together, phrase by phrase, line by line, resurrecting passages uttered over a decade before as a student actor, along with poems that constant repetition had made a part of me.

In the misery of the fighting—our small convoy was heavily ambushed on the second day, sixty miles north of Basra—and gnawing uncertainty, these passages at once consoled, pained, and protected me, often from myself.

One afternoon, in the driving rain, I was seated in a Pajero jeep, hot-wired and stolen by my Iraqi captors during the frantic flight from Kuwait City. We had stopped to fill our canteens from muddy puddles. All of the water purification plants had been bombed. The muck and rainwater had already turned my own guts inside out. As I made my way to the brackish pools I noticed a woman and two small children scooping up their hands to drink. I knew what such foul water would do to these innocents and in the cold downpour recited Auden's "Epitaph on a Tyrant" as a kind of quiet, unintelligible blessing:

> Perfection, of a kind, was what he was after,
> And the poetry he invented was easy to understand;
> He knew human folly like the back of his hand,
> And was greatly interested in armies and fleets;

When he laughed, respectable senators burst with laughter,
And when he cried the little children died in the streets.[7]

As the days wore on, sick, with little to eat, constantly under fire (at one point for sixteen hours), I began to fully appreciate the misery, pathos, and courage of professional soldiership.

One night, sheltering from rebel snipers behind an armored personnel carrier, some of my guards and I shared one can of peas and a jar of peach jam. Each of us got a few peas dropped into our dirt-caked palms and one plastic spoonful of jam. It was all any of us ate that day.

All great works of art find their full force in those moments when the conventions of the world are stripped away and confront our weakness, vulnerability, and mortality. For learning, in the end, meant little to writers like Shakespeare unless it translated into human experience.

"As long as reading is for us the instigator whose magic keys have opened the door to those dwelling-places deep within us that we would not have known how to enter, its role in our lives is salutary," Proust wrote. "It becomes dangerous, on the other hand, when, instead of awakening us to the personal life of the mind, reading tends to take its place."[8]

But when we write about warfare the prurient fascination usually rises up to defeat the message. The successful anti-war novels and films are those, like Elsa Morante's, that eschew battle scenes and focus on the heartbreak of violence and slaughter. It no doubt helped that Elsa Morante was a woman, less able to identify with and be seduced by war and the allure of violence. But in most wars women, if not engaged in the fighting, stand on the sidelines to cheer their men onward. Few are immune.

One of the most widely read works of Holocaust literature

in Israel is not the quiet, meditative reflections of writers such
as Primo Levi, who struggled to understand the capacity for evil
in all of us, but Ka'Tzetnik's six autobiographic volumes, published in the 1950s. What troubles the Israeli historian Omer
Bartov is that what "makes them so gripping: namely, their
obsession with violence and perversity."[9]

The main character of Ka'Tzetnik's sextet, *House of Dolls*, is a
young woman who is made into a prostitute for German soldiers.[10] The books were reissued in 1994 and handed out by the
Israeli Ministry of Education as recommended reading on the
Holocaust in high schools.

"Nothing could be a greater taboo than deriving sexual
pleasure from the fact that the central sites for these actions
were the concentration camps," Bartov writes. "Nothing could
be a greater taboo than deriving sexual pleasure from pornography in the context of the Holocaust; hence nothing could be
as exciting. That Israeli youth learned about sex and perversity,
and derived sexual gratification, from books describing the
manner in which Nazis tortured Jews, is all the more disturbing,
considering that we are speaking about a society whose population consisted of a large proportion of Holocaust survivors
and their offspring."[11]

The effects on society can only be guessed, he argues, but
there is little doubt that those subsequent generations "have not
been wholly liberated from this pernicious trap, whereby they
must have more of the violent and ruthless attributes associated
with the perpetrators so as not to become their victims (whom
on some level of consciousness they are still defending)."[12]

The conflict between the Israelis and the Palestinians has left
each side embracing death. They each believe that they are the
only real victims. There is a celebration of suicidal martyrdom
and justification of the tit-for-tat killing of noncombatants.

On a recent trip to the region, I visited the Khan Younis refugee camp in the Gaza Strip. As the searing afternoon heat and swirling eddies of dust enveloped the camp, I sought cover, slumping under the shade of a palm-roofed hut on the edge of the dunes. I was momentarily defeated by the grit that covered my face and hair, the jostling crowds, the stench of the open sewers and rotting garbage.

Barefoot boys, clutching ragged soccer balls and kites made out of scraps of paper, squatted a few feet away under scrub trees. Men, in flowing white or gray *galabias*—homespun robes—smoked cigarettes outside their doorways. They fingered prayer beads and spoke in hushed tones as they boiled tea or coffee on sooty coals in small iron braziers in the shade of the eaves. Two emaciated donkeys, their ribs outlined on their flanks, were tethered to wooden carts with rubber wheels.

It was still. The camp waited, as if holding its breath. And then, out of the dry furnace air a disembodied voice crackled over a loudspeaker from the Israeli side of the camp's perimeter fence.

"Come on, dogs," the voice boomed in Arabic. "Where are all the dogs of Khan Younis? Come! Come!"

I stood up and walked outside the hut. The invective spewed out in a bitter torrent. "Son of a bitch!" "Son of a whore!" "Your mother's cunt!"

The boys darted in small packs up the sloping dunes to the electric fence that separated the camp from the Jewish settlement abutting it. They lobbed rocks towards a jeep, mounted with a loudspeaker and protected by bulletproof armor plates and metal grating, that sat parked on the top of a hill known as Gani Tal. The soldier inside the jeep ridiculed and derided them. Three ambulances—which had pulled up in anticipation of what was to come—lined the road below the dunes.

There was the boom of a percussion grenade. The boys, most no more than ten or eleven years old, scattered, running clumsily through the heavy sand. They descended out of sight behind the dune in front of me. There were no sounds of gunfire. The soldiers shot with silencers. The bullets from M–16 rifles, unseen by me, tumbled end-over-end through their slight bodies. I would see the destruction, the way their stomachs were ripped out, the gaping holes in their limbs and torsos, later in the hospital.

I had seen children shot in other conflicts I have covered—death squads gunned them down in El Salvador and Guatemala, mothers with infants were lined up and massacred in Algeria, and Serb snipers put children in their sights and watched them crumple onto the pavement in Sarajevo—but I had never watched soldiers entice children like mice into a trap and murder them for sport.

All wars feed off martyrs, the mention of the dead instantly shutting down all arguments for compromise or tolerance for the other. It is the dead who rule. They speak from beyond the grave urging a nation onward to revenge.

Murad Abdel Rahman, thirty-seven, stared vacantly in front of him, mechanically standing up from one in a long line of purple plastic chairs placed in the street to shake the hands of mourners who greeted him. Posters of his dead eleven-year-old son Ali Murad adorned the walls. Black flags of mourning, green banners with Koranic verses, and signs from Palestinian factions surrounded the white canopy that had been spread out over the rutted, dirt street.

Men, seated in the rows, inclined their heads together to talk. A truck, manned by militants, sat parked. The bearded Islamists in white robes waited to turn the funeral into a piece of propaganda, with the boy's body as a prop.

The father said he had had no part in the decorations, which included posters of Saddam Hussein. He seemed indifferent to the elaborate display. He spoke slowly, his puffy eyes and uncomprehending gaze giving the lie to the rhetoric of sacrifice and glory that the militants would have the world believe marks such occasions.

"This is what I worked so hard to prevent," he said, his voice hoarse and low. "I took Ali with me every day to my restaurant at 6:00 in the morning on al-Bahar Street. I made him promise he would not go to the dunes to throw rocks. Yesterday he asked to go home at 3:00. He said he had to study for the make-up sessions they are holding for all the school closings this year. A half-hour after he left, people came running to tell me he was shot in the leg. I ran through the streets to the hospital. They would not let me in. They said he would be discharged soon. They told me he was OK. I forced my way inside and saw him lying in the corridor dead with a bullet hole in his heart. I fainted."

Several small boys stood glumly at the edge of the tent. They said they had called to Ali as he walked home to join them on the dunes.

"We all threw rocks," said ten-year-old Ahmed Moharb. "Over the loudspeaker the soldier told us to come to the fence to get chocolate and money. Then they cursed us. Then they fired a grenade. We started to run. They shot Ali in the back. I won't go again. I am afraid."

On the Sunday afternoon I witnessed, the Israelis shot four boys or young men, one of whom would die from his wounds the next day.

The residents in the camp, who had time to study the taunting, insisted that the Arabic accent over the loudspeakers was Lebanese. They believed that mercenaries from the South

Lebanese Army, once a Christian proxy army for Israel and long a bitter foe of the Palestinians, had been integrated into the Israeli force. The word in Palestinian Arabic for "shoot"—*ahousak*—was not used over the loudspeakers; in its place I heard the Lebanese word in Arabic—*atoohak*. And the camp residents said they heard Lebanese music coming from the guard posts.

Ali's small body was loaded onto the back of a truck. A cadre of young men, some bearded and in robes, others dressed in black and wearing wraparound sunglasses, marched with automatic weapons pointed in the air in three rows behind the bier. They fired rounds in the air. The crowd of several hundred, egged on by the speakers mounted on the truck, chanted Islamic and anti-Israeli slogans.

"Mothers of Jews!" they shouted. "We will make you weep like Palestinian mothers."

The funerals had added another dimension to the religious life of the camp, one that increased the reach of the Islamic militants. The truck, with a generator in the back and stacks of huge loudspeakers on the cab, lumbered ahead of the procession. It blasted out verses from the Koran, calls to die, and promises of glory for martyrs. Swarms of young boys ran along behind. The crowd passed the graphic murals and graffiti on the walls. One showed an Israeli bus, marked by a Star of David, on fire and smashed from an explosion. "Don't be merciful to those inside" read the slogan underneath. "Blow it up! Hit it!" It was signed "Hamas."

There was a frightening symbiotic relationship between the Israeli soldiers taunting children on the dunes and the Islamic militants who promoted martyrdom. It spun Gaza into an ever faster and more passionate dance with death.

Neamon Mohammed Faid, twenty, pulled up his shirt when I entered his hospital room in Nasser Hospital to reveal a flesh-colored bandage wrapped mummy-like around his torso. He had been shot below the heart. The bullet had spun out of his body in his lower back. Part of his kidney had been removed, along with much of his stomach and his spleen. His father and mother hovered over him.

"Yes, it was on the dunes," he said wearily. "The Jews were saying, 'Your mother is a bitch! Fuck your mother!' And then they would say, 'Come! Come!'"

He was with four others pitching stones at the jeep when the soldiers opened fire. He had been told moments before by the Palestinian police, who watched the daily shootings with resignation, to leave.

In Khan Younis's second hospital, al-Amal, thirteen-year-old Fahdi Abu Ammouna lay on a bed, his feet propped up on a pillow. Patches of dried blood covered the sheets. Late in the afternoon he had been throwing rocks at the jeeps. He said some of the rocks hit the army jeep, a claim I doubted.

"The soldier said over the loudspeaker that those who wanted to live should run," he said, "and those who wanted to die should stay. Then they swore at us. They said everyone who lives in Khan Younis is a dog. I started to run. I was shot. I never heard any shots. The bullet went through both of my legs. I crawled to the ambulance. It was the first time I went."

His mother, seated next to him and wearing a black head-scarf, slowly shook her head.

"He goes every day," she said softly. "I sent my older son to bring him home. And he was not home five minutes before he went back. I tell the boys it is useless, throwing stones and becoming a martyr will not make the Israelis leave. My sister has lost a son. My brother has lost a son. One of my uncles was killed and a cousin is dead. I tell them to look at the history of our struggle. All these deaths achieve nothing."

She began to talk about the first uprising, or *intifada*, that had led to the Oslo peace agreement. Her husband, Samir, who stood in a blue shirt, white pants, and sandals at the end of the bed, was at the time a prisoner in Israel. One morning Israeli soldiers burst into her two-room house in the refugee camp while she was baking bread. Fahdi was six months old. They turned the place upside down and threw Fahdi on the stove. He was severely burned. As she spoke she gently placed her fingers on her son's small arm, hooked up to an intravenous tube.

"The children are fed this hatred for the Jews from the day they are born," she said. "All they hear is that we have to get rid of the Jewish enemy. The call to fight is pumped out over the radio and the television. The trucks go through the streets of the camp praising the new martyrs and calling for more. The posters of the martyrs are everywhere. And the kids see their fathers, helpless against the Israelis, out of work, and admire the militants with guns. They want to fight."

The violent breakup of Yugoslavia, which was preceded by economic collapse, began in 1991. It was the same year that the government decided to permit hard-core sex films to be broadcast on public stations and that the first locally made pornographic film was produced. While the old Communist Yugoslavia did not censor love scenes in its state-run film industry, it condemned pornography as the exploitation of women and banned its production. The first graphic pictures of mutilated and dead from the war, along with the racial diatribes against Muslims and Croats, hit the airwaves at the same time Yugoslavs were allowed to watch porno films. The war was, like the sex films, about the lifting of taboos, about new forms of entertainment to mask the economic and political collapse of Yugoslavia. War and sex were the stimulants to divert a society that was collapsing.

The world, as it is in war, had been turned upside down. Those who had worked hard all their lives, put their meager savings into banks, and struggled to live on pensions or salaries, lost everything. The unscrupulous, who had massive debts, never had to repay them, lived off the black market or crime, used force to get what they wanted, and became fabulously rich and powerful. The moral universe disintegrated. There was a new code.

The criminal class, many of whom made their fortunes by plundering the possessions of ethnic Croats and Muslims who were expelled from their homes or killed in Bosnia during the war, had rented apartments where they sold stolen clothes from Italy. Huge outdoor fairs were held where you could buy stolen cars complete with fake registrations. Drugs, protection rackets, prostitution, not to speak of duty-free cigarettes (smuggled into Italy with speedboats from the Montenegrin coast), became the country's major businesses as state-run factories folded. In Belgrade, at the war's height, there were seventy escort services, three adult cinemas, and twenty pornographic magazines. After midnight the public television channels ran hard-core porno films.

Hedonism and perversion spiraled out of control as inflation ate away at the local currency. Those who had worked hard all their lives were now reviled as dupes and fools. They haunted the soup kitchens. The loyalty they had expressed to the state or to the institutions they worked for had left them beggars. They held worthless war bonds. They collected pensions, when they

were paid, that amounted to a few dollars. They sold rugs, tea
sets, china, paintings, anything they could dig out of their apartments at huge open-air flea markets. Their children, no matter
how well educated, worked in menial jobs abroad so they could
mail back enough for their parents to buy food. Distraught
teachers said they struggled to cope with children as young as
eleven who had been exposed to scenes of graphic sado-
masochism on television and copied the sexual acts they witnessed. Domestic violence, often by men who were out of
work or had not received their small salaries for months, was
widespread.

The ancient Greeks linked war and love. Aphrodite, the god-
dess of love and the wife of Hephaestos, the lame blacksmith
who forged the weapons and armor for the gods, became the
mistress of Ares, the god of war. It was an illicit affair. Ares,
impetuous, quarrelsome, and often drunk, was hated among the
gods. He loved battle for its own sake. His sister, Eris, spread
rumor and jealousy to whip up the winds of war. Ares never
favored one city or party against another. He frequently
switched loyalties, abandoning those he had once helped. He
delighted only in slaughter. It was only Eris and Aphrodite, who
had a perverse passion for him, who loved him. Hades honored
him because of the legions of slain young men he dispatched to
the underworld.

There is in wartime a nearly universal preoccupation with
sexual liaisons. There is a kind of breathless abandon in
wartime, and those who in peacetime would lead conservative
and sheltered lives give themselves over to wanton carnal relationships. Men, and especially soldiers, are preoccupied with little else. With power reduced to such a raw level and the
currency of life and death cheap, eroticism races through all
relationships. There is in these encounters a frenetic lust that

seeks, on some level, to replicate or augment the drug of war. It is certainly not about love, indeed love itself in wartime is hard to sustain or establish.

Casual encounters are charged with a raw, high-voltage sexual energy that smacks of the self-destructive lust of war itself. The erotic in war is like the rush of battle. It overwhelms the participants. Women who might not otherwise be hailed as beauties are endowed with the charms of Helen. Men endowed with little more than the power to kill are lionized and desired. Bodies, just as they lie scattered and immobile a few hundred yards away, become tools, objects to an end. The fleeting sexual encounters, intense, overpowering, and largely anonymous, deflate with tremendous speed and leave behind guilt, even disgust, and a void that expands into a swamp of loneliness. Stay long enough in war and real love, real tenderness and connection, becomes nearly impossible. Sex in war is another variant of the drug of war.

"If we are honest," the philosopher J. Glenn Gray wrote in *The Warriors: Reflections on Men in Battle,* "most of us who were civilian soldiers in recent wars will confess that we spent incomparably more time in the service of Eros during our military careers than ever before or again in our lives. When we were in uniform almost any girl who was faintly attractive had an erotic appeal for us. For their part, millions of women find a strong sexual attraction in the military uniform, particularly in time of war."[13]

The Polish journalist Ryszard Kapuściński in *Another Day of Life,* his book about the Angolan civil war, told of a twenty-year-old rebel soldier named Carlotta, a member of the Popular Movement for the Liberation of Angola (MPLA), the insurgent group backed by the Soviet Union and Cuba. A legendary fighter—and Kapuściński correctly pointed out that girls make much better child soldiers than boys because they are less prone

to hysterics—she met Kapuściński and his crew in a baggy
commando uniform with an automatic slung on her shoulder.
The men are besotted. They see her as endowed with "elusive
charm" and "great beauty."[14]

"Later when I developed the pictures of her, the only pictures of Carlotta that remained, I saw that she wasn't so beautiful. Yet nobody said as much out loud, so as not to destroy our
myth, our image of Carlotta from that October afternoon in
Benguela."[15]

"She seemed beautiful. Why?" he asked. "Because that was
the kind of mood we were in, because we needed it, because we
wanted it that way. We always create the beauty of women, and
that day we created Carlotta's beauty. I can't explain it any other
way."[16]

Those relationships that appear to extend beyond the erotic,
however, are also hollow. Many liaisons in wartime look and feel
like love, but they too have more to do with projection than
reality. Soldiers fall in love with women across a vast cultural
divide, although the linguistic barrier makes communication difficult. Here too war perverts the relationship. For in the soldier
lies absolute power, protection, and possibly escape. The
woman's appeal lies in the gentleness that is absent in war. Each
finds in the other attributes that war wipes out—tenderness or
security. But few of these liaisons last once the conflict ends.

The young are drawn to those who wield violence and
power. Why study to be a doctor or a lawyer when such academic toil was not rewarded, indeed often considered worthless? Why uphold a common morality, including hard work,
when the outcome was destitution? Why have any personal or
moral standards when these standards were irrelevant?

The killers and warlords became the object of sexual fantasy.

The paramilitary leader Zeljko Ražnatović, known as Arkan, was, according to Serbian opinion polls, one of the most desired men in the country.

War turned Belgrade, along with every other capital caught up in conflict, into Caligula's Rome. There was a moral lassitude in the air, bred of hopelessness and apathy. The city's best-known gangsters, sometimes in the company of Milošević's son Marko, who threatened bar patrons with automatic weapons, cruised the streets in BMWs and Mercedes. They filled the nightclubs of Belgrade, dressed in their expensive black Italian suits and leather jackets.

At the Lotus, one such club in the downtown area of the city, pulsating music thumped through the blue haze of cigarette smoke and strobe lights. Scantily clad strippers spun around poles and leapt into two huge floodlit animal cages with men and women from the dance floor. The young couples began to peel off their shirts and simulate sex with the dancers.

"Stay a little longer," a patron shouted at me. "The simulation is just the beginning."

Under a spotlight a stripper known as Nina, a star of Belgrade's violent and frenetic nightlife, descended a spiral staircase into the mayhem. Her lover and bodyguard, a stocky woman with closely cropped hair and a German Luger tucked in her belt, followed her menacingly from the shadows. Nina moved seductively around the dance floor bathed in light. She nuzzled up to the patrons.

War breaks down long-established prohibitions against violence, destruction, and murder. And with this often comes the crumbling of sexual, social, and political norms as the domination and brutality of the battlefield is carried into personal life. Rape, mutilation, abuse, and theft are the natural outcome of a world in which force rules, in which human beings are objects. The infection is pervasive. Society in wartime becomes atomized. It rewards personal survival skills and very often leaves those with decency and compassion trampled under the rush. The pride one feels in a life devoted to the nation or to an institution or a career or an ideal is often replaced by shame and guilt. Those who have lived upright, socially productive lives are punished for their gullibility in the new social order.

The wars in the Balkans saw the rise of rape camps, places where women were kept under guard and repeatedly abused by Serbian paramilitary forces. When this became boring—for perverse sex, like killing, must constantly entail the new and bizarre—the women were mutilated and killed, reportedly on video. Women were also held in very similar conditions, and later murdered, in Argentina during the Dirty War. Sexual slaves in Argentina were used and then discarded like waste, their drugged bodies at times dumped from helicopters into the sea.

At dusk in 1995, after being smuggled through Serbian lines ringing Sarajevo in the back of a jeep belonging to the United Nations High Commissioner for Refugees, I was taken to a large school in the Bosnian town of Zenica. There Bosnian Croats, in essence Bosnians who were Catholic, were huddled after being driven from their homes by Arkan's militia. They were some of the 10,000 Muslims and Croats who had been driven from their homes in Bosanski Novi, Sanski Most, and Prijedor over the last four days in one of the periodic waves of ethnic cleansing by the Serbs. As usual, the men of fighting age had been separated and detained. About 5,000 of them were now missing.

The displaced, robbed of every possession and then driven on buses to Muslim front lines, sat on the cement floor. Children wailed. The smell of cigarette smoke and unwashed bodies mingled in the dimly lit rooms. There was no electricity. Kerosene lamps provided a dim light. As I pushed through the crowd, hastily jotting down notes, it became clear that most small villages had lost nearly all their draft-age men. The men had been gathered in town squares and beheaded, beaten to death with sledgehammers, forced to dig their own graves and to watch as their daughters or wives were raped in front of them. I was not surprised.

The women who had been raped were easy to spot: sullen, broken, and uncommunicative. Most did not want to speak of the experience. I learned about it through others. The scene was typical. I looked into the blank, uncomprehending faces of the children and despaired for the next generation.

In town after town in Bosnia and Kosova, warlords turned universes upside down. They preyed on the weak to fulfill their own carnal lusts and desires. They stole and raped, murdered and abused, and their immoral universe proved ascendant. In village after village in Bosnia, Afghanistan, or the Congo, the killers and their militias ruled. They were once embraced as saviors, shielded by the myth of war, but they had become parasites.

These militias, without the discipline or military code of the professional soldier, were frightening. They were populated with criminals, misfits, and children who drive around with car trunks full of weapons they did not know how to use. They killed and tortured according to whims and moods. They enjoyed turning us into pawns, playing with our fear, holding us as "guests" while they unleashed a lifetime of bitterness upon those around them. Once in a village in Kosova I found a local warlord from the Kosova Liberation Army with enough weapons dangling off him to outfit three or four fighters. He began barking orders to his hapless followers and when they did not heed his demands started firing into the dirt. Blood began oozing out of one of his combat boots. Determined not to let his visitors see his self-inflicted wounds he clenched his teeth and limped away. It was among the rabble, the barbarians, that I longed for the Roman cohort, the drilled and organized mass that makes up professional armies.

In wartime nearly everyone becomes an accomplice. The huge dislocations, the millions who lose homes and property, are often compensated with the property of those that were forced out. Those who had their homes taken away from them in Srebrenica by the Bosnian Serbs were later given the homes of Serbs who fled the suburbs of Sarajevo. The moral destructiveness of ethnic cleansing, like the psychic wounds of war, thus reverberates throughout a society. Families who are stripped of all they own and then handed by the state apartments that were seized from others are complicitous, whether they like it or not, in the crimes of war.

These dislocations, a large and usually deliberate part of modern warfare, destroy communal structures and weaken ties to those beyond the immediate ethnic group. They create, as Hannah Arendt pointed out, a population of stateless individuals, refugees within their own countries, who to survive must share in the loot of war.[17] The policies of communist Russia revolved around such internal displacement. Political or moral dissent is silenced, since nearly all are forced to become accomplices. It is hard to condemn ethnic cleansing when you live in someone else's home.

Following the NATO bombing of the Bosnian Serb army in the fall of 1995, I accompanied several thousand Bosnian Muslim soldiers, backed by Croatian artillery, as they drove retreating

Serbs across central Bosnia. We pushed into town after town that had been abandoned often only hours before. The front lines became mixed up and confused, with soldiers from the two armies colliding into each other in messy little gun battles. In those few weeks, an estimated 100,000 Serbs were made homeless. In one village a desperate group of Serbs gunned down a family in a car, stole the vehicle, and fled.

The village of Ključ was a depressing collection of dirty stucco dwellings surrounding a muddy central square. I was there on a rainy September afternoon when five packed buses stopped along the road. Clutching his mother's hand, five-year-old Mirnes Mujaković descended from one of the buses. The boy searched for a place to sit on the sacks of clothing piled up along the street as the cargo was unloaded.

The boy's home, friends, toys, and neighborhood had all vanished eight days earlier in a confusing blur of loud threats, pushing, beatings, tears, and a bewildering night under the trees waiting for a boat to cross the Sava River into the Croatian town of Davor. For a week he and his Muslim neighbors had lived on the bus, shuttled from Croatia to Slovenia and now to Bosnia.

Two elderly people in his group had died. He saw their bodies. And strange, gruff men had handed out brown boxes with tins of food so everyone could eat. Now, a man with a clipboard was sending families off to empty houses, many with furniture, clothes, and the bloated bodies of farm animals lying haphazardly in the yards. The houses had been hastily marked with white numbers on the doors.

"Are you OK?" asked his mother, Rasema, as she pulled a sweatshirt from a bag and slipped it over her son's head. "What do you think?"

The boy did not answer. His mother looked up and offered an explanation.

"You see," she said, her hand shaking as she dabbed a piece of pink cloth below her eyes. "You see, his father went away."

Fathers often went away in this war. And fathers often did not come back. This was not the first Balkan war fought by men with memories like those being forged in Mirnes's mind. But for now, the boy sought only the solace of his mother's arms.

Soon the man with the clipboard came to the mother and son and took them down a dirt track to a small house that had been abandoned a week earlier by a Serb family. I walked with them. The house still had dishes with scraps of food on them, and clothes were strewn on the floor. A Serbian Orthodox icon hung on a wall. And a black and white wedding picture, apparently decades old, was tacked up over the bed.

"We are going to be getting a lot of these families," said Mehmet Makić, the head of the local displaced persons office, as he and I stood in the muddy yard. "The Serbs are pushing all the remaining Muslims around Banja Luka out. They are turning the houses of the Muslims over to the new Serb refugees. We expect to get about 11,000 people soon. The Serbs are taking the Muslim homes. We are putting the Muslims in the Serb homes."

The 300 people who arrived in Ključ on the buses were from the town of Prnjavor. Most had survived more than three years without work since the Serbs took control of their part of Bosnia. Most of them also had endured harassment and beatings and had seen their young men disappear. But in the last week, in the wake of the sweeping advance of the Bosnian Army, the mood got even uglier.

"We paid for this in advance," said thirty-nine-year-old Rifet

Ramović. "The Serb soldiers stood by the buses when we left and demanded that each of us pay them 150 to 300 deutsche marks. People had to beg their neighbors for help so they could afford to get out. By the time we left, most of us had nothing."

In the small living room of her new house, not far from where I had left Mirnes and his mother, Fatima Cura looked around. She and her husband started cleaning up the unfamiliar possessions scattered on the floor.

"I feel guilty," she said. "This is someone else's home. Is this right?"

Her husband did not answer as he knelt to pick up pieces of stale bread from the floor.

"We lived twenty-seven years together in our house," she said. "We expected something like this, so we sent our children out."

Their son was in Sweden and their daughter was in a refugee camp in Germany.

"Then one night last week the Serbs came and put a paper on our door saying we no longer owned the house," she said. "The police took our keys."

Eight days later they were driven out of Prnjavor. "We were beaten and pushed by the Serbs on the way to the buses," she said. "We wondered if we would make it over the river alive into Croatia."

Mirnes and his mother, like the others on the buses, prepared that night to sleep in a new, unfamiliar bed, still made up with the bedding used by the old owner and his wife. "All we have left from our old life together is each other, a few clothes, and Mirnes' stuffed bear," she said. "That bear has become the most precious thing we own."

Later that day, I wandered the streets of the town. The collective occupation of the houses was unsettling. On Ibre Hodzic Street one light shone from the rows of windows. I knocked on the door of the apartment and found three elderly women, two Serbs and a Muslim, intently listening to the news on a radio. The three friends were struggling, as they had for more than three years, to make sense of the latest diatribes unleashed by the Serbs or the Bosnian government, the political agreements that might augur peace, and the advances and defeats that marked the ebb and flow of war.

But in the end it had come down to this: The Bosnian government had just reclaimed this town from the Serbs, and nothing had changed except the victims. As a result of this reversal of fortune, Dursuma Medić, a Muslim, would now have to watch over her two Serbian friends—who for the last three and a half years had taken care of her.

"We are three old women trying to survive a war," said Burka Bakovik, fifty-two, a Bosnian Serb. "We have been friends since childhood. None of this hatred ever touched us. We all protected Dursuma when the Serbs ruled. Now she protects us. The only news we wait for is peace, and that hasn't come yet."

As we spoke I could see Muslim soldiers busy painting over the slogans left by the Serbs on the walls outside. "Only one Bosnia, all the way to the Drina" and "Victory is our destiny," they wrote.

"The war began with words," said Seka Milanovik, sixty-eight, the other Bosnian Serb woman, "but none of us paid any attention. The extremist Serbs and Muslims were misfits, criminals and failures. But soon they held rallies and talked of racial purity, things like that. We dismissed them—until the violence began."

The women said the extremist groups soon partitioned the

city and surrounding villages into Serbian, Croatian, and Muslim areas. And each religious group turned to thugs for protection.

"I live in this apartment for two reasons," said Medić. "One is to protect my Serb friends. The other is because the Serbs burned my house down. I know what can happen when desperate people seek revenge. This is why I have to always be here."

"My daughter and two grandchildren fled with the crowds," said Bakovik. "I did not even have time to say goodbye. In a moment they were gone. Now I am alone and afraid. I do not want to be by myself in my apartment, so I stay here. We are all women; we all felt the same pangs in childbirth. We do not believe in war."

The loss of such social ties, the dependence on the state to dole out homes or property that was stolen, has an insidious effect on even the good and the just. Many must live with guilt and shame. They feel powerless. And those who have been abused and humiliated often search for those even weaker than they to vilify and blame for their predicament. In ethnic warfare this response feeds the racist cant of nationalist warlords who are with one hand thieving on unprecedented scales and with the other blaming the hapless minorities they are persecuting for the economic collapse and misery.

Displacement is one of the fundamental tools warlords and states use to prosecute a conflict. This is why ethnic leaders are so displeased when members of their minority group remain behind. The Croat and Serb and Muslim leaders in Bosnia often made secret deals to "trade" minorities, whether these families wanted to leave their homes or not. Such disruption helped fuel the conflict and sever communal ties with other groups.

"No one ever forgets a sudden depreciation of himself, for it is too painful," wrote the Bulgarian essayist Elias Canetti. "And the crowd as such never forgets its depreciation. The natural tendency afterwards is to find something which is worth even less than oneself, which one can despise as one was despised oneself. It is not enough to take over an old contempt and to maintain it at the same level. What is wanted is a dynamic process of humiliation. Something must be treated in such a way that it becomes worth less and less, as the unit of money did during the inflation. And this process must be continued until its object is reduced to a state of utter worthlessness. Then one can throw it away like paper, or repulp it."[18]

In the Bosnian town of Višegrad there is a graceful 400-year-old bridge, hewn of large off-white stones, that spans the emerald-green waters of the Drina River. The Nobel laureate Ivo Andrić centered his novel, *The Bridge on the Drina*, around the pumice structure, which he could see from his window as a boy. The book chronicles, over 350 years, the turbulent and often violent history of Višegrad and Bosnia. And as Andrić pointed out, the bridge has served as a kind of public theater in times of war and upheaval. Brigands and criminals were once impaled and executed on its stone flanks. "In all tales about personal, family or public events," Andrić wrote, "The words 'on the bridge' could always be heard."[19]

The steep wooded hillsides that plunge to the river have for centuries produced killers of appalling magnitude. During the Bosnian war the latest arose from Višegrad, Milan Lukić, along with his group of some fifteen well-armed companions. They too used the bridge as a prop to exterminate a Muslim community that had been there for centuries. Of the 14,500 Muslims who lived in Višegrad before the war, 3,000 are missing or dead.

The others are scattered around Bosnia, many living in poverty in overcrowded rooms and refugee centers.

In April 1992, when the conflict between the Bosnian Serbs and Muslims began, Milan Lukić returned from Serbia to his hometown. He gathered together a group of men, including his brother Miloš, his cousin Sredoje, and a waiter, Mitar Vasiljević. Lukić, who often went barefoot, called the group the Wolves. He set about robbing Muslim homes. The plunder quickly turned to killing. On May 18, Lukić burst into Dzemo Zukić's home and shot his wife, Bakha, in the back, according to neighbors who saw the shooting. He drove the terrified husband away in the family car, a red Volkswagen Passat. Zukić was never seen again. But the car became a harbinger of death.

The killings quickly became frenzied and common. On one occasion, Lukić used a rope to tie a man to his car and dragged him through the streets until he died. On at least two occasions, he herded large groups of Muslims into houses and set the buildings on fire. Zahra Turjacanin, her face and arms badly marred by the flames, escaped from one burning house on June 27 and raced screaming through the streets. Townspeople said she was the only survivor of seventy-one people inside. She now lives in France.

Lukić and his followers raped young girls held captive at the Vilina Vlas spa outside Višegrad. Jasna Ahmedspahić, a young woman, jumped to her death from a window of the spa after being raped for four days. Then Lukić began to drive his captives to the center of the bridge. Lukić and his men taunted their victims, who were made to stand on the walls of the bridge, before pushing them into the water and opening fire with automatic weapons. He stuffed pork in the mouths of his Muslim victims and began to beat them to death with metal rods. Bodies, bloated and discolored from beatings and knife slashes, floated down the river, getting caught in the undergrowth along the banks. In one village, Slap, twelve miles down river from Višegrad, the villagers said they buried 180 bodies that floated up on the banks. One man was found crucified on the back of a door. On another occasion they found a garbage bag filled with human heads.

Human beings become pawns, manipulated and moved around a board like chess pieces. Those struggling to survive in a morally bankrupt universe find that there are few restraints left. The perversion seeps into the behavior of those who came with noble sentiments to help. The U.N. peacekeeping troops in Bosnia, just as aid workers in Africa did, used the money and power they wielded to frequent or even run prostitution rings. The most notorious prostitution ring in Sarajevo during the war, one that catered to the peacekeepers, the foreign community, and the gangsters—all those with hard currency—was run by Ukrainian troops. They had also cornered the market on black market diesel, although they had the annoying habit of mixing it with water.

The reporters, diplomats, aid workers, and peacekeepers who travel into war zones, without the restraint of law and amid a sea of powerless people, often view themselves as entitled. They excuse immoral behavior because of the belief that the work they carry out is for a greater good—the rescue of those around them—which outweighs impropriety. They become giddy with the admiration and social status that come with being protected and privileged. Diplomats who entered Sarajevo restaurants would be applauded. They had servants, new jeeps, nice houses, and clout. And they had power unlike anything they experienced at home.

The conflict created a new elite, foreign class. It was a class that fed off of war's lawlessness and perversion. Students who spoke English in Bosnia and later Kosova were soon making in a week more money than their teachers made in a year. Many lost all desire to study. It was not worth it. They paraded the new clothes and sunglasses they could buy with their dollars. Some began to look down on those around them with the same arrogance of those they worked for.

To those who are hungry, who spend all day in cold, gutted homes with no running water, who sleep on the concrete floors of overcrowded schools set up as refugee centers, who wake up and spend hours hunting for food or standing in long lines outside aid distribution centers, a little more humiliation is not much to endure. Many longed to enter the easy world of the elite. They would pay any price.

Many of those who set out to write their memoirs, or speak about the war, do so with shame. They know war's perversion. It corrupts nearly everyone. To be greeted by an indifferent public, by people who would rather not examine, in the end, their own darkness, makes the effort Herculean. After each war some struggle to tell us how the ego and vanity of commanders leads to the waste of lives and needless death, how they too became tainted, but the witnesses are soon ignored. It is not a pleasant message.

As would be the case with war literature in the millennia following its creation, *The Iliad* describes the bonds of honor between fellow warriors. Soldiers, while describing the closeness they feel in combat as friendship, are, as J. Glenn Gray wrote, probably deceived. The battlefield, with its ecstasy of destruction, its constant temptation of self-sacrifice, its evil bliss, is more about comradeship. The closeness of a unit, and even as a reporter one enters into that fraternity once you have been together under fire, is possible only with the wolf of death banging at the door. The feeling is genuine, but without the threat of violence and death it cannot be sustained.

There are few individual relationships—the only possible way to form friendships—in war. There are not the demands on us that there are in friendships. Veterans try to regain such feelings, but they fall short. Gray wrote that the "essential difference between comradeship and friendship consists, it seems to me, in a heightened awareness of the self in friendship and in the suppression of self-awareness in comradeship."[20]

Comrades seek to lose their identities in the relationship. Friends do not. "On the contrary," Gray wrote, "friends find themselves in each other and thereby gain greater self-knowledge and self-possession. They discover in their own breasts, as a consequence of their friendship, hitherto unknown potentialities for joy and understanding."[21]

The struggle to remain friends, the struggle to explore the often painful recesses of two hearts, to reach the deepest parts of another's being, to integrate our own emotions and desires with the needs of the friend, are challenged by the collective rush of war. There are fewer demands if we join the crowd and give our emotions over to the communal crusade.

The only solace comes from simple acts of kindness. They are the tiny, flickering candles in a cavern of darkness that sustain our common humanity.

There is a spiritual collapse after war. Societies struggle with the wanton destruction not only of property and cities but of those they loved. The erosion of morality and social responsibility becomes painfully evident in war's wake. Many feel used. By then it is too late. Those who drained the society flee, are killed, or live on in luxury from the profits of modern wars. Lethargy and passivity plague the populace that no longer has the energy or the moral fortitude to reconstitute society or fight back.

In the wake of war comes a normalization that levels victims and perpetrators. Victims and survivors are an awkward reminder of the collective complicity. Their presence inspires discomfort. So too with perpetrators, whose crimes were witnessed and even supported by many. But it is often the victims who suffer the worst bouts of guilt and remorse. They feel in debt to those who died. They know that it is not the best who survive war but often the selfish, the brutal, and the violent. Those who abandoned their humanity, betrayed their neighbors and friends, turned their back on their family, stole, cheated, killed, and stomped on the weak and infirm were often those who made it out alive. Many victims grasp, in a way the perpetrators do not, the inverted moral hierarchy. They see this inversion in their own struggle to survive. They realize, in a way that the perpetrators again do not, that the difference between the oppressed and the oppressors is not absolute. And they often wonder if they could have done more to save those who were lost around them.

"I might be alive in the place of another, at the expense of another; I might have usurped, that is, in fact killed," wrote Primo Levi, himself a survivor of the Holocaust.[22]

The physical marks of war are nearly erased from Sarajevo. Sheets of glass have been fitted into the high-rises, and the shell holes have been plastered over. The newly painted trolleys rumble noisily down the tracks of the central boulevard Zmaja od Bosne, known during the war as Snipers' Alley. Water, a commodity once so precious that mothers dashed under artillery fire to reach water trucks, gushes miraculously from the taps.

But the Bosnian capital, which once held together a blend of Muslims, Croats, and Serbs and hung on to life during almost four years of siege by the Bosnian Serbs, is a cultural wasteland. The city, once an artistic center, had a cosmopolitan feeling and a rich cultural and intellectual life. Marriages and friendships that crossed the ethnic divides were commonplace. Today, the ethnic mix and the liveliness it created are gone, along with hopes that the city would rekindle its old identity—hopes that have been disregarded by all three ethnic groups.

The $5.1 billion international reconstruction effort, which has physically mended Sarajevo, masks despair. The smooth, plaster facades of apartment blocks, painted purple, red, blue, and yellow, shelter people who for the most part survive on the beneficence of others.

Beneath the physical rehabilitation, however, there is another reality. Men, out of work, often wounded physically or emotionally, waste hours in dingy coffee shops. Many of the young gather in the lines for visas outside foreign embassies. At night they meet in jammed, smoky clubs like Fis or The Stage where they can buy marijuana, Ecstasy, and heroin. An army of war invalids lies trapped indoors. Most of them lack proper medical attention, and many spend their days alone in rooms, tended by elderly parents.

"My son is inside," said an angry seventy-year-old man, who would not give his name, as he stood outside his small house fitting new aluminum drainpipes to the roof. "He can't get up. Every night my wife has to go in and turn him over so he can go to the bathroom."

Thousands in the city, where half of the work force is jobless, live in apartments that belong to someone else, someone who lives across the ethnic gulf, still a universe away in this partitioned country.

Muslims now account for more than 90 percent of the population in this city of 350,000 and with the widespread uprooting of people during and after the war, only 20 percent of the city's residents are natives of the city. The siege and the drastic changes that followed it have left behind exhaustion and bewilderment that makes routine life daunting.

"I will never again be able to live such a strong, horrible, and wonderful life," said Boba Lizdek, thirty-two, a book translator. Lizdek, a Serb who stayed in Sarajevo through the war, said that since then she had lost her focus and purpose. "It is as if I see life through pieces of a mirror that lies in fragments," she said.

The suburb of Dobrinja, built as the athletes' village for the 1984 Winter Olympics, was on the front line during the war. Sections of the town are in ruins, the walls and roofs gone, the bricks and cement chewed up by shell and bullet holes. Crude grave markers poke up at odd angles from tiny, overgrown parks and lonely patches of ground.

The renovated buildings, often next to the ruins, gleam with spotless white plaster and terra-cotta tiled roofs. The balconies hold boxes of carnations. The streets are quiet.

Murdija Badzić, fifty-one, lived in a small apartment that she and her husband rebuilt for $10,000. It was clean, with new carpets, a semicircular blue sofa in the living room, and freshly painted walls.

In June 1992, Serbian troops occupied the Dobrinja area. Badzić was herded barefoot along with her children to a prison camp, where they were held for two weeks.

The family stayed away for four years out of fear, she said, and when she returned in 1996, all the mementos of her life, her photos, the children's favorite toys, the wedding gifts, and the collection of trinkets that remind couples of the passage of time together, had vanished.

The two-room apartment held nothing of the old life. The only photo on the wall was of her eldest son, Husein, a soldier killed in the war. She and her husband lived with their remaining two sons. The young men, unemployed since the end of the war, had applied to emigrate to the United States. When Badzić spoke of the war, her youngest son, Aladin, twenty-four, abruptly left the room.

"Forgive him," she said. "He cannot talk about the war. He cannot hear about it."

During the family's detention, Aladin, who was sixteen at the time, was severely beaten by Serbian soldiers and threatened with mock executions. He did not speak for two months after he was released.

In the empty street below, Huso Kovač, fifty-eight, swung himself forward with the help of hand-held aluminum crutches. He said he disliked spending days in his apartment, which previously belonged to a Serb. He moved laboriously about the neighborhood, resting at times on the cement walls and staring at the road.

Before the war Kovač worked in Sutjeska, the national park that was the site of a major Partisan battle against the Nazis in World War II. When he spoke of the yearly anniversaries, which always saw the arrival of Tito, the dictator, his eyes lit up. It was the only time he smiled.

He lost his leg in 1993 as he and his Muslim neighbors fled under mortar fire from Sutjeska over Mount Igman to Sarajevo. His only son died in the war. His daughter's husband was also killed. She cared for their two small children alone on her widow's pension.

"I don't trust anyone anymore," he said. "This is what the war has taught me, not to trust."

He shifted his hands to grip the handles of the crutches and moved away.

5

THE HIJACKING AND
RECOVERY OF MEMORY

> Our people's lives pass, bitter and empty, among
> malicious, vengeful thoughts and periodic revolts.
> To anything else, they are insensitive and inacces-
> sible. One sometimes wonders whether the spirit of
> the majority of the Balkan peoples has not been
> forever poisoned and that, perhaps, they will never
> again be able to do anything other than suffer vio-
> lence, or inflict it.
>
> •
>
> IVO ANDRIĆ
> *Conversation with Goya: Signs, Bridges*

HAGOB H. ASADOURIAN, LIKE MANY SURVIVORS OF
genocide, communes with shadows. Some are dark and
frightening, like the shades of Turkish soldiers, who in 1915
herded him and his family from his Armenian village, leaving
him to watch his mother and four of his sisters die of typhus in
the Syrian desert. Some are sweet, revolving around the raucous

Armenian-language plays performed in the 1920s at the Yiddish
Theater at Madison Avenue and Twenty-seventh Street in Manhattan. And some are poignant, like the reunion with his sole
surviving sister, thirty-nine years after they lost each other one
night near the Dead Sea as they fled with a ragged band of
Armenian orphans from Syria to Jerusalem.

But his battle to preserve memory, the theme of his fourteen
books, did not save him or his generation from the destructive
march of time. And time, to the rapidly vanishing community
of exiled Armenians, will soon finish the work that, he says, was
begun by the Turkish army more than eighty-five years ago.

The Turks have spent most of the past century denying, with
rather startling success, the Armenian genocide of 1915, when
the Ottoman Empire, fearing a nationalist revolt, forced two
million Armenians into the Syrian desert to die. The few surviving Armenians no longer ask to go home. They do not ask
for restitution. They ask simply to have the memory of their
obliteration acknowledged. It is a moral obsession, the lonely
legacy passed onto the third and fourth generation who no
longer speak Armenian but who carry within them the seeds of
resentment that will not be quashed.

Asadourian's latest book, *The Smoldering Generation,* was, he
said, "about the inevitable loss of our culture."

"No one takes the place of those who are gone," the ninety-
seven-year-old writer said when I visited him at his home in
Tenafly, New Jersey. He was seated in front of a picture window
that looked out on a carefully groomed garden. "Your children
do not understand you in this country. You cannot blame
them."

As he spoke, his middle-aged son, John, who has used a
wheelchair since a stroke, jerked himself into position behind

his father. He listened, his head cocked slightly to one side, with a grimace.

Although there were once ten major Armenian-language daily newspapers in the United States, there is just one left, published in California. Armenian clubs have closed, social societies have been disbanded, and cultural events have dwindled. Proceedings of Armenian meetings, when they take place, are usually in English (except at church affairs, where Armenian clergy nearly always speak in Armenian first, then English). Asadourian said that he had accepted that his writing would not halt the slide to obliteration of the language. (His two sons were raised speaking Armenian; his granddaughter speaks it, but does not write it very well.)

Rather, he writes to give a voice to the 331 people with whom he trudged into Syria in September 1915. Only twenty-nine of those people survived.

"You can never really write what happened anyway," Asadourian said. "It is too ghoulish. I still fight with myself to remember it as it was. You write because you have to. It all wells up inside of you. It is like a hole that fills constantly with water and no amount of bailing will empty it. This is why I continue."

His passion, however, burns deep. He refused to halt the painful story of his deportation despite having to reach for a bottle of pills. He took a deep breath before plunging into the last bit of detail, one he had left out of the lengthy chronology.

"When it came time to bury my mother, I had to get two other small boys to help me carry her body up to a well where they were dumping the corpses," he said. "We did this so the jackals would not eat them. The stench was terrible. There were swarms of black flies buzzing over the opening. We pushed her in feet first, and the other boys, to escape the smell, ran down the hill. I stayed. I had to watch. I saw her head, as she fell, bang on one side of the well and then the other before she disappeared. At the time, I did not feel anything at all."

He stopped, visibly shaken.

"What kind of a son is that?" he asked hoarsely.

I had seen and felt it before, the awful indifference to pain, even your own. But just because he did not feel anything at the moment he released his mother's body did not mean he did not care. He had spent his whole life honoring the memory of his mother. He had suffered, in later years, that moment of her hasty burial with an awful intensity. It was a display of the curious guilt of the victims who often carry with them torments not borne by the perpetrators of the crimes.

The house fell silent. Asadourian's son, as motionless as his father during the story, flipped the electric switch on his chair and rolled out of the room.

The Turkish government still vigorously denies the event. It says that some of the Armenians killed were rebels during World War I and others were victims of the fighting and the widespread famine. The Turks claim they escorted Armenians away from the fighting for their own safety. They concede only that, because of the war, some unfortunate incidents took place.

Much of the world of the Armenians, a people first mentioned by the ancient Greeks and Persians in the 6th century B.C., has been reduced to dusty, forgotten relics in present-day Turkey. After World War I, about 25,000 Armenians came to the United States. Some of their tales survive in small American collections of Armenian literature and poetry, like the 15,000 volumes in the Zohrab Center in New York. These books lie unread by all but a few scholars. Little of the work has been translated.

The murder of more than one million Armenians in Turkey is often cited as the opening act for the genocidal campaigns that convulsed the twentieth century. Although the Allied powers condemned the Turks during World War I, there was no effort to hold them accountable for actions against the Armenians. The magnitude of the deaths and ultimate indifference may have led Hitler, on the eve of the invasion of Poland, to remind his followers, "Who still speaks of the extermination of the Armenians?"

The globe is dotted with such anonymous burial pits. They are physical reminders of justice denied. Yet they have a startling power to plague the murderers decades after the event. These atrocities—denied by the perpetrators and sanctified by the victims—leave huge chasms between peoples. They serve to create two distinct and antagonistic histories. It is only with an historical consensus that there can be reconciliation.

The return of historical memory restores a common language to the one usurped by war. The 1991 exhumations in the Katyn Forest outside Kalinin for the thousands of Polish officers executed by the Soviets in World War II permitted an historical narrative that could be accepted by the Russians and the Poles. What followed, once the truth was exposed, was the collapse of the Soviet Union. The exhumations in Cambodia, El Salvador, and the Bosnian town of Srebrenica are part of the same process. It is these exhumations, these final acknowledgments, that bring down regimes and force the restoration of history. But until such a moment happens, the wartime regimes zealously guard the lie.

During conflicts, these hidden burial places are spoken of in hushed and nervous whispers. As wars wind to a close the killers make frantic and often futile efforts to hide their crimes. They bulldoze fields where bodies are buried, as they did in Srebrenica, dynamite mine shafts where bodies were dumped, or dissolve the corpses in acid. But the industrial-scale killing of the twentieth century makes such erasure difficult. And years later there often is a dogged and methodical effort, usually by lonely dissidents, to uncover the past. These statisticians wield with index cards the fate of despots, the return of historical memory and, finally, hope.

I was taken to a school in northern Iraq days after Iraqi soldiers withdrew from the region following the Gulf War. Kurdish rebels there told me that under the concrete in the schoolyard were hundreds of bodies. They vowed to smash through the concrete and dig them up.

When I moved across central Bosnia with advancing Muslim troops after the NATO bombing campaign of 1995, survivors would enter villages even while the fighting was still dying down and point out burial sites. These sites, one sensed, were as important as their houses and personal property. Muslim officials who traveled with the army carried long handwritten lists of names of missing from the war. They began, even amid the skirmishes, to hunt for the graves that held the bodies of hundreds, perhaps thousands, of victims massacred when the Serbs swept through this area to drive out the Muslims years earlier. I drove with them to several sites. I watched as they marked them off with rope for excavation. Near a hamlet called Pudin Han, we found a cave that had human bones poking up out of a large circular depression. Another site, known as Crvena Zemlja, or "red earth," had already given up bones and clothing. In Prhovo, a vacant ruin perched on a hillside about five miles north of Ključ, a man who witnessed a mass killing led these authorities to a spot where he told us dozens of victims of the massacre lay buried.

Senad Medanović, twenty-five, a factory worker turned sol-

dier, returned to his home with us after three years. He climbed
the steep dirt track leading to his village, in the company of
three other Muslims. All were armed with AK–47 assault rifles.
The men scanned the dense undergrowth for the pockets of
Bosnian Serb soldiers who were still hiding in the rolling, pine-
forested hills.

Medanović, ignoring the periodic crackle of small-arms fire,
headed for the spot, a rough plot of land across from the gutted
remains of his two-story house. He stood there and told me
about the day the Serbs came. It was on the morning of June
1, 1992. He saw several hundred Bosnian Serb militiamen and
Yugoslav Army troops surround the village of about two dozen
houses. They herded the families into the center of the village
and opened fire with automatic weapons and heavy machine
guns. Mingled with the group were Muslim families from some
neighboring villages.

"I was over here," said he, standing near the edge of a field.
"I did not trust the Serbs, and I stood as far away as I could. I
told my family they would kill us, but they did not believe such a
thing was possible. When they started to shoot I ran. I could
hear the screams of the women and the children. I could hear
the awful noise of the guns. I ran across the field into the
woods. The Serbs around the village fired at me, but I was able
to reach the woods and hide in the undergrowth."

The Serbs spent the night drinking and looting the houses in
the village, he said, and the next morning he watched as they
searched the woods for any survivors. They rounded up about
forty men, stripped them, and marched them down the road
with their hands tied.

"I saw them shoot two at the edge of the village," he said.
"When I was captured six days later, on the run, and taken to

the Manjača concentration camp, I found nine of the forty who had survived, including one of my brothers. The others had been murdered. The survivors told me where the mass grave was. They told me my mother, and the rest of my family, were dead. We ten are all that remain from Prhovo."

Lanky and bearded, he climbed through the window of his former house and began to search among the blackened debris. He pulled out the tattered remains of a blue shirt and hugged it.

"This belonged to one of my nephews," he said, "one of the twins."

The bloody campaign by the Bosnian Serbs to rid this part of Bosnia of Muslims, who had lived here for more than 500 years, left survivors vowing to take revenge. Medanović said he would hunt down the two Serbian commanders whom he said led the massacre.

"The two beasts who directed this slaughter were Marko Adamović and Ratko Buvac," he said. "We all knew the Serbian nationalists from Ključ before they came to kill us. We heard them preach hatred against the Muslims. And we saw them as they entered the village that morning to direct the killings."

But tempering his hatred was his relief at the chance to at least honor the memories of the family he lost, his mother, five of his six brothers, his only sister, his uncle, and two nephews.

He stood over the field that held the bodies.

"Here is where my family and my village lie now," he said. "And God has permitted me to survive to come back and give them a decent burial."

It was dusk and we were a small group, lightly armed, on a hill that still had bands of fleeing Serb soldiers. We started down the dirt track. But when Medanović saw the shattered black granite tombs of his father and grandfather, who died before

the war, he knelt. He tried to arrange the pieces of the headstones to spell out their names once again.

"Can you read their names now?" he asked me. "Can you see
who was buried here?"

Wartime leaders, who know that exposing the murders
means the loss of their own legitimacy and discrediting of the
myth, harass and denounce the Cassandras who cry out for justice and historical accountability. The effort to give a name to
the victims and killers begins a collective act of repentance, a
national catharsis. The process, as seen in South Africa's Truth
and Reconciliation Commission, is the only escape. And while
justice is not always done—in South Africa the full admission of
crimes saw killers granted an amnesty—dignity, identity, and
most important, memory are returned. This, for many families,
is enough.

Only rarely do some of the top leaders end up in jail. Usually
those who pay the price—if there is one to be paid—are the
lowly gunmen who are tried and imprisoned to take the heat off
of their commanders. Most of those who carry out war crimes,
however, are never punished. They are allowed to fade away in
retirement, whispered about but never finally condemned. There
are powerful institutions, security services, armed forces, and
ministries of the interior, that may permit some facts to be
exposed but will rarely permit a society to ascribe any responsibility to the actual state organs that directed the killings. Yet
despite the inevitable injustice of any investigation, the power
it has to restore memory is vital for recovery from war.

"The struggle of man against power," wrote the novelist
Milan Kundera, "is the struggle of memory against forgetting."[1]

I walked one afternoon over the cavernous pits and gorges
scattered throughout the hills above the Italian port city of Trieste. These hold dark secrets from the twilight days of World

War II, secrets that still disturb Italy and its Balkan neighbors.
The pits, covered with tons of debris, are believed to contain
hundreds, perhaps thousands, of corpses. The bodies are those
of Italians and Yugoslavs who opposed the Yugoslav Communist takeover of the city in May 1945, along with scores of captured German soldiers. But attempts to investigate, even after
five decades, have gone nowhere.

Trieste is a port city that for most of the twentieth century
sat on the edge of the volcanic upheavals that tore apart the
European monarchies and made up the front lines of the Cold
War. It changed hands a half dozen times. James Joyce and
Rainer Maria Rilke lived here. The notorious commander in the
Spanish civil war, Commandante Carlos, came from Trieste, as
did the writer Italo Svevo. The city, seedy, neglected, is no
longer of any geopolitical significance. But the scars of its past
infect the air. Old men with sad stories gather every afternoon
in the seaside coffee shops.

In May 1945, Tito's Communist Partisans in Yugoslavia, after
a bitter guerrilla war against the German and Croatian fascists,
pursued the retreating forces toward Italy. The Partisan army
seized the Istrian Peninsula, in the northern Adriatic, and raced
on toward Trieste. The Partisans' forty-day occupation of Trieste and their hunt for German soldiers, Italian and Croatian
fascists, and suspected opponents of Communism nearly led to
a clash with Allied forces. In June, the Yugoslavs withdrew to
the hinterlands, but Trieste was not handed back to Italy until
1954. Today the city has 230,000 people, many of them from
Italian families who were forced out of Yugoslavia after the war.

Trieste in May 1945 was a chaotic city filled with cornered
German, Croatian, and Italian soldiers who continued to fight
despite Italy's capitulation in 1943. Scores of accused fascists
were paraded daily by the Partisans through the cobblestone

streets to Yugoslav military courts. Most were quickly condemned to death and shot, or thrown alive into gorges and pits
around the city.

Many Slovenes in Trieste at the time, ecstatic at the downfall
of Italian fascism, greeted the Partisans as liberators and
assisted in manhunts by the Yugoslav secret police. During the
occupation, at least 3,500 residents of Trieste, along with an
unknown number of Yugoslavs, Italians, and Germans who
were trapped in the city, were shot and thrown into the fissures,
or *foibe*, of the Carso mountain range, the eastern end of the
Italian Alps. Thousands more were deported, and many perished in Yugoslav detention camps.

A secret British-American intelligence report of September
1945, made public just a few years ago, is filled with accounts by
witnesses to partisan atrocities. A Roman Catholic priest, Don
Sceck, told the investigators that on May 2, 1945, a group of 150
fascists were swiftly sentenced and then mowed down by partisan troops with machine guns in Basovizza, a small Slovene-
speaking village just outside Trieste. The corpses, he said, were
thrown into the huge Basovizza caverns, now a memorial to the
victims. The next day he saw a group of about 250 prisoners at
the mouth of the Basovizza pit.

"These persons were questioned and tried in the presence of
all the populace, who accused them," the priest said in the
report. "As soon as one of them was questioned, four or five
women rushed up to them and accused them of having murdered or tortured one of their relatives, or of having burned
down their homes. The accused persons were butted and
struck, and always admitted the crimes ascribed to them."

In war, death is often anonymous. When it is impossible to
find out whether someone is dead or alive there is no closure,
no way to fix the end of a life with a time and a place. The

atrocity is compounded by the atrocity committed against memory. The lack of closure tortures and deforms those who wait for an answer. This sacrilege against memory gnaws at survivors. Regimes use murder and anonymous death to keep their citizens off balance, agitated, and disturbed. It fuels war's collective insanity. But it must be rectified if healing is to take place.

The misery often spawns predators. Families in Iraq pay huge bribes to find out whether relatives are dead or alive. Occultists promise to put people in touch with those who are missing, often stringing families along for weeks as they pass on supposed messages from prisons, mines, or work camps. I have sat in on such encounters in El Salvador and Algeria, watching as tearful women struggle to believe that they are communicating with missing sons or husbands. These women, repeatedly rebuffed by the security forces and government bureaucrats, find comfort in mediums, although most realize after a few months that they have been had. Memory, even manufactured memory, seems better for a while than silence. Hope, however farfetched, is prolonged. But the ache over the missing eventually evolves into a single need—the recovery of the body.

A film by the French director Bertrand Tavernier, *Life and Nothing But* (1989), captured this need, with two women combing the remains of an old battlefield, looking for the same corpse. The Chilean writer Ariel Dorfman touched on the same theme in his novel *Widows*. He wrote of a village in Greece during World War II where a body is discovered washed up on a riverbank. It is battered beyond recognition. An elderly peasant woman, who has lost her two sons, her husband, and her father, claims the body and refuses to give it to the authorities. Soon thirty-seven women who have lost relatives also claim the body, setting off a struggle over the corpse and the military dictatorship that thought it could erase history.[2]

The violence of war is random. It does not make sense. And many of those who struggle with loss also struggle with the knowledge that the loss was futile and unnecessary. This leaves psychological wounds among survivors as well as veterans. Many of the soldiers who fought in Vietnam must grapple with the realization that there was no higher purpose to the war, that the sacrifice was a waste. It is easier to believe the myth that makes such loss noble and necessary, despite the glaring contradictions.

In Argentina in the 1970s and 1980s most of the 20,000 "disappeared" in the Dirty War were not armed radicals but labor leaders, community organizers, leftist intellectuals, and student organizers. Few of them had any connection to guerrilla campaigns. Indeed, by the time of the 1976 Argentine coup the armed guerrilla movements, such as the Montoneros, had largely been wiped out. They had never been a threat to the state, but the abductions spawned a vast underground prison system that soon existed mostly to extort money from the victims' families.

In Marguerite Feitlowitz's *The Lexicon of Terror*, she writes of the experiences of one Argentine prisoner, a physicist named Mario Villani.[3] The collapse of the moral universe of the torturers is displayed when, in between torture sessions, the guards take Villani and a few pregnant women prisoners to an amusement park. They make them ride the kiddie train. A guard, whose nom de guerre is Blood, brings his six- or seven-year-old daughter into the camp to meet Villani. Villani runs into one of his principal torturers a few years later, a man known in the camps as Julian the Turk. Julian recommends that Villani go see another of his former prisoners to ask for a job.

Julian the Turk was free because military pressure put a stop to the post-junta trials. After the convictions of five of the nine commanders, repeated military uprisings persuaded President Raúl Alfonsin to propose laws setting a time limit on prosecutions and exempting all men below a certain rank from any prosecution. The Argentine congress quickly passed both laws. Alfonsin's successor, Carlos Saúl Menem, then pardoned the commanders who had been convicted, along with several dozen other prisoners. In neighboring Chile, General Augusto Pinochet sits protected in his lifetime Senate seat, immune from prosecution.

Until the lie is discredited and history is recovered, societies continue to speak in euphemisms. They use words to mask reality. It was the Argentine junta that gave us words like *desaparecido* (disappeared person, almost always a euphemism for someone who had been secretly executed), *chupado* (sucked up, or kidnapped) and *trasladar* (transfer, a euphemism for take away to be killed). Terms like these blunt the campaign of terror. On the battlefield it is much the same. Soldiers get "waxed" rather than killed. Victims who are burned to death are "toasted."

The Soviet writer Vasily Grossman's novel *Life and Fate* was about the fight to remember and defeat anonymous death. The mother in the novel, based on Grossman's own mother, was massacred along with 30,000 other people, most of them Jews, by the Nazis in his native town of Berdichev in Ukraine during World War II. In one chapter he wrote the letter he believed his mother would have written to him before she was executed, a final message to her only child. The letter revealed the gaping wound that Grossman, who was unable to communicate with his mother before her execution, must have endured.

Describing neighbors who, given license by the Nazi occupiers, have turned her into a pariah, the mother wrote dispassionately. "I really don't know which is worse," she said, "gloating spite, or these pitying glances like people cast at a mangy, half-dead cat."

Then she wrote: "But now I've seen that the people who shout most loudly about delivering Russia from the Jews are the very ones who cringe like lackeys before the Germans, ready to betray their country for 30 pieces of German silver. And strange people from the outskirts of town seize our rooms, our blankets, our clothes. It must have been people like them who killed doctors at the time of the cholera riots. And then there are people whose souls have just withered, people who are ready to go along with anything evil—anything so as not to be suspected of disagreeing with whoever's in power."[4]

When *Life and Fate* was completed in 1960, four years before Grossman died, the K.G.B. seized the manuscript. He was never allowed to publish again.

It is rare that we are able to expose the crimes of a regime while it is still in power. This is usually part of the long recovery process once the killers have been ousted. But in Iraq we had the unique opportunity to peer inside the guts of Saddam Hussein's regime and confront a regime with its crimes.

After the Gulf War, the Kurds in northern Iraq were given a safe area that was under the protection of NATO warplanes. With the Iraqi military gone from the area, it became possible to investigate the crimes of Saddam Hussein's regime even as he remained in power. Mass graves, torture chambers, elaborate prison systems, and secret police files attested to the inner workings of one of the region's harshest dictatorships. Gravesites regularly contained hundreds of bodies of men, women, and children. I stood one afternoon as diggers uncovered the remains of 1,500 soldiers who had apparently been executed after refusing to fight in the war during the 1980s against Iran. Until the bodies were identified, the dead had "disappeared."

Kurdish leaders estimated that more than 180,000 Kurds had vanished at the hands of the Iraqi secret police. The Iraqis killed anyone, including young children, whom they believed supported the outlawed Kurdish guerrilla movement or belonged to a family that had ties with the Kurdish rebels. More than 4,000 villages—primarily those near the Turkish or Iranian borders that were regarded by the Iraqis as sanctuaries for Kurdish rebels—were demolished under the program, which reached its peak of intensity in 1987 and 1988, toward the end of the Iran-Iraq war.

The killing sites are often found a few feet from the mass graves. On Kalowa Hill, five tires filled with cement were all that remained of the spot where many people were shot to death. Earthen embankments bordered the site. Prisoners, blindfolded with their hands tied behind ten-foot metal poles, had their feet planted in the cement and were shot.

Of course those who lived nearby knew that something was happening. When I spoke with those in the vicinity of Kalowa Hill, they said they often heard screams and volleys of shots, but were threatened if they tried to peer into the high-walled compound. Stray dogs used to trot back with human bones or a fleshy limb, after getting inside the compound. The Iraqi guards began to shoot the dogs.

At Kalowa Hill I stood with my seven bodyguards. The Iraqi regime had put a price on the heads of all foreigners who worked in the Kurdish-controlled areas. Several had been shot and killed, including a German photographer I worked with. We watched a Kurdish woman, Pershan Hassan, clamber quickly up the dirt track leading to the site. As she hurried forward, she clutched to her chest a framed black and white photograph of a young boy. At the top of the rise, a crowd that had gathered parted silently as she stumbled forward.

She suddenly stopped and let out a gasp of pain and recognition. Before her, nine years after he had disappeared from a schoolyard, lay the skeletal remains of her thirteen-year-old son, Shafiq. A faded blue blindfold was tightly wrapped around his skull and spent bullets were scattered among his now dark-brown bones.

"I know him by his clothes," she whispered, her voice breaking as she lifted the garments and kissed them. "I raised him without a father."

In all such scenes there is grief. But there is also a palpable sense of relief. The lost son or husband is recovered. The salutary effect makes it possible to go forward in life. It took the efforts of Iraq's leading dissident, Kanan Makiya and Human Rights Watch, to make sure that truckloads of documents, including photographs and videotapes of executions, were transported out of northern Iraq to safety.

I leafed through the long, typewritten lists that were in abandoned secret police headquarters that chronicled killing after killing, sometimes for what seemed to be trivial offenses. One man was sentenced to death because he had a picture of a rebel Kurdish leader in his wallet.

A picture I found in a police file showed what appeared to be three Iraqi officials squatting like big game hunters next to the slumped body of a man who was recently killed. One of the Iraqis, wearing a beret, grinned while holding a knife to the corpse's neck. It was, once again, the strange need by killers to display human corpses as trophies.

I watched hours of videotapes shot by the Iraqi secret police of their own executions. Prisoners would be tied to poles, riddled with gunfire, and left slumped on the ground. There was a deadening sameness to it all and a strange and sickening fascination. The recording of such acts came out of a collapse of the moral universe, a world where right and wrong had been turned upside down. In the world of war, perversion may become moral; guilt may be honor, and the gunning down of unarmed people, including children, may be defined as heroic. In this world the "liquidation" of the enemy, with the enemy defined as simply the other, is part of the redemption of the nation.

The hill in northern Iraq began to draw hundreds of Kurdish women looking for lost children or husbands. The plaintive cries of those who recovered the remains of their loved ones would rise above the murmur of the crowd. Most, however, watched mutely day after day.

And circling the huge pit, a pit hacked at by men with shovels and pickaxes, were the gaunt survivors of the vast secret police prison network. They spoke of torture, beatings, hunger, and the long severance, sometimes for years, of all contact with the outside world.

A few weeks later, I traveled to Shorish, a suburb of Sulaimaniya, with Jamal Aziz Amin, a courtly forty-five-year-old headmaster. We entered a soundproofed room in the darkened remains of the Sulaimaniya central security prison, where he spent a year in detention. Large hooks hung from the ceiling where Amin, an Iraqi Kurd, was suspended during torture. He was handcuffed behind his back, he said, and hoisted onto the hooks at the wrist. He said he was stripped, questioned about his ties to Kurdish guerrilla groups, and given electric shocks until he fell unconscious.

"You would scream," he told me, "and it would sound as if you were yelling from the bottom of a deep, deep well."

The huge prison, its tiers of cells piled one on top of the other, stood bleak and deserted. When it was attacked in 1991 by Kurdish fighters and enraged civilians, 300 Iraqi secret policemen and guards, including the warden, held out for three days. None of the defenders survived.

Amin and his fellow Kurdish prisoners, after the attack, had the rare experience of standing over the bodies of many of their torturers.

"We wanted them to all come back to life," he said, "so we could kill them again."

At the prison, inmates subsisted on thin soup, bread, and weak tea. Amin said that by the time he was released, he had lost sixty pounds. The walls of the cells, many marked with crudely drawn calendars, carried the messages of those who tried to leave some testament, some record of their suffering.

"These were my friends, arrested with me," a prisoner named Ahmed Mohammed wrote, listing five names. "All were executed."

Another prisoner had written a message to his mother: "Oh, mother, in this dark room my dreams trouble me and I shake. Then comes the kicking against my door and a voice telling me to get up. It is time for my interrogation. I awake to the unconscious." Amin wound his way to the crude latrine, a hole in the cement, at the end of a corridor of cells.

"I wanted to show you this," he said, a small shaft of light streaming in from a tiny, barred window fourteen feet above him. "Here is where we would come at night so we could pull ourselves up the walls to hear the sound of the dogs barking in the distance. To hear the dogs, this was everything for us."

Historical memory is hijacked by those who carry out war. They seek, when the memory challenges the myth, to obliterate or hide the evidence that exposes the myth as lie. The destruction is pervasive, aided by an establishment, including the media, which apes the slogans and euphemisms parroted by the powerful. Because nearly everyone in wartime is complicit, it is difficult for societies to confront their own culpability and the lie that led to it.

But societies that do not confront the past remain trapped in an Oz-like world, a world whose most important truths are felt—then repressed—every day, a world where official lies are perpetuated by a vast bureaucracy. For the rift between Trieste's Slovene and Italian communities to be healed, the graves outside the city will have to be exhumed. The commissions set up in Chile, Argentina, and Brazil, as well as the international war crimes tribunal in The Hague, were created to give these nations a common vocabulary. Until then the factions will not communicate.

There probably can never be full recovery of memory, but in order to escape the miasma of war there must be some partial rehabilitation, some recognition of the denial and perversion, some new way given to speak that lays bare the myth as fantasy and the cause as bankrupt. The whole truth may finally be too hard to utter, but the process of healing only begins when we are able to at least acknowledge the tragedy and accept our share of the blame.

6

THE CAUSE

... all my means are sane, my motive and my object mad.

•

CAPTAIN AHAB IN *Moby Dick*

WHEN I STEPPED OFF AN ARMY C-130 MILITARY
transport in Dhahran, Saudi Arabia, to cover the Persian
Gulf War, I was escorted to a room with several dozen other
reporters and photographers. I was told to sign a paper that said
I would abide by the severe restrictions placed on the press by
the U.S. military. The restrictions authorized "pool reporters" to
be escorted by the military on field trips. The rest of the press
would sit in hotel rooms and rewrite the bland copy filed by the
pool or use the pool video and photos. This was an agreement I
violated the next morning, when I went into the field without
authorization. The rest of the war, during which I spent more
than half my time dodging military police and trying to talk my
way into units, was a forlorn and lonely struggle against the
heavy press control.

The Gulf War made war fashionable again. It was a cause the
nation willingly embraced. It gave us media-manufactured

heroes and a heady pride in our military superiority and technology. It made war fun. And the blame, as in many conflicts,
lay not with the military but the press. Television reporters hap-
pily disseminated the spoon-fed images that served the propaganda effort of the military and the state. These images did little
to convey the reality of war. Pool reporters, those guided
around in groups by the military, wrote about "our boys" eating
packaged army food, practicing for chemical weapons attacks,
and bathing out of buckets in the desert. It was war as spectacle,
war as entertainment. The images and stories were designed to
make us feel good about our nation, about ourselves. The Iraqi
families and soldiers being blown to bits by huge iron fragmentation bombs just over the border in Iraq were faceless and
nameless phantoms.

The notion that the press was used in the war is incorrect.
The press wanted to be used. It saw itself as part of the war
effort. Most reporters sent to cover a war don't really want to go
near the fighting. They do not tell this to their editors and
indeed will moan and complain about restrictions. The handful
who actually head out into the field have a bitter enmity with the
hotel-room warriors. But even those who do go out are guilty of
distortion. For we not only believe the myth of war and feed
recklessly off of the drug but also embrace the cause. We may
do it with more skepticism. We certainly expose more lies and
misconceptions. But we believe. We all believe. When you stop
believing you stop going to war.

The record of the press as mythmaker stretches at least from
William Howard Russell's romantic account of the 1854 charge
of the Light Brigade—he called the event "the pride and splen-
dour of war"—to Afghanistan after September 11, 2001. The
true victims of war, because we rarely see or hear them (as is

usual in most war reporting), faintly exist. I boycotted the pool system, but my reports did not puncture the myth or question the grand crusade to free Kuwait. I allowed soldiers to grumble. I shed a little light on the lies spread to make the war look like a coalition, but I did not challenge in any real way the patriotism and jingoism that enthused the crowds back home. We all used the same phrases. We all looked at Iraq through the same lens. And at night, when the huge bombers dropped tons of high explosives on Iraqi positions, lighting up the night sky with red fireballs, I felt immeasurable reassurance along with the soldiers.

It has been rare in every war I have covered to find a reporter who did not take sides. I believed—and still do—that in Bosnia and El Salvador, there were victims and oppressors in the conflict. But along with this acknowledgment comes for many a disturbing need to portray the side they back in their own self-image. The leftist Sandinistas in Nicaragua, the rebels in El Salvador and Guatemala, the African National Congress, the Muslim-led government in Sarajevo, or the opposition in Serbia were all endowed with the qualities they did not possess. The Christian ethicist Reinhold Niebuhr warned us that moral choice is not between the moral and the immoral, but between the immoral and the less immoral.

War finds its meaning in death. The cause is built on the backs of victims, portrayed always as innocent. Indeed, most conflicts are ignited with martyrs, whether real or created. The death of an innocent, one who is perceived as emblematic of the nation or the group under attack, becomes the initial rallying point for war. These dead become the standard-bearers of the cause and all causes feed off a steady supply of corpses.

Following the Iraqi invasion of Kuwait, it was widely disseminated that Iraqi soldiers removed hundreds of Kuwaiti babies from incubators and left them to die on hospital floors. The story, when we arrived in Kuwait and were able to check with doctors at the hospitals, turned out to be false. But by then the tale had served its purpose. The story came from a fifteen-year-old Kuwaiti who identified herself only as "Nayirah" when she tearfully testified before the Congressional Human Rights Caucus on October 10, 1990. She said she had watched fifteen infants being taken from incubators in the Al-Adan Hospital in Kuwait City by Iraqi soldiers who "left the babies on the cold floor to die." Nayirah turned out later to be the daughter of the Kuwaiti ambassador to the United States, Saud Nasir al-Sabah. She did not grant interviews after the war and it was never established whether she was actually in the country when the invasion took place.

Elias Canetti wrote, "It is the first death which infects everyone with the feeling of being threatened. It is impossible to overrate the part played by the first dead man in the kindling of wars. Rulers who want to unleash war know very well that they must procure or invent a first victim. It need not be anyone of particular importance, and can even be someone quite unknown. Nothing matters except his death; and it must be believed that the enemy is responsible for this. Every possible cause of his death is suppressed except one: his membership of the group to which one belongs oneself."[1]

The cause, sanctified by the dead, cannot be questioned without dishonoring those who gave up their lives. We become enmeshed in the imposed language. When any contradiction is raised or there is a sense that the cause is not just in an absolute sense, the doubts are attacked as apostasy. There is a constant act of remembering and honoring the fallen during war. These ceremonies sanctify the cause. As Americans we speak, following the September attacks, like the Islamic radicals we fight, primarily in clichés. We sound like the Serbian or Croatian nationalists who destroyed the Balkans. The official jargon obscures the game of war—the hunters and the hunted. We accept terms imposed upon us by the state—for example the "war on terror"—and these terms set the narrow parameters by which we are able to think and discuss.

The press, Michael Herr wrote in *Dispatches*, his book on the Vietnam War, "never found a way to report meaningfully about death, which of course was really what it was all about. The most repulsive, transparent gropes for sanctity in the midst of the killing received serious treatment in the papers and on the air. The jargon of the Process got blown into your head like bullets, and by the time you waded through all the Washington stories and all the Saigon stories, all the Other War stories and the corruption stories and the stories about brisk new gains in ARVN effectiveness, the suffering was somehow unimpressive."[2]

It is hard, maybe impossible, to fight a war if the cause is viewed as bankrupt. The sanctity of the cause is crucial to the war effort. The state spends tremendous time protecting, explaining, and promoting the cause. And some of the most important cheerleaders of the cause are the reporters. This is true in nearly every war. During the Gulf War, as in the weeks after the September attacks, communities gathered for vigils and worship services. The enterprise of the state became imbued with a religious aura. We, even those in the press, spoke in the collective. And because we in modern society have walked away from institutions that stand outside the state to find moral guidance and spiritual direction, we turn to the state in times of war. The state and the institutions of state become, for many, the center of worship in wartime. To expose the holes in the myth is to court excommunication.

Edmund Dene Morel, the British crusader against Belgian atrocities in the Congo, denounced World War I as madness.[3] He argued that through a series of treaties kept secret from Parliament and the public, Britain had become caught up in the senseless and tragic debacle. His fight against the war saw mobs break up his meetings with stink bombs and his banners ripped down. He finally could not rent a hall. His friends deserted him. Police raided his office and his home. The wartime censor banned some of his writings. He was flooded with hate mail. The government finally jailed him in 1917. It was only after 8.5 million dead and 21 million wounded that he was proven correct—the treaties did indeed exist. The war indeed was a needless waste. But by then the myth of war was no longer needed, since the fighting had ended.

The moral certitude of the state in wartime is a kind of fundamentalism. And this dangerous messianic brand of religion, one where self-doubt is minimal, has come increasingly to color the modern world of Christianity, Judaism, and Islam. Dr. James Luther Adams, my ethics professor at Harvard Divinity School, used to tell us that we would end our careers fighting an ascendant fundamentalist movement, or, as he liked to say, "the Christian fascists." He was not a scholar to be disregarded, however implausible such a scenario seemed at the time. There is a danger of a growing fusion between those in the state who wage war—both for and against modern states—and those who believe they understand and can act as agents for God.

History is awash with beleaguered revolutionaries and lunatic extremists who were endowed with enough luck and enough ruthlessness to fill power vacuums. The danger is not that fundamentalism will grow so much as that modern, secular society will wither. Already mainstream Christianity, Judaism, and Islam lie defeated and emasculated by the very forces that ironically turned them into tolerant, open institutions. In the event of massive and repeated terrorist strikes or an environmental catastrophe, an authoritarian state church could rise ascendant within American democracy. The current battle between us and our Islamic radical foes can only increase the reach of these groups.

But whether the impetus is ostensibly secular or religious, the adoption of the cause means adoption of the language of the cause. When we speak within the confines of this language we give up our linguistic capacity to question and make moral choices.

The cause is unassailable, wrapped in the mystery reserved for the divine. Those who attempt to expose the fabrications and to unwrap the contradictions of the cause are left isolated and reviled. We did not fight the Persian Gulf War to liberate Kuwait, but to ensure that we would continue to have cheap oil. But oil is hardly a cause that will bring crowds into the street.

I was with young Islamic militants in a Cairo slum a few weeks after the war. They no longer attended the state school because their families did not have the money to hire teachers to tutor them. The teachers, desperate for a decent income, would not let students pass unless they paid. These militants spent their days at the mosque. They saw the Persian Gulf War for what it was, a use of force by a country that consumed 25 percent of the world's petrol to protect its access to cheap oil. The message that was sent to them was this: We have everything and if you try to take it away from us we will kill you. It was not a message I could dispute.

We allied ourselves with some of the most despotic regimes

in the region during the war, including the Syrians, who sponsor an array of terrorist groups. Damascus demanded $3 billion as the price for sending its troops to support the war effort. The morning the invasion began, I traveled with a Marine detachment past the Syrian soldiers. They were drinking tea. They waved us forward. None of them ever saw any fighting. We did not see the Syrian soldiers again until they were passed through our lines after the combat was over so they, and our other Arab allies, could "liberate" Kuwait City. The ecological devastation to the region, the fact that Saddam Hussein remained in power to slaughter thousands of Shiites who rebelled with our encouragement against his regime and then were abandoned by us to their fate, the gross corruption and despotism of the Kuwaiti rulers, who did not move back to Kuwait City until their opulent palaces were refurbished, were minor footnotes to a stage-managed tale of triumph. As in most conflicts, the war, as presented to the public, was fantasy.

When those who commit crimes do so in the name of the cause, they often come to terms with the crimes through an ersatz moral relativism. Facts are trimmed, used, and become as interchangeable as opinions. The Muslims may say the Serbs shelled the marketplace in Sarajevo while the Serbs may say that the Muslims fired shells on their own citizens there to garner international support. Both opinions, if one sits in a café in Belgrade, may be valid. Both the facts and the opinions become a celebration of ignorance, and more ominously, a refusal to discredit the cause that has eaten away at one's moral conscience.

Destruction of honest inquiry, the notion that one fact is as good as the next, is one of the most disturbing consequences of war. The prosecution of war entails lying, often on a massive scale—something most governments engage in but especially when under the duress of war. The Serbs who were eventually able to admit that atrocities were carried out in their name explained away the crimes by saying that everyone did this in war. The same was true among the elite and the military in El Salvador. All could match an atrocity carried out by our side with an atrocity carried out by the enemy. Atrocity canceled out atrocity.

Hannah Arendt noted this attitude in Germany after World War II, calling it "nihilistic relativism." She believed it was a legacy of Nazi propaganda, which, unlike that of non-totalitarian states, was based on the concept that all facts could and would be altered and all Nazi lies should be made to appear true. Reality became a conglomerate of changing circumstances and slogans that could be true one day and false the next.[4]

Illusions punctuate our lives, blinding us to our own inconsistencies and repeated moral failings. But in wartime these illusions are compounded. The cause, the protection of the nation, the fight to "liberate Kuwait" or wage "a war on terrorism," justifies the means. We dismantle our moral universe to serve the cause of war. And once it is dismantled it is nearly impossible to put it back together. It is very hard for most of us to see the justice of the other side, to admit that we too bear guilt. When we are asked to choose between truth and contentment, most of us pick contentment.

Not long after the war in Bosnia, where most human rights monitors blamed the Serbian forces for perhaps 80 percent of the war crimes, a popular film was produced in Serbian called *Pretty Villages, Pretty Flames*. The movie showed images of drunken Bosnian Serb militiamen burning Muslim villages, killing elderly civilians, and carting away truckloads of loot—not a version of the Bosnian war that had been acknowledged

until then by many Serbs. Bosnian Serb fighters were portrayed
as petty criminals, thugs, and drug addicts. This, to a populace
that could still sit around and ask if it were true that Serbian
forces shelled Sarajevo, was a revelation.

The film dealt for the first time with the excesses of Bosnian Serb soldiers and the lies of the Serbian nationalist leaders
who fueled the war. It was seen as an opening, a frank and can-
did admission of what really happened. But it was also a classic example of the relativism that worried Arendt. The scramble
by some German historians to paint the crimes carried out by
Stalin as equivalent to the crimes carried out by Hitler absolved
the Germans of responsibility, for all were guilty. And under the
guise of candor, this film served the same purpose. It punctured
holes in the cause of Serbian nationalism. But it went on to say
that one cause was as rotten as the next, that just as the Serbs
had been manipulated by their own leaders, so had the Muslims
and the Croats. Not only that, the film made sure to bring Tito's
Yugoslavia and the international effort to rebuild Bosnia down
to the same depraved level.

The failure to dissect the cause of war leaves us open for the
next installment. When a cause is exhausted, or no longer
needed, it can only be invalidated in direct proportion to the
invalidation of the opposing cause. This is a scourge of war. We
can deflate our own cause but must deflate the cause of the
other as well.

Following the 1995 Dayton peace agreement, the Bosnian
Serbs were required to relinquish the suburbs around Sarajevo
to the Muslim-led government. A few days before the han-
dover, I stood with a group of ragged Bosnian Serb police officers in blue uniforms. They lined up in a small park and sang.
Their voices were barely audible over a scratchy recording of

the old anthem of the kingdom of Yugoslavia. The thunder of ammunition exploding in burning buildings drowned out whole stanzas.

The police officers lowered the Bosnian Serb flag from the front of the Grbavica police station, kissed the cloth, and folded it. Milenko Karisik, deputy interior minister for the Bosnian Serbs, proclaimed the officers "heroes" and reminded the few onlookers that the police were the first to raise the rebel Serbian flag in the suburb four years ago.

"We saved this area militarily but we lost it at Dayton," he said. "Maybe this generation of Serbs won't come back, but in future generations the Serbs will return."

The roaring fires in buildings, the bands of drunken Serbs cruising the streets in cars without license plates, and the fear etched on the faces of elderly people who peered through the plastic sheeting nailed across their window frames, illustrated that whatever authority these police officers had wielded disintegrated days ago.

More than a dozen fires sent billows of smoke and flames into a gray, overcast sky. Italian peacekeeping troops, who gunned their armored personnel carriers swiftly through the debris-strewn roads, did little to stop the looting and arson. Of the approximately 60,000 Bosnian Serbs from the five neighborhoods and suburbs that had been scheduled to be turned over to the federation, all but a few thousand had fled.

The repeated explosions came from setting alight the ammunition and grenades that arsonists had planted inside the buildings. Though some of the people who set the fires were vandals, others destroyed their own houses. An elderly Serbian couple who did not want to be identified were driven out of their apartment when a neighbor set his apartment ablaze, setting off explosions.

"What is happening now makes the thought of the Muslims coming here a relief," said the woman, fighting back tears. "We tried so hard to save our apartment. It was all we had in the world."

"People are burning their houses because they are bitter and angry," said Milorad Katić, the mayor of Grbavica. "They don't want to leave their houses for the Muslims to inhabit."

Most of the 2,000 or so Serbs who remained locked the doors of their buildings and barricaded themselves inside their apartments.

When one elderly woman unlocked the front door of her building that afternoon to let in a man who lived there, he brushed her aside and began to dump gasoline in the hallway. She ran desperately outside to find some Italian soldiers who rushed in and prevented the man from starting a fire.

But most were unlucky. I saw two women toss basins of water at a fire on a floor above them, but they soon had to flee as the fire spread.

"We struggled for so long, we endured so much over the last four years," said one woman, "and now we are burned out by our own people."

It was the final act of war, the self-destruction that comes at the end of the campaign of hate and death and violence. I wandered the streets nervously, trying to stay out of the way of drunken groups of armed police who fired rounds into the air. Reporters who had covered the siege of Sarajevo longer than I showed little pity. They muttered that it was what the "Chetniks" deserved, although the victims, from what I could see, were mostly elderly pensioners. This was the apocalyptic end of war, of all wars. The Serbs, like all who are defeated, were consuming themselves.

I made my way to the Vlakovo cemetery and met Nikola Ljesić. He carried with him several yellow candles, a small parcel of food, and a piece of brown wrapping paper filled with nails. He walked past the dun-colored mounds of earth beside several empty graves toward the wooden cross marked with the name of his son, Dragoslav. He said that the eighteen-year-old had been shot dead by a Muslim sniper in June 1992.

He kissed the cross. He knelt and kissed the dirt on the grave. He removed his brown wool hat and stood in silence.

"I would like to take him in my arms one more time, and kiss him and hold him," he said.

Ljesić lit the candles in front of his son's grave. He watched the flames flicker in the cold wind that whipped down from the barren, brown hills around him. On a weathered wooden bench he laid out two loaves of bread, a shaker of salt, smoked pork, a bottle of brandy, and a shot glass. The two grave diggers next to him, wearing blue work shirts over worn sweaters, ate the bread with salt and a piece of meat. They quickly downed the alcohol.

When the graveside mourning ritual was completed, Ljesić nodded for the men to begin hacking through the frigid earth until they reached the remains of his youngest child.

"I took a handful of tranquilizers before I came," he said.

"You don't know these Muslim fanatics," Ljesić said. "They have no morality. They would dig up my son and take his bones and burn them."

Cemetery officials were drawing up plans to unearth the some 1,000 dead who had been killed in the war and move all the bodies to a new cemetery in Sokolac, outside of Pale, the headquarters of the Bosnian Serbs.

"We only have three workers," said Jovo Kuljanin, the director of the cemetery, "so people often have to dig up their own graves. We don't have any hearses; people have to arrange for their own transportation. And everyone who wants a metal coffin must pay $140 for it. We can't provide one."

Ljesić, who had last visited the grave on January 9, his son's birthday, was unable to pay for a metal coffin. Instead he brought plastic sheeting, handed out by the United Nations High Commissioner for Refugees to cover windows. In the pocket of his black suit he carried nails to pound the coffin back together. He had paid Srdjan Manojlovic $70 to carry the coffin to Sokolac in his 1987 red Yugoslav Zastava van.

The war had shattered Ljesić's life. His two daughters left Bosnia—one for Germany and the other for France. His wife, whom he had not been able to contact for three years, was cut off from him in Muslim-held Sarajevo. His home, on the outskirts of the city, had been blasted into rubble. He had lost his job and lived alone in a small apartment in Doboj. Yet, even as he dug up the body of his son, he could not face the perfidiousness of what he had once supported. He knew it was rotten. He knew it was a waste. He was in deep despair, but always the Muslim enemy loomed above him, ready to violate the dead, his dead. No matter how horrible his own war was, no matter how corrupt and brutal his own leaders were, the cause could be justified if only by a negative, by the fear of the other.

"My wife does not know I am here today," he said. "She was not allowed by the Muslims to come to our son's funeral. She has never visited his grave. It would kill her to see this now."

Milivoje Matić, a burly man in a brown coat, stopped to take a shot of brandy and express his condolences to Ljesić. He listened patiently to the story of how the boy was killed. Matić told the story of his brother, Slobodan, who he said had been tortured to death in a Muslim jail in Sarajevo.

He then went to work a few feet away, swinging a pickax over his head to dig up his brother's grave.

Small beads of sweat collected on his forehead.

"His children called and asked me to get the body," he said breathlessly. "They asked me to dig him up."

When the coffin containing the remains of Ljesić's son was uncovered, the grave diggers brought in a small backhoe to lift it out of the ground. As it was hoisted up, the dilapidated brown-painted wooden box spewed water into the hole.

Ljesić removed his hat. He pulled the nails from his pocket.

"We can put it back together," he said softly to Zeljko Kneževic, one of the grave diggers. "Please do it for me. I will give you all the money I have. It is not a lot, but it is all that is left."

Kneževic pounded nails into the three planks of wood that once formed the lid. The corpse, wrapped in a gray, damp blanket, faced the open sky. Ljesić, as if he were putting his son to bed, gently laid a clean blanket over the remains. An American Chinook helicopter passed overhead.

"I will put this plastic around the coffin," he explained to the gravediggers. "We will tie it up with string."

When the coffin was repaired, Ljesić embraced Kneževic.

"I will never forget what you did for me," the father said.

The end of the coffin, covered with the milky white plastic sheeting, stuck out from the back of the van as it drove away.

Kneževic, seated on another grave, lit a cigarette.

"We have to do five graves tomorrow," he said. "I was here when they put the first body in the ground. It looks like I will be here when they pull the last one out. When the cemetery is empty, my job will be done and I will leave with everyone else."

7

EROS AND THANATOS

Beyond all this, the wish to be alone
However the sky grows dark with invitation-cards
However we follow the printed directions of sex
However the family is photographed under the
flagstaff—
Beyond all this, the wish to be alone

Beneath it all desire of oblivion runs
Despite the artful tensions of the calendar,
The life insurance, the tabled fertility rites,
The costly aversion of the eyes from death —
Beneath it all desire of oblivion runs.

PHILIP LARKIN

D URING THE WAR IN EL SALVADOR I WORKED WITH A
photographer who had a slew of close calls and then
called it quits. He moved to Miami. He took pictures of tepid
domestic stories for one of the newsweeklies. But life in Florida
was flat, dull, uninteresting. He could not adjust and soon came
back. From the moment he stepped off the plane it was clear he

had returned to die. Just as there are some soldiers or war correspondents who seem to us immortal and whose loss comes as
a sobering reminder that death has no favorites, there are also
those in war who are locked in a grim embrace with death from
which they cannot escape. He was frightening to behold, a
walking corpse. He was shot a few months later through the
back in a firefight. It took him less than a minute to die.

Sigmund Freud divided the forces in human nature between
the Eros instinct, the impulse within us that propels us to
become close to others, to preserve and conserve, and the
Thanatos, or death instinct, the impulse that works towards the
annihilation of all living things, including ourselves. For Freud
these forces were in eternal conflict. He was pessimistic about
ever eradicating war. All human history, he argued, is a tug-of-
war between these two instincts.

"The meaning of the evolution of civilization is no longer
obscure to us," Freud wrote in *Civilization and Its Discontents*. "It
must present the struggle between Eros and Death, between
the instinct of life and the instinct of destruction, as it works
itself out in the human species. This struggle is what all life
essentially consists of."[1]

We believe in the nobility and self-sacrifice demanded by war,
especially when we are blinded by the narcotic of war. We discover in the communal struggle, the shared sense of meaning
and purpose, a cause. War fills our spiritual void. I do not miss
war, but I miss what it brought. I can never say I was happy in
the midst of the fighting in El Salvador, or Bosnia, or Kosova,
but I had a sense of purpose, of calling. And this is a quality war
shares with love, for we are, in love, also able to choose fealty
and self-sacrifice over security.

Happiness is elusive and protean. And it is sterile when

devoid of meaning. But meaning, when it is set in the vast arena of war with its high stakes, its adrenaline-driven rushes, its bold sweeps and drama, is heartless and self-destructive. The initial selflessness of war mirrors that of love, the chief emotion war destroys. And this is what war often looks and feels like, at its inception: love. The ancient Greeks understood this strange relationship between love and death in wartime. When Achilles kills Penthesilea, the queen of the Amazons, in the Trojan War, he falls in love with her as she expires on the battlefield. Once she is dead, once love is dead, Achilles is doomed.

We are tempted to reduce life to a simple search for happiness. Happiness, however, withers if there is no meaning. The other temptation is to disavow the search for happiness in order to be faithful to that which provides meaning. But to live only for meaning—indifferent to all happiness—makes us fanatic, self-righteous, and cold. It leaves us cut off from our own humanity and the humanity of others. We must hope for grace, for our lives to be sustained by moments of meaning and happiness, both equally worthy of human communion.

During the first phases of the war in Kosova I moved about the countryside in an armored jeep. I slept in wooden sheds and barns or on the floors of peasant homes. One bitterly cold winter morning I woke at first light in a hut. I watched the wind blow snow through the slates over my sleeping bag. I heard from local rebels about a Serb attack on a nearby village. The victims would be buried in a few hours. As so often happened, I had to leave my vehicle behind because of the extensive Serb roadblocks. I walked to the site on foot. It was, as usual, a perilous game of cat-and-mouse, one I had played for five years with the military in El Salvador. During the funeral Serb snipers opened fire on the crowd. We darted for cover. I filed my story, quickly typed out and sent over the satellite phone I carried in my backpack. Then I walked out. To record the atrocities, even as I knew the killings would continue, was my task. But by then it was destroying me. I felt profoundly alone.

In the wake of catastrophe, including the attacks of September 11, 2001, there is a desperate longing by all those affected to be in the physical presence of those they love. When a heavy shell landed in Sarajevo, or an assassination took place in the streets of San Salvador, or a suicide bomber blew himself up in Jerusalem, mothers, fathers, husbands, wives, and children pawed through the onlookers seeking physical reunification with those they loved. This love, like death, radiates outwards. It battles Thanatos at the very moment of death's sting. These two fundamental human impulses crash like breakers into each other. And however much beyond reason, there is always a feeling that love is not powerless or impotent as we had believed a few seconds before. Love alone fuses happiness and meaning. Love alone can fight the impulse that lures us toward self-destruction.

The question is whether America now courts death. We no longer seem chastened by war as we were in the years after the Vietnam War. The Bush administration has revised its "Nuclear Posture Review" to give us "more flexible nuclear strike capabilities." Washington wants "more options" with which to confront contingencies "immediate, potential and unexpected," for smaller but more effective mega-tonnages to be deployed. This flirtation with weapons of mass destruction is a flirtation with our own obliteration, an embrace again of Thanatos.

There are few sanctuaries in war. But one is provided by couples in love. They are not able to staunch the slaughter. They are often powerless and can themselves often become victims. But it was with them, seated around a wood stove, usually over a simple meal, that I found sanity and was reminded of what it means to be human. Love kept them grounded. It was to such couples that I retreated during the wars in Central America, the Middle East, and the Balkans. Love, when it is deep and sustained by two individuals, includes self-giving—often self-sacrifice—as well as desire. For the covenant of love is such that it recognizes both the fragility and the sanctity of the individual. It recognizes itself in the other. It alone can save us.

I did not sleep well in war. I could rarely recall my dreams, waking only to know that they had been harsh and violent. When I left the war zones, the nightmares descended on me like furies. I had horrible visions of war. I would dream of being in combat with my father or young son and unable to protect them. But I could sleep in the homes of such couples. Their love spread a protective blanket over us. It was able to blot out the war, although the lure of combat, the distant rattle of automatic weapons beckoned us back, and we always went.

Aristotle said that only two living entities are capable of complete solitude and complete separateness: God and beast. Because of this the most acute form of suffering for human beings is loneliness. The isolated individual can never be adequately human. And many of war's most fervent adherents are those atomized individuals who, before the war came, were profoundly alone and unloved. They found fulfillment in war, perhaps because it was the closest they came to love. If we do not acknowledge such an attraction, which is, in some ways, so akin to love, we can never combat it.

We are all tempted to honor false covenants of race, nationalism, class, and gender. They sometimes compete for our loyalty. War, of course, is often—maybe always—a false covenant.

Sham covenants are based on exclusion rather than universality. All covenants that lack an adequate sense of humility and an acknowledgment of the sinfulness of our own cause are false covenants. The prophets warned us about them.

The cost of war is often measured in the physical destruction of a country's infrastructure, in the blasted buildings, factories, and bridges, in the number of dead. But probably worse is the psychological and spiritual toll. This cost takes generations to heal. It cripples and perverts whole societies, as Europe saw with the shattered veterans from World War I. But even for those who know the cost of war, it still holds out the promise of eradicating the thorny problems of life.

In the beginning war looks and feels like love. But unlike love it gives nothing in return but an ever-deepening dependence, like all narcotics, on the road to self-destruction. It does not affirm but places upon us greater and greater demands. It destroys the outside world until it is hard to live outside war's grip. It takes a higher and higher dose to achieve any thrill. Finally, one ingests war only to remain numb. The world outside war becomes, as Freud wrote, "uncanny." The familiar becomes strangely unfamiliar—many who have been in war find this when they return home. The world we once understood and longed to return to stands before us as alien, strange, and beyond our grasp.

In 1999 the British journalist Anthony Loyd published *My War Gone By, I Miss It So*, a book about his twin addictions to heroin and to the war in Bosnia. His account illuminates the self-destruction impulse that is fed by war and drugs as well as the highs that propel many into combat. For Loyd, like Michael Herr, war was the ultimate drug experience. It was the chance to taste extremes that would, he hoped, bring about a catharsis or obliteration. In times of peace, drugs are war's pale substitute. But drugs, in the end, cannot compare with the awful power and rush of battle. This was not why I went to war, but the twisted voyeurism and narcotic of war Loyd described attracted many to the battlefields and held them there.

> Deep down I was aware at the time that many of my motivations were fairly dark. On one level my sense of despair had been dispelled by therapy, yet on another it had not been replaced by either the desire for a future or the concept of one. I felt more aware of who I was, but that in itself—dominated as it was by sensations of fragmentation and isolation—filled me with no great hope, and in many ways only fueled an appetite for destruction.[2]

There are those for whom violence is sexual. They carry their phallic weapons slung low at an angle toward the ground. Most of these fighters are militiamen, those who stay away from real combat, have little training or discipline, and primarily terrorize the weak and defenseless. And they look the part, often with tight black fatigues, wraparound sunglasses, and big ugly jeeps or cars with tinted windows. For them war is about empowerment. They have turned places like the Congo into Hobbesian playgrounds.

These warlords rise to power with gangs who prey on minorities and the weak. When they are done, they turn on those they were fighting to protect. I was in the Bosnian Serb town of Banja Luka in the summer of 1995 not long after Serbian militias had driven out most of the ethnic Croats. Once the militias had finished looting the homes of the ethnic Croats and stealing their cars, they set up roadblocks to steal cars from the

Serbs who lived in the city. The cars were then driven over the border into Serbia for sale.

When the mask of war slips away and the rot and corruption is exposed, when the addiction turns sour and rank, when the myth is exposed as a fraud, we feel soiled and spent. It is then that we sink into despair, a despair that can lead us to welcome death. This despair is more common than many expect.

In the 1973 Arab-Israeli war, almost a third of all Israeli casualties were due to psychiatric causes, and the war lasted only a few weeks. A World War II study determined that after sixty days of continuous combat, 98 percent of all surviving soldiers will have become psychiatric casualties. They found that a common trait among the 2 percent who were able to endure sustained combat was a predisposition toward "aggressive psychopathic personalities."[3]

During the war in El Salvador soldiers could serve in the army for three or four years or longer, virtually until they psychologically collapsed. In garrison towns commanders banned the sale of sedatives because of abuse by troops. In this war the emotionally maimed were common.

Edilberto Ayala, a nineteen-year-old Salvadoran army sergeant, spent five years fighting, and suddenly lost his vision after his unit walked into a rebel ambush. The rebels killed eleven soldiers in the firefight, including Ayala's closest friend. A couple dozen soldiers were wounded. He was unable to see again until he was placed in an army hospital.

"I have these horrible headaches," he told me, sitting on the edge of his hospital bed. "There is shrapnel in my head. I keep telling the doctors to take it out."

But the doctors told me he had no head wounds.

J. Glenn Gray, a World War II combat veteran who taught

philosophy after the war, wrote: "Few of us can hold on to our real selves long enough to discover the real truths about ourselves and this whirling earth to which we cling. This is especially true of men in war. The great god Mars tries to blind us when we enter his realm, and when we leave he gives us a generous cup of the waters of Lethe to drink."[4]

This self-deception is powerful. It propels those in war forward. When it falls away, when we grasp war's reality, a universe collapses. Many of those who suddenly perceive the raw brutality and lie of war crumble into heaps.

Jon Steele, a cameraman who spent years in war zones, had a nervous breakdown in a crowded Heathrow Airport in 1994 after returning from Sarajevo, when for a moment he saw the cold reality of what he was doing, a reality that stripped away the self-righteous gloss and addiction to battle.

"I came back from Sarajevo," he said in an interview in the Israeli newspaper *Ha'aretz*. "We were in a place called Sniper's Alley, and I filmed a girl there who had been hit in the neck by a sniper's bullet. I filmed her dying in the ambulance and only after she was dead, I suddenly understood that the last thing she had seen was the reflection of the lens of the camera I was holding in front of her face. This wiped me out. I grabbed the camera and I started running down Snipers' Alley, filming at knee level the Bosnians running from place to place. I think that I broke down because I got things backward—I thought that because I was trying to be a hero and get exclusive pictures, people were dying."[5]

War is necrophilia. And this necrophilia is central to soldiering, just as it is central to the makeup of suicide bombers and terrorists. The necrophilia is hidden under platitudes about duty or comradeship. It waits, especially in moments when we seem to have little to live for and no hope, or in moments when the intoxication of war is at its pitch, to be unleashed. When we spend long enough in war it comes to us as a kind of release, a fatal and seductive embrace that can consummate the long flirtation in war with our own destruction. The ancient Greeks had a word for such a drive. They called it *ekpyrosis*—to be consumed by a ball of fire. They used the word to describe heroes.

War throws us into a frenzy in which all human life, including our own, seems secondary. The atavism of war creates us in war's image. In Chuck Sudetic's book *Blood and Vengeance* the former reporter for *The New York Times* writes of how he was eventually overpowered by the culture of death in wartime:

> I once walked through a town littered with the purple-and-yellow bodies of men and women and a few children, some shot to death, some with their heads torn off, and I felt nothing; I strolled around with a photographer, scratched notes, and lifted sheets covering the bodies of dead men to see if they had been castrated; I picked up a white flag from the ground near the twisted bodies of half a dozen men in civilian clothes who had been shot next to a wall, and then I carried the flag home and hung it above my desk. I once saw soldiers unload babies crushed to death in the back of a truck and immediately ran off to interview their mothers. I accidentally killed an eighteen-year-old man who raced in front of my car on a bike; his head was smashed; I held the door when they loaded him into the backseat of the automobile that carried him to the emergency room of Sarajevo's main hospital; I expressed my condolences to his father; then I got a tow back to my hotel, went to my room, and sent that day's story to New York.[6]

In Milovan Djilas's memoir of the partisan war in Yugoslavia, he too wrote of the enticement death held for the combatants. He stood over the body of his comrade, the commander Sava Kovačević, and found that

> Dying did not seem terrible or unjust. This was the most extraordinary, the most exalted moment of my life: death did not seem strange or undesirable. That I restrained myself from charging blindly into the fray and death, was perhaps due to my sense of obligation to the troops, or to some comrade's reminder concerning the tasks at hand. In my memory I returned to those moments many times, with the same feeling of intimacy with death and desire for it, while I was in prison, particularly during my first incarceration.[7]

War ascendant wipes out Eros. It wipes out all delicacy and tenderness. And this is why those in war swing from rank sentimentality to perversion, with little in between. Stray puppies, street kids, cats, anything that can be an object of affection for soldiers are adopted and pampered even in the midst of killing, the beating and torture of prisoners, and the razing of villages. If the pets die they are buried with elaborate rituals and little grave markers. But it is not only love, although the soldiers insist it feels like love. These animals, as well as the young waifs who collect around military units, are total dependents. They pay homage to the absolute power above them. Indeed, it may be that at times they please or they die.

In the midst of slaughter the only choice is often between hate and lust. Human beings become objects, objects to extinguish or to provide carnal gratification. The widespread casual and frenetic sex in wartime often crosses the line into perversion and violence. It exposes the vast moral void. When life becomes worth nothing, when one is not sure of survival, when a society is ruled by fear, there often seems only death or fleeting, carnal pleasure. This is why Lady Ann in Shakespeare's *Richard III* goes to Richard's bed. She sleeps with Richard because her moral universe has been destroyed. This kind of love is the product of the impersonal violence of war.

In war we may deform ourselves, our essence, by subverting passion, loyalty, and love to duty. Perhaps one could argue that this is why Virgil's Aeneas appears so woefully unhappy in *The Aeneid.* Despite his love for Dido he must leave her to found the empire in Italy: *hic amor, haec patria est*—there is my love, there my country. Yet in moments of extremity to make a moral choice, to defy war's enticement, to defend love, can be self-destructive. Shakespeare shows it in Antony in *Antony and Cleopatra*, as he does in the final defeat of Coriolanus. Antony embraces love and passion and loses empire. Like Dido, by giving himself to love, he dooms his empire and cuts his life short. He is no match for Octavius's bloodless thirst for power.

In the rise to power we become smaller, power absorbs us, and once power is attained we are often its pawn. As in *Richard III,* the all-powerful prince, can swiftly fall prey to the forces he thought he had harnessed. So too in war. Shakespeare's Lear and Richard III gain knowledge only as they are pushed down the ladder, as they are stripped of all illusions. Love may not always triumph, but it keeps us human. It offers the only chance to escape from the contagion of war. Perhaps it is the only antidote. And there are times when remaining human is the only victory possible.

Kurt Schork, a Reuters correspondent who spent a decade in war zones before being killed in an ambush in Sierra Leone, wrote a story out of Sarajevo about Bosko Brckić, a Serb, and

Admira Ismić, a Muslim, both twenty-five. They had been sweethearts since high school. The lovers tried to flee the besieged city in May 1993, a year after the war started, but were gunned down by Serb snipers.

They died together on the banks of Sarajevo's Miljacka River. Bosko fell dead instantly. Admira was badly wounded. She crawled over and hugged him. She expired in his arms. Bosko lay face-down on the pavement, his right arm bent awkwardly behind him. Admira lay next to him, her left arm across his back. Another corpse, that of a man shot five months earlier, lay decomposing nearby.

Their bodies lay there for four days, sprawled near the Vrbana bridge, a pitted wasteland of shell-blasted rubble, downed tree branches, and dangling power lines, before they were recovered.

They are buried together, under a heart-shaped headstone, in the Lion's Cemetery for the victims of the war. Kurt is buried next to them. Kurt, brilliant, courageous, and driven, had been unable to break free from the addiction of war. His entrapment, his long flirtation with Thanatos, was never mentioned at the memorial service staged for him in Washington by the Reuters bureaucrats he did not respect. Everyone tiptoed around it. But those of us who knew him understood that he had been consumed by his addiction. I had worked with Kurt for ten years, starting in northern Iraq. Literate, funny—it seems the brave are often funny—he and I passed books back and forth in our struggle to make sense of the madness around us. His loss was a hole that will never be filled.

I flew to Sarajevo and met the British filmmaker Dan Reed. It was an overcast November day. We stood over the grave and downed a pint of whiskey. Dan lit a candle. I recited a poem the Roman lyric poet Catullus had written to honor his dead brother.

By strangers' coasts and waters, many days at sea,
I come here for the rites of your unworlding,
Bringing for you, the dead, these last gifts of the living
And my words—vain sounds for the man of dust.
Alas, my brother,
You have been taken from me. You have been taken from me,
By cold chance turned a shadow, and my pain.
Here are the foods of the old ceremony, appointed
Long ago for the starvelings under the earth:
Take them: your brother's tears have made them wet; and take
Into eternity my hail and my farewell.[8]

It was there, among a few thousand war dead, that Kurt
belonged. He died because he could not free himself from war,
from the death impulse. He was in Africa searching for new
highs. He was trying to replicate what he had found in Sarajevo.
But he could not. War could never be new again. I had tried for
years after El Salvador to make it come back. It was never the
same. Kurt had been in East Timor and Chechnya. Sierra
Leone, I was sure, meant little to him. Miguel Gil Morano, a
Spanish cameraman, who had also covered the wars in Bosnia
and Kosova, died with him. They were, like all who do not let
go, consumed by a ball of fire. But they lit the fuse. And they
would be the first to admit it.

Viktor Frankl, in *Man's Search for Meaning*, writes of the grim
battle between love and Thanatos in Auschwitz. He recalls
being on a work detail, freezing in the blast of the Polish winter,
when he began to think about his wife, who had already been
gassed, although he did not know this at the time.

A thought transfixed me: for the first time in my life I saw
the truth as it is set into song by so many poets, proclaimed

as the final wisdom by so many thinkers. The truth—that
love is the ultimate and the highest goal to which man can
aspire. Then I grasped the meaning of the greatest secret
that human poetry and human thought and belief have to
impart: The salvation of man is through love and in love.[9]

The Thanatos instinct is a drive toward suicide, individual
and collective. War celebrates only power—and we come to
believe in wartime that it is the only real form of power. It preys
on our most primal and savage impulses. It allows us to do what
peacetime society forbids or restrains us from doing. It allows
us to kill. However much soldiers regret killing once it is finished, however much they spend their lives trying to cope with
the experience, the act itself, fueled by fear, excitement, the pull
of the crowd, and the god-like exhilaration of destroying, is
often thrilling.

I have watched fighters in El Salvador, Nicaragua, Guatemala, the Sudan, the Punjab, Iraq, Bosnia, and Kosova enter villages, tense, exhausted, wary of ambushes, with the fear and
tension that comes from combat, and begin to shoot at random. Flames soon lick up from houses. Discipline, if there was
any, disintegrates. Items are looted, civilians are battered with
rifle butts, units fall apart, and the violence directed toward
unarmed men, women, and children grows as it feeds on itself.
The eyes of the soldiers who carry this orgy of death are
crazed. They speak only in guttural shouts. They are high on the
power to spare lives or take them, the divine power to destroy.
And they are indeed, for a moment, gods swatting down powerless human beings like flies. The lust for violence, the freedom
to eradicate the world around them, even human lives, is seductive. And the line that divides us, who would like to see ourselves as civilized and compassionate, from such communal

barbarity is razor-thin. In wartime it often seems to matter little where one came from or how well-schooled and moral one
was before the war began. The frenzy of the crowd is overpowering.

Bob Kerrey, a former United States senator who won the
Medal of Honor for his military service in Vietnam, once led a
combat mission that caused the deaths of thirteen to twenty
unarmed civilians, most of them women and children. When
this story was first revealed in the spring of 2001, there was,
among an unknowing public, an expression of shock and an
effort to explain such behavior. But the revelation was, rather
than an anomaly, an example of how most wars are fought. It
was a glimpse into the reality of war that many in the public,
anxious not to see war's sordid nature, worked hard to shut.
Kerrey, in a speech at the Virginia Military Institute soon after
the incident was made public, said: "I have been haunted by it
for thirty-two years."

The raid, which took place in 1969, saw Kerrey, then a twenty-
five-year-old lieutenant who had arrived in Vietnam a month earlier, lead a group of six Navy Seals—the informal name for
Sea-Air-Land units—behind enemy lines. They hoped to capture
a Vietcong leader who was reported to be holding a meeting that
night. The unit was ferried to the spot by boat. They encoun-
tered a thatched hut and killed those inside. There were, those in
the unit said, women inside. They ran into more huts. More
women and children were killed, although Kerrey says he and his
men came under fire. "The thing that I will remember until the
day I die is walking in and finding, I don't know, 14 or so, I don't
even know what the number was, women and children who were
dead," he told *The New York Times Magazine*.[10]

In an interview with *The Wall Street Journal*, Kerrey said, "This is killing me. I'm tired of people describing me as a hero and holding this inside."[11]

The military histories—which tell little of war's reality—crowd out the wrenching tales by the emotionally maimed. Each generation again responds to war as innocents. Each generation discovers its own disillusionment—often after a terrible price. The myth of war and the drug of war wait to be tasted. The mythical heroes of the past loom over us. Those who can tell us the truth are silenced or prefer to forget. The state needs the myth, as much as it needs its soldiers and its machines of war, to survive.

To say the least, killing is nearly always a sordid affair. Those who carry such memories do so with difficulty, even when the cause seems just. Moreover, those who are killed do not die the clean death we see on television or film. They die messy, disturbing deaths that often plague the killers. And the bodies of the newly slain retain a disquieting power. The rows of impersonal dead, stacked like firewood one next to the other, draped on roadsides, twisted into strange, often grimly humorous shapes, speak. I have looked into the open eyes of dead men and wished them shut, for they seemed to beckon me into the underworld. You will be me, the eyes call out, see what you will become. Even hardened soldiers drape cloth over such faces or reach out and push the eyelids shut. The eyes of the dead are windows into a world we fear.

Goodbye Darkness, William Manchester's memoir of the Pacific war in World War II, has an unvarnished account of what it feels like to shoot another man. Nothing is more sickening in war than watching human lives get snuffed out. Nothing haunts you more. And it is never, as outsiders think, clean or easy or neat. Killing is a dirty business, more like butchering animals.

Manchester describes, in the opening pages of his memoir, the only time he shot a Japanese soldier he could see.

Not only was he the first Japanese soldier I had ever shot at; he was the only one I had seen at close quarters. He was a robin-fat, moon-faced, roly-poly little man with his thick, stubby, trunk-like legs sheathed in faded khaki puttees and the rest of him squeezed into a uniform that was much too tight. Unlike me, he was wearing a tin hat, dressed to kill. But I was quite safe from him. His Arisaka rifle was strapped on in a sniper's harness, and though he had heard me, and was trying to turn toward me, the harness sling had him trapped. He couldn't disentangle himself from it. His eyes were rolling in panic. Realizing that he couldn't extricate his arms and defend himself, he was backing toward a corner with a curious, crablike motion.

My first shot had missed him, embedding itself in the straw wall, but the second caught him dead-on in the femoral artery. His left thigh blossomed, swiftly turning to mush. A wave of blood gushed from the wound; then another boiled out, sheeting across his legs, pooling on the earthen floor. Mutely he looked down at it. He dipped a hand in it and listlessly smeared his cheek red. His shoulders gave a little spasmodic jerk, as though someone had whacked him on the back; then he emitted a tremendous, raspy fart, slumped down, and died. I kept firing, wasting government property.

Already I thought I detected the dark brown effluvium of the freshly slain, a sour, pervasive emanation which is different from anything you have known. Yet seeing death at this range, like smelling it, requires no previous experience. You instantly recognize the spastic convulsion and the rattle, which in his case was not loud, but deprecating and concil-iatory, like the manners of civilian Japanese. He continued to sink until he reached the earthen floor. His eyes glazed over. Almost immediately a fly landed on his left eyeball. It was joined by another. I don't know how long I stood there staring. I knew from previous combat what lay ahead for the corpse. It would swell, then bloat, bursting out of the uni-form. Then the face would turn from yellow to red, to pur-ple, to green, to black. My father's account of the Argonne had omitted certain vital facts. A feeling of disgust and self-hatred clotted darkly in my throat, gagging me.

Jerking my head to shake off the stupor, I slipped a new, fully loaded magazine into the butt of my .45. Then I began to tremble, and next to shake, all over. I sobbed, in a voice still grainy with fear: "I'm sorry." Then I threw up all over myself. I recognized the half-digested C-ration beans drib-bling down my front, smelled the vomit above the cordite. At the same time I noticed another odor; I had urinated in my skivvies. I pondered fleetly why our excretions become so loathsome the instant they leave the body. Then Barney burst in on me, his carbine at the ready, his face gray, as though he, not I, had just become a partner in the firm of death. He ran over to the Nip's body, grabbed its stacking swivel—its neck—and let go, satisfied that it was a cadaver. I marveled at his courage; I couldn't have taken a step toward that cor-ner. He approached me and then backed away in revulsion, from my foul stench. He said: "Slim, you stink." I said noth-ing. I knew I had become a thing of tears and twitchings and dirtied pants. I remember wondering dumbly: Is that what they mean by "conspicuous gallantry"?[12]

There is among many who fight in war a sense of shame, one that is made worse by the patriotic drivel used to justify the act of killing in war. Those who seek meaning in patriotism do not want to hear the truth of war, wary of bursting the bubble. The tensions between those who were there and those who were not, those who refuse to let go of the myth and those that know it to be a lie feed into the dislocation and malaise after war. In the end, neither side cares to speak to the other. The shame and alienation of combat soldiers, coupled with the indifference to the truth of war by those who were not there, reduces many societies to silence. It seems better to forget.

"I, too, belong to this species," J. Glenn Gray wrote. "I am ashamed not only of my own deeds, not only of my nation's deeds, but of human deeds as well. I am ashamed to be a man."[13]

When Ernie Pyle, the American war correspondent in World War II, was killed on the Pacific island of Ie Shima in 1945, a rough draft of a column was found on his body. He was preparing it for release upon the end of the war in Europe. He had done much to promote the myth of the warrior and the heroism of soldiering, but by the end he seemed to tire of it all.

But there are many of the living who have had burned into their brains forever the unnatural sight of cold dead men scattered over the hillsides and in the ditches along the high rows of hedge throughout the world.

Dead men by mass production—in one country after another—month after month and year after year. Dead men in winter and dead men in summer.

Dead men in such familiar promiscuity that they become monotonous.

Dead men in such monstrous infinity that you come

almost to hate them. These are the things that you at home need not even try to understand. To you at home they are columns of figures, or he is a near one who went away and just didn't come back. You didn't see him lying so grotesque and pasty beside the gravel road in France.

We saw him, saw him by the multiple thousands. That's the difference.[14]

Discarded veterans are never a pretty sight. They are troubled and some physically maimed. They often feel betrayed, misunderstood and alone. It is hard to integrate again into peacetime society. Many are shunted aside, left to nuture their resentment and pain.

I found Kazem Ahangaron in Naushahr, on Iran's Caspian coast, not long after the end of the eight-year war with Iraq. He was once a disciple of war. But the violence he turned on Iraqi soldiers he had turned against himself.

"I tried to do it with pills, Valium and depressants, mostly," the gaunt twenty-eight-year-old veteran said, seated on a white pebble beach. "They pumped my stomach out at the hospital. But twelve of my friends have killed themselves this year."

The Caspian resort city, skirted by jagged mountains and towering fir trees, was once the summer capital of the shah. Its faded yet elegant whitewashed villas belonged to the officials of the monarchy before the 1979 Islamic revolution.

When I visited the seedy remains of Naushahr it had one of the highest rates of suicides in Iran, most by unemployed and disillusioned veterans of the war with Iraq. Figures in Iran are hard to come by and often unreliable, but doctors in the city told me that there had been 400 suicides of the town's 80,000 people in the past year. The men, out of work and alienated from the puritanical rule of the clerics, were unable to find a home or marry. They looked back on the raw carnage of the war with bitterness and ahead with despair. Drugs took the place of battle. Suicide took the place of heroic death.

Many of the suicides in Naushahr were caused by Phostoxin, small phosphate tablets known as "rice pills" that were used in granaries to kill insects. The tablets would paralyze the nervous system and send the young men into a coma. The city did not have a psychiatrist. Many rice merchants, in an effort to curb the suicides, had stopped selling the German-made tablets.

The Islamic clerics who took over Iran sought to reshape the country into a nation of devout Muslims. They spurned the decadence of the West, including what the clerics condemned as the West's loose sexual mores, drug use, and thirst for sensual gratification.

Naushahr's dance halls and bars had been turned over to shopkeepers or boarded over. The beaches were segregated by sex and patrolled by squads of morality police. At the crest of a hill, the lavish Chinese Horse casino, which once glittered through the night like a huge ocean liner, lay in rubble.

But rather than build a new generation of believers, the fundamentalist leaders created a generation of men who were alienated and infected with the hopeless despair of war and violence.

"Life has become a charade," Ahangaron said. "We carry out one life in public and another in private."

The war, once, captured their imaginations. But the years of slaughter had left them listless and addicted to hashish and opium. Many were volunteers who believed that they were not only defending their nation but helping to create a new society in the war with Iraq. The disillusionment was total.

"Iran's best wrestlers come from Naushahr," said Ramazan Gharib, a thirty-five-year-old veteran, "and the army recruiters, very cleverly, used this. When the war started we were all exhorted to show our strength, our manliness, and we went down to enlist."

But the front lines, where Iranian units were butchered en masse as they tried to sweep in human waves across the mud flats, held little glory. And many who survived the war, which began in 1980 and ended in 1988, returned changed and unsettled by the senseless carnage.

The town's leading cleric, Mohammed Masha Yekhi, had called on young people to choose life rather than suicide. He said he would not allow those who committed suicide a Muslim burial.

I sat one morning with two war veterans on the porch of a dilapidated villa overlooking the Caspian. The men, who fished and used their boats to take people water skiing, were slumped in wicker chairs drinking cups of sweet tea.

The two men told me that they had easy access to the drugs, homemade beer, and grain alcohol that was sold on the beach. They smuggled out tins of caviar from the state-run packaging plant and traded it with Russian sailors, anchored offshore, for vodka. For a price they guided couples to secluded beaches, where women could swim in bathing suits and embrace their boyfriends, activities the clerics had forbidden. The money they earned was swallowed by their addiction.

"I will never be normal again," said one of the men, who spent twenty-three months at the front. "I am nervous. I can't control my anger. If anything disturbs me, like a minor car accident, I explode."

The second man, who was a lieutenant in the war, looked out

over the water and said in a monotone, "My battalion was ordered across the flats early one morning. Within a couple of hours 400 soldiers were dead and hundreds more wounded. It was a stupid, useless waste. When we got back they called us traitors."

In the shade of a stone wall, just in front of the villa, with its collection of drooping cots and dirty shag carpets, a young man, dressed in a black shirt and pants, stared blankly at the water.

"He comes here every day," one of the veterans said. "He just finished his army service, but he has no job and nowhere to go. He smokes hash and watches the surf."

The men said they lived on the margins of existence, sometimes sleeping under grass-roofed huts. The pittance the men earned, the psychological burdens they bore, and their inability to afford a place to live had crushed them.

"All we have left is the sea," a former officer said, "and the sea is what keeps us here. But then one day even the sea isn't enough."

As long as we think abstractly, as long as we find in patriotism and the exuberance of war our fulfillment, we will never understand those who do battle against us, or how we are perceived by them, or finally those who do battle for us and how we should respond to it all. We will never discover who we are. We will fail to confront the capacity we all have for violence. And we will court our own extermination. By accepting the facile cliché that the battle under way against terrorism is a battle against evil, by easily branding those who fight us as the barbarians, we, like them, refuse to acknowledge our own culpability. We ignore real injustices that have led many of those arrayed against us to their rage and despair.

Late one night, unable to sleep during the war in El Salvador, I picked up Shakespeare's *Macbeth*. It was not a calculated decision. I had come that day from a village where about a dozen people had been murdered by the death squads, their thumbs tied behind their backs with wire and their throats slit.

I had read the play before, but in my other life as a student. A thirst for power at the cost of human life was no longer an abstraction to me. It was part of my universe.

I came upon Macduff's wife's speech made when the murderers, sent by Macbeth, arrive to kill her and her small children: "Whither should I fly?" she asks,

I have done no harm. But I remember now
I am in this earthly world—where to do harm
Is often laudable, to do good sometime
Accounted dangerous folly.[15]

Those words seized me like furies and cried out for the dead I had seen lined up that day in a dusty market square, the dead I have seen since, the dead, including the two thousand children who were killed in Sarajevo. The words cried out for those whom I would see later in unmarked mass graves in Bosnia, Kosova, Iraq, the Sudan, Algeria, El Salvador, the dead who are my own, who carried notebooks, cameras, and a vanquished idealism and sad addiction into war and never returned. Of course resistance is usually folly, of course power exercised with ruthlessness will win, of course force easily snuffs out gentle people, the compassionate, and the decent. A repentant Lear, who was unable to love because of his thirst for power and self-adulation acknowledges this in the final moments of the play.

Shakespeare celebrates, at his best, this magnificence of failure. When we view our lives honestly from the inside we are all failures, all sinners, all in need of forgiveness. Shakespeare lays bare the myths that blind and deform our souls. He understands that the world of the flesh and the world of the spirit are indivisible, that they coexist in a paradox, ever present.

Shakespeare reminds us that though we may not do what we want, we are responsible for our lives. It does not matter what has been made of us; what matters is what we ourselves make of what has been done to us.

I returned from the Balkans to America in the fall of 1998, to a Nieman Fellowship at Harvard, after fifteen years abroad mostly reporting wars. I no longer had the emotional and physical resilience of youth. The curator of the Nieman program, Bill Kovach, suggested that I see James O. Freedman, the former president of Dartmouth, for advice on how to spend the year. Freedman recommended the classics and urged me to take Greek or Latin.

I had studied Greek in seminary so I opted for Latin. Of course, there is nothing sacred, or necessarily redeeming, about ancient texts. The German and Italian fascists used and misused classical literature, especially Virgil's *Aeneid*, in their propaganda. The Greeks and Romans embraced magic, slavery, the subjugation of women, racial triumphalism, animal sacrifice, and infanticide. The Roman emperors staged elaborate reenactments of battles in and outside the arena that saw hundreds and at times thousands of prisoners and slaves maimed and killed for sport. At lunchtime, in between shows, they publicly executed prisoners. Any democratic participation was the prerogative of male citizens and was snuffed out for long periods by tyrants and near-constant warfare.

But the classics offer a continuum with Western literature,

architecture, art, and political systems. Our country's past, our political and social philosophy, and our intellectual achievements and spiritual struggles cannot be connected without great holes in the fabric, and failures of understanding, if we are not conversant in the classics.

"All literature, all philosophical treatises, all the voices of antiquity," Cicero wrote, "are full of examples for imitation, which would all lie unseen in darkness without the light of literature."[16] Thucydides, knowing that Athens was doomed in the war with Sparta, consoled himself with the belief that his city's artistic and intellectual achievements would in the coming centuries overshadow raw Spartan militarism. Beauty and knowledge could, ultimately, triumph over power.

As my year at Harvard progressed, I devoured the classical authors but wasn't always as sure about taking on a dead language. One of my favorite professors, Kathleen Coleman, stopped me one morning and announced that I needed a purpose behind my slog through Latin. Once a week, she instructed, I would appear at her office prepared to do a translation of a poem by Catullus or passage from Virgil. I had never read Catullus, but came to love him.

Carrying my books, I retreated in the afternoons to the Smyth Classical Library within Widener Library, with its huge oak tables and sagging leather chairs. My fondest memories revolve around this sanctuary with its well-thumbed volumes, noisy heating system, and glass cases with dusty displays of items like Roman table legs. I was freed to step outside myself, to struggle with questions the cant of modern culture often allows us to ignore.

All idylls must end. Mine was shattered on March 24, 1999, when NATO began its bombing of Kosova. I had come to

Cambridge from Kosova. Kosovar Albanians I had known for
three years disappeared following the mass arrests or were murdered. Fehmi Agani, a gentle and erudite man who I often met
in Pristina, was shot and left on the side of a road. I slept little. I
was chained to the news reports. My translator in Kosova,
Shukrije Gashi, a poet whose boyfriend had been killed by the
Serbs, had to flee the country. The horrors of Kosova were
abstractions to most people in Cambridge. I held a communion,
in my final weeks at Harvard, with the long dead.

I had memorized a few poems by Catullus and parts of *The
Aeneid.* I woke one morning well before dawn, haunted by a
Catullus poem written to Calvus, whose lover Quintilia had
died. Calvus had abandoned her, as I felt I had abandoned
friends in Kosova and an array of other conflicts. His grief was
mingled with his guilt. In the end, these words give me a balm
to my grief, a momentary solace, a little understanding:

> If anything welcome or pleasing, Calvus, can be felt
> by silent tombs in answer to our grief,
> from that painful longing in which we renew old loves
> and weep for friendships we once cast away,
> Surely Quintilia does not lament her early death
> as much as she rejoices in your love.[17]

To survive as a human being is possible only through love.
And, when Thanatos is ascendant, the instinct must be to reach
out to those we love, to see in them all the divinity, pity, and
pathos of the human. And to recognize love in the lives of
others—even those with whom we are in conflict—love that is
like our own. It does not mean we will avoid war or death. It
does not mean that we as distinct individuals will survive. But

love, in its mystery, has its own power. It alone gives us meaning that endures. It alone allows us to embrace and cherish life. Love has power both to resist in our nature what we know we must resist, and to affirm what we know we must affirm. And love, as the poets remind us, is eternal.

NOTES

INTRODUCTION

1. Orwell, George, *1984* (San Diego: Harcourt Brace Jovanovich, 1949), p. 35.
2. Homer, *The Odyssey*, translated by Stanley Lombardo (Indianapolis: Hackett, 2000), p. 138.
3. Arendt, Hannah, *The Origins of Totalitarianism* (San Diego: Harcourt Brace Jovanovich, 1979), pp. 380–381.
4. García Márquez, Gabriel, *Chronicle of a Death Foretold* (New York: Knopf, 1983).

CHAPTER 1
THE MYTH OF WAR

1. LeShan, Lawrence, *The Psychology of War* (New York: Helios, 1992), Chapter Two.
2. Weil, Simone, '*The Iliad*' or '*The Poem of Force,*' (Wallingford, PA: Pendle Hill Pamphlet, 1993), p. 11.
3. Shakespeare, William, *Troilus and Cressida*–"Dramatis Personae," (Boston: Riverside Shakespeare, Houghton Mifflin, 1974), p. 448.
4. Ibid., Act V, sc. ii, p. 486.
5. Caputo, Philip, *Rumor of War* (New York: Holt, Rinehart & Winston, 1977), p. 345.
6. Shakespeare, William, *Troilus and Cressida*, (Boston: Riverside Shakespeare, Houghton Mifflin, 1974), Act I, sc. i, p. 450.
7. Mowat, Farley, *And No Birds Sang* (Toronto: Seal, 1987), p. 195.

8. Shakespeare, William, *Troilus and Cressida*, (Boston: Riverside Shakespeare, Houghton Mifflin, 1974), Act V, sc. viii, p. 490.

9. Weil, Simone, *'The Iliad' or 'The Poem of Force'* (Wallingford, PA: Pendle Hill Pamphlet, 1993), p. 36.

10. *London Observer*, November 18, 1822, quoted in Samuel Hynes, *The Soldiers' Tale* (New York: Penguin, 1997), p. 17.

11. Myrivilis, Stratis, *Life in the Tomb* (London: Quartet Books, 1987), p. 137.

12. Freud, Sigmund, *Civilization and Its Discontents* (New York: W. W. Norton, 1989), p. 72.

13. Orwell, George, *Homage to Catalonia*, quoted by F. Dyson, *Weapons and Hope* (New York: Harper & Row, 1984), p. 129.

14. Lasch, Christopher, *The Culture of Narcissism* (New York: W. W. Norton, 1979), pp. 7, 15.

15. See Shakespeare's *Henry IV, Part One, Henry IV, Part Two*, and *Henry V*.

CHAPTER 2
THE PLAGUE OF NATIONALISM

1. Kiš, Danilo, *On Nationalism*, in the Appendix to Mark Thompson's *A Paper House* (London: Vintage,1992), p. 339.

2. Todorov, Tzvetan, *Facing the Extreme: Moral Life in the Concentration Camps* (New York: Metropolitan /Owl Books, 1996), p. 228.

3. Levi, Primo, *The Drowned and the Saved (I Sommersi e i Salvati)* (London: Abacus, 1991), quoted by Todorov, Tzvetan, *Facing the Extreme* (New York: Metropolitan/Owl Books, 1996), p. 238.

4. Duras, Marguerite, *The War: A Memoir* (New York: Pantheon, 1986), p. 48.

CHAPTER 3
THE DESTRUCTION OF CULTURE

1. Ignatieff, Michael, *The Warrior's Honor: Ethnic War and the Modern Conscience* (New York: Henry Holt, 1998), p. 56.

2. Shakespeare, William, *Othello* (Boston: The Riverside Shakespeare, Houghton Mifflin, 1974), Act IV, sc. i.

3. Sachs, Susan, *Newsday*, October 22, 1995, p. A04.

CHAPTER 4

THE SEDUCTION OF BATTLE AND THE PERVERSION OF WAR

1. Bartov, Omer, *Mirrors of Destruction* (New York: Oxford University Press, 2002), p. 45.

2. Remarque, Erich Maria, *All Quiet on the Western Front* (New York: Fawcett Crest, 1975), p. 114.

3. Browning, Christopher, *Ordinary Men: Reserve Police Battalion 101 and the Final Solution in Poland* (New York: HarperCollins, 1992), Ch. 18.

4. Ibid.

5. Ibid., p. 85.

6. Morante, Elsa, *History: A Novel (La Storia)*, (New York: Aventura/Vintage Books, 1984).

7. Auden, W. H., *Selected Poems* (London: Faber & Faber, 1981), p. 80.

8. Proust, Marcel, quoted in Alain De Botton, *How Proust Can Change Your Life* (London: Picador,1997), p. 197.

9. Bartov, *Mirrors of Destruction*, p. 189.

10. Ka'Tzetnik 135633, *House of Dolls* (London: Muller, Blond & White, 1986).

11. Bartov, *Mirrors of Destruction*, p. 193.

12. Ibid.

13. Gray, J. Glenn, *The Warriors: Reflections on Men in Battle* (Lincoln: University of Nebraska Press, 1998), pp. 61–62.

14. Kapuściński, Ryszard, *Another Day of Life* (London: Picador, 1988), p. 56.

15. Ibid.

16. Ibid., p. 57.

17. Arendt, Hannah, *The Origins of Totalitarianism* (New York: Harcourt Brace, 1979), Ch. 9.

18. Canetti, Elias, *Crowds and Power* (New York: Viking Press, 1962), p. 187.

19. Andrić, Ivo, *The Bridge on the Drina* (Chicago: University of Chicago Press, 1977), p. 15.
20. Gray, *The Warriors: Reflections on Men in Battle*, p. 90.
21. Ibid.
22. Levi, Primo, *Survival in Auschwitz (Se questo è un uomo)* (New York: Collier, 1961).

CHAPTER 5

THE HIJACKING AND RECOVERY OF MEMORY

1. Kundera, Milan, *The Book of Laughter and Forgetting* (New York: HarperPerennial, 1996), p. 4.
2. Dorfman, Ariel, *Widows* (New York: Aventura, 1983).
3. Feitlowitz, Marguerite, *The Lexicon of Terror* (New York: Oxford University Press, 1998).
4. Grossman, Vasily, *Life and Fate* (New York: Harper & Row, 1980), p. 82.

CHAPTER 6

THE CAUSE

1. Canetti, Elias, *Crowds and Power* (New York: Viking, 1962), p. 138.
2. Herr, Michael, *Dispatches* (New York: Vintage International, 1991), p. 215.
3. For an expansive portrait of Morel and the Congo, see Adam Hochschild, *King Leopold's Ghost* (Boston: Houghton Mifflin, 1998).
4. Arendt, Hannah, *The Origins of Totalitarianism*, discussed by Omer Bartov in his book, *Murder in Our Midst* (New York: Oxford University Press, 2000), p. 72.

CHAPTER 7
EROS AND THANATOS

1. Freud, Sigmund, *Civilization and Its Discontents* (New York: W. W. Norton, 1989), p. 82.s
2. Loyd, Anthony, *My War Gone By, I Miss It So* (London: Doubleday, 1999), p. 136.
3. Grossman, Dave, *On Killing: The Psychological Cost of Learning to Kill in War and Society* (Boston: Little, Brown, 1996), pp. 43–44.
4. Gray, J. Glenn, *The Warriors: Reflections on Men in Battle* (Lincoln: University of Nebraska Press, 1998), p. 21.
5. *Ha'aretz*, English Edition, May 4, 2001, p. B3.
6. Sudetic, Chuck, *Blood and Vengeance* (New York: W. W. Norton, 1998), pp. xxxii–xxxiii.
7. Djilas, Milovan, *Wartime* (New York: Harvest Books, 1977), p. 280.
8. Fitzgerald, Robert, *In the Rose of Time: Poems 1931–1956* (New York: New Directions Books, 1956), p. 148.
9. Frankl, Viktor, *Man's Search for Meaning* (New York: Simon and Schuster, 1984), p. 48.
10. Vistica, Gregory L., "What happened in Thanh Phong," *The New York Times Magazine*, April 29, 2001, p. 51.
11. Farney, Dennis, *The Wall Street Journal*, April 25, 2001.
12. Manchester, William, *Goodbye Darkness: A Memoir of the Pacific War* (London: Dell, 1980), pp. 17–18.
13. Gray, *The Warriors*, p. 207.
14. Pyle, Ernie, *Ernies' War–the Best of Ernie Pyle's World War II Dispatches* (New York: Simon and Schuster, 1987), p. 419.
15. Shakespeare, William, *Macbeth* (Boston: Riverside Shakespeare, Houghton Mifflin, 1974), Act IV, sc. ii.
16. Cicero, *Pro Archia*, 2.3. 14–16, quoted in Bernard Knox, *The Oldest Dead White European Males* (New York: W. W. Norton, 1993), p. 83.
17. Goold, George, *Catullus* (London: Duckworth, 1983).

BIBLIOGRAPHY

Andrić, Ivo. *The Bridge on the Drina*. Chicago: University of Chicago Press, 1977.

———. *Conversations with Goya: Bridges, Signs* London: Menard Press, 1992.

Armstrong, Karen. *The Battle for God*. New York: Knopf, 2000.

Arendt, Hannah. *The Origins of Totalitarianism*. New York: Harcourt Brace, 1976.

Auden, W. H. *Selected Poems*. Boston: Faber & Faber, 1979.

Bartov, Omer. *Mirrors of Destruction*. New York: Oxford University Press, 1996.

———. *Murder in our Midst*. New York: Oxford University Press, 2000.

Blunden, Edmund. *Undertones of War*. London: Penguin, 1984.

Browning, Christopher. *Ordinary Men*. New York: HarperCollins, 1992.

Canetti, Elias. *Crowds and Power*. New York: Viking, 1962.

Caputo, Philip. *A Rumor of War*. New York: Holt, Rinehart and Winston, 1977.

Carroll, Lewis. *Alice's Adventures in Wonderland*. New York: Oxford University Press, 1971.

Céline, Louis-Ferdinand. *Castle to Castle (D'un Chateau l'Autre)*. New York: Carroll & Graf, 1988.

———. *Journey to the End of the Night* (Voyage au Bout de la Nuit) New York: New Directions, 1983.

Conrad, Joseph. *Heart of Darkness*. New York: Knopf, 1993.

———. *Lord Jim*. Evanston, Illinois: Harper & Row, 1963.

———. *Victory*. New York: Doubleday, 1957.

De Botton, Alain. *How Proust Can Change Your Life*. London: Picador, 1997.

Djilas, Milovan. *Wartime*. New York: Harcourt Brace Jovanovich, 1977.

Dorfman, Ariel. *Widows*. New York: Aventura, 1984.

Duras, Marguerite. *The War: a Memoir*. New York: Pantheon, 1986.

Eliot, T. S. *What Is a Classic?* New York: Faber & Faber, 1950.

Feitlowitz, Margarite. *A Lexicon of Terror: Argentina and the Legacies of Torture.* New York: Oxford University Press, 1998.

Ferguson, Niall. *The Pity of War*. London: Allen Lane, 1998.

Fitzgerald, Robert. *In the Rose of Time; Poems 1931–1956*. Norfolk, Conn.: James Laughlin, 1956.

Forster, E. M. *Two Cheers for Democracy*. New York: Harcourt Brace, 1951.

Frankl, Victor. *Man's Search for Meaning*. New York: Simon and Schuster, 1984.

Freud, Sigmund. *Civilization and Its Discontents*. New York: W. W. Norton, 1989.

———. *On Creativity and the Unconscious*. New York: Harper & Row, 1958.

Fussell, Paul. *The Great War and Modern Memory*. Oxford, England: Oxford University Press, 1977.

García Márquez, Gabriel. *Chronicle of a Death Foretold*. New York: Knopf, 1983.

Graves, Robert. *Goodbye to All That*. Middlesex, England: Penguin, 1986.

———. *The Greek Myths I and II*. London: Penguin, 1960.

Gray, J. Glenn. *The Warriors: Reflections on Men in Battle*. Lincoln: University of Nebraska Press, 1998.

Grossman, David. *On Killing: The Psychological Cost of Learning to Kill in War and Society*. Boston: Little, Brown, 1996.

Grossman, Vasily. *Life and Fate*. New York: Harper & Row, 1980.

Halbwachs, Maurice. *La Mémoire Collective*. Paris: Albin Michel, 1950.

Herr, Michael. *Dispatches*. New York: Vintage International, 1991.

Hochschild, Adam. *King Leopold's Ghost*. Boston: Houghton Mifflin, 1998.

Hollander, Paul. *Political Pilgrims*. New York: Harper Colophon, 1981.

Holmes, Richard. *Firing Line*. London: Pimlico, 1994.

Homer, translated by Stanley Lombardo. *The Iliad*. Indianapolis: Hackett, 1997.

———. *Odyssey*. Indianapolis: Hackett, 2000.

Hume, David. *A Treatise on Human Nature*. Oxford, England: Clarendon Press, 1968.

Hynes, Samuel. *The Soldiers' Tale.* New York: Penguin, 1997.

Ignatieff, Michael. *The Warrior's Honor.* New York: Henry Holt, 1997.

Jones, James. *From Here to Eternity.* Glasgow: Collins, 1987.

Junger, Ernst. *Storm of Steel: From the Diary of a German Storm-troop Officer on the Western Front.* New York: Fertig, 1996.

Kapuściński, Ryszard. *Another Day of Life.* London: Picador, 1988.

Ka'Tzetnik 135633. *House of Dolls.* London: Miller, Blond, & White, 1986.

Keegan, John. *The Face of Battle.* London: Jonathan Cape Ltd., 1976.
———. *A History of Warfare.* London: Random House, 1994.

Knightley, Phillip. *The First Casualty.* New York: Harcourt Brace Jovanovich, 1975.

Knox, Bernard. *The Oldest Dead White European Males.* New York: W. W. Norton, 1993.

Koestler, Arthur. *Scum of the Earth.* London: Eland, 1991.

Kundera, Milan. *The Book of Laughter and Forgetting.* New York: Harper Perennial, 1996.

Larkin, Philip. *Collected Poems.* New York: Farrar, Straus and Giroux, 1989.
———. *Required Writing.* Boston: Faber & Faber, 1986.

Lasch, Christopher. *The Culture of Narcissism.* New York: W. W. Norton, 1979.

LeShan, Lawrence. *The Psychology of War.* New York: Helios, 1992.

Levi, Primo. *The Drowned and the Saved (I Sommersi e i Salvati).* London: Abacus, 1991.
———. *Survival in Auschwitz (Se questo è un uomo).* New York: Collier, 1987.

Loyd, Anthony. *My War Gone By, I Miss It So.* London: Doubleday, 1999.

Mailer, Norman. *The Naked and the Dead.* London: Panther, 1984.

Manchester, William. *Goodbye Darkess: A Memoir of the Pacific War.* New York: Dell, 1980.

Manning, Frederic. *The Middle Parts of Fortune.* London: Penguin, 2000.

Marshall, S. L. A. *Men Against Fire.* Norman: University of Oklahoma Press, 2000.

Melville, Herman. *Moby-Dick.* New York: W. W. Norton, 1967.

Morante, Elsa. *History: A Novel (La Storia).* New York: Aventura, 1984.

Myrivilis, Stratis. *Life In the Tomb.* London: Quartet, 1987.

Niebuhr, Reinhold. *The Children of Light and The Children of Darkness.* New York: Charles Scribner's Sons, 1972.
————. *Moral Man and Immoral Society.* New York: Charles Scribner's Sons, 1960.
————. *The Nature and Destiny of Man Vol. I and II.* New York: Charles Scribner's Sons, 1964.
Orwell, George. *Homage to Catalonia.* New York: Harcourt Brace Jovanovich, 1952.
————. *1984.* New York: Harcourt Brace Jovanovich, 1977.
Owen, Wilfred. *Selected Poems.* London: Bloomsbury, 1995.
Pyle, Ernie. *Ernie's War.* New York: Simon and Schuster, 1986.
Remarque, Erich Maria. *All Quiet on the Western Front.* New York: Fawcett Crest, 1958.
Roth, Joseph. *Hotel Savoy.* Woodstock, N.Y.: Overlook Press, 1986.
————. *The Radetzky March.* London: Penguin, 1974.
Shakespeare, William. *The Riverside Shakespeare,* edited by G. Blakemore Evans. Boston: Houghton Mifflin, 1974.
Silkin, Jon (ed.). *The Penguin Book of First World War Poetry.* London: Penguin, 1996.
Sudetic, Chuck. *Blood and Vengeance.* New York: W. W. Norton, 1998.
Thompson, Mark. *A Paper House.* London: Vintage, 1992.
Thucydides. *A Comprehensive Guide to The Peloponnesian War,* edited by Robert B. Strassler. New York: Touchstone, 1998.
Todorov, Tzvetan. *Facing the Extreme: Moral Life in the Concentration Camps.* New York: Metropolitan/Owl Books, 1996.
Wiesel, Elie. *Night.* New York: Avon, 1960.
Zimmerman, Warren. *Origins of a Catastrophe.* New York: Times Books, 1996.

ACKNOWLEDGMENTS

IT HAS BEEN NEARLY TWENTY YEARS SINCE I GRADUATED from Harvard Divinity School and left Cambridge to cover the war in El Salvador. This book is not only the result of my work in various war zones, but is a product of the education I received, especially in English literature and Christian theology, at Colgate University and Harvard University. I owe much of what I am to great professors—Coleman Brown, Margaret Maurer, Krister Stendhal, G. Blakemore Evans, W. Jackson Bate, Robert Coles, and Robert Pinsky. They taught me how to read and write and most importantly how to think critically. I have carried their wisdom, their love of books, and their moral probity with me. I have tried to live a life by the standards they set.

Peter Osnos, the publisher of PublicAffairs, conceived of the book idea and pushed me to make it work. He then went on to publish it. He turned me over to his executive editor, Paul Golob, whose talent and good humor carried me through. It is a much better book for Paul's willingness to read and reread with such care and intelligence. David Patterson at PublicAffairs ironed out all the kinks and made the logistics work. Lisa Bankoff of International Creative Management shepherded me through the world of book publishing with grace and wisdom.

My editors at *The New York Times*, Jon Landman, Ann Cronin, Christine Kay, and Bill Goss are not only immensely talented but blessed with infinite patience. Moreover, they stand up for the reporters who work for them. I want to thank colleagues and editors at *The New York Times* over the years, including Bernie Gwertzman, whose decency and equanimity made him truly loved, Andy Rosenthal, Bill Keller, Chris Wren, Ethan Bronner, Eric Eckholm, Helen Verongos, Marie Courtney, Cynthia Latimer-Ortiz, Kathy Rose, Steve Weisman, Tom Feyer, Eric Schmitt, Steve Kinzer, Jeanne Moore, Ed Marks, Chris Drew, and Susan Sachs. The editors at *Harper's* magazine, in particular John R. MacArthur, Lewis H. Lapham, and Ben Metcalf, keep alive the marriage between great writing and great thought and somehow make my pieces sing. I would also like to thank the editors I work with at *Foreign Affairs*, especially James F. Hoge Jr. and Celia Whitaker, along with Fareed Zakaria, now with *Newsweek*. Also, my colleagues at New York University, especially William and Judy Serrin, Carol Sternhell, Michael and Beth Norman and Cathleen Dullahan, all keep alive great journalism traditions. Eva Sanchez, Puja Vaswani, and Caroline Clare Binham worked tirelessly as researchers. They, and the staff at the New York University library, were vital. My NYU library privileges are among my most precious possessions.

Coleman Brown, Peter Meineck, Kim Parham, Jack Wheeler, who lent his considerable intellect as well as his experience as a professional soldier, Linda McNell, and Claudia Wassmann worked on the manuscript and made many important changes and corrections. They gave it greater clarity and depth. I owe a huge debt to the colleagues I worked with over the years—especially Lajla Veselica and Wade Goddard in Croatia and Ivana Sekularac in Serbia; these three kept me balanced and were able, when I most

needed it, to make me laugh at myself. Boba Lizdek in
Sarajevo and now Paris, Shukrije Gashi, my translator in
Kosova, Alija Dedajić, whose wits saved both our lives dur-
ing the war in Bosnia more than once, Jadranka Milanović,
the late Miladin Zivotić, and Serif Turgut were priceless com-
panions. Tom Gjelten and Neal Conan at National Public
Radio, Kanan Makiya, Tony Horwitz and Geraldine Brooks,
Jim Landers, Michael Ignatieff, Iliriana Bajo, Ivo Banac,
Malika Berak—who introduced me to two of my favorite
writers, Marcel Proust and Louis-Ferdinand Céline—Rina
Castelnuovo, Omar Othman, Gamal Mohei al-Din, Michael
Georgy, Carlos Ramos, Emma Daley, Chuck Sudetic, Max
Marcus, Kit Roane, Hani Sabra, Edward Said, and Alan Chin
all contributed to my understanding and became close
friends. Kurt Schork and Miguel Gil Morano, two brave and
fine war correspondents, who were killed in May 2000 in an
ambush in Sierra Leone, will remain with me always. I want
to also thank Michael and Yora Kisch, Douglas and Ellen
Davidson, Robert Kaplan, Sören and Charlotte Liborius,
Alina Margolis, Daniel Reed, Walter and Ann Pincus, Ward
Pincus and Iobel Andemicael, Christine Hauser, Ravi Sidhu,
David and Yael Amir, Patricia Diermeier, Elise Colette, and
the great and very funny political cartoonist Joe Sacco.

I spent the academic year 1998–1999 at Harvard as a
Nieman Fellow thanks to generosity of Joe Lelyveld and *The
New York Times*. During the year I developed a close friend-
ship with the curator, Bill Kovach, an inspirational man and
one of the finest journalists I have ever known. Bill, along
with Julie Felt, Chris Marquis, Mary and Lawrence Walsh,
Kathy Coleman, Richard Thomas, Frank and Margo Lindsey,
Zeph Stewart, James and Sheba Freedman, Lily Galily, and
Susan Reed, made that year one of the richest of my life.

I owe more than I can repay to Josyane Séchaud, who endured the long absences, the danger, and frequent uncertainty from El Salvador to Kosova, with Swiss stoicism and unwavering understanding and support. My mother, Teddy Hedges, a professor of English, imparted to me a love of books and writing. She was the first one to publish my work, in a booklet she typed and bound when I was a child. My aunt and uncle, Miriam and Ellsworth Blair, make our retreats to Maine possible and somehow put up with my wildnesss. But my greatest thanks go to Thomas and Noëlle, who remind me every day that my chief role, and the one I value most, is as a father. I hope they never do what I did.

INDEX

Achilles, 12, 29, 159
Adamović, Marko, 129
Adams, James Luther, 147
Aeneas, 168
The Aeneid (Virgil), 168, 182, 184
Afghanistan, 105
   casualties of war in, 13
   language of war and, 8
   myth of war and, 22, 23
Afghans, 9
Africa, 10
African National Congress, 144
Ahangaron, Kazem, 177, 178
Ahmedspahić, Jasna, 113
Al-Adan Hospital, 145
al-Amal Hospital, 97
Alfonsin, Raul, 135
Algeria, 2, 133
   casualties of war in, 13
   killing of children in, 94
   willingness to kill and, 88
All Quiet on the Western Front
   (Remarque), 87
al-Sabah, Saud Nasir, 145
Amazons, 159
America. See United States
American Council of Trustees and
   Alumni, 72
Amin, Jamal Aziz, 138–39
Ammouna, Fahdi Abu, 97

Andrić, Ivo, 64, 112, 122
Angola
   casualties of war in, 13
   civil war in, 24–25, 101–102
Ann, Lady, 168
Another Day of Life (Kapuściński),
   101
Antony and Cleopatra (Shakespeare),
   90, 168
Aphrodite, 100
apocalypse, redemption through, 85
Arab-Israeli war (1973), 164
Arafat, Yasir, 24
Arendt, Hannah, 15, 150, 151
Ares, 100
Argentina, 47, 141
   Dirty War and, 43–45, 134
   nationalism and, 59–60
   rape camps in, 104
   torture in, 134–135
   willingness to kill and, 88
Aristotle, 161
Arkan, 27, 103
Armenians, genocide of, 122–125
Arnedt, Hannah, 106
art, significance in wartime, 62–63
Asadourian, Hagob H., 122–125
Asadourian, John, 123–125
Athens, 183
Auden, W. H., 90

Augustan age, 26
Austerlitz, 31
Australia, 6
Ayala, Edilberto, 164
Ayios Demetrios Church, 66

Badzić, Murdija, 119–120
Bakovik, Burka, 110, 111
Baldizón, Alvaro José, 36
Balkans, 13, 66, 161
    culture destruction and, 77
    myth of war and, 21, 26, 31–32
    rape camps in, 104
Banja Luka, 107, 163
Bartov, Omer, 86, 92
Basovizza, 132
Basra, Shiite uprising in, 89–90
BBC, 59
Belgrade, 103
Belgrade Circle, 55
Belgrade University, 55
Berdichec, 135
Bible, 27
Bildt, Carl, 79
bin Laden, Osama, 8
Bisbua, casualties of war in, 13
Blood, 134
Blood and Vengeance (Sudetic), 166
B'nai B'rith, 70
Bosanski Novi, 104
Bosnian War
    aftermath of, 117–120
    attraction of war and, 6–7
    cause of, 149–156
    Communist hierarchy in, 4
    culture and, 62–63, 69–73, 76–80
    displacement and, 106–112

end of, 151–153
killing in, 9, 86–87, 88
memory recovery and, 128–130
myth of war and, 20–21, 25, 26
nationalism and, 14–15, 48–58
Serbian warrior and, 20
sex and, 104–106
U.S. intervention in, 16, 20
UN and, 1, 16, 32, 104
war as drug and, 163–164
Brandt, Willy, 57
Brazil, 141
Brckić, Bosko, 169
The Bridge on the Drina (Andrić), 112
Britain, 44, 147
Browning, Christopher, 87–88
Buenos Aries, 59
Burundi, casualties of war in, 13
Bush, George W., 4, 160
Buvac, Ratko, 129

Cairo, 148
California, 5
Caligula, 103
Calvus, 184
Cambodia, 126
Camino Real Hotel, 8
Canada, 49
Canetti, Elias, 112, 145
Caputo, Philip, 26
Carlos, Commandante, 131
Carlotta, 101–102
Casa Rosada, 59
Cassandra, 25
Catholic Church, 46
Catullus, 170, 183, 184

cause
  of Bosnian War, 149–156
  language of, 148
  myth of war and, 146–147
  of Persian Gulf War, 142–146,
    148–149
  war and, 142–156
Ceaușescu, Nicolae, 2
Central America, 13, 24, 35, 161
Chechens, 9
Chechnya, 13, 16, 170
"Chetniks," 14, 153
children, war and, 93–98
Chile, 44, 141
Christianity, 147–148
Chronicle of a Death Foretold
    (Márquez), 16
Cicero, 183
Civilization and Its Discontents
    (Freud), 158
Clark, Wesley K., 16
Clerides, Glafkos, 66
Clinton, Bill, 20, 34
Cold War, 15, 131
Coleman, Kathleen, 183
Colombia, 2, 13
communism, 27
Communist Partisans, 131–132
Congo, 105, 163
Congress, 5
Congressional Human Rights
    Caucus, 145
Conrad, Joseph, 90
Contras, 24, 36
Conversation with Goya: Signs, Bridges
    (Andrić), 122
Coriolanus (Shakespeare), 83, 168

Ćosić, Dobrica, 48
Costa Rica, 6
Crimean War, 22
Croatia, 14
  Catholic Church in, 46
  Education Ministry in, 33
  gangsters and, 27–28
  myth of war and, 20, 21, 26,
    32–34
  nationalism and, 70–71
  victimhood and, 64
  See also Bosnian War
Cromwell, Oliver, 19
Crvena Zemlja, 127
Cuba, 35, 102
culture
  Bosnian War and, 62–63
  destruction of, 62–82
  memory and, 123
  nationalism and, 62
  state and, 62
  war and, 3, 62–82
The Culture of Narcissism (Lasch), 37
Cura, Fatima, 109
Cyclops, 12
Cyprus, Turkish invasion of, 64–67
Czechoslovakia, 57

Damascus, 149
Dante, 1
Davor, 107
Dayton peace agreement (1995),
    151–152
death
  abuse of, 89, 137
  anonymous, 135
  media and, 146

U.S. and, 160
war and, 89, 144–146, 157–158,
     165–167
democracy, terrorism and, 9, 148
Denktash, Rauf, 67
desaparecido, 135
Desdemona, 72
Dhahran, 23, 142
Dido, 168
Dirty War, 43–45, 134
Dispatches (Herr), 146
displacement, 106–112
Djilas, Milovan, 57, 63, 167
Doboj, 155
Dobrinja, 119–120
Dorfman, Ariel, 133
Dragan, Captain, 27
Dresden, 28
Drina River, 112
drug of war, 17, 25, 87–88, 101,
     162–164, 173
Dulcinea, 27
Durant, Will, 10
Duras, Marguerite, 60

East Timor, 170
Egypt, 77
ekpyrosis, 166
Eliot, T. S., 90
El Salvador, 2, 133, 144, 150
     civil war in, 86
     death squads in, 8
     exhumations in, 126
     killing of children in, 94
     myth of war and, 25, 35, 39–42
     revolutionary movements in, 35,
          39–42

war in, 5–6, 164
willingness to kill and, 88
Enzensberger, Hans Magnus, 67
"Epitaph to a Tyrant" (Auden), 90
Eris, 100
Eritrea, 13
Eros, 101
     Thanatos vs., 158–185
Ethiopia, 13
Euripides, 28

*Facing the Extreme: Moral Life in the
     Concentration Camps* (Todorov),
     48–58
Faid, Neamon Mohammed, 97
Falkland Islands, 43, 59
Falstaff, 38–39
Farabundo Marti National Libera-
     tion Front (FMLN), 40
fear, war and, 83–85
Fejzić, Fadil, 50, 52–53
Fietlowitz, Marguerite, 134
FMLN. *See* Farabundo Marti
     National Liberation Front
foibe, 132
Fortinbras, Prince, 79
France, 3, 10, 55, 155
Frankl, Victor, 170–171
Franz Ferdinand, 77, 80
Free Belgrade University, 58
Freedman, James O., 182
"freedom fighters," 24
Freud, Sigmund, 32, 158, 162
friendship in war, 115–116

galabias, 93
Gani Tal, 93

Gashi, Shukrije, 184
Gaza, 2–4, 35, 93–98
Germany, 16, 109, 150, 155
Gharib, Ramazan, 179
Glavaš, Branimir, 27
god, war as, 10–11
Goodbye Darkness (Manchester), 173–175
Goražde, 50
Grand Illusion (film), 85
Grant, Ulysses S., 16
Gray, J. Glenn, 101, 115, 116, 164–165, 176
Grbavica, 153
Greece, 16, 133
Greeks, 166, 182
    Armenians and, 125
    war and, 10, 26
Green Line, 65, 66–67
Grossman, Vasily, 135–136
Grujić, Branko, 76
Guatemala, 2
    casualties of war in, 13
    killing of children in, 94
    rebels in, 144
Gulf War. *See* Persian Gulf War

Ha'aretz, 165
The Hague, 141
Hamlet (Shakespeare), 78–79
Hanoi, 8
happiness, meaning and, 159
Harvard Divinty School, 147
"Harvest Festival," 88
Hassan, Pershan, 137–138
Hector, 29
Helen, 26

Henry V (Shakespeare), 25, 26, 38–39
Hephaestos, 100
heroism, myth of war and, 83–86
Herr, Michael, 146, 162–163
High Commission for Refugees, 104, 155
Hiroshima, 28
History: A Novel (Morante), 89
Hitler, Adolf, 126, 151
Holocaust, 70, 77, 92
Homer, 26, 29
House of Dolls (Ka'Tzetnik), 92
Human Rights Watch, 138
Hume, David, 19
Hungary, 16
Hussein, Saddam, 13, 95, 136–137, 149

Ie Shima, 176
Ignatieff, Michael, 71
The Iliad (Homer), 11, 12, 90, 115–116
Impasses of Historical Reality (Tudjman), 70
innocents, violence against, 8
intifada, 98
Iran, 2, 10, 177–178
    Islamic revolution (1979), 177
Iraq, 77, 127, 144–145
    killing sites in, 136–141
    Kurdish rebellion and, 2
    language of war and, 8
    willingness to kill and, 88
Iraqi Republican Guard, 2
Ireland, 13, 66
Islam, 47, 147–148

Islamic fundamentalists, 5
Islamic University, 68
Ismić, Admira, 169
Israel, 77
   alliances with, 8
   Palestine and, 4, 13, 14, 24, 47,
      92–98
   United Nations and, 68
   war of independence in, 47
Istrian Peninsula, 131
Italy, 131–132

Jerusalem, 4
Jews, 70
   Egypt and, 77
   Israeli war of indepence and, 47
   massacre of, 135
   World War II and, 87–88
jihad, 4
Jordan, 77
Joyce, James, 131
Judaism, 147–148
Julian the Turk, 134–135
Jünger, Ernst, 85

Kalinin, 126
Kalowa Hill, 137
Kapuściński, Ryszard, 101, 102
Karadžić, Radovan, 50, 58, 69
Karisik, Milenko, 152
Katić, Milorad, 153
Katyn Forest, 126
Ka'Tzetnik, 92
Kerrey, Bob, 172–173
KGB, 136
Khafji, 23
Khan Younis refugee camp, 93–98

Khartoum, 39
Kigali, 16–17
killing
   in Bosnian War, 9
   impersonal, 84–87
   war and, 173–177
King Lear (Shakespeare), 28,
      181–182
Kiš, Danilo, 45, 63
kleos, 12
Ključ, 107, 127
Kneževic, Zeljko, 156
Kopaci, 52
Korea, 21
Kosova, 2, 13, 75
   myth of war and, 25
   NATO and, 184
   sex and, 105–106
   U.S. intervention in, 16
   willingness to kill and, 88
Kosova Liberation Army, 105
Kovać, Huso, 120–121
Kovačević, Sava, 167
Kovach, Bill, 182
Krstović, Dejan, 79
Kuljanin, Jovo, 155
Kundera, Milan, 130
Kurdish rebellion, 2
Kuwait, 25, 38, 144–145, 148
Kuwait City, 85, 90, 149

Lang, Jack, 55
language of war, 8, 148
Larkin, Philip, 157
Lasch, Christopher, 37
Lebanon, 69
Ledra Palace Hotel, 66–67

Lee, Barbara J., 5
Leipzig, 31
LeShan, Lawrence, 21
Levi, Primo, 53, 117
The Lexicon of Terror (Fietlowitz), 134
Liberia, 13, 16, 25
Libya, 2
Life and Fate (Grossman), 135, 136
Life and Nothing But (film), 133
Life in the Tomb (Myrivilis), 31
Light Brigade, 143
Lizdek, Boba, 119
Ljesić, Nikola, 154–156
Lloyd, Anthony, 162
London Observer, 30–31
Lotus, 103
love, war and, 100, 158–185
Lozano, Hernán, 37
Lukić, Milan, 113–114
Luxembourg, Duke of, 19

Macbeth (Shakespeare), 28, 181
Madrid, 6
Mahdi, Sadek, 39
Majdanek, 88
Makić, Mehmet, 108
Malvinas, 43
Man's Search for Meaning (Frankl), 170
Manchester, William, 174
manhood, heroism and, 84
Manjaca concentration camp, 129
Manojlovic, Srdjan, 155
Márquez, Gabriel García, 16
Mars, 165
Marx, Karl, 56
Matić, Milivoje, 155–156
Matić, Slobodan, 156

McNamara, Robert, 8, 11
meaning, war and, 158–159
Medanović, Senad, 128, 129
media
    death and, 146
    myth of war and, 22–23, 143
    war and, 20, 142–144
Medić, Dursuma, 110–111
memory, recovery of, 122–141
Menem, Carlos Saúl, 135
Middle East, 35, 77, 161
A Midsummer Night's Dream (Shakespeare), 45
Mikaya, Kanan, 138
Milanović, Seka, 110
Milošević, Marko, 103
Milošević, Slobodan, 9, 48, 103
    Bosnian War and, 21, 55, 60–61
Mladić, Ratko, 58
Mobutu, Joseph-Désiré, 10
Mohammed, Ahmed, 140
Moharb, Ahmed, 95
Montoneros, 134
Morano, Miguel Gil, 170
Morante, Elsa, 89, 91
Morel, Edmund Dene, 147
Mostar, 48, 73
Mount Igman, 1, 121
Mowat, Farley, 28
MPLA. *See* Popular Movement for the Liberation of Angola
Mujaković, Mirnes, 107–109
Mujaković, Rasema, 107–109, 109–110
Murad, Ali, 94
Muslims, 9
    Balkans and, 66

Islam and, 47
myth of war and, 20, 26, 32–34
nationalist rhetoric and, 14–15
Serbs and, 129
as victims, 64
Myrivilis, Stratis, 31
myth
nationalism and, 45–50
racism and, 24
of Serbian warrior, 20
of war, 3, 11, 17, 19–42, 134,
141, 143, 173
My War Gone By, I Miss It So (Lloyd),
162

Nagasaki, 28
nationalism
Bosnian War and, 14–15, 48–58
culture and, 62
Dirty War and, 43–45
myth of war and, 45–50
problem with, 58–59
September 11 and, 15
symbols of, 63
war and, 43–61
Native Americans, 47
NATO. *See* North Atlantic Treaty
Organization
Naushahr, 177–178
Nayriah, 145
Nazis, 135
Nestor, 11
New York City, 8, 125
New York Times, 58, 166
New York Times Magazine, 173
Nicaragua, 2, 24, 34–37, 144
Nicosia, 64, 65, 66

Niebuhr, Reinhold, 17, 144
nihilistic relativism, 150
Nina, 103
1984 (Orwell), 9
Nixon-Eckersall, Richard, 65
North Atlantic Treaty Organization
(NATO), 107, 136, 184
"Nuclear Posture Review," 160

Octavius, 168
odussomai, 12
Odysseus, 12
The Odyssey (Homer), 12
Ohio, 36
Olympus Hotel, 65
Ordinary Men (Browning), 87
The Origins of Totalitarianism
(Arendt), 15
Orwell, George, 9–10, 35
Oslo peace agreement, 98
Othello (Shakespeare), 72
Ottoman Empire, 123
Outcast of the Islands (Conrad), 90

Palestine, 9
culture and, 67–70
Israel and, 13, 14, 24, 47, 92–98
uprising in, 4, 154
Pandarus, 25
patriotism
myth of, 141
soldiers and, 14–15
war and, 10, 14–15, 176
Patroclus, 29
Pavelić, Ante, 34
Pavle, Patriarch, 56
Penthesilea, 159

Persian Gulf War, 2, 13
    cause of, 142–146, 148–149
    impersonal slaughter of, 84–85
    Kuwait and, 148
    myth of war and, 23, 25
    nationalism and, 61
    NATO and, 136
Persians, 125
Philistines, 30
Phostoxin, 178
Pinochet, Augusto, 135
pity, 89
Plato, 1
Plaza de Mayo, 59
Pledge of Resistance, 36
Poland, 16, 87
Poniatowa, 88
pool reporters, 142, 143
Popular Movement for the Libera-
    tion of Angola (MPLA), 102
Pretty Villages, Pretty Flames (film),
    150–151
Prhovo, 127, 129
Prijedor, 104
Princip, Gavrilo, 77–78
Prinjavor, 107
Pristina, 75
professional soldiership, 90–91
Proust, 91
The Psychology of War (LeShan), 21
Pudin Han, 127
Punjab, 2
Pyle, Ernie, 176–177

Quintilia, 184
quislings, 14
Quixote, Don, 27

racism, 24
Rahman, Murad Abdel, 94
Ramovic, Rifet, 109
rape camps, 104
Rayyan, Nezar, 68–69
Ražnjatović, Zeljko, 27, 103
Reagan, Ronald, 24
reality, mythic vs. sensory, 21–22
recovery from war, 12, 129–130,
    133–134, 162
redemption, apocalypse and, 85
Reed, Dan, 169–170
relativism, nihilistic, 150
religion, 14
Remarque, Erich Maria, 87
Republika Srpska, 58
responsibility, ethics of, 16–17
rice pills, 178
Richard III (Shakespeare), 168
Rilke, Rainer Maria, 131
Riyadh, 23
Romans, 10, 182
Rome, 89, 103
Roth, Joseph, 85
Rumor of War (Caputo), 26
Russell, William Howard, 143
Russia, 9, 34, 102, 106–107
Rwanda, 16, 88

Saigon, 8
Sandinistas, 36–37, 144
San Salvador, 8
Sanski Most, 104
Sarajevo, 1–3, 20, 94, 121
Saudi Arabia, 142
Saul, 30
Savic, Obrad, 55

Savimbi, Jonas, 24
Sceek, Don, 132
Schork, Kurt, 168–169
Senate, 5
September 11, 4–5, 8, 15, 44–45
Serbia
  Balkans and, 66
  Muslims and, 129
  myth of war and, 20, 26, 32–34
  nationalism and, 14–15
  victimhood and, 64
  World War I and, 48
  See also Bosnian War
Serbian Orthodox Church, 46, 56
Serbian warrior, myth of, 20
Serbo-Croatian, 32
Šešelj, Vojislav, 27
sex, war and, 99–106, 163, 168
shabab, 4
Shakespeare, William, 25, 28–30, 83,
    90, 91, 168, 181–182
Shiite rebellion, 2
Shorish, 138
Sierra Leone, 13, 16, 169, 170
Slavica, 48–49, 53
Slovenia, 107
The Smoldering Generation
    (Asadourian), 123
Smyth Classical Library, 183
Sniper's Alley, 165
Sokolac, 154, 155
soldiers
  patriotism and, 14–15
  professional, 90–91
  qualities of, 16
Somali, 13
Somoza, Anastasio, 37

Sorak, Rosa and Drago, 50–53
South Africa, 129
South Lebanese Army, 96
Soviet Union. *See* Russia
Spain, 66
Spanish Civil War, 131
Sparta, 183
Special Investigations Commission,
    36
Srebrenica, 16–17, 105, 126
Sri Lanka, 13, 16
Stalin, Joseph, 151
state
  culture and, 62
  displacement and, 111–112
  myth of war and, 22, 23
  victimhood and, 64
Steele, Jon, 165
Suchitoto, 40
Sudan, 2, 13
Sudetic, Chuck, 166
suicide, 171, 177–180
Sutjeska, 120, 121
Svevo, Italo, 131
Sweden, 109
Syria, 124, 149

Taliban, 13, 24
Tavernier, Bertrand, 133
Temraz, Hyam, 68
terrorism
  democracy and, 9, 148
  myth of war and, 22
  nuclear, 28
  Syria and, 149
  war on, 4–5, 8–9
Thanatos, Eros vs., 158–185

Thersites, 25
Third Reich, 59
Thucydides, 183
Tito, Josip Broz, 14–15, 56, 77, 120,
    151
    Communist Partisans of, 131
    myth of war and, 20
Todorov, Tzvetan, 50
Tokyo, 28
Torah, 77
total war. *See* war
Trawniki, 88
A Treatise on Human Nature (Hume),
    19
Trieste, 130–131, 141
Troilus and Cressida (Shakespeare),
    25, 26, 28–30
Trojan War, 28, 159
Troy, 12
Truth and Reconciliation Commis-
    sion, 129
Tudjman, Franjo, 21, 33, 34, 69–70
Turjacanin, Zahra, 113
Turkey, 13
    Armenian genocide and,
        123–126
    invasion of Cyprus by, 64–67
    Kurdish rebellion and, 2

Ukraine, 16, 135
Ulysses, 25
United Nations (UN)
    Bosnian War and, 1, 16, 20, 32,
        104
    Cyprus and, 65, 66
    High Commission for Refugees
        of, 104, 155
    Israel and, 68

United States
    Armenians and, 125
    Bosnia and, 16
    Bosnian War and, 20
    death and, 160
    Kosova and, 16
    nationalism and, 61
    September 11 and, 44–45
    war on terrorism and, 4
University of Belgrade, 58
Ustashe, 14, 70

Varosha, 65
Vasiljević, Mitar, 113
victimhood, 64
Vietnam, 11, 17, 160
    language of war and, 8
    myth of war and, 21, 22
    nationalism and, 61
Vietnam Veterans Memorial, 11
Vilina Vlas spa, 113
Villani, Mario, 134
violence. *See* killing
Virgil, 26, 168, 182, 183
Virginia Military Institute, 172
Višegrad, 112, 113

Wall Street Journal, 173
war
    aftermath of, 30–32, 106,
        117–121, 164–165
    anodyne of, 5
    attraction of, 3–10, 84
    casualties of, 12–14
    cause and, 142–156
    children and, 93–98
    crimes of, 129
    as crusade, 4–5

culture and, 3, 62–82
death and, 89, 132–134, 144–146, 157–158, 165–167
dislocation and, 106–112
drug of, 17, 25, 87–88, 101, 162–164, 173
Eros and Thanatos in, 158–185
as false covenant, 161–62
fear and, 83–85
friendship in, 115–116
as god, 10–11
killing and, 8–9, 21, 84–88, 173–177
love and, 100, 158–185
meaning and, 158–159
media and, 20, 142–144
memory recovery and, 122–41
modern, 8, 28, 106
myth of, 3, 11, 17, 19–42, 83–86, 134, 143, 173
nationalism and, 43–61
as necrophilia, 165–166
patriotism and, 10, 14–15, 176
recovery from, 12, 129–130, 133–134, 162
sex and, 99–106, 163, 168
suicide and, 177–80
on terrorism, 4–5, 8–9
warlords
in Bosnia, 30, 163
displacement and, 111–112
in Somali, 13
The Warrior's Honor: Ethnic War and the Modern Conscience (Ignatieff), 71

The Warriors (Gray), 101
Waterloo, 31
Weil, Simone, 21, 30
West, 20, 27
West Bank, 2, 4
West Point, 11
Wheeler, John, 11
Widener Library, 183
Widows (Dorfman), 133
Witness for Peace, 36
Wolves, 113
World War I, 31, 48, 85
World War II, 87, 89, 131, 133, 150

Yale Law School, 11
Yeats, William Butler, 90
Yekhi, Mohammed Masha, 179
Yemen, 2
Yorkshire, 31
Yugoslavia, 15
breakup of, 98–99
Communist Partisans in, 131–132
myth of war and, 20, 27, 33
nationalism and, 46
partisan war in, 167
Tito and, 151

Zagreb, 33, 34
Zagreb University, 70
Zaire, 25
Zenica, 104
Zivotić, Miladin, 57–58
Zohrab Center, 125
Zukić, Dzemo, 113